★ "Elegant prose, a veritable Chinese box of puzzles, and authentic, well-rounded characters make this a standout."
—*Publishers Weekly*, Starred Review

"First-class fiction, a multilayered and original mystery under-scored by fine writing, fully developed characters, and a wonderful sense of place. Doug Burgess writes with humor and poignancy while creating an eerie, atmospheric tale that is sure to please."
—Michael Koryta, *New York Times* bestselling author

"Drop everything and read this book. A terrific story in a terrifically honest voice—it's intelligent and original, hilarious and heartbreak-ing, evocative and charming. A beautifully written tale of murder, dementia, family, love—and surprises! Standing ovation."
—Hank Phillippi Ryan, award-winning bestselling author

"If only we all had friends like the Laughing Sarahs: fiercely loyal, mordantly funny, and murderously clever. Doug Burgess's book brings a wildly original amateur detective to the table of the most secretive small town in New England. I can't wait to go back."
—Francine Mathews, author of the Merry Folger Nantucket Mysteries and several spy thrillers

"Readers…will find Burgess's debut strongly evocative of a dis-tinctive place, presented in a compelling first-person voice that manages to be beyond illusions but never cynical."
—*Kirkus Reviews*

"Burgess handles the revelations with an effective mix of wry humor and tough-guy violence."

—*Booklist*

"Nonfiction author Burgess's debut novel is an entertaining kaleidoscope of a mystery, replete with New England maritime history, a love story, ghosts, and humor."

—*Library Journal*

Also by Doug Burgess

Seize the Trident
The Pirates' Pact
The World for Ransom
The Politics of Piracy
Engines of Empire
Dark Currents (originally published as *Fogland Point*)

When Hope and History Rhyme

A
Legacy
of
Bones

Doug
Burgess

sourcebooks landmark

Published by Sourcebooks Landmark, an imprint of Sourcebooks
P.O. Box 4410, Naperville, Illinois 60567-4410
(630) 961-3900
sourcebooks.com

Library of Congress Cataloging-in-Publication Data

Names: Burgess, Douglas R., Jr., author.
Title: A legacy of bones / Doug Burgess.
Description: Naperville, Illinois : Sourcebooks Landmark, [2023]
Identifiers: LCCN 2022028706 (print) | LCCN 2022028707
(ebook) | (trade paperback) | (epub)
Subjects: LCGFT: Novels.
Classification: LCC PS3602.U7453 L44 2023 (print) | LCC PS3602.U7453
(ebook) | DDC 813/.6--dc23/eng/20220616
LC record available at https://lccn.loc.gov/2022028706
LC ebook record available at https://lccn.loc.gov/2022028707

Printed and bound in Canada.
MBP 10 9 8 7 6 5 4 3 2 1

For Tonmoy Hassan, Aloha Mau

PROLOGUE

The 'i'iwis began chattering in the banyan tree outside old Mr. Po's window before dawn. Their conversation was muted at first, a polite exchange of greetings, but quickly gained tempo as more and more neighbors joined in. By daybreak it was an argument. Mr. Po cursed them, as he always did. The 'i'iwis answered back good-naturedly, clicking and ruffling their feathers.

Breakfast waited on the table: a cut papaya under a mesh dome and a handful of granola that his daughter told him would keep him regular. He acquiesced on this because she didn't know about the cigarette that followed, savored on the lanai in the cool blue light. In Mr. Po's mind, one canceled out the other. He ate his meal and dressed himself in an old pair of khakis, baggy round the knees, and sandals. He rarely wore anything else.

"Come on, Sadie. Come on, old girl."

Mr. Po named his dog, Sadie, after his dead wife. People thought that strange, even disrespectful, and he didn't bother to explain. Truth was, he had been saying her name for almost sixty years, and now she was gone he found he couldn't bear not saying it anymore. The present Sadie was a fat and cheerful yellow Labrador. She kept by his side as they walked out into the valley, following a dirt trail that Mr. Po had cleared himself in his younger days. Now his sandaled feet kept it smooth. The path snaked behind the house into a dense grove of trees. The ground was moist; it had rained last night.

"Good, very good," muttered Mr. Po. He spoke to himself all the time now, though usually pretended he was talking to Sadie. Sauntering along beside him, one ear cocked for prey, she pretended to listen.

In the foothills the trees were sparse, revealing long vistas that stretched all the way to the sea. Mr. Po followed the same route as the ancients, and the symmetry of his footsteps and theirs passing over sacred ground pleased him. Once there had been a village at the bottom of the valley where all rivers met. The rivers were still there, but the village was gone, drowned in a storm, rebuilt, and devastated once again. Now there were only a few scattered trailers half-hidden by palms. Mr. Po's daughter lived in one of them. He didn't visit her often; didn't want to know what it looked like inside. He had come once, unannounced, and the smell of rotten garbage and worse things—things he wasn't even sure he could name—left him depressed. Sadie had been a forceful woman, matriarch of her family, but Sadie was dead. Now his daughter did as she pleased, and the rest of the clan moved to Oahu looking for work.

Best not to dwell on such matters. Mr. Po breathed deep the morning air and saw ahead the object of his walk. The *heiau* was old, older than Kamehameha, older even than the first kings. Its black lava walls were tall and forbidding, more like a fortress than a place of worship. Mr. Po lit his second cigarette of the day, not as satisfying as the first but still a comfort, and saluted the temple. Sadie disappeared into the underbrush.

The light around him bled from blue to silver to deep rose. Like a child waking from a deep sleep, he thought, as he always did. At eighty-three years old his thoughts moved down the same well-worn paths as his feet. Now both led him inside the black walls to a spot he loved. Sadie had found it first—his wife, that is—and showed him when they were both children playing in this grim, abandoned castle. At the very center of the complex was another stone outcropping, forming a rough square and sitting some five feet higher than the rest. "This is the castle keep," Sadie told him, and scrambled up to take possession. He didn't know what a "keep" was, and neither did she, but it seemed a likely enough spot. Here wild plants flourished: snowbushes and monstera and a curious curly-headed burst of foliage called star of India. This was the spot Mr. Po came every morning to greet the day. He looked at the sky and thought of his wife.

The golden crown was just passing over the rim of the cliffs. The morning god Lono spread his broad arm, and light fell from his hand. At that moment the trees seem to draw breath. The warmth of the sun penetrated their canopy, waking the animals within and stirring the ground itself. The day had begun. Old Mr. Po turned and found Sadie just below him, staring with a puzzled expression. She wagged her tail and whined.

"What is it?"

She shifted on her feet, agitated. Mr. Po followed her gaze and saw that where the sun had reached the ground it glowed lurid red, almost scarlet. A long shadow appeared. It came from the statue of the old *haole* preacher who settled on these islands many years before. The statue stood a few yards away from the temple, surmounting a cylinder of lava rock. Mr. Po tried not to look at it; the thing was hideous. He watched its shadow instead. Outstretched arms extended, forming a crucifix. The sign of the cross now covered the old *heiau*, as was intended. But then other shadows appeared. For a moment Mr. Po thought light had caught the trees, but there were no trees here. Human figures, distended, restless, writhing. The old man had seen such things before. "Come on," he urged the dog. "Come on, girl. Come away from there." But Sadie, showing a tenacity that reminded him of his late wife, obstinately followed her nose. The shadows covered her now. She paused, whimpered. Her fur stood as if electrified. Mr. Po took a hesitant step toward her, and their eyes met. Black lips drew back from teeth, and she uttered a low but unmistakable growl.

"Sadie?"

Suddenly the old dog threw back her head and howled. But it was not her voice Mr. Po heard.

Chapter 1

MOKUPUNI POINO, THE CURSED ISLAND

Hawaiians think of the Big Island as young compared to its siblings. The oldest, Kauai, is green and soft-shouldered and pleasantly senescent. Oahu, the middle child, is all things to all people. But the Big Island of Hawaii is sharp-edged and prickly with a teenager's mood swings. On the western side, Kona smiles warmly while to the east Hilo grumbles under a perpetual, sodden cloud. The roads upcountry to Mauna Kea veer from lunar landscape to Western prairies; in the south, lava flows from a bottomless cauldron into the sea.

Kaumaha Island lies about fifteen miles off the Kona coast, a long boat ride or a short seaplane trip. The tectonic convulsions that birthed it were incomplete: instead of a single mountain, the sea tossed up a crescent-shaped ridge, giving the island the shape of an apple with one bite missing. Fishermen once lived in the valley but a tsunami in the seventeenth century nearly wiped them out. The survivors came down from the cliffs, buried their dead, and rebuilt. Five years later they were consumed by a second flood. The few who escaped decided that the gods had cursed this place and abandoned it for good. They left its name as a warning to others: *Kaumaha*, Misery Island.

Reverend Amyas Lathrop knew nothing of this when he

purchased the land from King Kamehameha III in 1847. He thought he got a bargain. Kamehameha promised him there wouldn't be a soul there; he could do just as he liked. The king was known to have a lively sense of humor. The reverend built his plantation house of lava rock, smoothed and shaped into a respectable counterfeit of brick. It had two stories and a roof of green tin, encircled by a lanai with koa wood columns and piecework railings that recalled the Mississippi steamboats then coming into fashion. The paint, originally yellow, had weathered into a kind of dusky tan flecked with black spots where the lava shone through. It looked like mottled skin.

Ogden Lathrop stood on the lanai of Lathrop House with a whisky in one hand and a cigar in the other. He squinted in the sunlight, but the view never changed. The valley, a few outcroppings of black lava ruins and, in the foothills, a more prominent cluster capped by the stark bronze figure of old Uncle Amyas. Yet through the myopia of sunlight and sweat he saw a mirage of what was to come. Excavators would cleave the virgin ground; the river would be covered in concrete. The hills would disappear forever behind a white balconied citadel. Ogden wanted to hear the sound the earth made when Tanaka's heavy equipment began to rip it apart. He wanted to see it flying through the air, denuded, powerless. The land. The valley. That wretched incubus on every male Lathrop for almost two hundred years. "Just look at it, Oggy," his father would say, standing on the veranda and sweeping his hand before him, "Have you ever seen anything so beautiful in your life?"

Ogden had, every day, all four years he spent at the University of Pittsburgh getting his business degree. He would have happily traded every one of those hills for a decent pizza delivery. Instead he came back, hung his diploma on the wall, rolled up his sleeves and went out to fix the tractor. For the first few years his father had been with him, querulous, disapproving. A series of strokes slowed his movements and speech, but his eyes were expressive. *Those furrows aren't straight, can't you see that? And the refinery is falling down. Whole place is turning to shit.* Then the old man died and there was nothing to prevent his son from transforming a genteelly unprofitable plantation into a completely disastrous hotel.

Remnants of that experiment surrounded him. A brass-railed luggage cart lay on its side near the porch steps. The gardeners had been using it as a wheelbarrow until one of the wheels snapped. A velvet rope cordoned off the back stairs with a sign that read FAMILY ONLY. *That might be my epitaph,* Ogden Lathrop thought.

"Dad?" His son Roger poked his head through the screen door. "You out here? Gran wants you."

"What for?"

Roger manfully resisted rolling his eyes. He returned from his first year at Hawaii State to discover both his parents somehow diminished in his sight. His father knew perfectly well that Eleanor Lathrop, materfamilias, did not provide a reason for her demands. It was enough to make them known. She was born a Fisk, and the Fisks held almost mystical power on the islands since they first arrived with Captain Cook in 1778. But Roger had also learned a few things. He cast a sharp glance at the plimsoll line in his father's glass. Three-quarters full, which was good—assuming this was the first and not the fourth. "Dunno. But she seemed pretty insistent."

Ogden grimaced. He stubbed out his cigar on one of the railings and kept tight hold of the whisky. "Okay, I'm coming."

The house was a center-hall Colonial of the Federal style, with doors at either end. To the left of the entrance were the front parlor, library, and study. To the right were the music room, dining room, and back parlor, which the family kept for themselves as a den. The front parlor, with its straight-backed

Hepplewhite chairs and uncompromising horsehair settees, was little changed since the late Reverend's wife, Prudence, arranged it to her liking. It was reserved for holidays and occasions of state.

Eleanor waited for them in the front parlor. She sat in the most angular chair and looked as if she might have grown out of it. Though she was nearly ninety, her back was unbent, and her pale blue eyes glittered with a fierce intelligence. She favored her son with a glance of cold disapproval that took in his unkempt, thinning hair, empurpled face and the drink sweating in his hand. "It's only ten thirty," she said.

"For God's sake, Ma, it's blazing outside."

Seven generations of Lathrops had been born on this island, yet Ogden still blistered every time he opened the front door. His face was never without a sheen of perspiration, and he had a habit of running his palm over it like a baker kneading dough. His nose resembled an overripe strawberry.

"Sit down," she ordered.

Ogden sat next to his wife, Marnie, who smiled at him in a bemused sort of way. A thin, colorless woman of fifty, she seemed to blend into whatever background she found herself in. Eleanor observed that she had chosen exactly the wrong shade of green patterned dress against her pale skin. "Marnie," she said impulsively, "don't you own anything besides pastel? You look like a watercolor left out in the rain."

Roger chuckled and was promptly contrite. Marnie smoothed her hands over the fabric as though to erase the pattern. "Oh, this? I saw it in the window at Mauna Loa, and it seemed nice, and the material is very breathable..."

Eleanor cut her off without remorse. "Ogden, if you put one more of your damn cheroots out on my railings, I will impale you with them. You think I can't see the scorch marks? If you want to burn the place down to collect the insurance, for God's sake do it properly." This was wicked, for they both knew he had many times considered doing exactly that.

"Why are we here, Gran?" Roger asked. "If you just wanted to stick pins in us, couldn't we do it in the den, where it's more comfortable?"

Eleanor looked at him kindly. *Thank heaven*, she thought, *that the grandkids have a little spunk.* "At the moment, dear, we're waiting."

"For what?"

"The rest of the family, of course."

Ogden made a noise between a growl and a gurgle. "You don't mean..."

"I certainly do."

Just then the front door opened and shut with a bang. A tall, well-muscled Hawaiian woman entered the room in two long strides, swinging a rucksack from one shoulder. In a tank top and denim she still managed to look regal. Her black hair was pulled into a braid, revealing a heart-shaped face with eyes as dark as caverns. She tossed the sack negligently into the corner and announced, "Hello, family!"

Eleanor was amused. "Lani, dear. Come take a pew." Another figure loomed in the door. "Ah, I see you brought reinforcements."

He was a few years older, just under thirty, with curly black hair tumbling over his shoulders and an expression that was both engaging and insolent. "This is Peter Pauahi," Lani announced casually. Peter wore nothing but a pair of board shorts that looked as if they had been mauled.

"You remember him, Ma," Ogden said with loathing. "He's the one who told the Honolulu papers we were all murderers and rapists."

"I didn't say *all*," Peter corrected with a grin.

"Please sit down, both of you." Eleanor waited as they

settled on the Regency divan, directly across from a smolder-
ing Ogden. "Actually, I'm glad you came, Peter. It makes things
easier." She adjusted herself slightly and looked around at the
assembled company. "Anyone want tea? There's some guava
cake in the fridge."

No one wanted tea.

"All right, then," Eleanor continued, "this has gone far
enough. It was one thing when it was just family, but now Tanaka
wants to bring in outsiders to manage us like little *keiki*. We are
not children. So we're going to end this here, today."

"It's not that easy, Gran," Lani answered evenly. "It's gone
beyond us now."

"It has not. That's what I brought you here to tell you. But
we'll come to that later. First, Ogden, would you please remind
us how you got us into this mess?"

Her son sputtered, "That's a hell of a way to talk about a
twenty-million-dollar deal..."

"Oh, is it that much?" purred Lani. "I didn't realize."

"It's none of your fucking business, that's what it is."

"Enough." Eleanor's tone was sharp. "Very well, as my son is
incapable of coherent speech, I'll tell it for him. Some months
ago he was approached at the Pacific Club by this fellow David
Tanaka. Apparently, they play golf together. Tanaka heard of our
difficulties and offered to come to the rescue. By the end of that
afternoon, they had agreed to sell Kaumaha, and afterward it
was in the hands of the lawyers. Am I right so far?"

Ogden flushed but did not speak.

"My son, as you all know, is managing director of the
Lathrop House Hotel, as well as a trustee in the overall estate.
As managing director, he had every right to sell the hotel..."

"To destroy our village!" Peter interjected hotly.

"...but, as a trustee of the Lathrop Estate, he had no right
to sell the land." She paused and glanced around. Dead silence

greeted her. "Am I not making myself plain? The hotel and the land beneath it are two properties, not one."

Roger cleared his throat. He spoke slowly, choosing each word. "So that means Tanaka paid twenty million dollars for... this house?"

"Correct." She smiled at him like a fond pupil. "Oh, the bill of sale covers the whole island. But there are two trustees for the Lathrop Estate, and the terms of the trust make it clear that both must consent to any sale. I did not give my consent. I *do not* give my consent. Not yet."

Ogden stared at her with glazed eyes. His mouth was open. "What are you talking about?" he finally croaked. "It's done. It's all done."

"Not at all. Your father left you the house, but we own Kaumaha jointly. Your sale never happened."

Ogden crumpled. "But I did it already," he muttered into his chin. "It's done..."

Lani had been silent. Suddenly she leapt to her feet with a war whoop that startled them all. "It's done, all right!" she yelled, triumphant. "Overdone! Burnt to a crisp! Hooray!"

Peter looked at her as if she had gone mad. "But the hotel," he reminded her, "the hotel is sold..."

"The hotel doesn't matter! It's just bricks, and Tanaka can have them. Kaumaha is saved!" She rushed to embrace her grandmother, who held up a monitory hand.

"Not so fast. I haven't finished yet. You'd better take a seat." She waited for a moment, then went on: "I am, as I said, a trustee to the Lathrop estate. I have a responsibility to the island. But I also have a responsibility to my family. *All* of my family," she added, looking at Lani. "The fact is, the hotel is a flop, and sugar isn't coming back. We've made a go of this place for almost a hundred and eighty years, but I don't see how we can keep on. I have to think of the next generation...you and Roger. My dear, this is an enormous amount of money. I know perfectly well that my miserable son will hoard his share. But if you drop the arbitration demand and allow the sale to proceed, you can have mine and distribute it among the villagers as you see fit. What do you say?"

Lani stood irresolute, towering over her grandmother. Her hands dropped limply. "I…I don't know…"

"I do," snapped Peter. "I'm one of those villagers you're talking about. And you want to buy us off. But we still don't get a say. Families that have been here for generations!"

"The island will be sold, no matter what, Peter," Eleanor told him. "If not by us, then by the government, after they claim it for taxes. Better to get something out of it for yourselves. Protesting only makes it worse for your people."

"First you try to buy us off, now you blackmail us. We shut our mouths, or you'll take our homes away. That's it, isn't it? Some kind of *lolo* choice!"

Roger, observing this scene, thought he understood. Until now, Peter Pauahi's life had been singularly free from achievement. He had dropped out of school in Kona at fifteen, drifted back to the island and had remained in limbo ever since. Peter was supposed to be a mechanic's apprentice, floating about the garage with an oil rag dangling from his belt, but no one had ever actually seen him fix anything. Mostly he just hung around the piers and smoked dope with his friends. This fight brought him notoriety, respect. He would not relinquish it easily.

Eleanor continued to look at her granddaughter. Though hardly alike, there was a certain shared quality to their faces. "It's your decision," Eleanor said softly.

Something hardened in Lani, and the kinship faded. "No," she answered. "I can't. It may be the right thing to do, and it may have to happen. But I can't be the one who does it. You must understand that."

Eleanor nodded. "I do."

"WELL, I FUCKING DON'T!" Ogden screamed. He rose from his chair, spittle dribbling down his chin, and turned on Lani. "Where do you get off, anyway? You've never wanted anything to do with us. Always hanging out in the village, down there with *them*. Think I'm going to let you ruin my life, my son's future? You're not even part of this family!"

A moment later there was a sharp sound, like a gunshot. With astonishing speed Eleanor had stood and slapped her son across the mouth. He looked stunned. "That's enough now, you hear?" she hissed. "That girl is your dead sister's child and every bit as much a Lathrop as you or Roger. She may not look like you, but that's to her credit, not yours."

"Of course she's part of the family," Roger put in. He liked his cousin. They played together as children. Less so after the crash, when Lani went to live with grandparents in the village. But she had always been kind to him, in a big-sister sort of way. "Sit down, Dad," he added.

Ogden sat, rubbing his jaw. Marnie patted his knee gently, like a mother comforting a small child. "Do be quiet and listen, dear," she murmured.

But Peter was still nursing an earlier grievance. "We'll fight you!" he vowed. "That arbitration commission, they'll understand. I'll make them understand. You're all nothing but a bunch of rotten *haoles*!"

Eleanor still looked at her granddaughter. Their eyes met for a moment, then Lani looked away. Eleanor sighed and spread her hands in resignation. "Well, that's that, I guess. The decision is mine after all. I won't stop the sale, but I won't encourage it, either. It will go to arbitration."

Ogden looked from one to the other, confused. "I don't understand," he said. "What's happened?"

"Nothing," his mother told him. "Nothing at all, apparently."

———

Mrs. Winnie Te Papa sat at her desk in her usual position: squarely, both feet on the floor, toes in sensible rattan sandals pointed at exact right angles to her body. Her hands gripped the arms of her chair, which left a pendulous fold of flesh draping each side like a bed skirt. Her head tilted back to catch faint breezes from the oscillating fan, which harassed only a few wisps in the disciplined iron braid that hung down her back. Her face was round and serene, carved of koa wood with cracks and seams running cross-grained around a generous mouth, broad nose, and twinkling gray eyes the color of sunlight on water. Reading glasses dangled from a chain around her neck, but these were merely for show; she put them on the tip of her nose when she wished to emphasize a point. In fact, at seventy years old, her eyesight was as good as a girl's.

At the moment she was dictating. *"Dear Professor Chilters, Regarding your letter of Thursday last, I have examined the article in question and it is without doubt a fraud. A genuine tiki would bear rough edges characteristic of a particular kind of native chisel..."*

Even as she spoke, half her mind was on the letter unfolded before her on the desk. The paper was creamy yellow and more cloth than pulp; at the top it bore the legend *Diamond Head Holdings,* with the ubiquitous mountain arcing between the *D* and *H.* The signature at the bottom was a flourish that took up nearly a quarter of the page. *David Tanaka, President and CEO.* In between these two imposing figures was a short, neat paragraph, formally requesting Mrs. Te Papa's honored presence to help arbitrate the sale of Kaumaha Island for the new Royal Poinciana Resort. Her hand slowly crept toward the paper, of its own will, and crushed the soft vellum between thumb and forefinger. Finally, she could bear it no longer. "Marybeth, there is a letter here..."

"Yes, missus."

Her assistant, granddaughter of an old friend, could usually be relied on to spare Mrs. Te Papa the usual requests. These included state lunches, dedication ceremonies, serving as local color—pun, Mrs. Te Papa would say, intended—for visiting dignitaries and, most especially, groundbreakings. These she objected to on principle. "Our ground," she once told the president of a large American hotel chain, "is broken enough." But this, this, was something else again. Mrs. Te Papa adopted the manner mild. "I thought, my dear, that I made it understood that I do not respond to corporations. However well-intentioned they may be."

"Yes. I thought it would interest you."

The unabashed tone intrigued her. She picked up the letter and examined it again. *Yes,* she decided, *I see what the child means.* In the second paragraph was a curious request. *"I hope that we might ask your counsel on certain matters which, though not directly related to development, have raised significant concerns."*

"But why," she mused, "would Tanaka want *my* help?"

Strictly speaking, it was not Marybeth's job to answer her employer's rhetorical observations, but in this instance, she had specific facts. Silently she handed Mrs. Te Papa that day's copy of the *Honolulu Star-Advertiser*. The page had been thoughtfully folded. "Dispute Over Statue Halts Development Plans," the headline blared. Mrs. Te Papa reclined slightly and began to read.

A statue raised over the site of a purported ancient structure is causing headaches for Honolulu hotelier David Tanaka and driving a wedge within the tiny island community of Kaumaha. The island has long been the property of the Lathrop family, though a native Hawaiian village has existed since the mid-19th century. Virtually unknown for decades, the island leapt to prominence last January when Mr. Tanaka, president and CEO of Diamond Head Holdings, submitted an offer for purchase to

the Lathrop family. The decision to sell was made public only this month and has sparked an outcry among the island's residents.

At the center of the dispute, literally, is a statue of Reverend Amyas Lathrop. Erected as a memorial in 1863, it was originally thought to sit on a disused well. But research by famed anthropologist Dr. Robert Ackerman, published in 1975, revealed the cylindrical structure to be the remains of an ancient meeting house that was of central importance to the island's long-lost indigenous population. Mr. Tanaka does not propose to destroy the statue or its base, but it would be incorporated within the hotel complex. This does not sit well with residents. A local action committee, Save Kaumaha, petitioned the State of Hawaii for an injunction to prevent any construction on the site. They also insist the statue be removed. "He's standing atop my culture, my people," says Peter Pauahi, chairman of Save Kaumaha. "It's as if they replaced my history with theirs. And now they're trying to do it again."

Mr. Tanaka disagrees. "These are not Mr. Pauahi's people," he recently stated. "The tribe which built these structures has been dead for centuries. Mr. Pauahi's family came, along with many others, to settle Kaumaha after it had already been purchased from the Kingdom of Hawaii by Reverend Lathrop." Faced with mounting opposition and negative publicity, however, Mr. Tanaka today announced he would be willing to submit the matter to arbitration.

Mrs. Te Papa let the paper fall to her desk with a slap. Her official title was cultural director for the Office of Hawaiian Affairs. It meant, they both knew, a great many committees. "Who else is on the arbitration board?" she asked.

"That professor, for one. Ackerman. And some judge." So, Mrs. Te Papa thought, academia and justice have their voice. And I shall speak for the dead. "They want you there on Saturday," Marybeth added.

The old lady grunted. "That seems presumptuous."

"I already accepted for you and booked the flight."

Mrs. Te Papa swiveled in her chair. *Really, this was getting out of hand.* "Marybeth! It may be the mark of a good assistant to anticipate the desires of her employer, but you go too far! What on earth makes you think I'd want any part of this?"

Marybeth Kualua was of Māori descent, like Mrs. Te Papa's late husband, Winston, and many of their friends. She had a pleasant face, incapable of guile. She also knew her employer better than any person alive and loved her like a mother. "Really, missus! A sacred ruin, an evil developer, and all the natives and *haoles* scrabbling over it? How could you resist?"

Mrs. Te Papa's lips thinned in displeasure, especially as the girl was right. "But I have commitments, meetings... I haven't packed... I'll need to bring myself up to date on the whole business..."

Her assistant was almost smug. "I cleared your schedule and compiled a dossier for you to read on the plane. I'll even read it to you, if you want."

"You?"

"I'm going, too, of course. The stipend was plenty big for two tickets. Who else would run errands for you?"

Mrs. Te Papa realized she was in the grip of forces larger than herself. Still, she protested feebly, "Where will we sleep?"

"The Lathrops are giving their house over for the conference. No other guests except the committee members. They say you will be very comfortable." Marybeth went on to list the arrangements as her employer nodded absently. But in her own mind, Mrs. Te Papa was not comfortable. *Misery Island,* she thought. *A place that drowned its inhabitants.* And another corner of her ever-shrinking homeland that was soon to be sacrificed to the insatiable tourist dollar.

No, she was not comfortable at all.

Chapter 2

I KE AWAWA, THE STATUE IN THE VALLEY

The seaplane was loud and rattled a great deal. Mrs. Te Papa, who had, as she herself described it, a "sufficiency of flesh," felt various parts of it jiggle as if trying to break free. "Not long now!" the pilot shouted over the roar. Next to her, Marybeth was engaged in a kind of pas de deux with the papers in her lap. They tumbled to the cabin floor, she gathered and began to sort them, and with another lurch, they fell again. "Just leave it!" Mrs. Te Papa yelled.

"What?!"

The plane's wing dipped as it made a long arc over Kaumaha Island. She saw the crescent ridge of hills, the long valley, the cluster of houses—more like trailers, from the looks of them—near the water. Lathrop House sat by itself like a sentry post where thick jungle opened into grassland. She tried to spot the famous statue, but the plane was already too low, skidding along the surface of the waves until it came alongside the jetty with a thump.

A welcoming party awaited them. Most of the village had turned out, men in straw hats and baggy shorts and their wives in gaily patterned muumuus. Few were younger than sixty. It was the same with all these little villages, Mrs. Te Papa thought sadly. The young left to find better work, and the old had to fend for themselves. But the boy who came forward to help her with her bags could not have been more than twenty. "Mrs. Te Papa? Welcome to the island. I'm Roger Lathrop."

Mrs. Te Papa was indulgent toward the young and decided she liked this one. He had a warm smile, a splash of freckles on his nose, and calm gray eyes that betrayed surprising maturity. She noticed Marybeth furtively running a hand through her frizzed hair. "Before we head up to the house," Roger told them, "there are a few people who'd like to meet you." An elderly gentleman dressed in a gray linen suit tottered forward and took her hand.

"Gilbert Kapiaho. I'm delighted, Mrs. Te Papa. I've read all your work, of course."

"Really?" Mrs. Te Papa was startled.

"Mr. Kapiaho is our cultural historian," Roger explained. "As well as mayor and grocer, too. I guess you could say he looks after the villagers."

"What's left of them," Kapiaho added ruefully. "May I present my wife, Agnes? And these are the Kupu'ulus..." With almost Victorian courtliness, Kapiaho introduced them all. Mrs. Te Papa shook hands, tried to find something pleasant to say, feeling rather like she was on a royal tour. When it was done, they climbed into the battered jeep as Roger loaded the bags into the back. Marybeth looked chagrined at relinquishing the seat next to Roger, but age and authority won out.

A single road led from the pier through the village and finally to Lathrop House. Mrs. Te Papa looked around her with interest, but there was little to be seen. The village told its familiar story of high aspirations and slow decay. The road was wide and straight with ornamental hitching posts every fifty feet or so, capped with equine bronze figureheads. Here and there were the desiccated remains of a school or post office; a banyan tree had all but consumed the tiny library. Of the original houses, most were nothing but foundations. Kaumaha's current residents lived in shacks built from scrap lumber and lava rock with rusting tin roofs or plastic tarps to keep out the rain. A few sprouted makeshift plywood lanais. Few windows had glass. The only automobile in sight was an ancient Chevrolet resting on cement blocks.

Roger heard Mrs. Te Papa sigh. "Yes," he agreed, "it's been hard for them since the refinery closed."

But as the jeep turned left, a church came into view. Not much bigger than a storage shed, it was freshly painted white with dark green trim and shutters. Window boxes held bouquets of fresh geraniums. There was even a tiny bell and steeple, and the legend *To the Glory of God, 1848* spelled out in gold letters above the doors. "How lovely!" she exclaimed.

"Isn't it? That's all that's left of the original mission. There's a cemetery behind where Uncle Amyas and his wife are buried. Gilbert Kapiaho tends the graves and keeps the church tidy. That's his house next door." He gestured toward a charming periwinkle cottage surrounded by flower beds.

"Do the villagers still use the church?" Mrs. Te Papa wondered.

Roger chuckled. "Kinda. Gilbert runs a general store out of the vestry, and the nave is his own little museum of local culture. But there are still weddings and funerals. More of the latter these days, I'm afraid."

The road took another turn, leading them into a dense jungle that formed a kind of natural barrier between the village and valley. "Are the others here yet?" Mrs. Te Papa asked.

"Tanaka's coming by helicopter later this afternoon. Judge Chan and Professor Ackerman both arrived this morning. The hotel hasn't been this full in years." He made a wry face.

Mrs. Te Papa believed in coming directly to the point. "What," she demanded, "is your opinion of the sale?"

With both hands on the wheel, Roger shrugged. "Well, we

can't afford to keep it, that's for sure. The old place lost money for years as a sugar plantation. Then Dad tried to make a go of it as a hotel. Fired all but a handful of the workers and turned the rest into maids, cooks, desk clerks. Most of them quit after a couple weeks. Now we just have old Agnes, who comes round whenever we have a guest. That's Gilbert's wife, whom you met." Mrs. Te Papa nodded. "We opened up with a big fanfare two years ago," Roger continued, "and it rained for two weeks. Things pretty much went downhill from there." As if in agreement the jeep gave a sudden lurch. They were in a dense thicket of banyans, through which the sun filtered dimly.

"So you are in favor of selling, out of necessity," Mrs. Te Papa summed up.

"Yeah, but not like this. Dad's doing the same thing he did with the plantation. Never told anyone his plans, just handed all the villagers their pink slips. This, too. He announced one afternoon that he'd sold the place to Tanaka, and we were all going to be millionaires."

"How did the rest of the family react?"

"Mom doesn't react much to anything. Gran was properly steamed, but she knows how to hold her fire."

"There are no other children or grandchildren?"

Mrs. Te Papa wondered if it was her imagination or did Roger pause for a moment before replying? "Yes," he said evenly, "my cousin. Ailani Kapiaho."

"The same as..."

"My Aunt Rose married their son, Billy, so Lani is Gil and Agnes's grandchild. Her parents were both killed when their plane went down in the bay during a hard landing. After that she was pretty much raised by the Kapiahos, and by Gran of course." His eyes darkened. "Lani saw it happen. She was only eight."

"How terrible for her," Mrs. Te Papa condoled.

"I saw it, too," Roger went on, as if he couldn't help himself.

"It was a bad storm; they shouldn't have been flying at all. But Billy was my dad's overseer. He ran the plantation. He was on the Big Island for a few days, but Dad wanted him back. Something to do with the accounts. And Billy was worried, because even then Dad was talking about shutting down the farm…" His voice trailed off. "There's the house," he added abruptly.

Lathrop House came into view through a break in the trees. There was a small knot of people standing on the front porch; Mrs. Te Papa saw their heads swivel round with the sound of the jeep's engine approaching. Since some comment was clearly expected of her, she said, "It looks like a very fine house."

"Gran can tell you the history if you want. Although I expect that's why you're here, right?" He winked in a friendly way.

The figures were becoming clearer. A short, paunchy man in a Hawaiian shirt was explaining something to a very thin, very angry old man. In his white polo, white billed cap, and shorts flapping about his meager shanks, the old man looked nothing so much like an irritable stork. The paunchy man was sweating profusely. He made a placating gesture, which the other waved away. Next to them, an elderly lady sat watching the scene with undisguised amusement.

Sounds of the argument reached them before the car rolled to a stop. A high, thin, Oxonian voice was complaining, "No, dammit, you are not hearing me. I have a conference in Cincinnati on Tuesday. Do you know how far that is? I have to prepare an entire presentation on Kotekan earthenware. Forty-five minutes, plus questions. Which leaves me exactly one night to clear up this nonsense and go."

"But, Professor," Ogden Lathrop's voice was a balance of supplication and panic, "Mr. Tanaka expected *three days* of deliberation!"

"Then Mr. Tanaka will learn to live with disappointment."

Mrs. Te Papa joined them on the lanai. Ogden turned to her

with real relief. He swiftly introduced himself and his mother, and added, "This is the famous Dr. Robert Ackerman, who I'm sure you've heard about."

"Naturally," said Mrs. Te Papa, and shook his hand.

Ackerman was not mollified. "Dear lady," he told her, "you have been deceived. Swindled. Inveigled under false pretenses. You were, I expect, told that you would serve on a committee to decide this island's fate?"

"I was."

"Ha!" Ackerman was triumphant. "No such thing! We are not commissioners. We are mere advisers. The decision rests elsewhere."

"I see," said Mrs. Te Papa coldly.

"I expect you do! Moreover, they expect us to remain on this godforsaken island singing its praises for *three whole days.*"

"So I understand."

"But there is so much history to consider…" Ogden interjected in vain.

Dr. Ackerman turned on him wrathfully. "Let me give you some history to consider. I spent six months on this rock in 1972, turning over every leaf and pebble. I know this place better than anyone ever will. I know, for example, that the hot water heater predates the Great Depression, and the shower pressure is on par with the piss stream of an eighty-year-old with an enlarged prostate. I also know that there is not a single screen in this entire house without a dime-sized hole in it, through which all nature comes every night to torment me. I won't even mention the execrable condition of the kitchen or the lack of air-conditioning. Tell me, have you remedied these defects?"

It was plain from Ogden's face he hadn't.

"I am prepared to accommodate Dr. Ackerman's schedule," Mrs. Te Papa informed them. "But I do not like that I have been tricked into coming." Ogden opened his mouth to protest, but she silenced him. "And I should like to know who will have the final authority."

"That would be me," said a cheerful voice.

They all turned. And looked down. Mrs. Te Papa was unhappily conscious of her lack of inches, but this woman could scarcely be taller than five feet. In a periwinkle-blue caftan with gold lace on the cuffs, she looked like an Asian fairy godmother. Her black hair was streaked with gray and pulled into an untidy bun, and her round face beamed with pleasure. "Winnie Te Papa! I'm so excited to finally meet you! I'm Rosalind Chan." The hand that grasped Mrs. Te Papa's was as tiny as a doll's, but its grip was surprisingly strong.

"Judge Chan, I am honored."

"Nonsense, it's me who should be honored. I saw your lecture at Manoa last year. It was fascinating." She went on to quote a large portion of the talk almost verbatim, then politely explained it to Ogden and Dr. Ackerman. Ogden's mouth hung slack. "But what I'm still puzzled about," she persisted, "is your description of the funerary rites. Why should there be so much disparity between the Oahu and Kauai peoples..."

"We were discussing your role here, Judge," Dr. Ackerman cut in ruthlessly.

"Oh, that." The corners of her mouth turned down slightly. "There was a mix-up there somehow. I explained it all *very* carefully to David. When both parties request arbitration, it's a judge—me—that makes the final decision. But I promise you, Mrs.—may I call you Winnie? Yes. I promise you, Winnie, I will make no decision at all until I have heard everything from you and Dr. Ackerman. And I will weigh your testimony very carefully indeed. After all, you're the experts." She bobbed her head to both of them.

"That is very gracious of you," Mrs. Te Papa responded. Ogden looked grim.

A head popped through the front door. A middle-aged woman in an unbecoming lavender blouse looked momentarily startled to find so many people gathered on the porch. "Your rooms are all ready, if you'd care to rest a while," she said in a whispery voice. "Mr. Tanaka telephoned that he is just taking off now, so he'll be here in an hour or so."

Ackerman drew breath for some fresh protest, but Mrs. Te Papa thanked her and led the way into the house. "There's clean towels on each bed and more in the linen cupboard on the landing," Marnie added. "And you'll find a basket of soaps on the sink." Looking sideways at Dr. Ackerman as he passed by, she murmured, "Please let me know if you need anything, anything at all. We hope you'll be very comfortable here."

"Comfortable, hell!" the professor declared, and disappeared up the stairs.

———

Mrs. Te Papa's room was large and sunny with steep dormers and a view of the sea. A quick glance through the windows confirmed the professor's prognosis on the screens, but mosquitoes rarely bothered her. The bed was a four-poster of venerable age, perhaps original to the house. With a practiced eye, Mrs. Te Papa noticed the sheets were thin and worn, but exquisitely clean. She laid down to rest. Only a few minutes passed before there came a gentle knock on her door. She answered it and found Eleanor Lathrop standing there in a floppy sun hat.

"I hope I'm not intruding. Just wondered if you'd care for a walk."

"Certainly."

Eleanor led her down the back stairs and out into the grounds. The sun had reached its zenith, but both ladies were used to the heat. Where sugarcane once grew now stood reeds as high as a man's shoulder that whispered to one another in the light breeze. In contratempo came the low shurr of crickets and the occasional derisive call of a *puaiohi*. The trail wove past rusted remains of farming equipment: scythes, threshers, even the skeletal frame and axle of an automobile. "We used to have a refinery here, too," Eleanor explained, "but it was corrugated tin and ugly as death, so Ogden tore it down after the farm closed. You can still see the foundation over to the left." Mrs. Te Papa marveled at the old lady's agility as she stepped lightly over roots and stones along the narrow path. "Are there many trails like this?" she asked.

"A dozen, maybe. There's some that cut through the valley and one that goes along the cliffs. We carved out a few ourselves, but most date back to the original tribe. This is one of those."

They turned a corner and found more equipment. A backhoe gleamed in the sun, surrounded by a pile of odd-looking implements. "This can't be from the farm?" said Mrs. Te Papa.

"No, no. That's Tanaka's. Brought it over after the sale—the *alleged* sale. It's not construction equipment, just a few things to clear the weeds. I could have stopped them but... Well, it's easier than paying someone to mow the grass, right?" Eleanor grinned.

"And these?" Mrs. Te Papa held something that looked like a Chinese firework wrapped in clear plastic.

"Careful with that! Those are blast caps. Dynamite. They use them to blow out tree stumps."

Mrs. Te Papa replaced it gently on the pile. "Not exactly mowing the grass," she remarked.

"Well, they haven't started yet, have they?"

They walked a bit more before Mrs. Te Papa asked, "What do you know about Mr. Tanaka?"

Eleanor's shrug was the same as her grandson's. "He's local, from Honalo, above Kona. Went to Kahakai Elementary with my friend Eunice's grandson. But when he was twelve or thirteen some relatives swooped in from Japan and carried him off. That was the last anyone heard until about five years ago. Then one spring day he drops down on Honolulu like the Count of Monte Cristo. Penthouse at Koolani, private jet, big cabin cruiser docked at Ala Moana, the works. Even has a kind of ninja that follows him around as a bodyguard."

"A self-made man," Mrs. Te Papa said, though she believed that no man was ever entirely self-made. "And in person?"

Mrs. Lathrop paused to consider. "Smooth," she said finally. "Confident but not arrogant. Excellent manners in a feudal sort of way. He stands up when a lady enters the room. And he's good looking, too, if that matters."

Mrs. Te Papa smiled. "That always matters. Do you know what he plans to do with the island?"

"You'll hear for yourself presently. Come along."

The reeds and tall grass fell away, and they found themselves standing on a hillock facing the sea. Lathrop House seemed very far now. "This is where the ruins begin," Eleanor explained, "but they're all over the place. It must have been quite a town in its day. The star attraction is just over here." They passed the remains of a great *heiau*, which Mrs. Te Papa dated to the fifteenth century. Just beyond it, obscured by its mass, was the statue of Reverend Amyas Lathrop.

The first impression it gave was sheer ordinariness; the second, incongruity. Set against Technicolor hills and among the blackened ruins of a lost tribe, Reverend Lathrop looked like a tourist from Poughkeepsie. He stood with his feet slightly apart and arms outstretched. The gesture was meant to invoke the crucified Lord, but something in the Reverend's stance suggested he had just slipped on ice. In his face Mrs. Te Papa saw the original plan, as it were, of Ogden Lathrop. Both men shared a high forehead, heavy jowls, and small, close-set eyes. But the Reverend's were innocuous, their expression serene.

"Roger, thank God, looks like my side of the family."

"What can you tell me about him?" Mrs. Te Papa asked, gesturing to the statue.

"Old Amyas? I'm surprised no one's told you that story already." She settled on a stone ledge, drew out a collapsible fan, and fanned herself vigorously. "Well, first of all, Amyas and his wife, Prudence, were Baptists. He had a small church near Boston, but the missionary fever hit them, and they came to Honolulu around 1847. By that time, as you probably know, the Mormons had cornered the market. So Amyas had a word with the king and ended up with Kaumaha. He brought a handful of converts, maybe thirty in all. It was they who built him this house and the little chapel in the village. Amyas tried to follow the example he'd seen on Oahu and planted the valley with sugarcane. The first two crops failed. The villagers started drifting away, and Amyas began to wonder if God had a different plan for him.

"Then measles hit the islands in 1848. Brought into Hilo by an American gunboat. Figures, right? It was the worst outbreak Hawaii had ever seen. Thousands died. A hard death, too. Not just the pox but whooping cough and influenza. Not even the royal family was spared. They lost their little girl, their hanai daughter, Princess Ka'imina'auao."

"I remember that story," said Mrs. Te Papa. "Her sister became Queen Lili'oukalani. The family never recovered from the child's death and remained in mourning the rest of their lives."

"They weren't the only ones. Everywhere was bad, but the Big Island was worst of all. Whole towns and villages disappeared. People wandered into Kona from the jungle and the plains, trying to find a doctor, and died right in the street. There were so many that they ran out of coffins. Just dug a great pit, sprinkled some lye on top, and covered them up."

Mrs. Te Papa shook her head sadly. The ravages of Western disease were well-known to her.

"It wasn't long before news reached Amyas. To their credit, he and his wife, Prudence, went to the Big Island at once and volunteered. Amyas prayed over the sick and did what he could. But Prudence had nurse's training in Boston. She was a dynamo. The only large, well-ventilated building on the entire island was Hulihe'e Palace. She went at once to its owner, Prince William Pitt Leleiohoku, and found him being carried out the door in a burlap sack. From that moment Prudence took charge. She ordered all the bedding burned and fresh linens brought down from the attic. She had the servants put all the furniture on the lawn and lay down straw matting in every room. Then she selected five or six ladies-in-waiting and gave them a crash course in nursing. By the end of that day, Kona's first hospital was up and running.

"Of course there wasn't much she could do except wipe their foreheads and give them water, not in 1848. But for the first time the sick were quarantined from the healthy. New cases began to decline. The epidemic burnt itself out, taking with it a third of the native population. And Amyas and Prudence were heroes."

"Amyas, too?"

"He did his share. While Prudence nursed their fevers, Amyas comforted them and gave the Christians among them last rites. He put up a tent in the lawn and began encouraging the survivors to pray. My guess is they didn't need much encouragement. His tent revivals became famous, and even after the epidemic ended, droves of people were still coming to hear him speak. When the time came to return to Kaumaha, Amyas offered a home on the island to anyone who wished to come. About three hundred or so families took him up on it. Maybe they were ardent Baptists, or maybe they figured an island off by itself might be a good place to wait out the next scourge. Either way, they came. And Amyas had his labor force."

Mrs. Te Papa thought for a moment. "That is very interesting, but it does not explain how his statue came to be here. If anything, I should have thought his wife deserved one."

"So she did. But it didn't work out that way. You see, Amyas was murdered."

Eleanor seemed to lose breath on the last word and garbled it. "Did you say martyred?"

"Martyred *and* murdered, yes. About twelve years or so after he came back from Kona. There had been another outbreak of fever on the island—they came every year—and the Hawaiians started praying to Kane, as they always did. Amyas told them this was forbidden. He had overlooked it before, but after a decade I guess he figured they would have embraced the Lord and Savior by now. Once that maggot was in his mind, so to speak, he started looking into everything, trying to see just how deep the rot had gone. He must not have liked what he found. That Sunday he gave a pretty little speech. Told them that they were heathens and savages and not a single one of them would enter the Kingdom of Heaven. Even now, he said, after all these years, he had uncovered a practice among them so revolting that he could not even bring himself to say it aloud."

"Surely he could not just mean a prayer to Kane?" Mrs. Te Papa objected.

"I don't know, and the record doesn't say. Maybe he found something else. The villagers went home properly chastened, but not convinced. Then one of the children became ill, and the Reverend had him quarantined to prevent any spread. The parents objected fiercely, broke into the sick house, and brought him back to the village. But then, of course, the boy died. The villagers wanted to prepare the body in the traditional way: remove the liver and feed it to a bird, salt the body, and wrap it in *kapa* before burning it on a pyre. Amyas was appalled. He came down to the funeral with a Bible in one hand and a musket in the other and ordered them to disperse. They did. But that night someone crept into his bedroom and put an *ihe* through his heart."

An *ihe* was a sharpened wooden spear. It was, Mrs. Te Papa had to admit, a dramatic touch. "They did not harm the rest of the family?" she asked.

"Oh, no. There was only one son, and he had gone to the mainland to fight for the Union. Prudence and Amyas slept in separate rooms. Prudence took his death with real Christian fortitude. The next morning she called one of the overseers to help her, and together they buried Amyas behind the chapel. Prudence said the prayers herself. She must have been furious with the Hawaiians, but she never stopped trying to convert them. Maybe that's why she had the statue made—so that they would never forget. As you can see it's solid bronze and must weigh a ton. I heard it was cast in New York, then lashed to the mainmast of a whaler bound for Hilo."

Mrs. Te Papa turned from the statue to examine its pediment. It was made of the same black volcanic stone as everything else on the island, shaped into a rough cylinder that stood about four feet high. At its base the rocks formed a kind of pyramid that anchored the structure. One of these bore a quantity of cuts and slashes, so worn down by time as to be almost indistinguishable from the rough surface. Mrs. Te Papa crouched until her nose nearly touched but could make no sense of them. "These markings," she called, "what are they?"

"Those are old Ackerman's pride and joy," Eleanor answered with a smirk. "He wrote a whole book about them. You can see they're not Hawaiian, but they were made with Hawaiian tools. He explained to me what it all means—something about the Oceanic Diaspora, I think. Anyway he'll be gassing about it tonight, you can be sure."

It was past midday. Shadows began to creep across the barren ground. Mrs. Te Papa was conscious of a strange unease that she could not, for the moment, place. There was something—not in the rocks, but in the air. Something missing. "Listen," she said suddenly. "Do you hear that?"

Eleanor was still seated on the rock ledge. She cupped her hand over her ear. "I'm a little deaf. What should I hear?"

"The birds."

"I don't hear any birds."

"Nor do I." All the cheerful, busy sounds of the valley had stilled. It was as if something had crowded them out. Mrs. Te Papa barely had time to register this fact before into that hollow shell came the dry crackle of footsteps. "Who's there?" she called, and was irritated by the panic in her voice.

"Where?" Eleanor asked, confused.

An old man shambled out into the sun. He wore patched dungarees and a cotton shirt of indefinable age. His nut-brown face seemed to have collapsed on itself. Next to him trotted a fat and amiable Labrador, who greeted Mrs. Lathrop like an old friend. But when she saw where Mrs. Te Papa stood, she lowered her rump and pretended great interest in a twig.

"This is Mr. Po," Eleanor explained. "One of our residents."

"You're that culture lady?" he demanded. His voice was hoarse, as if he was unaccustomed to using it. "The one from Honolulu?"

"I am Winnie Te Papa," she replied.

"Okay, well you best leave this place alone. It is *kapu*, cursed."

Eleanor rolled her eyes, but Mrs. Te Papa asked seriously, "How do you know it is *kapu*?"

The old man threw a sidelong glance at Mrs. Lathrop and answered in Hawaiian, the phrases tumbling out of his mouth so quickly that even Mrs. Te Papa, who was fluent, had difficulty keeping up. *"I have seen things. Many things. Ever since I was born on this island and my grandmother told me to beware this place, that there were spirits here. But I could not ignore them. They came to me and showed me things. How the village once looked, before the floods. How the priests honored their gods. I was not afraid.*

"But there is something else. Something I cannot see, but it is there. It bubbles up from the earth. This whole ground, if you could see it, is black like a stain. Infected. It comes not as a vision in my eyes but a feeling in my stomach. I used to get this feeling once in a while, not often, like a cramp. Now it is constant. Whatever haunts this ground is rising to the surface like a volcano about to explode."

"What is this feeling?"

"Pain," he answered at once. *"And rage. Hopelessness. Like drowning. And being unable to drown."*

Mrs. Te Papa looked closely into his face. He averted his gaze. *"That is not all,"* she said. *"There is something else. What is it?"*

The man was silent for a moment. He drew a ragged breath, and she was astonished to see tears well in his eyes. *"Hilahila!"* he burst out. *"Shame, terrible shame. I cannot bear it. It suffocates me. All around, everywhere, in the air and earth and water. I tried to help. I tried to help. But I did not know!"* He broke down into sobs and buried his face in his hands. Turning, he fled into the forest. The dog looked at the two women for a moment, as if apologizing, then loped off after her master.

"Gracious me, that was something." Mrs. Lathrop still sat with her legs tucked like a Buddha on the stone ledge. It was impossible to interpret her expression. "Did you understand all of it?"

"The words, yes. But the meaning…"

There was a sound like a wasp buzzing above their heads. They both looked up just as a sleek white helicopter breached the cliffs at low altitude, its body gleaming. Mrs. Te Papa could just make out the Diamond Head Holdings crest on the tail. The pilot executed a long arc that moved the copter's shadow over the entire valley before turning toward the harbor and disappearing out of sight.

"We'd better go back," Eleanor said.

Chapter 3

KA HĀLĀWAI, THE HEARING

Almost unconsciously, Mrs. Te Papa formed an image in her mind of the mysterious Mr. Tanaka. When he was finally revealed, the similarity was so uncanny that she wondered if she had second sight. He stood as she entered the room, just as Eleanor said he would.

He was tall, over six feet, but so slender that he seemed taller still. "Winnie Te Papa," he said with a broad smile, "I am so pleased to meet you at last." The hand that took hers was beautifully made. Like a concert pianist's, she thought. He was conscious of his height and inclined slightly so that it did not seem as though he were towering over her. The face that peered down at her could have done credit to any billboard in Honolulu.

"Mr. Tanaka," she managed.

"David, please. I believe you know my great-aunt, Mildred Hayakawa?"

"Yes, she is one of my oldest friends." Mrs. Te Papa marveled at the skill with which he established intimacy so quickly. She also suspected Tanaka could dredge up an uncle or at least a second cousin to match every person in the room.

"Now that we're all here..." Ogden began, but his mother cut him short.

"Really, Ogden, that's the second time you've forgotten your own niece! I think you're going senile."

They did not have long to wait. Lani arrived, again with Peter in tow, and Ogden handled the introductions with bad grace. Mrs. Te Papa was reminded at once of the paintings she had seen in Iolani Palace. Ailani Kapiaho had the high cheekbones and aristocratic features of her grandmother Eleanor, but there was something of her grandfather Gilbert in her warm, kind eyes. She was tall and muscular, of almost the same dimensions as the local man with her. Her dark hair had been allowed to follow its own whim today and tumbled about her shoulders. In her face Mrs. Te Papa saw forcefulness, intelligence, and great anxiety. Peter, the "boyfriend," she immediately wrote off as a *nunoao*, an idiot. He had condescended to wear a shirt to these proceedings, though it was gray with age and bore several oil stains. His manner oscillated between swagger and truculence.

Some unseen hand had laid out a generous buffet in the dining room, but only Mrs. Te Papa and Dr. Ackerman attacked it with any enthusiasm. Judge Chan joined them at one corner of the long table. "I feel," she said, "like I have wandered into one of those awkward Thanksgiving dinners that end in chaos. If there were mashed potatoes, I expect they'd be throwing them soon."

Ackerman, his mouth full of pork, nodded agreement.

"As far as I can tell," the judge went on, "Ogden Lathrop is the driving force behind the sale. What his mother thinks is anyone's guess. His son and wife accept it as a necessity—which, judging by the financial statements I've seen, it is."

The professor swallowed. "Oh?" he asked interested.

"They owe nearly a decade's worth of taxes. Frankly, I'm surprised there hasn't been a lien placed on them yet."

"That's the one I am interested in," said Mrs. Te Papa, gesturing with a chicken leg.

"The granddaughter? Yes, it's tragic, isn't it? Like those

families that had a foot in both camps during the Civil War. The poor child is obviously near to collapse."

Lani did not look near to collapse. She sat in what Mrs. Te Papa thought of as the "children's corner," between Roger, Marybeth, and Peter. She was talking animatedly. But Mrs. Te Papa noticed her hands twisting themselves in her lap. Eleanor, caught in the middle of an intense discussion between Ogden and Tanaka, had seen it, too. A worried frown appeared on her brow.

Tanaka broke free of Ogden and brought his plate over to join them. "I hope this isn't a breach of etiquette," he said with a smile.

Judge Chan slid over to make room. "Fortunately, arbitration is not a lawsuit. We can allow a little informality here. In fact, I must say it makes a nice change from my day-to-day."

Dr. Ackerman asked politely, "What is your usual—is 'practice' the right word?"

"Close enough. Family court. Compared to a disputed custody case, this lot are blowing kisses at one another."

"Money," said Mrs. Te Papa, "has ruined more families than infidelity or drink. In my experience."

Tanaka grinned. "I'll try not to take that personally, Winnie."

The dining room door opened and Marnie flitted in. She cast her gaze over the assembly before darting over to Tanaka. "I'm so sorry," she said breathlessly, "but I wonder if your man—I mean, the gentleman you came with—I know he's upstairs now, but do you think he might…possibly…be…hungry?" Her voice faded into a whisper.

"That is very considerate of you, Mrs. Lathrop. I will make sure he eats something."

Marnie made a jerking motion toward the door, but Rosalind Chan held her arm. "My dear," she said, "I have only just realized. Do we have you to thank for this wonderful meal?"

Some women blush when paid an unexpected compliment; Marnie went pale. "Oh. Yes. I mean, thank you. And you're welcome. Of course." She broke free and nearly ran for the exit.

Dr. Ackerman bit off another piece of chicken and chewed it thoughtfully. "You know," he said, "I think that woman's crazy."

"She's a very good cook," Mrs. Te Papa allowed. "But, yes, she is certainly afraid. I wonder why."

"I think it's Dr. Ackerman here," said Tanaka mischievously. "He bullies her."

"I? I never said a word to her. I was addressing myself to that dunderhead of a husband."

Tanaka's face darkened. "I'd like to know what *he's* afraid of. He latched on to me like a limpet the moment I arrived. But he has to know it's out of my hands now. What's he playing at?"

The quartet turned their gaze on Ogden Lathrop, who at that moment was shoveling French fries into his mouth morosely. "Did you bring your man with you?" Judge Chan asked Tanaka. "I didn't know we could bring spouses. Why doesn't he want to eat with the rest of us?"

Tanaka chuckled. "I think Mrs. Lathrop means Kaito. He is my bodyguard. And not, incidentally, my type."

"I can't imagine you would be in much danger here," Ackerman remarked. "Except from dengue fever or rheumatism."

"On the contrary, I am in much greater danger here. My home, office, and car are all well-protected. Here, I am quite exposed."

Mrs. Te Papa frowned. "You have enemies, Mr. Tanaka?"

"David, please," he repeated. "Yes, Winnie. Every businessman has enemies. There are those who would kidnap me for ransom. And there are competitors who stand to lose millions if I succeed."

"Including this project?"

"Certainly. There is, for example, a very powerful Filipino

developer named Rodrigo Roxas who purchased several hundred acres near Kailua. If I build first, his resort will be redundant."

Mrs. Te Papa was intrigued. "Would he really kill for something as petty as that?"

"He has done so before," Tanaka answered gravely. There was an uncomfortable pause.

"Where is your room?" Ackerman wanted to know.

"On the west side, facing the sea. Why?"

"Good. Mine faces the valley." He took another bite of chicken, swallowed. "Just don't want the ninjas to get confused."

———

Judge Chan called the hearing informal, yet Mrs. Te Papa felt an odd frisson as she entered the library and saw a semicircle of chairs facing a single, throne-like seat. The judge lifted herself onto it, feet dangling like a child's. "Now," she began, "I think it would be helpful to set a few ground rules, don't you? First, I propose to hear from our esteemed experts, Dr. Ackerman and Mrs. Te Papa, on the historic and cultural significance of the site. Then I shall hear from Mr. Tanaka on his development plans. If the Lathrop family have anything to add, they may, of course, do so. But I ask that there be no interruptions, and any questions should be addressed to me. Are we agreed?"

Everyone nodded. Mrs. Te Papa leaned over to Marybeth next to her. "You have your notepad? Write down what everyone says." Marybeth pulled out her pencil just as the judge said, "Dr. Ackerman, you may begin."

Ackerman spoke at exhaustive and exhausting length. He brought slides. His audience was treated to a frame-by-frame depiction of Kaumaha, with parenthetical comparisons to similar ruins at Kaniakapupu, Mo'okini, and Hikiau. When he finally came to the slides of the statue column, his eyes lit with zeal. "Now this," he said, "is truly fascinating. You will note these markings *here* and *here* and *here*. At first glance they resemble early Hawaiian glyphs, but do not correspond to any known system in the Polynesian pictorial lexicon. As you can see, they are much eroded. When I first came to study the site in 1972, I assumed that other defining marks had worn away. But on comparison with..."—he named five or six other Oceanic tribes as his listeners' eyes glazed—"...I ultimately determined that they were identical with those of the Asmat tribe of Papua New Guinea!" He paused, as if waiting for applause.

"That is most interesting, Professor," Judge Chan said politely. "Would you mind elaborating?"

Ogden stifled a groan.

"Certainly. The Asmat were voyagers. We have already charted their diaspora throughout the Oceanic world as far as Tonga. But the discovery of these glyphs proves that they made it all the way to Hawaii—they were, in fact, the original tribesmen on this island."

"And you were able to decipher the markings?"

"Indeed, yes. There are three of particular interest. This figure here represents a meeting house or temple. Its literal translation is "where they are gathered." The second signifies bone and flesh. The third, just below, represents quantity or plenty. Taken together, these symbols correspond to a site of great significance to the Asmat people, the House of the Bone Feast."

"Christ!" Ogden burst out suddenly. "They were cannibals!"

Dr. Ackerman gave him a withering look. "That is irrelevant, sir. Guinean tribes mark the passage into manhood through a ritualized ceremony, the most important of a man's life. A great hall is constructed and decorated with effigies of the recently deceased. This is the bone feast house, or *emak cem*. Young boys are kept isolated within the ritual house for several months—"

"Months!" bleated Roger, horrified.

"So that they may commune with the spirits of the dead, yes," Ackerman answered impatiently. "After which time the boys are released, one by one. They are made to crawl on their bellies over *wuramon*, ritual canoes bearing animal carvings. Each animal represents a dead relation. By crossing over them, the boys ingest a part of their essence. After which, they are seized by a tribal artisan who carves designs into their bodies with a hot blade. The scar tissue becomes a kind of tattoo."

He looked around triumphantly. There were several seconds of appalled silence.

"Do you have any idea what the other marks on the column mean?" asked the judge finally.

Ackerman shrugged. "They appear to be some kind of numerological measurement. But as to the purpose, it is impossible to know."

"So it is your belief that the statue base once formed a part of this bone feast house?"

"There is no question. The pyramidic shape is identical to the framing structures found in Papua New Guinea. Were it not for that horror of a statue, you might well see even more defining characteristics on the cap."

"So I presume you favor its removal?" An idea came to the judge. "Perhaps," she suggested brightly, "we could transfer the statue to a *different* location on the island…"

"No," said Ackerman flatly. Feeling this might be somewhat harsh, he condescended to explain. "Unfortunately, a quantity of liquid concrete was poured onto the base and into the aperture, which I believe was hollow. The statue is affixed to that concrete. Consequently, any attempt to remove it would result in its destruction. More importantly, it would also destroy the site." He glared at Ogden as if it was all his fault.

"Oh, I see." Judge Chan looked disappointed. "Thank you, Professor. Mrs. Te Papa, what are your thoughts?"

Mrs. Te Papa rose from her chair and spoke briefly. "As to the historic significance of the site to the Hawaiian people, I defer to Dr. Ackerman's excellent analysis. There can be no doubt this is a place of great importance. But that importance does not lie only in its past. Today there are tragically few native villages left on these islands, a fact of which I am sure you are aware. Most have been relocated or destroyed for precisely the same reason as this one: to make way for tourists. I would not call the village on Kaumaha pretty. It is not picturesque. But it has existed here for over one hundred and seventy years, and I think that deserves consideration."

The judge rubbed her chin thoughtfully. "It's a singular case, though," she mused. "The Lathrop family has been here just as long as the villagers. Neither could be described as indigenous. Am I to favor the Hawaiians simply because they are Hawaiian?"

"No, Judge. But consider the circumstances. The Lathrops own the land, for which the villagers have paid rent since time immemorial. Their situation is comparable, I think, to the English feudal system. The seigneur has certain responsibilities that run with the property. Among them, surely, is the obligation not to arbitrarily deprive people of land which their great-great-great-grandparents tilled."

Roger looked rather startled at being described as a lord, but Eleanor dropped her gaze sadly. "That is very true," Judge Chan admitted. "I must think on that."

Ogden was on his feet at once. "Judge, we have papers... rental contracts...bank statements... Some of these people haven't paid rent in years. Here, let me show you." He almost shoved the file under her nose. Judge Chan turned the pages over one at a time. "Yes, I see that. You have also chosen to cut off their access to electricity, which you yourself supply."

"That turbine costs me six hundred dollars a month!" he protested. "Am I supposed to just eat the cost?"

Peter, who had remained unusually silent until now, spoke up. "It's not just the electricity!" he shouted. "He turns our water off, too. And the houses are falling down, no repairs at all. Some of them even have tar paper for roofs!"

"I believe," the judge said mildly, "I asked for no interruptions. That means you, too, Mr. Lathrop." She turned to Tanaka, who had been idly studying the ceiling. "You had a statement to make?"

Startled, he leapt to his feet. "Yes, Judge. It is just this. After some consideration, I have decided to alter the blueprints for the Poinciana Resort. The original design, as you know, extended to the cliffs and incorporated the ruins. If I may, I'd like to show you these." He unfurled a large sheet of drafting paper. It was a map of the island, gorgeously colored. On it were depicted several buildings resembling long huts with thatched roofs. The rusty pier was gone, a sparkling marina in its place. "As you see, the proposed buildings lie between Lathrop House and the sea; the valley is unencumbered."

"But the village?" the judge asked.

"The area where the village presently sits will be needed. But, aside from the old chapel, there are no historic dwellings, nothing at all of the original settlement. I propose to build a condominium complex that will house all the residents. They will pay exactly the same rents as they do now, in perpetuity."

Judge Chan took the blueprints and examined them for some time. She looked to Lani and Peter. "This seems a much more equitable plan. Does it alter your views at all?"

Lani was thoughtful. "May I see those?" The judge handed the plans to her. After a long moment, Lani turned to her grandmother. "Does your offer still stand?"

"Yes, dear. Of course it does."

"Then..."

"NO!" Peter was on his feet, wild-eyed. "How can you do this? How can you sell us out?"

"Peter, I'm not. The island will have to be sold anyway, don't you see? This way the villagers can stay."

"In a frigging condo?"

"A home, yes," continued Lani. "But I also plan on dividing up my share, thanks to Gran. They won't have to work another day for the rest of their lives."

For a moment Peter was speechless.

"You claim to represent the villagers," the judge pressed gently. "Surely you could ask them how they feel?"

"I…I don't…" he sputtered.

"I'll ask them," Lani said. Her expression had hardened.

Peter looked at her as if he had never seen her before. Without another word, he stormed out of the room. They heard the front door slam.

"Whew," Ogden said, mopping his brow with a handkerchief. "You sure know how to pick 'em, Lani."

But Lani was not listening. Her gaze was still fixed on the door, a small frown creasing her forehead.

———

Down in the village, Mr. Po was having a bad day. He wondered whether it was right to speak to the culture lady as he did. He had looked like a fool. Or a madman. Since there no one to share these worries with, he muttered to himself. Sadie watched him from the couch as he shuffled around the tiny shack, meticulously wiping and re-wiping the furniture. The pain in his stomach was worse tonight. Odd thoughts kept popping into his mind: bits of conversation, images of places and people he had never seen. Once he turned toward the bathroom and had the distinct feeling of dropping his foot into freshly fallen snow. For one moment he saw a narrow lane lit with kerosene lanterns, everything glowing electric blue in the dusk. Heard the sound of a church bell tolling the hour. *Evensong,* his brain told him, even though had no idea what evensong meant. Then it was gone.

Lately he felt as if his entire body were a poorly tuned transistor radio. He had no control over the dial. There was even a moment just now when he lurched into the library at Lathrop House, heard the professor with the frizzy white hair saying, *"Unfortunately a quantity of liquid concrete..."* He also heard what the professor was *not* saying: *"Such a waste of time. Terrible place, don't know why I came. If I get up at six, I can call for the seaplane at nine and be back in time to catch the Lakers..."* Then Mr. Po felt a terrible stabbing pain in his chest and fell, as it were, back into himself.

Sadie got up from the couch, waddled over, and put her cold nose in his hand. It was all she could think of to do. But it worked. Mr. Po stroked her head, smiled. "Good girl," he said. "Good girl." She gazed up at him adoringly.

It was then he heard the first crack of thunder, not outside but in his mind. This was another useless skill: he knew the weather before it came. Somewhere out at sea the clouds were gathering, like an army preparing to march. In an hour or two they would arrive. Mr. Po checked to make sure the screens were down and sandbags in all the doorframes. "Ku," he said aloud. But then he thought: *Ku?*

"Ku demands a sacrifice."

It was a complete thought this time, as legible as if he were taking dictation. His brain sent signals to the lips and tongue, which formed the words and spoke them. Only then did he know what he had said. Sadie thumped her tail on the floor, looked at him expectantly.

Mr. Po felt an enormous pressure in the back of his head. He staggered to the couch and fell facedown. His sight was gone; he believed he was having a stroke. Sadie nuzzled him worriedly.

But he was already miles beneath the earth. It pressed down until his chest collapsed, and he could no longer breathe. The earth, or rather the black, shapeless thing that lived within the mud and rocks and roots, was speaking. *"KU DEMANDS...."*

The eruption came. It roared up from the core, molten and furious. At the center of its white-hot light a brilliant kaleidoscope of images formed and reformed endlessly. Every voice he had ever heard sounded at once. The light and sound broke through the surface and shot, geyser-like, toward an opening sky. In his tiny cabin, Mr. Po fell from the couch and began to rock back and forth. He was screaming, but there was no breath left to scream.

———

Judge Chan shuffled the pile of papers in her lap. "Very well," she said in her bright chairwoman voice, "let's see where we stand. It seems to me that there are two separate issues here: the proposed development and the removal of the statue. As to the first, the only equitable choice seems to be to let the villagers themselves decide if they would be willing to trade their homes for—as I understand it—a lump sum and a new dwelling. If a majority agree, then the sale may go forward."

Ogden had not followed much of the previous half hour, but he understood this at once. "And if they vote against?" he demanded.

The judge answered calmly, "Then it will not."

Ogden turned furious eyes on Tanaka, but the other man merely shrugged. "It seems only fair," Tanaka said. "Miss Kapiaho, will you have a word with the residents and find out if they are agreeable?" Lani nodded.

"Splendid," said the judge. "That just leaves the statue. I take Dr. Ackerman's point about the concrete, but assuming it *could* be removed, we must decide whether it should be."

Tanaka had gotten what he wanted. He knew the villagers would vote for the sale, despite Ogden's palpitations. Now he stretched his limbs like a cat. "I don't give a damn about the thing either way," he said lazily. "It doesn't add much to the landscape."

This rather cold appraisal seemed to shake Lani free of her trance. "It needs to go," she burst out. Turning to her grandmother, who sat next to her, she apologized. "I'm truly sorry, Gran, but I can't think of a more glaring example of cultural defilement. Amyas Lathrop might have been a good man, but he did his best to destroy my ancestors' culture and religion and replace them with his own. Seeing him perched atop that sacred place, all smug and triumphant—honestly, after everything that's happened, I can't bear to look at the thing."

"You've managed to look at it for twenty-five years," Ogden growled.

"I wasn't the one who brought us to this point. You did, Uncle. But since we are here and a decision must be made, it's important that we make the right one. The village is lost, and I know that's my doing more than anyone's. So maybe this is my way of atoning. I don't know. But I say it should come down."

"You have nothing to atone for," Eleanor said sharply. She took her granddaughter's hand in both of her own. "You hear me? *Nothing*. This should never have been your fight."

The judge looked upon this domestic scene with motherly approval. "Well, that about settles it. Unless someone would like to make a case for letting the statue remain?"

Mrs. Te Papa looked to Ogden, but it was Roger who got to his feet. He cleared his throat nervously. "I know how Lani feels," he said, his voice barely above a whisper. "I know how I would feel if it were my people down there in the village. But I'm a Lathrop. So if we're discussing culture and history, I think maybe mine should matter, too. Like Lani said, Amyas Lathrop was a good man. He and his wife helped a lot of people. And as *you* said, Judge, the natives who came with Amyas to this island came willingly. They believed in its mission. Maybe he was wrong and they were wrong, but that doesn't really matter, does it? Whoever put that statue there was asking that Amyas be remembered, nothing more. Don't we owe him that? My family is a part of this island's history. I want to be able to bring my kids back here someday and tell them that story. Why should we say one people deserve to be remembered and another doesn't?"

Roger looked around the room for approval but was met with glares. Stammering, he soldiered on, "I mean, it would be terrible if they tore down one monument to build another. But if I understand what Dr. Ackerman was saying, they just put the statue on top. It's kinda like that church I read about in Rome—a medieval church built over an early Christian basilica, over an old Roman temple..."

"San Clemente," Ackerman supplied.

"Right, that. It's just layers of history. Each one doesn't destroy or disturb the other. It's just there. So I say we...leave it there." Roger coughed and accidentally caught his cousin's eye. He sat down abruptly.

There was a long silence. Mrs. Te Papa leaned over to Marybeth and whispered, "Did you get all of that?" Marybeth nodded. Next to her, Eleanor looked thoughtfully at her grandson, who blushed and kept his eyes on his sandals. Lani seemed lost once again in some private contemplation. Ogden fidgeted. His wife stared at her own reflection in the dark window glass.

But Judge Chan had been thinking. Her head rested on the palm of her hand like a contemplative cherub. She wrote a few lines on the legal pad in her lap, sighed, and donned a pair of half-moon reading glasses. "I'm ready to make my ruling now," she said.

Everyone in the room sat a little straighter in their chairs. The judge turned to Marybeth. "You, miss, I'm so sorry I don't know your name. Are you taking notes? Very good. I'll try to speak slowly. In the matter of the sale and development of Kaumaha Island, the parties are agreed that a poll will be taken among the current residents, and if a majority favors the sale— along with the stipulations made by Mr. Tanaka on behalf of Diamond Head Holdings—the transfer and development may proceed. Should the question fail to reach a majority, we will reconvene at a later date to discuss options." Both Tanaka and Lani nodded.

"The statue of Amyas Lathrop is a thornier question. Monuments are frozen in time, representing the hopes, beliefs, and even prejudices of those who built them. But, at bottom, they are a cry for remembrance into the endless unknowable void. That cry reaches us now, at this moment. We must decide whether future generations will hear it as well.

"Dr. Ackerman has indicated that significant damage may result to both statue and site if the attempt is made. Moreover, while I take Miss Kapiaho's remarks to heart, I agree with Mr. Lathrop that it is unwise to put a hand too firmly on the scales of history. Let us say this. At one time this island was settled by a tribe of voyagers, late of New Guinea. At another time it was settled by a Christian missionary and his converts. I see no reason why both stories may not be told. It is my judgment that the statue remain in place."

———

The storm Mr. Po predicted arrived exactly when he knew it would. Mrs. Te Papa heard the first rumble of thunder in her room, where she was resting. It was just past seven o'clock, and the sun still shone through the windows. A moment later it was gone. She rolled over and saw the cloud, black as death, hurtling toward her. "Good," she said to herself. "It will clear the air." With that satisfactory thought she fell asleep.

Eleanor had taken up her customary perch on her bedroom lanai. She liked to watch storms. The weather in Hawaii was wonderfully dramatic, shouting its lines to the back of the theater and chewing up scenery. When the first lightning bolt streaked, Mrs. Lathrop let out a pleasurable sigh.

Lani joined her. They watched the storm in silence for a few moments until Lani said, "I hope you're not mad at me." The clatter of the rain nearly drowned her words.

"Why should I be?"

"The statue. The sale. Everything. I know I'm still half a Lathrop; you don't need to remind me. But being half of both is the same as being neither."

"I'm not sure about that. What does your grandpa say?" Gilbert Kapiaho was a sensible man and a good man. Over the years Eleanor had come to recognize many of his best qualities reflected in Lani.

"He doesn't want to lose his home, but he knows the island will end up getting sold anyway. He said we should make the best deal we can."

"I told you the same thing."

Lani sighed. "I know. It just seems so...overwhelming. Like everything is coming to an end. Not just the island. Everything."

"Peter?" Eleanor asked intelligently.

"I don't *understand* him. At first it all made sense, when we thought we'd lose the village after the sale. But then it seemed like the more Tanaka gave, the more inflexible Peter became."

The perfect definition of a nitwit, Eleanor said to herself. Aloud she asked, "Was it his idea to go after Uncle Amyas?"

"Yes. He said it was like a back door. For the statue to be removed, the land under it would have to be declared significant or sacred. If that happened, Tanaka couldn't build. He said the statue was the key to the whole thing."

Eleanor was surprised. "That's actually rather clever."

"I thought so, too. Then once Tanaka caved, it didn't matter anymore. But by then the statue was already in the crosshairs… I'm sorry. I know the family matters a lot to you."

"Does it matter to you? You're a Lathrop, too."

"Am I?" Lani seemed genuinely puzzled. "Most of the time I feel like someone's unwanted bastard, the one that shows up for family picnics and spoils everything."

Her grandmother's eyes narrowed. "Has anyone besides Ogden ever made you feel that way?"

"Never…deliberately."

Mrs. Lathrop stared at her granddaughter for a long moment. "Come with me," she said, rising. "I want to show you something."

Eleanor reached under her bed and drew out a slender object about two feet long, wrapped in oilcloth. She laid it on the desk and pulled back the fabric delicately. "Do you know what this is?"

Lani thought it looked rather like an arrow, except shaft and blade were made from a single piece of ebony, honed sharp. The edge was serrated and there were markings along its length. Halfway down was a handgrip of bone ringed with feathers, now yellowed with age. The thing was ancient and terrible and beautiful.

"It's called an *ihe*," Eleanor explained. "Sort of a cross between a dagger and a spear. The tribes used them for close combat. Would you like to hold it?"

Gingerly, Lani took the weapon in her hands. "It's so light," she said wonderingly.

"It's the one that impaled old Uncle Amyas."

Lani gave a tiny cry as her fingers uncurled. The *ihe* seemed to writhe in her hand like a snake. "How did you get this?" she asked, her eyes wide.

"Well, that's rather the story, dear, isn't it? Come, sit down. Bring that with you."

They sat next to one another on the chesterfield, the spear between them. The rain continued to beat a staccato tempo against the roof, drowning out all other sounds. "It is time you knew your true inheritance," Eleanor said so quietly that her granddaughter had to lean in to hear. Then, speaking softer than the rain, Eleanor began to tell her.

> *"A True Account and Journal of the Settlement of New Boston Island, Formerly Kaw-maw-ha, Begun This 23 of January, 1848, by Reverend Amyas Lathrop," EXTRACTED (Courtesy of the Fisk Collection at the University of Hawaii, Manoa. A gift of Mrs. Eleanor Lathrop)*

March 3, 1848 in Kona-Town

My purpose holds fast; I am resolved. The plague that infects these islands can only be the work of Almighty God—for have I not seen myself how fire burns a forest clean, that new growth may emerge? So it is here. The fever shall burn away all blasphemies. Let them pray to their false idols and see what good it does them. "These be thy gods, O Israel, which have brought thee up out of the land of Egypt!"

I purged my bowels again this morning. It is a source of ceaseless wonder to me that my body incorporates all the foul sustenance of this place, strange fruits, and seeds, and converts all into that which is wholesome and good. Except for certain bilious attacks, indigestion, and flatulence. I recommend a similar diet of barley water and hourly prayer to any Christian white man who ventures upon the Sandwich Isles. Certain emetics like bayberry or mustard may also be introduced to keep the system vital.

I prayed over nine men today and showed eight of them the glories of Christ before their spirit parted from their bodies. The peace and satisfaction writ upon their faces was wonderful to see. I may sleep tonight with the knowledge that eight souls rest in the bosom of our Redeemer—not a bad day of work! Of the ninth I am disconsolate. Earnestly I entreated him, prayed with him, read him the comforting words of Paul to the Ephesians. "And you hath he quickened, who were dead in trespasses and sins; wherein in time past ye walked according to the course of this world, according to the prince of the power of the air..." Yet through it all he continued to cling to some revolting graven object and muttered the same rites until he became delirious from the fever, and I could no longer reach him. I fear his soul is cast to perdition. If only there had been more time.

Chapter 4

AHI, THE BONFIRE

Mrs. Te Papa awoke to darkness. She fumbled for her wristwatch on the nightstand, saw it was past ten. Her windows were open and revealed nothing except the familiar ribbon of sea, now lit by a waxing moon. But her sensitive nose smelled woodsmoke and from somewhere below came the unlikely sounds of a party. She heard footsteps pass her door. Popping her head out into the corridor, she encountered Marnie heading toward the landing with a large silver punchbowl in her hands. "Oh!" Marnie cried, and dropped it, sending cups skittering in every direction.

Gallantly, Mrs. Te Papa helped her recover them. "I hear voices outside," she said. "What's happening?"

"I'm so sorry!" That seemed to be Marnie's default setting. "You see, Oggy—my husband—thought we should all celebrate the agreement with a bonfire, just to show no hard feelings. And I knew I should tell you, but then it seemed rude to wake you, but then I thought if you *did* wake up because of all the noise—"

"Not at all," said Mrs. Te Papa firmly, cutting her off midstream. "I will be down in a moment." But she did wonder if this bonfire was merely a backdrop for Ogden Lathrop to indulge his favorite pastime.

Her prediction was correct. In the yard beyond the lanai,

Ogden presided over the bar and helped himself liberally. He expounded at length on the iniquities of the island to the only sympathetic listener he could find, Dr. Ackerman. "See, it's the lack of mineral content in the soil," he was saying in a too-emphatic voice, "Nothing grows right. Like moon dust. And the hotel didn't work cuz it's too damn far away and the house needs a ton of repairs…"

"You need hardly tell me that," Ackerman answered snappishly. "I've killed five mosquitoes in my room, and I'm sure that's not the last. In fact," he added with a kind of gloomy relish, "I brought my old copy of Ridgeway's Latin Lexicon from when I was here in '72. Best thing in the world to squash the little bastards."

Ogden muttered something about repellent, but Ackerman scoffed. "That does nothing! Nothing at all! If I even *hear* one buzzing…."

Further from the house, Roger sat on a felled log with Marybeth. They stared into the fire and their hands almost touched. "Will you miss all this?" she asked him.

Roger thought for a moment, shrugged. "I suppose we all miss the place we grew up."

"But not everybody gets to grow up *here*." Marybeth's clannish Māori family occupied a block of flats in a seedier part of Honolulu. She had shared a room with five cousins, two cats, and a parakeet until she was eighteen.

"It's not all that great," Roger assured her. "There's no Wi-Fi, the water tastes like sludge, and the electricity sputters. A big house like this is basically a ship sinking one inch at a time. There's always something falling off or rusting through. The roof, the drains, the floorboards, the wiring…it goes on and on. And nobody to fix it but us."

Marybeth was not fooled. "You love this place," she said intelligently. "You don't want to lose it."

"I don't. But I will. No matter what happens, I'll be the last Lathrop born on Kaumaha." He ran a hand though his sandy hair. "It's not even that, not really. But we all worked so damned hard for so many years. Mom especially."

"Your mother?" Marybeth had noticed Marnie in the way that someone does a house cat, and she felt rather guilty about it.

"She's a Lathrop, too, distant cousin or something. Grew up on the mainland but used to come here once a year for the big family reunions. I guess this place was like fairyland to her. Sometimes I think she married Dad just to be able to finally call it home." Roger laughed ruefully. "What a white elephant that turned out to be. All those years of hammering away, keeping it all going on a shoestring or less, and now—nothing."

"But with the money from the sale..."

"Which may not happen. I have a feeling Lani's going to try to make the villagers vote against it. To be honest, I don't blame her. Even if it does go through, Mom and I will never see a penny anyway. Dad's convinced he's a real estate genius. He's already talking about investing in some dog track in Manila. The rest will go to bookies, booze, and that woman in Hilo he thinks I don't know about."

Instinctively, Marybeth grasped his arm. "It may not be as bad as all that."

"The one I really feel sorry for is Lani. If it was up to Dad, she and her grandparents would be kicked off the island without a backward glance. But this is worse, in a way. Because now she's the one who pulled the trigger."

They both saw Ailani standing alone on the porch, staring out at the valley. In the firelight it was impossible to read the expression on her face. As they watched, Peter Pauahi materialized out of nowhere and tugged her arm. She spun around, startled. He seemed to be entreating. She raised a hand in protest, but he was insistent. Finally they disappeared into the house.

Rosalind Chan and David Tanaka were also watching this curious scene, and their reactions mirrored Roger's. "That poor kid," Tanaka commented.

"I know. But what else could we do?"

"Dunno. I almost wish I'd never heard of this place."

The judge cocked an eyebrow. "Second thoughts, David? That doesn't seem like you."

"Oh, I get them all the time, Rosie. But usually it's just business. This feels different, somehow."

"Nothing's been finalized yet. You could walk away..."

"I could, sure. But then what? Roxas will just snap it up the moment I leave. And he won't be as gentle. At least I gave them the choice."

Judge Chan knew more than she liked about Rodrigo Roxas. From narcotics to child prostitution, there wasn't a dirty bit of business on the islands that he didn't have a hand in. But so far nothing stuck. "If you get your way, the site is preserved, and the villagers get something. Not a bad deal all around."

"I know, I know." But Tanaka still looked troubled. Judge Chan patted his arm in a motherly kind of way.

"It'll all be over soon," she promised him.

———

When Roger came into the house to fetch a soda from the fridge, he found his cousin in the library with her elbows propped on the table and her head in her hands. "Lani! What's wrong? What happened?"

"Go away, Rog."

"Like hell." He sat down next to her and put a hand on her shoulder. "Tell me," he said. "Was it Peter? Did he hurt you?"

Her face was concealed beneath a dark bell of hair, but she shook her head. "It's not like that. It doesn't matter. Honestly."

"Of course it matters. This has all been too much for you."
He sighed. "And I made it worse. I'm sorry. You must hate me
right now."

Lani looked up. Her eyes were reddened from crying, but
they had a glint of surprised amusement. "Don't give yourself so
much credit," she said.

"You mean you're not angry with me?"

"For defending your family and your birthright? Yeah, I'm
fucking furious." She took his hand and squeezed it affectionately. "Come off it, Cuz. You did what you had to do. You're a
Lathrop."

"You're a Lathrop, too."

Her fingers clenched and she drew her hand away. "No,
I'm not."

"Don't say that! You are just as much a part of this family—"

"*No!*"

Roger was astonished by the vehemence in her voice and tried
to understand. He answered haltingly, "You are, though. I know we
haven't always treated you like it. You should've stayed in this house
with me. It was your right. Gran said so. But the Kapiahos lost their
only child that day, and they wanted you so much. You probably
didn't know it, but the day they took you from here down to the
village was the saddest day of my life. I felt like I lost my sister."

Lani murmured, "I felt that way, too. Remember I used to
call you Little Bra? You thought it meant sibling, and when I
left for school you'd go running through the house screaming
'*Where's my bra? I want my bra!*'"

They both laughed. "Yeah, Dad had some serious doubts
about me for a while. You were Princess Mud-In-Your-Eye, as
I recall." He sighed. "We should've grown up together, Lani.
Maybe then you'd see things differently. Maybe I would, too.
But you must know how I, how we... *Goddammit!*" he burst out
suddenly, "I'm not Dad. I don't give a crap about the money."

"I know, braddah."

But something had changed. There was a barrier between them now that had never been there before. "Can't you tell me what's wrong?" he urged. "Maybe I can help."

Again she shook her head, but more gently. "Thanks, but you can't. We're part of something much bigger than either of us. It has a momentum of its own."

He thought he knew what she meant. "It's all happened so damn fast. Like I can't process it yet. I keep looking out toward the village and seeing all the trees rooted up, big white condos like sagging wedding cakes. A swimming pool in the valley. Even this house…"

"Don't," she begged him. "Don't say any more."

"You know, I always figured when my turn came, I'd share it with you. No more Lathrops or villagers. Just Kaumaha and the people who love it."

"*Ae*, that sounds wonderful," Lani said wistfully.

"Instead, we're both exiles. We have that in common, at least. The last generation." Roger was thoughtful. "Maybe that's why we're both fighting so hard over that stupid statue. I mean, who cares about a hunk of bronze and some old rocks? The past only matters when there's no future left."

Lani looked down at the book before her. "You're wrong, Cuz. The past always matters."

"Does it have to? When I was speaking my piece tonight, I started to wonder if I sounded like some redneck trying save a statue of General Lee. Still fighting for the Old Cause. God, I hope I'm not like that."

"Oh, Rog." She gave him an odd look, exasperated and affectionate. "You could never be like that. But there's so much you don't understand."

"Such as?"

For a moment it looked as though she would answer. Her

eyes lit with a sudden fire. But then, as if some ancient *kapu* laid its hand over her mouth, she demurred. "You're right. It doesn't matter. What is it all, anyway, except stories we tell to make ourselves feel better?"

"You don't believe that," Roger said perceptively.

"Maybe I want to. It would make the rest easier to bear." Suddenly she looked exhausted. "Go back to the party, Cuz. I need to be alone for a bit."

Roger obeyed, still troubled. Lani's eyes dropped and stared unseeingly at the page before her.

"*Wahi hewa*, this terrible place," he heard her mutter. "Maybe it deserves to be destroyed."

———

At seventy, Mrs. Te Papa knew there were certain things she could no longer trust. Bathtubs were one. Stairs were another. The process of going up or down was so laborious that she developed the odd habit of counting each stair, which her steel-trap mind then automatically filed away. The Prudential Life Insurance building, for example, had seventeen steps between lobby and mezzanine. Hawaii State Library had twelve. The old Honolulu Court House, where she spent many hours giving depositions, had a whopping thirty-seven steps and no elevator.

In a robin's-egg blue muumuu and lace shawl, she negotiated the steps of Lathrop House one at a time. Only when she reached her terminus did Mrs. Te Papa dare take her eyes off her feet, and discovered the path was blocked. Standing in the open door was a man she had never seen. He had his back to her, facing the bonfire, but she could see tattoos encircling his neck and peeking out the cuffs of his starched white shirt. Scarlet dragon scales against whorls of green and blue. The rest lay decently concealed, yet it was not hard to imagine him covered from chin to ankles. His hair was pulled into a samurai's topknot and his bulging shoulders filled the doorframe. Then the old boards complained under her weight, and he spun around, hand reaching for the bulge in his hip pocket.

Mrs. Te Papa raised her own hands. "I surrender," she said.

The guard relaxed but did not smile. His face was set in permanent fury, eyes bulging, lips compressed. She had seen faces like that on Kamakura scrolls from the twelfth century, with swords raised either to decapitate some unfortunate or commit hara-kiri themselves. A line from Gilbert and Sullivan ran inanely in her head: *"Behold the Lord High Executioner! A personage of noble rank and title/A dignified and potent officer, whose functions are particularly vital!"*

"You must be Mr. Tanaka's... er, you must be Kaito?"

He nodded briefly. "May I pass?" she asked, and with equal courtesy he moved to one side, bowed, and made a sweeping gesture with his arm. But as soon as she reached the lanai, she felt his shadow slide back into the doorway again.

The tableau on the lawn had shifted. Marybeth and Roger rejoined the group. Dr. Ackerman, freed at last of his incubus, chatted with them amiably. Tanaka and Judge Chan sat side by side on wicker chairs. Eleanor Lathrop was nowhere to be found.

Ogden had not strayed far from the punch bowl. His face was brick-red and his eyes bloodshot. At his side, Marnie remonstrated. "You're too hot out here, dear. You should come in away from the fire for a bit. I think the smoke is getting in your eyes." She tugged on his arm, and he swayed toward her in acquiescence. "Hot," he muttered thickly. Ogden took two tottering steps, overbalanced, and fell, taking both the punch bowl and his wife down with him. Tanaka and Roger rushed to assist, while Ackerman mock-clapped.

"So much for the Lathrops," said a voice at Mrs. Te Papa's elbow. She turned and saw Lani, face twisted with disgust.

Unfortunately for everyone, Ogden had heard. He staggered to his feet and shrugged off both men. His hamlike face peered up at the lanai. "Oh, it's you, is it? You've got a hell of nerve. What have you been up to, anyway? Trying to convince the natives that they're better off in those fleabag trailers?"

Lani's eyes blazed with tears. "If I thought there was any chance of convincing them of that, Uncle, I would. If only to see the look on your face."

Ogden smiled nastily. "I'll bet. That's what you wanted all along, isn't it? You don't give a crap about the villagers. You just want to see us destroyed."

"Dad!" Roger protested, but Lani gripped the rail with both hands and snarled, "And if I did, so what? Don't you deserve it? You took all their jobs away and made them live in filth. Now you want to kick them off their island. You've done nothing but wreck these people's lives, and now you expect them to be grateful—my God, *grateful*—that they get a few crumbs that aren't even coming from you anyway."

"That's more than they deserve!" His piggy eyes narrowed. "Why do you think the crops failed? Why did the hotel fail? Because your precious, lazy-as-fuck villagers couldn't move their asses and get things done. It's always been me. It's always been the Lathrops. Without us your crowd would have starved and died a hundred years ago."

"The Lathrops!" Lani's voice rose to a scream. "Wow, you guys really get off on thinking you're our saviors, don't you? Bring us here, make us work your fields and serve your food and wipe your ass and worship your God. And be thankful for the privilege. Do you know what you are? You're leeches. All the way back to the King Leech himself. You don't get it, do you, Uncle? I don't want your house or your money, and I sure as hell don't want your name. Good God, if I could open my veins right now and drain out every precious polluted drop of Lathrop blood…"

Ogden was on the steps, narrowing the distance. He no longer needed to yell, for the silence around them was absolute. Even the crackle of the fire seemed hushed. "Well, that's lucky for you then, sweetheart," he hissed. "Because you've never been one of us. Don't forget, I was *there*. That wasn't some fucking Romeo and Juliet story between Rose and Billy. Just a barnyard fling. Hell, for all I know, he probably raped her. What I *do* know is she was all set to marry Phil Townsend, and *his* family owned most of Kauai. Would have saved us all. But then you came along, and Ma told Billy he had to go through with it. So there we all were. If you want to come for us, baby, you'd better know the truth. You were what ruined this family. Can you imagine?" He shook his head in disbelief. "One hundred and fifty years of hurricanes, floods, droughts, and diseases, and the whole show falls apart because of one filthy fucking half-breed—"

Mrs. Te Papa's *kupuna* instincts asserted themselves. She threw a protective arm over Lani and interposed her considerable bulk between the combatants. Her carefully modulated speech was tossed aside. "How dare you speak to her like that, you fat, sweaty *ho'opailua* hog! You come after *hapa*, you gotta come through me! I'll lay you flat myself!"

But someone else was quicker. Ogden felt a hand on his shoulder and turned directly into David Tanaka's fist.

———

Emotional outbursts occur for any number of reasons—rage, sorrow, or joy—but the aftertaste is always the same: embarrassment. Society rushes to fill the void with comforting platitudes. So it was not surprising that, after Ogden was carried insensible into the house, and Lani ran toward the village in tears, Dr. Ackerman should turn to Judge Chan and ask politely whether she had any children of her own, and what were their names. Just one daughter, she answered with an equal show of calm. Gwendolyn.

"She was in my class," Roger added helpfully.

Mrs. Te Papa saw Marybeth advancing on her, some vapidity bubbling on her lips, and fled into the house. The back parlor had become a recovery room, and Kaito was perched on the stairs looking martial, so she retreated into the library and closed the door. Books always soothed her. She had a vague idea of finding a novel and disappearing into her room, which she had no intention of leaving until the seaplane came tomorrow morning.

The titles on the shelves were the usual hodgepodge that one finds in most home libraries: detective thrillers, cookbooks, how-to manuals, a complete set of Encyclopedia Britannica from 1974, a handful of romance novels, and a few popular histories, mostly of the military sort. She noticed with interest that among these was, incongruously, *The Farthest Reaches: A Study of New Guinean Settlement in Hawaii*, by Dr. Robert Ackerman. It was signed by the author himself to *"My dear friend Eleanor Lathrop, for her many kindnesses."* Someone had been reading it recently, for there were bookmarks with notations in blue ink. Mrs. Te Papa deciphered one: *"National Trust maybe. Try UNESCO?"* Another in green ink attached to the copyright page was even more obscure: *"Nixon?"*

She replaced the book on its shelf and lingered for a moment among a collection of Bibles and devotionals with leather spines that had cracked with age. She selected the most imposing, black leather and large as a paving stone with gold embossed lettering, and found the scrawled signature of *Reverend Amyas Lathrop* on the flyleaf. *June 2, 1829*. He had brought this with him when he came. She flipped to the back, curious. It was the custom among Victorians, Mrs. Te Papa knew, to use their family Bibles to record such events as births, deaths, and marriages. So it was here. Under BIRTHS, a strong, clear hand had written *Louisa Alva, May 23, 1831, Thomas Boyle, November 5, 1833, William David, 1836, Elizabeth Rose, October 21, 1840.* Yet each of these names bore a small black cross next to it. Had they died at birth, or infancy, or even in the womb? Such things were sadly common then. But at last came success: *John Joseph, August 1, 1842.* That was the boy, she remembered, who went off to fight for the Union. He must have returned, for the next page listed his own children. His marriage to Catherine Bishop Howell was duly noted under MARRIAGES, along with those of his sons, grandsons, great-grandsons, and so on. Nothing about the daughters, Mrs. Te Papa noticed. She turned, at last, to DEATHS. At the very top a small, spidery hand had written *Amyas Boyle Lathrop, October 15, 1861.* Underneath was another phrase, so crabbed as to be almost illegible. It was not English. It was, she decided after a moment, Latin.

   Destrui a Daemonibus

   Mrs. Te Papa studied Latin at university. It was an elegant language of great compactness and precision—not unlike Hawaiian. The words and phrases came floating back, until at last she had it: *"Destroyed by Devils."* Well! So Prudence had not been quite so forgiving after all! But one could scarcely blame her. Not far below another hand, John Joseph's presumably, had added, *Prudence Lorrimer Lathrop, June 5, 1875. Protector of this Island, Beloved by All.* A fitting epitaph, Mrs. Te Papa thought, which she would be proud of herself.

   She was just replacing the Bible on its shelf when she noticed a scrap of paper peeking out between two hymnals. Anthropologists and archaeologists are trained to catch incongruities: tiny ridges in the sand, an odd-shaped mound, even a particular species of plant growing where it should not. Over time this becomes second nature. Thus Mrs. Te Papa perceived that the hymnals were covered in a thick layer of dust which an unseen hand had recently disturbed. The paper could not have been there long. Curious, she tugged until it released. A newspaper cutting from the *Honolulu Star-Advertiser*, not yet yellowed. She unfolded it gently. The photograph showed a young man with a cheeky grin, glasses, and dark hair that stuck up all over his head as though he'd been electrocuted. It looked like a high school graduation photo. *Steven Shimazu*, the paper identified him. The headline read, *"Yakuza Suspected in Beating Death of Honolulu Teenager."* Underneath this someone had scrawled in large black letters:

"I KNOW WHAT YOU DID."

———

None of them slept well that night. A light shone in Eleanor's room long after the others' had been extinguished. Downstairs on the sofa, Ogden tossed fitfully and muttered. His wife sat watching him without expression, a book open in her lap. After several hours, she sighed, closed the book, and left. Roger Lathrop stared at the wallpaper of his bedroom— silver swans against a blue summer sky—and imagined the room transformed into the office of the assistant manager of food and beverage for the Royal Poinciana Resort. Nearby, Marybeth stared at her own wallpaper and thought of Roger. Judge Chan read case reports until her glasses slid gently from her nose. Tanaka carefully checked the latches on all the doors and windows before drawing out a Colt .45 from its holster and placing it on the nightstand. Across the hall, Dr. Ackerman chased an errant mosquito around his bedroom until finally, with a howl of triumph, he dispatched it against the wardrobe. Then he looked up at the ceiling and saw three more.

At her grandparents' house in the village, Lani dreamt of a great *heiau* with koa pillars and a palm-thatched roof. Priests surrounded her. They were chanting. But their words were drowned by the sound of the storm outside, which screamed like a demented thing. It tore the thatched roof from the temple and extinguished their torches with a cold wet hand. The wind spoke a single name, again and again. She woke with it on her lips as well: *"Ku."*

Mrs. Te Papa's dreams were untroubled until, sometime in the night, a clap of thunder brought her back to wakefulness. She opened her eyes and turned her head toward the window. *Don't cry, Winnie,* her grandmother told her when she was little, *Thunder is just Lono bringing down his staff on the clouds to make the rain.* She thought of her grandmother, smiled. She waited for the rain.

But the rain did not come.

"A True Account…"

April 25, 1848

The fever has done its worst. We hear intelligence that on the outer isles whole villages are emptied and bodies lie naked in the streets as carrion. Praise God I have not seen such horrors here. Kona Town is holding fast, and thanks to our efforts it may soon be possible to return to the home island where, I fear, we shall find the crops in sad disrepair.

Of great and glorious moment, I now count some three hundred living souls among the saved. Each morning I lead the faithful in a prayer of thanksgiving before we set to work among the sick. The native temperament can be a hard trial, and it is the devil's own work to set their minds upon a single task, but once directed they are quick and clever as monkeys. They have learned the paternoster and Nicene creed, and soon I shall endeavor to instruct them in hymns. Prudence does splendid work in the hospital, though I fear her efforts are now directed to comforting the dying. She is tireless and quite distraught when another succumbs.

It is not for me to reprove my wife, especially when she does such good service for the Lord, but I cannot help but feel she too much favors body over spirit. What matter, in the end, whether these unfortunates have a few more years in this vile world? It is but dross compared to the everlasting salvation that awaits the faithful in Christ. Rather than tend their sickly bodies she would better tend their sickly spirits, as I do. But I am only one man, and I grow weary.

Chapter 5

MOHAI, THE SACRIFICE

The late Winston Te Papa had been an unsatisfactory man in many ways. Mrs. Te Papa knew them all, yet in her most vulnerable moments—like that treacherous time between sleep and consciousness—she still called his name. Reached for his warm, massive body in the sheets. Was forever surprised that he was not there. It was then she truly awoke and looked around. Amber light filled the bedroom at Lathrop House. She stretched, reached for her wrap, and padded over to the window. The 'i'iwis were making their usual racket but had not yet reached full volume. Mrs. Te Papa guessed it was not long after dawn, perhaps seven o'clock. Her wristwatch confirmed this.

The rest of the house was silent. Good, she thought. She had no desire to make polite conversation. Pulling on a pair of sandals, she slipped into the landing and down the stairs. This time there was no samurai blocking her path. She opened the front door quietly, letting it close behind her with a soft click. For now, at least, the island was hers.

She followed the same trail as before, past the rusting farm tools and Tanaka's glittering machines. But the morning light made everything softer, greener, kinder. This was Mrs. Te Papa's favorite time of day. She was a woman who ate what she liked and carried her pleasures around with her, yet the cardiologist said she had the heart of a sixteen-year-old girl. A miracle, he said. She credited these daily walks.

It was not the statue she wished to see. That had long since lost any attraction. But the *heiau* had several interesting features that reminded her of Mo'okini, and anyway she was unlikely to see it again. The seaplane was due at ten. The thought gave her a momentary flutter of joy. Mrs. Te Papa did not like this place. She had not seen the spirits Mr. Po saw, but she felt them. Well, she felt *something*. And Kaumaha's current residents were disquieting enough, never mind the dead ones.

The *heiau* loomed ahead. Mrs. Te Papa quickened her pace. But there was something—woodsmoke?—in the air. No, it was sharper and, though very faint, acrid. For some reason she thought of a battlefield. The sun was brighter now, and she could see past the temple to the hills beyond. Perhaps it was a trick of the light, or her mind still groggy with sleep, but for a moment the vista appeared in double exposure: what she saw, and what she expected to see. There was something out of focus, something impossible. Like those games one played as a child: *How many things are different in this picture?* She paused with her hand on her hip before it came to her.

The statue was gone.

Now she was running, fists clenched, her whole body bent forward in the effort. And there, beyond the temple walls, she saw. Only a small mound of earth remained to mark the place where Amyas Lathrop stood. But the ground was studded with bits of lava rock and twisted metal, some as far as fifteen feet from the center. Her feet tripped over the shards, and once she looked down she saw a hand protruding from the dirt, fingers extended toward the sun. The sight nearly made her faint. But of course it was only old Amyas, or a piece of him.

Some powerful explosive had done this, and Mrs. Te Papa

thought at once of the blast caps. How had they worked? A fuse? She fancied there was some kind of timing instructions on the package, so perhaps they had an internal fuse like a grenade. But however it was done, it was done well. It looked as if the very Hammer of God had come down and obliterated the thing out of existence.

She saw another soot-covered hand and a bit of leg obscured by a large boulder. Beyond that a long and narrow shard of about four feet had burrowed itself into the ground. It looked like a piece of modern art. But even as she considered it, her filing-cabinet mind was trying to get her attention. *The nails, Winnie. Look at the nails.* She turned back to the hand and saw that its fingernails had dirt caked under them. Almost against her will she began to move toward the boulder. As she did, other details came into view. The hand became an arm, the arm attached to a figure in a shapeless gray wad of cloth and cargo shorts. One bare leg was drawn slightly above the other, as if frozen in the act of running. Dark, matted hair tumbled around the shoulders. Streaks of gray dirt ran through the locks, save for the area around the wound, which was clotted black.

Mrs. Te Papa knew there was no hope, but nevertheless felt for a pulse. She rose slowly, hands on her knees. The sun felt hot on her face. From somewhere very far away came the sound of footsteps, quickening as they approached. Then they stopped, and she heard a low, guttural moan.

"As I feared," said Mr. Po, "Ku has taken his sacrifice."

Ku was the god of war. Mrs. Te Papa knew that in ancient times the Hawaiian peoples sacrificed to him, but that was centuries ago. She was about to ask him what he meant when another figure appeared. Rosalind Chan crested the trail dressed in a paisley blouse and white slacks. A straw hat shielded her eyes. Gently she removed it and laid it across her chest. "So," she said, "it's happened."

"Yes."

The judge peered closer. "I wondered if he might try something like this. But he must not have known…"

"Who?"

"That boy Peter, of course."

Mrs. Te Papa shook her head. "That is not Peter." In a voice of infinite sadness, she added, "It's Lani."

———

Returning to Lathrop House they were greeted by the friendly sound of clattering china and the smell of bacon. A buffet had been laid out in the dining room, and everyone except Eleanor was there. She preferred a tray in her room. "Ah, Winnie," said Tanaka, resplendent in a scarlet silk bathrobe, "come sit by me. We saved you some toast."

Mrs. Te Papa experienced a moment of weightless panic as her stomach seemed to fly into her mouth. She looked from one face to another, watching their expressions melt from contentment to alarm, and finally turned to Roger. "I'm terribly sorry," she said, willing her voice to remain steady, "but I'm afraid there has been an accident. Judge Chan is telephoning the police now."

"What's that?" Ogden exclaimed, rising slowly and wiping butter off his chin. His face was blotched and one eye empurpled. He looked and was, in fact, in considerable pain. "What sort of accident?"

Mrs. Te Papa answered carefully, still looking at Roger, "It appears as though someone tried to destroy the statue last night. There was an explosion. We found Lani Kapiaho in the rubble."

"My God," Roger whispered. His face drained of color. "Is she…?"

"Yes, I'm afraid we were too late to help her."

There was a shocked silence. Then Ogden Lathrop brought

his fist down on the table. They all jumped. "Good riddance!" he shouted. "So she blew up old Amyas, eh? Serves her right."

"Shut up, you moron!"

If Mrs. Te Papa had not heard for herself, she would never have believed Marnie capable of making such a sound. She was on her feet, facing her husband, fists clenched. They looked absurdly like two mismatched sumo wrestlers. Then Marnie dissolved into tears, buried her face in her hands and fled the room.

"Mr. Lathrop," said Tanaka, his voice as calm as water over rocks, "I suggest you go to your room and stay there. Kaito can help you if you need assistance."

Ogden shot a terrified look at Kaito, who still managed to look fierce behind a plate of scrambled eggs. He left without another word. Kaito, catching a signal from his employer, discreetly followed.

"Someone should tell Ellie," Professor Ackerman said. His white hair was disheveled and he wore a tweed jacket over a pair of striped pajamas. "I'll do it, I guess."

"No," said Roger suddenly. "I will." Marybeth reached her hand toward him, but he did not notice. He drew a deep breath and marched out. The judge appeared a moment later, looking frazzled.

"Just got off the phone with the Staties." She stared at the toast rack for a moment, weighing the ethics, then finally helped herself to a slice. "Took forever to explain it all. But they're sending someone from Honolulu, a detective. And a forensics team."

"Are we supposed to just hang around here till they arrive?" Ackerman growled.

"They're taking a helicopter, Bob. Should only be a couple hours."

Ackerman was only slightly mollified. "I know I'm not supposed to ask," he began waspishly, "*de mortuis* and all that, but did you happen to notice if there was anything left of the bone feast house?"

The judge looked scandalized, but Mrs. Te Papa answered, "Not really. It was quite a large detonation, Professor. Enough to dislodge lava rock cemented in concrete and send it hurtling fast enough to crush a human skull fifteen feet away."

"Excuse me, I don't feel well," said Marybeth, and fled.

But Dr. Ackerman's professional instincts were outraged. *"Fifteen feet?* What the hell did she use? Fertilizer?"

"I am not sure. But there were a number of blast caps on the island. Construction equipment. I saw them yesterday."

She was not looking at Tanaka, but heard the air expel from his lungs. "Oh, Christ," he muttered.

"What makes you so sure it was Lani that set the blast?" the judge demanded angrily of Ackerman. "You didn't see the body. We did. She might have simply witnessed it and not run away in time."

"That's quite true," said Mrs. Te Papa thoughtfully.

Ackerman was unabashed. "Again, I don't wish to appear heartless. But there were only two people on this island who wanted that statue gone, and one of them…"

"Peter!" The exclamation burst from the judge's lips.

Mrs. Te Papa had already thought of this. "The police will tell him, I'm sure. But it might be better if one of us broke it to the Kapiahos."

The other three regarded her stonily.

"Very well," she sighed. "I'll go now."

———

When Marybeth reached the upstairs landing she saw Eleanor's door was still open. The old woman sat on her lanai, a cigarette in her hand. It was an attitude of repose, until one noticed the long trail of ash, the absolute stillness of the figure. Sunlight sparkled on the ocean, but Eleanor Lathrop stared into it unblinking. She might have been made of wax.

Roger's door was closed. Marybeth put a hand on the knob, withdrew it, then with a little spurt grasped the handle and twisted it firmly. She half-fell into the room.

He was lying with his face turned to the wall. Quietly, Marybeth closed the door and sat on the bed. "I'm sorry," she said. It sounded hideously inadequate. But what could one say to someone's whose cousin accidentally blew herself up trying to destroy the statue that he, Roger, was desperate to save? Not even Emily Post had an answer for that. "I know you were close," she added.

"We should have been closer." His voice seemed very far away. "She was like a sister to me. We were together in the big house until the crash, did you know that? Then she went away."

"But you still saw each other, didn't you?"

"Holidays, mostly, and only because Gran insisted. Otherwise it was like Lani didn't exist. She was never welcome here again, not really. I'll never forgive him for that."

"Your dad?" Marybeth asked intuitively.

"Yeah. I was too little to understand, but even when Rose and Billy were still alive he always acted weird around them. Like there was a bad smell whenever Billy came into the room. And Rose was so kind, I wish you'd known her. So patient with him, even when he got loaded and called her filthy names, stuff I can't even repeat. When they all lived here Dad treated Lani like a servant's kid, or worse. Like she was a mistake. Then, after…it was horrible. Gran still tried to bring Lani up here as much as she could, but Dad gave her the stink eye every time. Finally, when Lani was sixteen, she started giving it back."

"Your cousin seemed pretty fierce," Marybeth admitted.

Roger rolled over and looked at her. His tear-stained face was wistful. "She was always a mouthy kid," he recalled affectionately. "And Dad's got no filter at all, especially when he's been drinking. You saw last night."

Marybeth nodded, embarrassed.

"Lani gave as good as she got. She was the only one that really stood up to him, including me. I was terrified of my old man, and I had reason to be. The kind of guy who wore a leather belt with shorts, just in case. But even when Lani was still in high school I remember her calling him a useless drunk one Christmas and breaking a chair on his back. She didn't come around much after that."

Marybeth was torn between consolation and baser curiosity. "Why did he hate her so much? Just because she was *hapa*? Heck, everybody's mixed race in Hawaii. I'm Māori, but my gran says I'm one-fourth Filipino."

Roger smiled slightly. "Sure, but not everyone's a Lathrop. Dad's idea of blood lineage is almost *Game of Thrones*. But I don't think that's the reason, not really. Dad hated his brother-in-law because they both knew it was Billy Kapiaho who ran the plantation. My grandpa trusted him, loved him...maybe even more than his own son. All that resentment got transferred to Lani after Billy died."

"A little girl?" Marybeth was incredulous.

"You don't know my father. There's no one alive he can't find a way to be an asshole to."

She believed it, readily.

"The truth is," Roger mused, "Lani was everything my dad wished he could be: strong, independent, fearless. And completely attached to this island. I think that's the core of it. Dad hates Kaumaha, always has. And Lani *was* Kaumaha."

Marybeth recalled her first vision of Ailani Kapiaho, looking as if she had sprung from the earth itself. Indestructible.

Or so it seemed. "She knew you didn't feel that way. You or your grandmother."

Gently she laid a hand on his shoulder. He grasped it. "Thanks for that," Roger said. "Gran's broken up, says it's all her fault. I feel the same. But I wish to Christ I hadn't fought Lani on that goddamn statue. I would have blown the thing up myself if it meant keeping her."

"I know you would."

He sighed, and added quietly, "You see, she was everything I wished I could be, too."

———

The last two hours were among the longest of Mrs. Te Papa's life. The Kapiahos had been horrified and incredulous at first, then heartbreakingly kind, which was worse. Agnes went in the other room to lie down while Gilbert made ginger tea and calmly asked questions. How had his granddaughter been struck? Where? Had her death been instantaneous? Would the police let him see her? Mrs. Te Papa answered as best she could, her voice still quavering, and after she was done he said simply, "*Mahalo*. I must go be with my wife now."

When she returned to Lathrop House Mrs. Te Papa found a helicopter parked in the valley and a dozen or so officers moving about the grounds. A detective who introduced himself as Randall Roundtree met her at the door. He was a paunchy, morose man in his late fifties with close-cropped graying hair and a bushy mustache that needed trimming. It drooped to match his mood. "My chief speaks very highly of you," he said surprisingly. "He asked to be remembered when he found out you were here. William Chao."

"Willie!" Mrs. Te Papa exclaimed. "I wrote his recommendation letter for the academy. But that was a hundred years ago."

Roundtree smiled. "I guess you're hard to forget. He said you knew people. Not like having connections, but that you knew *people*, understood them from the inside out, the way some do horses or money."

Mrs. Te Papa laughed uncomfortably. "I'm not sure that's much of a compliment."

"From him it is. He said that you were bound to know more about what went on here than anyone, and that I'd be a damn fool not to ask your help." Chief Chao had said other things as well. *If she's anything like she used to be, Randy, you'd better just deputize her and be done with it. The woman's a beaver in human form; you won't keep her away from this. My advice, don't try. Keep her happy and ask her opinion. She may look like someone's sweet kama'aina granny, but she's smart as hell and tough as old boots.*

Mindful of this advice, Detective Roundtree led Mrs. Te Papa to the library and sat her down. With infinite courtesy he drew out the entire story: her summons to the island, the dispute over the statue, the flare-up at the bonfire last night. He also got her impressions of each of the participants in this strange little drama. They were vivid and, he was sure, accurate.

"The chief was right about you," Roundtree said approvingly after she'd finished. "That was a very comprehensive picture you've drawn for me. The family wanted the statue to stay, the judge said it could stay, and only Lani and Peter Pauahi objected?"

"Yes. I would have preferred it removed myself, but Dr. Ackerman testified that it could not be done without damaging the structure underneath."

"That's true enough," the detective agreed. He had seen for himself. "All those lava rocks were fixed with concrete. Seems a stupid thing to do, really; the statue didn't need that much support."

"Perhaps not, but people didn't think too much about

historic preservation back then. I doubt anyone would have known or cared about the Bone Feast House. To them it was just a convenient foundation."

Roundtree made another note. "There's one thing I don't understand," he said. "According to what I've heard so far, Lani opposed the sale until Mrs. Lathrop offered to give her a share, which she could then distribute to the villagers. And Mr. Tanaka was going to allow them to remain on the island, albeit in a new construction."

"That's correct."

"So the main issue was always the village, not the statue?"

"Certainly. All Lani's efforts were directed toward the fate of Kaumaha. That was the primary concern of the Lathrops and Mr. Tanaka as well."

"Yeah, twenty million dollars has a way of clarifying one's thinking," Roundtree said wryly.

"Well, yes. Certainly no one cared much about old Amyas. Even Dr. Ackerman thought it was an excrescence. And Tanaka said he didn't give a damn about it one way or the other."

The detective nodded. "That's what puzzles me. By the end of the night Ailani Kapiaho had a commitment from Tanaka that he would not build unless a majority of villagers approved the sale. Sounds like a victory, doesn't it? Why would she jeopardize all of that a few hours later by destroying the statue?"

Mrs. Te Papa considered. "Lani was very agitated," she said at last. "Ogden attacked her, called her filthy names and accused her of being the cause of the island's misfortunes. And I suspect she may have quarreled with Peter Pauahi, though I just saw them go into the house and didn't hear what was said."

"We'll check that out," Roundtree promised.

"But from what I observed, she was not thinking rationally. She was enraged, and rightly so. I was mad at Ogden myself," she admitted with a fine show of candor. "It might have been the sensible thing to leave the statue alone, but for Lani Kapiaho, that might not have been possible."

"Would she have known about the blast caps?"

"Probably. I saw them yesterday, even picked one up. I gathered they'd been on the island for a couple weeks."

"Yeah, Tanaka was careless about that."

"I expect almost everyone noticed them," she added. "They were hard to miss." Mrs. Te Papa leaned forward. "Detective, I don't know if I'm allowed to ask, but are you *sure* it was Lani that set the explosion? Isn't it possible she simply arrived at the wrong time?"

Roundtree spread his hands. "No way to tell yet, ma'am. Forensics are up there now, taking a look. From the angle of the body, it looks like she was trying to run away, but that doesn't prove anything. On the other hand, who else would want to blow it up? Other than Mr. Pauahi, of course."

"We keep coming back to Peter," Mrs. Te Papa sighed.

"That's right, you met him. What did you think?"

"Not much," she admitted. "Blustering, irrational, pig-headed. A great deal like Ogden Lathrop, in fact."

"The sort who might blow up a statue out of sheer obstinacy?"

"More likely than Lani, from what I saw of him. But there was something else..." She thought for a moment. "He *seemed* genuinely outraged. And yet there was something forced, unnatural about it. I could have sworn he wasn't so much angry as *anxious*. As if the conversation had gone in a way he didn't expect, and was dangerous to him." She shrugged. "It was no more than a feeling."

Roundtree nodded and made a careful note. He opened his mouth to speak again when an officer appeared in the door. "Sorry, sir, the coroner's asking for you. She's at the site."

"What's up?"

The officer cast an uncertain glance at Mrs. Te Papa. "There are some…discrepancies," he answered guardedly.

Detective Roundtree's mustache drooped even more. *Nothing's ever easy*, he thought. "Okay." Then he turned to Mrs. Te Papa and began, "Perhaps we could…"

"Continue this conversation at the site?" She stood and gathered her purse. "Naturally."

They both knew that was not what he was going to say. *Human beaver*, Roundtree reminded himself. He managed a smile. "After you, ma'am," he said politely.

———

The coroner, Dr. Alice Kepple, was a woman in her middle forties with long, prematurely gray hair and the demeanor of an ex-hippie. She greeted Mrs. Te Papa without surprise as they gazed down solemnly at what had, a few hours ago, been a beautiful and willful young woman. "Such a waste," Mrs. Te Papa murmured sadly.

"It always is."

"But I wish you could have seen how beautiful she was. Like a princess. Not all broken in a heap—it seems so unnatural, doesn't it?"

"Unnatural," Dr. Kepple repeated. "Yes, it does." She was about to say more, then thought better of it.

"And so foolish."

The coroner raised an eyebrow. "Foolish?"

Mrs. Te Papa widened her eyes in innocence. "Isn't it likely that she set the fuses but didn't know how far away to stand? Or how long it would take them to blow?"

"It strikes you that way, does it?"

She nodded. "My nephew had a similar accident with a firework. He misjudged the fuse and it shot right into his eye.

Pau! He was nearly blinded." It was a frequent trick of Mrs. Te Papa's to volunteer an objectionable statement and wait to be corrected. Invariably, she was. "Doesn't it strike you that way, too?" she goaded.

"It could, it certainly could." Dr. Kepple removed a silver pencil from her vest and gestured with it. "Here she is, all splayed out like she's running away, even has one arm extended to catch her fall. Clothes are pretty much where they should be. And the rock that did it is right next to her head." She indicated a lethal-looking chunk the size of a grapefruit. "The body was like this when you found it, right? Did you get a good look at the wound?"

Mrs. Te Papa had not. Nor had she wanted to.

The coroner leaned over the corpse and pointed. "You can see where it struck, right here. There's a sharp bit that went deeper, which corresponds to the rock. How do you suppose that bit drove in like that, if the rock hit her flat on the back of the head?"

Mrs. Te Papa heard a sharp intake of breath from Detective Roundtree. It was followed by a long, regretful sigh. *Never, ever easy.* "It's a downward blow," he said sadly. "Lani wasn't struck on the back of the head but the top. The greatest impact is at the base of the wound."

Dr. Kepple beamed. "You got it. Which means?"

"Someone standing right behind her."

The implications of this were obvious, and horrifying. "But that would be murder!" exclaimed Mrs. Te Papa.

"Yes." Randall Roundtree's nature had been shaped by thirty years on the force. The perfidy of humanity, he knew, was infinite.

"Eh, eh, not so fast," the coroner corrected. "It *might* have been murder. It might also have been a stone dislodged by the blast which flew almost straight up and then fell on top of her."

"Just like Pompeii," Mrs. Te Papa mused. The other two stared, uncomprehending. "Pumice stone shot out of the caldera during the eruption, then hit the atmosphere and...oh, never mind." Strangely, she found herself wishing Dr. Ackerman were present. He, at least, would know about Pompeii.

Detective Roundtree was doggedly following his own train of thought. "That could mean any of three things."

"Murder, accident...or, what?" Dr. Kepple was puzzled. "Surely not suicide?"

This was an inspired thought which Roundtree had not yet considered. He filed it away for later. "No, no, I didn't mean that," he answered. "I meant that if it was murder, it had to be one of three ways. First, Miss Kapiaho set the explosion and was killed by someone afterward. Second, she came upon the scene and saw who did it, with the same result. Third—"

"She was killed *first*, and the explosion was staged to hide the evidence of the crime!" Mrs. Te Papa had recovered some of her old ebullience.

"That's about the size of it."

The coroner ran a hand through her wiry hair. "Seems a lot of fuss over an old statue," she remarked.

Detective Roundtree shook his head, but it was Mrs. Te Papa who answered. "No, I'm afraid not. The detective and I were just talking about that. If Lani blew up the statue and died accidentally, that's one thing. But if she was murdered...well, it's entirely possible it had nothing to do with the statue at all."

Dr. Kepple was curious. "What else was there?"

"Oh, about twenty million dollars."

The coroner whistled. "So that's where the wind lies."

"Keep digging, Alice," Roundtree instructed. "See if there's anything else here to identify whether the victim set the blast or not. And Mrs. Te Papa," he said, turning to her with an apologetic smile, "I'm afraid we're going to have to go over your testimony again, in light of new developments. You may have to stay on the island a bit longer that we thought."

Mrs. Te Papa understood. If Lani Kapiaho's death was a tragic accident, then she herself was a vital witness. But if it was murder, a very different word applied.

Ho'onani i ke akua, she was a suspect.

"A True Account..."

June 5, 1848 in New Boston, formerly Kaw-Maw-Ha

I have only time for the briefest of memorials. We are safely arrived back on our island with some eighty native persons in tow. The captain of the schooner which gave us passage is accustomed to charge 25p for every Christian head but 50 for heathen, on account of sanitary arrangements. I told him my flock were Christians and had them recite the paternoster in unison. He said he'd never seen Christians like these and reciting a bit of scripture didn't make them know how to use a privy for what God intended. I gave 30 per head and said I'd take responsibility for their cleanliness. He did not seem convinced, but fortunately they are a well-turned-out lot, in the main.

There being no habitable structures on the island other than the great house, I put the converts at once to work building a refinery for cane sugar, in which they may take shelter until such time as they are able to build proper dwellings for themselves. Presently I shall have a chapel raised, and such other buildings as needs must.

The first day of our new settlement, I performed a small service of benediction and thanksgiving on the shore. Mindful of those who knelt in prayer over Plymouth Rock, I was pleased to christen the island

New Boston. I can only hope our small community of the faithful may prove worthy of that august name. And so, thankfully, to bed.

May God bless this most noble and Christian colony and keep all its congregants true to His Most Holy Word.

Chapter 6

KĀNALUA, THE SUSPECTS

Mrs. Te Papa did not enjoy being told that she could not leave the island until certain matters had been sorted out, a process which had no precise definition or end. Nor, for that matter, did Judge Chan or David Tanaka. Their reactions were mild, however, compared to that of Dr. Ackerman. His squawking filled the house.

Detective Roundtree spent the afternoon conducting interviews in the library. But the results were negligible. David Tanaka provided a clear and detached precis of the events leading to the bonfire, including his own confrontation with Ogden. He was inclined to downplay the latter. "I saw a drunk and unstable man acting aggressively toward a young woman," he said with a shrug. "Something needed to be done."

"Very chivalrous of you," Roundtree congratulated him.

"Not really. Ackerman is too old, and, naturally, Roger couldn't strike his own father. I was the only one."

"What about your bodyguard? Wasn't he actually on the lanai with them?"

Tanaka allowed himself a tight smile. "Kaito doesn't act unless I tell him to. And if he had, Ogden would never have gotten up again."

But it was Ogden Lathrop who entered next, sporting a brilliantly scarlet eye almost swollen shut. As he passed Tanaka, he flattened himself against the doorframe. Tanaka took no notice of him at all. Ogden answered Roundtree's questions with monosyllables and rested his elbows on the desk. Roundtree, who had some experience, diagnosed a severe hangover. But he later amended that to include general awfulness. "Bitch got what she deserved," was Ogden's considered analysis. "Should have read the directions better, shouldn't she?"

"It may not have been the blast that killed her, Mr. Lathrop." He paused to let this sink into Ogden's alcohol-soaked brain. "Maybe someone who got up in the night, saw her heading to the statue and followed. Someone who was so outraged at what she'd done that he brained her right there."

Ogden's one good eye widened. "I was asleep," he said quickly and with surprising clarity. "Passed out on the couch. Thanks to Tanaka. And the booze, I guess. Marnie'll tell you."

"Your wife told us that she remained with you until about one a.m. We believe the explosion happened sometime after two." Ogden broke down into gibberish and left soon after.

The hardest was the matriarch. Detective Roundtree had no intention of forcing her to come downstairs, but when he arrived in her bedroom he found her dressed and seated on the lanai. The ravages of grief showed on her face. "Roger tells me that you believe Lani was murdered," she said by way of introduction.

"It's a possibility we are considering."

"No, it is not possible. *Aole loa.*" She was definite.

Randall Roundtree had not built a forty-year career on contradicting witnesses, especially grief-stricken old ladies. "Is that so, ma'am?"

He expected to hear that none of the Lathrops or their friends would hurt a fly, but Eleanor surprised him. "You think that the explosion was just a blind, don't you? That someone else did it?"

Roundtree was noncommittal. "Those are also possibilities, yes."

"No. Lani set the explosion and died doing it."

The detective shifted a little. "If you don't mind me asking, how can you be so sure?"

"I saw her."

"Ah." He leaned back and opened his notebook. "What time was this?"

"Hard to say for certain. I was in my room until around two. Couldn't sleep. Came out here and sat on the lanai after that. I didn't go back inside till dawn."

"You spent the whole night out here?"

"I often do. With a blanket on my lap it's comfortable enough and I had…a lot on my mind."

Detective Roundtree was tempted but let it pass. "What exactly did you see?"

"For the first ten minutes or so, nothing. Then I saw Lani come up from the village. The path crosses right under the house before it turns into the forest."

"You're sure she was headed to the statue?"

"That trail only leads one place."

Roundtree made a note. "And no one was with her? No one came afterward?"

"No. She was quite alone. No one could have come later or I would have seen them go up. I'd certainly see them come back down."

"Did you hear the explosion?" He remembered something Mrs. Te Papa told him. "It might have sounded like a thunderclap."

"No, I didn't hear a thing. But I am quite deaf."

Roundtree was thinking. "It's still possible that someone

could have been at the site already, before you came out of your room. Then they found another way to leave that doesn't go past the house."

"Look around you, Detective," she answered with a sweep of her hand. "It's a valley. The only way would be to scale the cliffs and walk along the ridge until they reached the village. But even then I'd have seen whoever it was come back into the house. The other door is chained and bolted. The only way in is under your feet right now."

Unless the murderer was in the village, Roundtree thought to himself. He made another note. "You were very close to your granddaughter," he said gently. It wasn't a question. "In fact, you probably knew her better than anyone here. Anything you can tell me about her would be a great help."

Eleanor stared at the valley for so long that he thought she must not have heard him. But then she whispered, "It was my fault."

"I'm sorry?"

"It was *my* fault," she repeated. "After the hearing I could see she was conflicted. She felt she had betrayed her people. I took her aside and told her that was nonsense. She was protecting her people the only way she could. I told her..." The old woman's composure finally broke and her voice became ragged. "I told her she was...a warrior. God help me, I even showed her the weapon."

Weapon? Roundtree wondered, but Eleanor was not finished.

"I said she would always be a part of two worlds, but tonight she had done credit to both. I was only trying to comfort her. But then later...at the party...those terrible things my son said..."

"Yes," The detective's face was grim. "I heard about what your son said."

"Can you blame her, then? After hearing that she was the

reason this whole crisis came about, simply by being born? Can you blame her for lashing out?"

But there had been several long hours between the bonfire and explosion, Roundtree thought. Could Lani Kapiaho have been so enraged at her uncle and his family as to deliberately, in the dead of night, sneak up and undo all the good work she had done earlier? Sure, it was possible.

But for his money, it was not good enough.

———

Often during the previous day Mrs. Te Papa had felt like an unwanted houseguest caught in the middle of a domestic squabble. Now she, Judge Chan, and Dr. Ackerman had been abandoned entirely. They gathered in exile on the lanai and reviewed their position. "It's outrageous," Ackerman declared. "We came here to advise on this wretched sale, nothing more. We have nothing to do with these people or their affairs. I couldn't give a tinker's damn who gets Kaumaha or whether old bloody Amyas stayed aloft for another three hundred years. I'm sorry that the site is gone, but I saw enough of it fifty years ago to last a lifetime. I told the police everything I know, which is practically nothing. I spent the whole damn night swatting mosquitoes, and the bodies are still on the ceiling to prove it. *So why am I still here?*"

"Are you so sure, Robert," the judge asked with mischief in her eye, "that you didn't blow it up out of sheer pique?"

"If only I'd thought of it. But I would have made sure there were no witnesses around, if so. That poor girl."

Mrs. Te Papa put a hand to her chin. "The police seem to think the statue might have been destroyed afterward, to conceal the crime of her death."

Judge Chan paled. "*Ko'u akua!* But that would be murder!"

Ackerman, however, was unfazed. "Even more reason to let us go. I, for one, never saw any of these people before in my life—except Eleanor, of course, and that was decades ago. I don't say I wish the rest of them ill, but…"

"The police wouldn't keep us here for no reason," the judge said firmly. "But it does seem rather silly to just hang about with nothing to do."

"My God! This place is like Calvinist purgatory. All the beauty you could want and not so much as a deck of cards to pass the time. And I need to be in Cincinnati…"

Mrs. Te Papa cut him off swiftly. They had heard, many times, about Cincinnati. "I am not sure our time here has to be purposeless," she said, thinking aloud. "We could, I suppose, pool our resources…"

"What resources?" the professor demanded. "I don't even have a wireless signal."

"No, no, I don't mean that. But we were present at the party last night, which the police seem to have seized on as being important. We've been observing these people at close quarters. Maybe we know something already."

"Are you suggesting," Dr. Ackerman seemed prepared to put a toe in, "that we *outfox* the police…"

"And solve the crime ourselves!" Judge Chan finished.

Mrs. Te Papa was horrified. "Not at all!" she protested. "Whatever information we may find we will, of course, turn over to them."

"Oh, I suppose so," the judge agreed, a trifle wistfully.

Ackerman's natural irritability was matched by a rigorous scientific mind. "The first thing we should do," he declared, "is exonerate ourselves." He turned to Rosalind Chan. "Do *you* have an alibi?"

"*Gao shenme gui!*" The judge was startled into Mandarin.

"I'm afraid he's right," said Mrs. Te Papa. "It's no good

pretending this has nothing to do with us. We are guests on an island where a murder may have been committed. As theatrical as that sounds, it's a fact. I know, for example, that I had no reason at all to kill Lani Kapiaho, but there is no possible way *you* could know that about me."

"Fair enough," Judge Chan sighed.

"I'll go first," Ackerman volunteered. "I came up to my room around midnight, worked on some papers for about half an hour, then tried to sleep. But the damn mosquitoes kept me up for hours."

"I could hear you swatting them," Chan confirmed. "And swearing."

The professor's grin was surprisingly boyish. "Well, it was a good fight. Anyway, that probably lasted until two or three, I'm not sure. Then I tried to read again but mostly just tossed and turned until daybreak. No witnesses, of course." He looked mischievous.

"Did you happen to hear a loud noise?" Mrs. Te Papa asked. "It might have sounded like thunder."

Ackerman considered. "Come to think of it, I do remember hearing something. It didn't sound like thunder, though. It was sharper, more like a car backfiring. That's what I thought it was."

"What time was this?"

He frowned. "Sometime after two? I'm not sure. Did you hear it, Judge?"

"I heard a noise, but thought it was a door slamming—or you, Dr. Ackerman, if you'll pardon me."

"Not an unreasonable assumption," he admitted.

"I take it neither of you left your rooms?" Mrs. Te Papa asked.

They both shook their heads. "I sleep lightly, as a rule," said the judge. "Dr. Ackerman's antics woke me up a couple times, but that was all. Oh, and once I went to the toilet. But that was later, around four or five."

"I, too," Mrs. Te Papa concurred. "Such is age."

"Well, that rules us out," Judge Chan said, with a hint of amusement. "If any of us was a murderer, we'd certainly have given ourselves an alibi."

"What about the rest of them?" Ackerman wondered.

"Ogden Lathrop was out cold on the sofa when I passed by the study," Chan offered, "but I can't account for anyone else."

Mrs. Te Papa was thinking. "Perhaps we should go over the events of last night, the conversations we overheard, and see if anything stands out."

The others concurred. Yet an hour later the only thing they had achieved was distracting themselves for an hour. "Are you *sure...*"

"Yes, dammit!" Ackerman snapped at Judge Chan. "We've been through every scrap of conversation, twice. Other than Ogden Lathrop's enormities, I saw no one else threaten Lani since I arrived."

"Peter sure wanted to talk to her, though," she answered thoughtfully. "I'd give a lot to know what they said to one another."

"I, too," Mrs. Te Papa admitted. "She looked at him very strangely during the hearing. Almost as if she didn't know who he was. Or, more precisely, who he had become."

Ackerman was unimpressed. "That doesn't make sense. Of all the participants in the hearing, his were the only views that never changed."

"Exactly. But the circumstances did. Anyone could see the deal Lani was being offered was far better—including Lani herself. So why couldn't he?"

"Sheer bloody-mindedness, I suppose."

No one who had met Peter could deny that, but it still seemed unsatisfactory. Marnie appeared in the doorway with a pitcher of iced tea and glasses. "I'm sorry you've been left alone so long, but what with the police and all... Anyway, I thought you might be thirsty."

"You are an angel in the house," Dr. Ackerman told her gravely.

She poured them each a glass. The judge was looking at her with sudden interest. "Marnie," she said, "you were inside most of last night during the bonfire, weren't you? I didn't see you until…" Until she went to rescue Ogden from himself. "…until later."

"Oh, no, no," Marnie twittered. "I don't like fires much. Oggy loves them, but they give me allergies. Most of the time I just sit in the library and read."

"Is that where you were when Lani came back in with her young man?"

"Yes, I saw them go by. Into the study. They closed the door."

"Ah, well," said the judge sadly.

"—But they couldn't close the pocket doors, not all the way. They've been out of alignment for years now. I've tried to fix them a dozen times, but…"

There was a moment of respectful silence. "Marnie," Mrs. Te Papa said slowly, "are you saying you heard their conversation?"

"Not *all* of it," she averred. "Just what came through the doors. I wasn't trying to listen, of course."

"Certainly not. But what did you hear, exactly?"

Mrs. Te Papa saw the consternation on the woman's face as she stood irresolutely, clutching the pitcher. On the one hand she was a decent creature who didn't like to speak ill of others, especially the dead. On the other, this might be the first time in decades when anyone was interested in what she had to say. Temptation beckoned, and she fell. "They were arguing. Screaming, really. It started off quietly enough but by the end they were both shouting their heads off. Lani kept saying the same thing over and over. '*I saw the statements! I saw the statements!*'"

"Statements?" the judge repeated blankly. "Whose statements? What about?"

"I don't know. But he kept trying to calm her down. Denying it, whatever it was. I don't think she believed him, though."

"Oh? Why not?"

"Because she kept saying, '*Everyone here is a liar!*' And when she left, and he was still in the den, she turned around and said—very quietly, but I could still hear—'*The two people I trusted most both betrayed me tonight.*' I don't think she'd say those things if she believed him, would she?" None of them had an answer. After a moment Marnie bustled away.

"'But behold, the hand of him that betrayeth me is with me on the table!'" Dr. Ackerman intoned, "'Woe unto that man by whom he is betrayed!'"

"*Two* people," Mrs. Te Papa repeated. "Who was the other?"

The judge, however, looked satisfied. "Well, at least we can be pretty sure who one was," she said smugly.

———

The police, as it happened, were also very interested in Peter Pauahi at that moment. The man himself sat before Detective Roundtree in the same dirty gray shirt he had worn the day before. His hair was tangled and his eyes bleary. He said, for the fifth time, "I dunno what you want with me. I don't know nothing 'bout Lani. Except I can't believe she's gone."

Roundtree was a patient man. He merely asked again, "A whole crowd of people saw you pull Lani into the house last night. What did you need to talk to her about so urgently?"

"I told you, nothing, nothing man. I just wanted to say *ainokea*, no hard feelings about how the hearing went down, that's all."

"People heard an argument."

"Well, she was mad at me, so what? It was a difference of opinion. I wanted to keep *katonk* developers off my land, is that such a crime?" Even now Roundtree perceived the ghost of a swagger that must have made Peter intolerable yesterday.

"No," he said pleasantly, "that's not a crime. So you got your answer and went home, and that was it? You didn't see her again that night?"

"'Course not. Figured I'd let her sleep and cool off. Then we could talk again tomorrow." He crossed his legs and wiggled his sandaled foot nervously.

Roundtree had a map of the village in front of him. "Your place," he said, "lies on the road between the Kapiahos and Lathrop House. Lani must have passed you when she went up to the statue. Are you sure you didn't see her? It would be very helpful if we could narrow down the time," he added politely.

"I told you, I told you, I was asleep. I didn't see nobody. Who do you see when you're asleep?"

Only the dead, Roundtree thought. But he said merely, "I understand. So you would be willing to swear that you have not been up to the statue site since before yesterday afternoon?"

"Sure, because it's the truth. Why the hell would I go up there? I hate that place."

"Yes, we know. And now it's been blasted off the face of the earth."

Peter stared at him. He wiped a hand across dry lips. "Look," he said earnestly, "I loved Lani. I really did. We grew up together. And maybe what we had wouldn't have worked, not forever. But I would never hurt her, not for anything. Why would I?"

Detective Roundtree spread his hands and smiled. "Well, I can't think of a reason at the moment. So I guess we're done here." Peter started to leave when Roundtree added, "Just wait for a moment at the door, would you? Sergeant Collins needs your left shoe."

Peter's mouth dropped. "Why the hell?"

"Because there's a bit of Amyas Lathrop stuck to the sole. Thanks so much for coming."

After Peter Pauahi had left, or rather fled, Detective Roundtree slumped in his chair. It was getting on evening now, and he was tired. He called to Sergeant Collins to get him a Pepsi. "And tell the crew to start packing it in. We're done here for the day."

"What about the guests, sir? Ackerman and the others?"

Roundtree shrugged. "No reason to keep them now. If we need 'em again they can just come to the station. Tell that kid Roger he can schedule the seaplane for tomorrow morning."

"They'll like that," Collins said with a grin.

At that moment another officer burst through the door and, finding his chief seated before him, came rather awkwardly to attention.

"At ease, son, this isn't the Navy."

Officer Terry Kipu, who actually *had* been in the Navy, nodded. "Right, sir. Just got back from the crime scene. The coroner wanted me to tell you that the body has been photographed and plotted and is ready for transfer, if you'll give the go-ahead. She says they're losing the light."

"Very well."

"She'd also like you to tell her what she should do with the others."

Roundtree passed a hand over his face, paused. "The other what?"

"The other bodies, sir. Skeletons, more like. The coroner says she doesn't have enough plastic bags, and if she leaves them out, she thinks the animals might get at them, so she's wondering if we could lay down a tarp or something?"

The detective took a long gulp of Pepsi and waited until it hit the bottom of his stomach before he asked, faintly, "How many?"

"I think they're still pulling them up, sir." Kipu considered for a moment, as his chief grasped the desk in front of him with hands that were suddenly sweaty.

"I'm pretty sure the count when I left was thirty-two."

"A True Account..."

December 23, 1849

There are no seasons here. Nothing marks the passage of time. If it were not for the calendar I should have no idea of the month, much less the day. I wonder that this is why the Hawaiian people are at the same time indolent and savage. Nature imposes no demands on them. They have only to strew seed in the ground for crops to grow, reach their nets into the sea for fish to swim willingly into them. Some might see this as a sign of God's blessing, but I know better. It is a curse. With no trials to overcome, they have never progressed beyond beasts in the wild. It is travails that make a man, a race, a civilization. If I should give one gift to the people of these islands, it would be winter. Let them shudder and freeze, so that they may learn to build stronger homes. Let them scratch for food, so they should be thankful for abundance. I miss the snow.

The fever has returned again, not as bad as last time, but we lost three persons—the widow Berenice, young Jack Hi'o and the newborn babe of the Andersens. Seven others are ill, and I have sent to Kona for medicines and supplies. I dread these occurrences, for they bring out the very worst in the natives—a touch of fear drives them mad, and at once they clutch for their wretched tikis and begin making offerings to their gods. This they do in secret, but I am well apprised of it. There is one amongst them, a fine strapping lad of twenty-two who came with the name Kapiaho. He is

Guinean by birth, captured as a slave and brought to the Sandwich Islands on a packet boat. Escaping these confines he took refuge in Hilo with a local family and adopted their ways. He has even picked up the rudiments of the Christian faith, though I regret his instruction came from a Papist and is thus lacking. I named him Melchior after the King of the Persians. It is a pleasure to exchange verses of Scripture with him, and he is a ready student. He has shared his concerns with me—namely, that the villagers are not fully conversant in the true faith and, worse still, are becoming recidivist. It now appears many amongst them do not profess Christianity at all, but merely accepted passage to New Boston that they might escape a second wave of plague. This is dispiriting news indeed. But I take heart. There are some faithful amongst them, Melchior assures me, and under my guidance I have no doubt the rest shall see the error of their ways.

He really is a splendid fellow. I have a mind to appoint him overseer of the field hands, as a measure of my trust. Prudence agrees.

Chapter 7

LUKU, THE MASSACRE

Roger did not, after all, call for the seaplane.

"Now," said Roundtree slowly, "what I need to know is, are we looking at a crime scene or an archaeological dig?"

The dead were laid out in rows. Some were complete skeletons, others nothing more than a skull or rib cage. It was morning again, and with a sick feeling of déjà vu, Winnie Te Papa found herself standing among the ruins of Kaumaha. Judge Chan and Robert Ackerman were at her side: Ackerman for his expertise, and the judge because no power on earth could keep her from coming.

"Describe to me how you found them," Ackerman demanded. His tone was unusually muted.

"The cylinder that supported the statue was hollow. I think you said as much, Professor. Turns out it was not only hollow but deep, like a well or a cistern. We measured the depth to about twenty feet. The cavity was only about four feet in diameter, so the bodies landed on top of one another in a more-or-less vertical position. The skeletons at the top were complete and identifiable. The ones toward the bottom were…less so."

Ackerman nodded. "Yes, they would have compacted over time, especially with the added weight. Ossuaries in places like New Orleans are much the same. Any clothing or jewelry?"

"None. But, as you can see, they are all…"

"Children." The judge's voice was a horrified whisper.

"That's right. By their heights, I'd say none older than eleven or twelve. Some much younger. I think you said this place was called the House of the Bone Feast, Professor?"

Color returned to the old man's face. "That is *not* what that means!" he snapped. "The bone feast house was a ceremonial place, a gathering. The bones were animal, for God's sake, not human."

"But then how can you account…"

"I can't account for it! I only know what it was built for."

Mrs. Te Papa cleared her throat. "A sacred space may have many uses over time, according to the society that inhabits it. Just think of what Roger was saying the other night about San Clemente." Roundtree cocked an eyebrow, and she explained. Ackerman added his agreement.

"So," Roundtree said thoughtfully, "that means this could have been a meeting hall built over the site of an ancient sacrifice, or a later society that used the ruin for its own dark purposes. Any idea which?"

Mrs. Te Papa shrugged. "Human sacrifices were known to continue on the islands until the nineteenth century. Captain Cook witnessed one. A French journalist depicted another around 1819. But this many…it would have taken time. This was not done in a day, nor even a year." She shuddered. Another voice rang in her ears: *Ku has taken his sacrifice.* But there could not be a connection, surely.

Because, and she put this very frankly to herself, the gods did not exist. This was not a statement she dared to make aloud, as it was disrespectful and—paradoxically—invited disaster. Part of her role as cultural director was visiting schools and teaching the *keiki* about the Hawaiian pantheon. Invariably, she was asked the big question, and her answer was always the same: gods are lessons, and those lessons are important. They define who we are as a people. They gave our ancestors a way to understand the universe and teach their children to be good. The gods are important. But they are not anything to be frightened of.

Except, of course, that they were. The ancient Hawaiians were in mortal terror of their gods, and of Ku, god of war, most of all. Every depiction of him showed a grimacing face calling down destruction from the heavens. Kana, Lono, Kanaloa, and Papa were all creators; even Pele, goddess of fire, used her power to make new land. But Ku was the negation. Hawaiians sacrificed to him to slake his blood lust and leave them unharmed. But *this many*? What kind of terror or madness had infected these people?

Detective Roundtree interrupted her thoughts. "Any idea how it was done?"

She and Ackerman peered closely at one of the better-preserved skeletons Ackerman saw it first. "Those nicks there, see them? That looks like a blade did that."

"Yes. Their throats were cut."

She heard the judge mutter, "How horrid!" but Ackerman's professional curiosity was aroused. "Pity they laid them all out like this. It would have been helpful to see them in situ."

Mrs. Te Papa agreed. "There is so much we don't know. Were they buried naked, or did all the clothing rot away? Was this done over years, or decades?"

"Or even centuries?"

Roundtree cleared his throat politely. "I'm sorry to interrupt," he said, "but my interest in this may be a bit different from yours. If this horror is as old as you say, then it can't possibly have anything to do with the murder, right?"

"Oh, I wouldn't say that," Judge Chan objected. They all turned to her. "Well, think what's going to happen now.

You have just uncovered a significant burial site. Naturally, the sale and development of the island will be put on hold until experts like yourselves make sense of all this. And while ruins may not be enough to stop a hotel, sacred burial grounds definitely are."

"Not to mention," Mrs. Te Papa agreed, "that no Hawaiian developer in his right mind would ever build on top of or even near one." There had been the old Kamehameha Hotel in Kona which burned mysteriously to the ground three times before its owners simply padlocked the site and fled. Gods were one thing, but spirits—especially *angry* spirits—were another.

"So," Roundtree summed up, "you're suggesting someone might have blown this thing up just to expose what lay beneath?"

"It's a possibility, right? They might have been hoping that we did it ourselves, by removing the statue. Once that wasn't going to happen, they took matters into their own hands."

Ackerman thought of an objection. "But that would mean whoever it was already knew about the bodies. And if they've been sealed for centuries, how could he?"

None of them knew the answer.

———

Peter Pauahi slept in the crawl space above his parents' garage. It was a tiny wedge of stale air not more than five feet high, littered with magazines, food cartons, and cigarette butts. But it had a telephone.

The phone rang at precisely nine that evening. Peter answered it at once. *"You failed,"* it told him.

"Wha...what are you talking about?"

"We gave you specific instructions. They were not carried out. Now our client has to deal with this personally."

The hand that held the receiver was slick with sweat. "I

tried!" he almost shouted. "How could I know he'd change the deal like that? Christ, what was I supposed to do?"

"What we paid you for."

"Look, the deal is off. That's what you wanted, right? There's no way the island will be sold now. Do you know what they found under that statue?" Briefly he told them.

There was a pause of empty static. *"You are certain?"*

"Of course I am! It couldn't have worked out any better. Wait…" A terrible thought occurred to him. "Did…did you know?"

Another pause. *"We'll be in touch."*

The connection was severed. Peter stared at the phone for a moment, disbelievingly. There was a rustling sound from below. "Dad!" Peter shouted, "Goddamn it, I said I wanted to be alone."

"I think you'd better come down, son."

But it was not his father's voice. Peter peered over the edge and saw Detective Roundtree standing there with two officers. Peter's parents were behind them, holding hands and staring fixedly at the ground. They all had the same expression, like mourners at a funeral.

Peter Pauahi screamed.

"A True Account…"

January 3, 1850

Was awoken last night by the most dreadful sound, a kind of high keening shriek. Prudence did not stir, but she is much fatigued of late. I put on my dressing gown and performed a search of the house, but found nothing amiss. The sound comes from the valley. I can hear it quite distinctly. At first I supposed it to be an animal, for the desperation in its cry reminds me of the noise a coyote makes when caught in a trap. But the note is sustained indefinitely, I assume by multiple voices that take up the chant. There are no words, not even Hawaiian ones, but odd dips and ululations that carry the form of language without its substance.

I stood on the porch and looked out into the valley, expecting to see a bonfire with men dancing round it. But there was no light at all save the stars, and nothing stirred. I was of half a mind to set out on foot then and there, but good sense prevailed. It is likely a few of the village boys making mischief. I shall speak to Melchior about it on the morrow.

February 24, 1850
The sound comes every night. I have brought Prudence and Melchior and even my small son, John, onto the porch to listen, but that is the cunning of the thing—it stops the moment they emerge. I cannot account for it. Melchior has made inquiries and learned nothing: the natives refuse to admit their complicity in what, I am now certain, is a foul and dirty trick to deprive me of my sleep and make me lax in my obligations. But it may be worse still. The tenor of the cry is familiar to me—I did not recognize it at first, but it is very like the call of the Hawaiian priests when they invoke their great god, Kane. I heard a ceremony thus performed at my last visit to Honolulu. It is now plain that some person or persons on this island are deliberately challenging Christianity itself, mocking the Faith and me.

I have set Melchior a task. He shall conceal himself along the village road at nightfall and keep watch over each and every dwelling. None may step out but that he shall see them, and none can reach the valley by any means but the road. "Put on the whole armour of God,

that ye may be able to stand against the wiles of the devil."
If there is a pagan element among my flock, I shall root it
out. I shall.

February 25, 1850

   Melchior remained at his post throughout the night
but saw and heard nothing. None emerged from their
homes. But the cry came regardless and I am at my
wit's end.

Chapter 8

KAHUAI, THE BROTHERHOOD

Three days later Mrs. Te Papa was back at her desk in the featureless, factory-like Office of Hawaiian Affairs. Marybeth sat across from her. The weather outside was a perfect seventy-six degrees and sunny. Indeed, to the untrained observer, it would appear as if everything had returned to normal.

But Mrs. Te Papa could tell that Marybeth was distracted. She answered her employer's questions readily enough but added nothing of her own. And when she thought Mrs. Te Papa was not looking, her gaze drifted wistfully toward the window.

Marybeth could tell Mrs. Te Papa was distracted also. The old woman's face, normally as clear as a tide pool, looked troubled. She frowned and muttered to herself. She mislaid her favorite coffee cup three times and came perilously close to accusing Marybeth of concealing it.

The thoughts of both women returned, as if compelled, to Kaumaha.

"I heard they arrested that boy today," Mrs. Te Papa said as casually as she dared.

Marybeth dropped her pencil. "Not Roger?"

"No, no, the other one. Peter."

"Oh. What makes them think he did it?" Now she sounded almost indifferent.

"He lied about being at the site. There was a piece of the statue lodged in his shoe. Then there was the argument Marnie overheard. Lani kept yelling at him about 'the statements.' That got the police thinking. They checked his bank statements and found he had been making some very large deposits recently. They began when he started to protest the sale of Kaumaha."

"Wow." Marybeth considered this for a moment. "So did he blow up the statue, too?"

"Apparently. The working theory is that he told Lani to meet him there late that night on some pretext or other. He came along the ridge path from the village so no one would see him. When she arrived, he struck her down and then staged the scene to make it appear is if she had set the explosion and died in the attempt. Then he went back along the same ridge trail. Old Mrs. Lathrop only saw Lani, remember."

"That makes sense."

Yes, Mrs. Te Papa agreed, it did make sense. Nice and efficient. No need to worry about dozens of skeletons trapped underground, or drunken relatives, or newspaper cuttings with threatening messages tucked into library shelves... *"Yakuza Suspected in Beating Death..."*

"Marybeth," she said suddenly, "have you ever heard of Yakuza?"

There was a long pause. "What do you want with them?" Marybeth asked, her voice flat.

"I don't want anything with them. I don't know who *they* are."

"That's because no one does. They like it that way."

Mrs. Te Papa was losing patience. "My dear, I have no idea what you are talking about."

"Oh!" Marybeth rushed to explain. "The Yakuza are Japanese mafia. Like the Tongs in China, but much more powerful."

"I see." She considered this. "Are they active in Hawaii?"

Marybeth nodded. "Very. In fact, they're the only criminal organization that operates here. They chased the others out."

But the girl was still holding something back. What was it? Not a family member, certainly: the Luatua clan were Māori and self-contained. But hadn't there been... "Your ex-boyfriend?"

"It was never proved! I never knew! My *kupuna* was furious when she found out about Hiro!"

Mrs. Te Papa believed that. Gertrude Luatua was one of her oldest friends, and Marybeth was her favorite grandchild. "Okay, okay," she said placatingly. "*Ho'omaha*, I won't say a word to Gertie, I promise. Or anyone else. But this may be very important, dear. Tell me what you know."

Her eyes, steel-gray and unblinking, were like searchlights. Marybeth hesitated for only a moment, then dropped her gaze. Mrs. Te Papa began to take notes.

The Yakuza, she learned, began during the Edo dynasty in the 1600s as a guild of street peddlers, the lowest strata of Japanese society. Spit on, beaten, and hounded from one town to the next, they finally organized and fought back. Over centuries the guild became a vast criminal organization which controlled everything from gambling halls to black market goods. Despised by the nobility, denounced by the government, they clung to power from one dynasty to the next. During the Second World War—with everything from rice flour to bricks in desperately short supply—the Yakuza came into their own. They formed construction companies, shipping companies, grocery chains. In the decades that followed they became almost respectable. They purchased baseball teams and invested in the stock market. After the Kobe earthquake they sent hundreds of trucks with food, water, and medical supplies. They contributed to political campaigns—discreetly, of course—and even had fan magazines written about some of their more colorful members.

The Japanese government regarded them much as the Edo emperors had: embarrassing, but inevitable. The Yakuza were fine with that.

"But how does one become a member? Is it like a gang?"

More like a fraternity, it appeared. Membership was by invitation only, and there were numerous rituals and rites of passage. The Yakuza were ferociously loyal and protective of one another. In matters of business they were ruthless but never capricious or cruel. Within their ranks they forbade theft, battery, and all petty crime. The *saiko-komon*, or bosses and underbosses, maintained an almost feudal sense of honor and duty. Marybeth met one of these men and came away impressed. "He treated me like a princess," she said wistfully. When Hiro failed to pull back her chair, he earned a tongue-lashing that would have made even her grandmother proud.

"Yes, yes," Mrs. Te Papa thought Marybeth had become rather starstruck by what was, after all, a bunch of gangsters. "But are there identifying marks? How can you tell when you're talking to one? The Tongs have a gang sign on their wrist, I believe…" Actually, she remembered it from a James Bond movie.

"I don't know about that, but they sure have a lot of tattoos," Marybeth answered. "Like a biker gang. You wouldn't know it, though, because they always wear long-sleeve shirts and trousers, even on hot days. But I heard that they take them off when they play *Oicho-Kabu* and they're covered from chin to ankles."

Oicho-Kabu was a card game not unlike baccarat. Mrs. Te Papa had played it herself. She was silent for a moment, staring out the window at the parking lot, thinking of a warm night and a tattooed figure framed against the light of a bonfire. "Do you know where Diamond Head Holdings is located?" she asked finally.

Marybeth didn't, but after fifteen seconds on Google maps, she did. She sometimes worried that Mrs. Te Papa would embrace the internet and Marybeth would be out of a job. "It's in the Queen Kalama tower. Fifteenth floor. You want me to make you an appointment?"

"No. I will go myself. He'll either see me or he won't."

———

The Queen Kalama was part of a cluster of buildings adjacent to the First Hawaiian Center. Its glass-walled anonymity could have been found in Shanghai or Zurich or Chicago. Mrs. Te Papa approached the guard and asked if she could speak with Mr. Tanaka of Diamond Head Holdings. No, she didn't have an appointment. But perhaps his assistant could let him know she was here. The guard looked incredulous but reached for the intercom. As he did, she noticed the brilliant whorls of green ink under his sleeve.

Ten minutes later she was being ushered through a series of high-ceilinged, white-painted rooms, each with a single Japanese scroll or sculpture featured prominently. Thick carpeting absorbed the sound of her feet. The place had an almost monastic stillness, and she wondered whether all business was transacted in whispers. At the end of the hallway was a door marked DAVID TANAKA, CEO.

Tanaka was seated in a large leather chair, his legs tucked under him, reading. He rose as she came in. "Winnie! This really is an unexpected pleasure. Please sit."

The office was...just an office. White walls, beige carpet, and a partner's desk set before a sheet of glass that looked out imperially over Mamala Bay. Tanaka offered her tea, which she refused. "What are you reading?" she asked curiously.

Tanaka picked up the book and handed it to her. *The Pullman Strike.*

"I remember this," she said thoughtfully.

"I doubt it. The strike happened in 1894."

Mrs. Te Papa shook her head. "I meant, I heard about it. Pullman cut his employees' wages in half and raised their rents at the same time. Then he got the U.S. Army to shoot the strikers. Thirty-four dead, in all." She sighed. "The sugar barons did much the same here around that time."

Tanaka grinned. "There's some justice, though. Pullman dropped dead of a heart attack two years later. His widow was so afraid the socialists would come for him that she had the poor old boy encased in a lead-lined coffin with three tons of concrete poured over the top. When the trumpet sounds, George Pullman is going to have a heck of a time answering the call. I hope Mrs. Pullman put in a jackhammer."

"Ko'u akua!" cried Mrs. Te Papa, startled. "It's an idea, that."

"I'm sorry?"

"Nothing." She shook herself slightly. "I have come," she told him, "to ask you three very impertinent questions."

He grinned delightedly. "And here I thought my day was going to be boring. Fire away."

"First is this. Why did you seek my presence at the ground-breaking, and why did you want me on the committee?"

Tanaka was unsurprised. "That's actually two questions. But the answer is the same. Kahakai Elementary School, class of 1999." He smiled at her puzzlement. "You came to speak at my eighth-grade commencement. I'm sure you don't remember, why would you? You told us that we were part of a sacred trust, being Hawaiian. That it wasn't about blood or ancestry. Everyone born on these islands was an inheritor of the same spirit as Kamehameha and had an equal duty to protect their people. And that the very essence of being Hawaiian was twofold: diversity and tolerance."

"I often say that," Mrs. Te Papa admitted. "No one is 'pure' Hawaiian. We are all *hapa*. Accepting diversity is part of tolerance."

"Yes, it is. I was valedictorian that year. You gave me an award and told me how proud you were of me. I'd never heard those words before. And that's why I whispered up at you, 'Does diversity mean other things besides skin? Like who we love?' And you leaned down—I was a lot shorter then—and said, 'Yes, little 'anela, diversity means you may love whomever you want, and tolerance means everyone will accept that love.' I never forgot it. So when I needed advice on whether I was being a true Hawaiian, you were the first person I thought of."

Whatever Mrs. Te Papa was expecting, it was not this. She sat in her chair for a few moments, breathing hard. "I am really very...touched," she said.

"Don't be. I bet half the kids in Honolulu could tell you a story like that. What's the second question?"

For a moment she hesitated. She looked at David Tanaka in his starched white shirt and paua shell cuff links and imagined the scrawny eighth grader he once had been. She drew a breath, let it out slowly, and asked: "Do you have any tattoos?"

The smile remained fixed in place, as if he'd forgotten it was there. "Why do you want to know?" His voice was carefully neutral.

"If the reason doesn't matter, you will have no difficulty answering the question."

But he did not answer. Instead, he sat back in his chair and linked his hands behind his head. He drew in a great lungful of air and expelled it toward the ceiling. "It was Kaito, I suppose. I keep telling him he needs a better tailor."

"Partly him, yes. His are distinctive and cover his entire body. Just out of curiosity, do yours as well?"

"Not...quite as much," Tanaka answered. The ghost of a smile returned. "I assume there's a reason you want to know, that it's not just idle curiosity. You don't strike me as that kind of person."

"I'm not. There is a reason." She tried to keep her voice as calm as his.

"Okay, then." He leaned forward and put his hands on the desk. "I'm going to try to explain this. I've never said these words before, and if it was anyone other than you...well, they never would have made it past the guard. But here goes." He sighed. "My parents were coffee-growers in Honalo. Field hands. Just like theirs had been, and so on, for five generations. Hard people. Hard-shell Baptists, too, like old Amyas Lathrop. But my people came from Kyoto about thirty years after he was dead, so I can't blame him for that.

"They wanted me in the fields, but until I turned sixteen the law kept me in school. And school was magical. Everything came easily: algebra, history, literature. I was a pretty decent forward on the soccer team, too." He grinned in remembrance. "But nobody in my house cared about that, or the grades. To them I was just wasting time. Maybe if they'd been the least bit proud— well, I can't change the past. But it certainly meant I couldn't tell them the other things I was discovering about myself."

"You told me instead," Mrs. Te Papa said with a tiny smile of her own.

"Yes. That was supposed to be my last day of freedom. After that I went out to the fields. But I had a friend at school—I won't tell you her name; she was Japanese and her father had taken an interest. He was very rich—Kona rich, anyway. Always asked me about my studies, what I wanted to do after, was I going to go to college here or on the mainland? So finally that summer I told him the truth, just so he would stop asking. The next day I came back and found my father and this man talking over the kitchen table. Two weeks later I had a one-way ticket to Tokyo.

"I didn't know if he bribed or just threatened my parents, and I didn't care. I had a new family now. They put me through high school and college, paid for everything, even my MBA. I lived with my Tokyo *oyabun* and his wife and children. This is the word they use for boss, but it literally means foster parent. That's what he was. For the first time in my life, I knew real love. All he asked in return was complete honesty. So, when he finally asked the question, I told him the truth. The next week he started setting me up on dates with the *kobun* guards. Some of them were pretty cute." Tanaka began to laugh. "You know what? It turns out they knew all along. Even my Kona friend's father. He asked if I was her boyfriend, and she told him the truth. All of it, including the crazy Baptist parents. So he rescued me even more than I realized.

"That's what they do. The whole outfit is full of exiles, kids thrown out of their homes for one reason or another. They take them when no one else will. Oh, I know what you're thinking. That they just saw me as raw material they could use. I don't deny it. And I don't deny I was grateful, and loyal. But that's just the beginning of the story. For years now they've watched over me, protected me, encouraged me. And I learned a lot from them. I saw how they gave each person justice and took care of their communities. How they prized honor and responsibility above all. The truth is, whatever morality I've got is theirs, not my Bible-thumping parents'. And that's the truth." He sat back in his chair and spread his hands, as if daring her to contradict him.

She didn't. In fact she was thinking how similar the Yakuza sounded to the *ohana* of her childhood: families that were more like clans, with strict rules of deportment and frequent, sometimes astonishing displays of affection. All gone now, alas. She spoke the thought that was in her mind: "You were lucky."

David Tanaka beamed. "Yes. I was. Thank you for understanding that. And the third?"

"I beg your pardon?" For once, Mrs. Te Papa was caught off guard.

"You said there were three questions."

"Three *impertinent* questions," she corrected. "And I'm

afraid the third is the most impertinent of all." Mrs. Te Papa reached into her handbag and drew out the newspaper cutting. She handed it to him without a word.

Tanaka opened the fold, saw what was inside. *I KNOW WHAT YOU DID.* She watched his face intently. She expected to see recognition followed by guilt, perhaps an attempt to conceal both. What she saw instead was profound and genuine shock. He looked from the paper to her, then back again. He stared at it as if he did not quite believe it existed. "What *is* this?" His voice was almost a gasp.

"I was hoping you could tell me. I found it in the library at Lathrop House, tucked between two books. I think it was put there the day of the hearing or not long before."

Color rushed back into David Tanaka's cheeks. It was remarkable, Mrs. Te Papa thought irrelevantly, how emotions transformed the human face. Shock had given way to rage. His eyes bulged, and a muscle in his neck began to twitch. "You found this?" he said, so quietly that she had to strain to hear him. "Are you sure?"

Suddenly, Mrs. Te Papa realized she was in real danger from this man. It was a rare sensation, but not unknown. "I am not a blackmailer, David," she said, as calmly as she could. "I don't want anything from you at all, except the truth. I found that cutting exactly as I told you. I was hoping you could tell me something about it."

Slowly, very slowly, Tanaka shook his head. "I cannot help you," he told her. "I cannot tell you anything about this at all. I'm sorry." He pressed a button on his desk, and a moment later his assistant appeared. "We're done here, Nancy."

Recognizing her cue, Mrs. Te Papa gathered her things and stood. For once David Tanaka's manners failed him, and he did not rise as she left. He remained in his chair, staring after her with a curiously blank expression.

——

When she stepped off the elevator into the lobby, Mrs. Te Papa realized she had been holding her breath. She exhaled with a burst, surprising the security guard. Turning to apologize, she caught sight of a familiar figure moving toward the elevators. Dr. Robert Ackerman had traded his polo shirt and shorts for a rather ancient linen suit. His head was down and he clutched a tattered leather bag to his chest. Mrs. Te Papa nearly hailed him, but something in his manner suggested he did not wish to be disturbed. There was an intensity of purpose that she had not seen while he was in Kaumaha. The elevator arrived, and Ackerman got on it. The doors closed.

Only much later did it occur to Mrs. Te Papa that this was Tuesday, the day Dr. Ackerman was supposed to be in Ohio.

"A True Account..."

May 3, 1850

The sickness is upon us again. I know not how it arrived, for there has been no contact with the outside world save the single cutter that brings us our necessities. Four persons are infected, one gravely so. I begin to become convinced that some part of the community has been making clandestine trips to Kona Town. As none will admit to this, the purpose can only be to maintain contact with those so-called "priests" of the pagan cult whose influence, I fear, still remains strong among my flock.

Melchior tells me this is not the case. He assures me, again and again, that the people are true and loyal converts to Christ. But I now confess I have my doubts about his fidelity. He quite failed to discover the source of the cries that plagued us last winter, and it may well be because he himself was the author. His manner to me is equal parts fawning and truculent, depending upon whether he agrees with the order he is given. When I instructed him to render punishment on five laborers whom I found to be shirking their work at the refinery he became insolent, simply because they were children. The Hawaiian people have, I may say, a great fondness for children, which manifests itself in overindulgence and lassitude. Discipline is unknown to them. The laborers were discovered by me in a corner of the factory playing a kind of game with pebbles and shells. I ordered they be caned at once, fifteen lashes each, which is Melchior's task. He did not refuse but rather tried to find excuses for this behavior, and when I insisted, he delivered the blows in a lackadaisical manner. I was ultimately forced to thrash the boys myself.

This trifling incident now seems laced with portent. It may be that I am to blame. I rose him above his station and showered him with affection, made him overseer of the fields and deacon of the church. I relied too much upon his professed good nature and love for Our Savior. If I have been mistaken it was a grievous error, as he is now powerful among the villagers and may yet do me harm. "Men should be what they seem; or those that be not, let them seem none." Ay, a veritable Iago, with the face of the Moor!

I have shared my suspicions with no one, not even Prudence. She is quite taken with the lad and made it her special project to educate him in all things from practical science to philosophy. This education has, I regret to say, only made him more intractable. But he learns with great alacrity, for he is not unintelligent. I must proceed with care.

Chapter 9

KAHAKAU, THE DUKE

At Lathrop House, Roger hung up the hall phone and found both his parents standing behind him. Ogden was ashen.

"That was Tanaka," Roger told them. "He's pulling out of the sale."

His father's face crumpled into anger, but Marnie remained impassive. "Did he say why?" she asked in a surprisingly tranquil voice.

"He said *we*—" He looked at Ogden accusingly, "—misrepresented the legal status of the property. That he did not pay twenty million for the house alone, so therefore the previous contract was invalid. And he doesn't wish to renew the offer."

"We'll fucking sue!" Ogden declared.

"Who'll pay for the lawyers?" Roger went on: "He also said there's a strong chance the State of Hawaii may declare Kaumaha a state park and burial ground, so that it can never be sold or built upon."

Ogden's mouth hung slack. "They can't do that!"

"They can. Tanaka filed the application himself."

There was a moment of shocked silence. *"Good for him!"* Marnie suddenly shouted. She hiccuped once and then began to laugh uncontrollably. Tears streamed down her face.

Both men stared as if the hall rug had suddenly burst into song. "What did you say?" Ogden asked hoarsely.

"I said good for him. You did everything you could to destroy this place, Oggy, and I'm glad someone's finally had the balls to stop you."

Ogden was white to the lips. "Do you realize what this means, woman? We owe ten years in back taxes. The state doesn't need to buy Kaumaha, they can just take it. We'll be homeless."

"It's no more than we deserve." Marnie spoke almost incoherently, the words tumbling out of her as if a dam had burst: "I remember your grandpa saying this island was a sacred trust, handed down from one generation to the next. So for twenty years I patched and painted and cleaned until my fingers were raw. But what have you done? Thrown all the money away on liquor and whores and playing a big shot at the club. In the meantime, the house went to hell, the valley is nothing but weeds, and the villagers lost their jobs. Now that everything's gone, you thought you could turn Kaumaha into condos and walk away. And I let you!" She shook her head in disbelief. "God help me, I deserve this as much as you do."

"And Roger?" Ogden was pleased to see that smug look fall off her face. "Does he deserve this brave new future of yours?"

"Don't worry about me," Roger said quickly. "Not that you really would anyway. I think I'll enjoy having to make it on my own." For some reason, at that moment he thought of Marybeth.

Ogden stared at his wife and son as if he'd never seen them before. From behind them came a peal of soft laughter. He turned and saw Eleanor Lathrop paused on the stairs, one hand on the rail.

She had not come down since the tragedy. But this afternoon her hair was tied into a neat bun and she wore her usual outfit of a peasant smock and jeans. Except a certain pallor and thinness, she seemed almost herself. "Are you satisfied now, boy?" Eleanor asked Ogden, a wry smile lighting up her face. "Did you get everything you ever wanted?"

"Did *you*?" he shot back, stung. "You love this, don't you? Seeing me humiliated. You and Dad. I wouldn't be surprised if you arranged this whole damn thing."

"No, no, this one is all yours." She came down and took her grandson's hand. "But you're right, I am happy. Lani died defending Kaumaha, and now her legacy will be honored forever. I'm proud of *both* my grandchildren." She turned to Marnie. "Do you think you could get me a sandwich and a cup of tea, dear? I'm feeling a bit hungry."

"Of course!" Marnie said automatically. She hurried into the kitchen.

Eleanor looked back to her son. "Just so you know, Roger will not be penniless. I have enough savings to see him through the rest of his studies. And a bit left for Marnie, too, if she needs it."

"But what about you, Gran?" Roger asked, concerned.

"I've made arrangements for myself, too, don't worry." She patted his hand reassuringly until the frown disappeared, then changed the conversation to other matters. Ogden wandered off into the den and closed the door. Eleanor and Roger went out to the lanai.

It amused Eleanor Lathrop sometimes to tell the truth. She had indeed made arrangements, yet saw no reason to share them. Dr. Schiavo had been quite clear at her last visit. A decent hotel in Kona would do for the next few weeks.

After that, she wouldn't need much space at all.

———

Whenever Mrs. Te Papa had a particularly unpleasant duty to perform, she preceded it with a lavish meal. Eating calmed her. She enjoyed good food, and at this time of life it was one of few pleasures left.

Her café of choice was a small place on Beretania and Punahou called Louie's Broke Da Mouth. Its current proprietor was a Samoan named Wendell, but he had been there for so long that everyone called him Louie and he didn't mind. The restaurant was tucked into the front rooms of an old prewar bungalow painted Pepto Bismol–pink and surrounded by dreary stucco offices. Over the years the staff learned to gauge Mrs. Te Papa's mood by her order. The loco moco plate lunch was her baseline. If she had it with a diet soda and salad instead of macaroni, she had just come from the doctor's. If she received unexpected good news, she asked for half-and-half kalua pork. If she was in a particularly foul temper, she added Spam musubi and a side of tempura shrimp.

That was her order today. The servers exchanged a raised eyebrow. "And an Assam tea," she added, "with a Lilikoi Passion on ice." These were two bottled drinks, found everywhere on the islands, which to her certain knowledge existed nowhere else. She unfurled a copy of the *Honolulu Star-Advertiser* and began to read slowly, thoroughly. The wasubi arrived. As Mrs. Te Papa ate, a warm feeling of contentment spread gradually through her. She could think clearly now. Her first thought was of Dr. Ackerman. From her cavernous purse she drew out, after some effort, the "smart" phone that Marybeth convinced her to buy. She cordially loathed the thing and was sure the feeling was mutual. It never did anything she wished, but periodically a muffled and aggrieved British voice emerged from the depths of the bag: *"I'm sorry, I did not understand. Could you please repeat the question?"*

She pressed the green icon which she knew meant "text,"

and the screen appeared. So far, so good. Holding the phone like a slice of bread, she began punching letters with her stubby index finger one at a time:

> marybeth findout if there s a conference in Cincinnati or not and see if robt ackermaN is suppose to SPEak ther*e

After a few moments she had her answer:

> Checked every scheduled academic conference, nothing at all in Cincinnati. Anthropological conferences scheduled this month in Miami, Chicago, and Dallas, but Robert Ackerman not listed as speaker at any.

Mrs. Te Papa was too generous to resent her assistant's effortless ease with these machines. But she did notice it. She thought for a moment, then began telegraphing her reply: need list of all officers in queen kalama tower. Pleased with herself, she hit "send," and waited.

There was a long pause. Finally the reply came back: ?.

Damn. She tried again: *officers. Wait. OFF Ice s.

Another long pause. Then something popped up, not text but a kind of picture. With some trepidation, she touched it. At once, miraculously, it expanded into a list. Squinting slightly, Mrs. Te Papa scanned the names. Diamond Head Holdings occupied twelve floors in the tower; something called Oceania Properties had eleven. Besides these were the usual collection of accountants, shell companies, law offices, and doctors—three cardiologists, an oncologist, and a podiatrist. But Mrs. Te Papa was intrigued by Oceania. She sent the name to Marybeth with a query and waited. Thirty seconds later the reply came: Rodrigo Roxas, CEO.

Ko'u akua! Roxas, the homicidal *manong* developer! Imagine him and Tanaka in the same building. Did they ever get caught in the elevator together? Or fight for the same parking space? On the other hand, Mrs. Te Papa reflected, perhaps it was not so remarkable after all. Honolulu was not New York; there weren't that many glittering office towers here. Queen Kalama was among the newest and tallest. Perhaps rich businessmen naturally gravitated toward the same offices as they would the same gym or club.

But, more to the point, which man had Robert Ackerman come to see, and why?

———

When Mrs. Te Papa paid her bill and left, her good humor was restored. She arrived at the police station in the same cheerful mind, which not even its gray walls, linoleum, and persistent smell of socks could dampen. Somewhere deep within her, the musubi and tempura shrimp continued to radiate waves of reassurance. "I am here to see Peter Pauahi," she told the desk guard confidently.

"Are you his attorney?"

"I am with the Office of Hawaiian Affairs. I need to ask him a few questions." She flashed an important-looking badge that had the state seal and a great many numbers on it. After a few calls she was shown upstairs. Mrs. Te Papa favored the guard with a smile and pocketed the badge. It worked great for getting free museum passes, too.

She found Peter in a small cell near the lavatory. Oahu has a proper prison, of course, but its municipal police station has a handful of such rooms that are usually kept for pickpockets, drunks, domestic abusers, and other transients. Peter still wore the same stained gray shirt and shorts. His hair was flattened on one side where he had slept on it. His face had been drained of all belligerence; he looked puzzled, and very young. "Auntie?" he said, using the slang term for elder. "I thought...are you my lawyer?"

"No, Peter. But I can get you one, if you'd like."

He shrugged. "Yeah, I think so."

She sat down on the narrow cot across from his. "I will try to help you," she said. "But you must tell me everything first. Understand, I am not the police. I am not acting for anyone else. I just need to know the truth. Did you kill Lani Kapiaho?"

He shook his head vehemently. "No, *aole loa*. I loved her. I really did."

"But you lied to her."

He clasped his hands between his knees and stared at the floor. "Yes," he said, very quietly, "I lied to her. I didn't mean to. I figured it would be okay, since we wanted the same thing, just for different reasons. That's what *he* said, anyway."

"Mr. Roxas?" Mrs. Te Papa ventured.

He didn't seem surprised she knew the name. "Yeah. Right after Tanaka went public with the plans for the sale. I didn't know who Roxas was at first, just this little *buk buk* with thick glasses and a really ugly Hawaiian shirt. He came up to me at the bar at Uncle Billy's in Kailua. You know the place?"

She knew it.

"He was real nice. Said it was terrible what the Lathrops were trying to do, and how could we let them get away with it? Shoot, I agreed but said we couldn't do much, with no money and no pull. He said he could help with both. Then this *pake* fishes out a roll of bills and hands me a thousand dollars, right there. 'Start-up costs,' he calls it. I should have known—I *did* know. But I figured maybe this was how things were done in the real world. Every action group has sponsors, right?" Mrs. Te Papa nodded but said nothing. "I thought it would be okay," Peter went on. "I started Save Kaumaha and got most of the villagers on my side. Lani was real proud of me. It was like that for a while. But then Roxas started making demands. He called them suggestions."

"Including using the statue?"

"Yeah, that was all his idea. Or maybe his lawyers', who knows? He said that if we could get the site under the statue declared *kapu*, nobody could build on it. But the only way to do that was to get the statue itself removed. Something about restoring the site back to its original use. He knew all about the bone feast house, or whatever it was. Said it could be the most important piece of the puzzle."

"Did he know about the bodies buried underneath?"

Peter shrugged again. "Dunno. If he did, he never told me."

Mrs. Te Papa was thoughtful. "Do you know if he had anyone else…helping him? Dr. Ackerman, for instance?"

"He never mentioned. But he said he figured Tanaka would try to rig the commission somehow."

"Then Tanaka altered his plans so that only the village would be affected, not the site."

"Yeah, and Roxas went *lolo*! He kept telling me I had to stop the sale no matter what. He said he knew where my family lived, and wouldn't it be too bad if…" Peter trailed off, horrified. He took a deep breath and went on: "The night of the hearing, he called me at my house. I told him what happened. He was real quiet at first, just asking questions. Then he said I had better deal with this, or else. I panicked. I promised him I'd fix it somehow. But he hung up.

"I didn't realize Lani had come in. She must've heard. All I know is she went into the bedroom and locked the door, and when she came out she stormed right past me. I caught up with her at the party. That's when she told me she'd found the bank statements. Roxas always paid me in cash, but it was a lot of money."

"Did she say anything else?"

"She said everyone on this island was a liar, that none of us were who she thought we were. She said she'd already been betrayed once that night and I was the second, and worst. Those were her last words."

He paused, as if he couldn't go on. "And later?" Mrs. Te Papa prompted gently.

"I couldn't sleep. Who could? I was lying awake when I heard the explosion. It was sometime after two, I couldn't say exactly when. I threw on my clothes and started running up the path, toward the statue. And when I got there…"

"Yes?"

"It was just as you saw it. The statue was gone, and Lani was dead. I was shocked, heartbroken. At first I figured she did it herself. But then I thought, what if it was Roxas? He said he would deal with the problem. At the very least, blowing up the statue would keep the controversy going. And then I thought of something even worse."

Mrs. Te Papa nodded understandingly. "You thought you had been set up."

"Hell, yeah! I was the one that really went beef for that statue to come down. I was the head of Save Kaumaha, for Christ's sake. There I was standing in the rubble, with my girlfriend's body lying at my feet. I panicked. I didn't know if anyone had seen me come up the path, but I went home over the ridge trail that leads right to the village."

"Do you still think it was Roxas that set the explosion?"

"Shoot, it had to be. Look what happened afterward. Once they cleared away the debris and found all those skeletons, the site became a *kapu* burial ground. Nobody can build on it now. It's all turning out just like he planned. Including me," he added ruefully.

"But surely you can tell the police all this?"

"I did, but where's the proof? Like I said, it was all cash. And even if they believe it was Roxas giving me the money, there's nothing to say he didn't order me to blow up the statue, too. They're claiming I did it and then killed Lani because she knew what I was up to."

It wasn't a bad theory, Mrs. Te Papa admitted. Nevertheless... "I believe you," she told him solemnly. "I will do what I can."

Peter studied her for a moment. "Auntie, why are you helping me?" His voice sounded genuinely confused.

"Because an old friend told me to."

This was true. What Winnie Te Papa did not say, however, was that she regarded it as a sacred trust to help any of her people, no matter how undeserving they might be.

Or that her friend had been dead since 1968.

———

When Winnie Hulikohola was nine years old she won a prize from the Queen Ka'ahumahu Elementary School for the best piece of English composition. The topic was: *This week Hawaii became the 50th State in the United States. How does that make you feel?* Most children wrote how proud they were to be American citizens, how their parents cried with joy when they heard the vote in Congress had passed. Winnie wrote: "For eighty years we were controlled by the American plantation owners. They were Republicans. But now that we are a state, we can vote Democrat and get our own people into government. Not very many, though. I think we are still a colony, but maybe a colony with some rights, like the Americans wanted from the British in 1776. So that is a good thing. But we will never be our own country again. Just a tiny part of theirs, very far away. I hope they forget about us."

When the day came for the ceremony, the entire school was

abuzz with news: Duke Kahanamoku was coming to present the award. This was a very big deal, like President Eisenhower or Mickey Mantle or Cary Grant. Except that Duke was all of those, and he was Hawaiian. Born just before the turn of the century, he had already lived the equivalent of ten ordinary lives. In 1911 he was the fastest man in the world underwater, so fast that the snooty Amateur Athletic Union refused to believe his recorded time. He won gold medals for freestyle swimming in the 1912 and 1920 Olympics, then placed just behind Johnny Weissmuller in Paris in 1924. Weissmuller went on to become the first Tarzan. Duke traveled the world, teaching people how to surf. He brought surfing to Australia and California. He met the Prince of Wales and Rudolph Valentino, and stayed in Hollywood long enough to make friends with all the movie stars and become an actor himself. He was tall, bronzed, and handsome, with a body that looked like it had been sculpted from onyx. One day he saw a fishing boat capsize in Newport Beach. He took his board and swam out to the vessel, picking the fishermen off one at a time, eight trips in all. He received an Award for Valor, and lifeguards all over the world began using surfboards.

Duke came back to Honolulu in 1934. People talked about him running for governor, standing up against the Big Five, the American corporations that ran everything. These same people pointed out that Duke was both a Kahanamoku and a Paoa, two families of Hawaiian nobility. Instead, Duke chose to become the police chief of Honolulu. "Because," he said, with a wide-toothed grin, "if I'm governor, I'll have to work for those men. But if I'm police chief I can arrest them."

That morning in 1959 the entire elementary school was gathered in the schoolyard, even the teachers. A police siren announced his arrival. The patrol car was a prewar Buick, somewhat worse for wear. Duke climbed out of the passenger seat, unfolding his long body slowly in a single fluid motion. How an angel might get out of a car, Winnie thought. He was tall and very thin and looked exactly like the pictures of him winning the gold medal all those years ago, except that his hair had gone completely white. He was dressed in a gray suit with a Shriners pin in his lapel. He waved cheerfully to the children, who screamed with joy. "Duke!" "Duke!"

Duke punctiliously shook hands with the school principal and all the teachers, several of whom dropped into a half-curtsy. "Now," he said, looking around the schoolyard, "which of you is Miss Winifred Hulikohoa?" His voice was surprisingly gentle.

Shyly, Winnie raised her hand. Duke flashed his famous smile. "Well, come on over here, young lady." She obeyed, and Duke dropped a medal around her neck. He handed her a book, *The Songbird* by Mayella Anderson, and a check for twenty-five dollars. A man from the *Advertiser* snapped their picture. Winnie stepped away, waiting for him to get back into the patrol car and leave. But Duke kept a firm hand on her shoulder and leaned down until his enormous face was in hers. "Winifred," he said, "have you ever rode in a police car?"

She shook her head. "Would you like to?" She nodded, a little hesitantly.

"K'den. Hop in." Winnie made for the back, but once again the hand came down. "It's more fun in the front," Duke told her seriously. He climbed into the back seat while Winnie slid in next to the driver. He let her switch the siren on as they pulled out.

They dodged and darted through Honolulu traffic. The siren was very loud and made Winnie's ears hurt, but Duke didn't seem to mind it. She watched him through the wire grille as he pulled out an old leather briefcase and began making notes. "Are you working on a case?" she asked in a small voice.

Duke looked up, smiled. "Yes," he told her. "But not a hard one. A foolish man stole some money and hid it where he thought no one would find it."

"But you found it?"

"Yes."

"Where?" Winnie asked, imagining a secret cave with dynamite traps.

"In a bank."

They pulled up in front of an ochre building with an orange portico that looked like a Moorish castle. Duke got out and opened the door for her. But a moment later another patrolman was on the steps, drawing him away in conversation. The driver took her hand and led her into the station. He introduced her to a secretary with the whitest blouse Winnie had ever seen. She smelled like almonds and gave Winnie a coloring book with images from *Sleeping Beauty*. Winnie sat in the lobby for some time, filling every line. The sun dipped into the windows, turning the room a rich gold.

"Miss Hulikohoa?"

The secretary was back. She led Winnie down a long corridor, up a flight of stairs, down another passageway. Policemen rushed about, phones jangled, typewriters clacked. Once Winnie looked through an open door and saw a man sitting in a metal chair holding a reddened cloth to his forehead. Blood trickled between his fingers and down his sleeve. The secretary opened a frosted glass door and gently ushered Winnie inside.

Duke Kahanamoku sat in his shirtsleeves behind a desk covered in files. The office of the chief of police was not what Winnie was expecting. She imagined something large and booklined with maybe a flagstaff or two. Duke's office was scarcely bigger than her principal's, and much shabbier. There was only the desk, two chairs, and a green metal filing cabinet. She looked to the walls, expecting to see pictures of Duke with all the famous actors and politicians he'd met. But there was just a big map of Honolulu held in place with tacks. The only photographs in the room were on the filing cabinet. His children.

Winnie realized too late that Duke had been waiting for her to finish her inspection. "Well, little sistah," he said, leaning back and cupping his hands behind his head, "so you hope the Yanks leave us alone, eh? Do you think they will?"

She had always been a truthful child. "No."

"Neither do I." He gestured for her to sit. "You know, I read the newspaper every day. I listen to the wireless. I talk to people. So I figure I've heard four, maybe five hundred different opinions about this statehood thing. Yours was the best."

Winnie scarcely knew what to say to this. She waited.

"You are right, of course. We're still a colony. I saw it better once I left. Everywhere I went, they wanted to shake my hand, feel my bicep. But they always acted real surprised that I could speak as well as them. Almost," he amended with a grin. "And Hollywood was worse. There's some great people there; don't let anyone tell you different. It's not all phonies. Clark Gable, he's a real swell guy. But the studio directors! All they wanted was to put me in a loincloth and make me stand around on the beach talking a bunch of *pookela* to Gig Young." Duke shook his head, sighed. "Do you know why I became a cop?" he asked abruptly.

Winnie didn't, but ventured instead, "To catch bad people?" Then she felt stupid.

Duke considered this. "That's part of the job, sure. But we don't just catch bad people. We protect good people. That's really what it's about. I wanted to protect my people. Can you understand that?"

"Yes," said Winnie in her small voice.

"I think you can. I think that's what you were trying to say in that essay of yours. But it's not easy. And this," He made a vague gesture out the window, where an American flag fluttered, "this doesn't make it much easier. But you're young, and I'm old. It may be different for you. In the end, though, our people will always need someone to protect them. Someone like you." He smiled again, and his eyes twinkled. A moment later the secretary came in and hustled her away.

"*E hoʻomanaʻo i kou poʻe kānaka*, Winifred Hulikohola!" Duke shouted through the door. He waved.

For years Winnie played that scene again and again in her mind. Was he just being kind? Did he really see something inside of her that she scarcely knew herself? As she grew older, Winnie began to ask with each decision what Duke would say or do. He became her conscience. When she graduated summa cum laude, with a scholarship to study Hawaiian culture at the university, she wanted to write and tell him. But Duke Kahanamoku had died of a heart attack a few months earlier. She was among the crowd that watched his funeral cortege pass by, sobbing and tossing her lei onto the coffin.

Years later, after her marriage and career were getting along nicely, Mrs. Te Papa made a discovery. Friends encouraged her to practice meditation, and the results were startling. She found that if she concentrated very hard, closed her mind to everything else, she could bring herself back to that office. Duke was still there. She spoke to him, and he answered back. When she emerged and described this to her friends, their reactions were unhelpful. Some called it daydreaming, or hallucination, while others congratulated her for breaching the spirit world. Truthfully, Mrs. Te Papa didn't know herself. She only knew that when she reached the frosted door, Duke was on the other side of it.

Tonight she lit a candle, placed it on the floor, and sat beside it. She gazed into the flame. Gradually it spread, filling the room with warm afternoon light. Sunlight streamed through the windows of the dingy office, catching dust motes whirling in the air. Duke smiled at her. "Winnie," he said, gesturing to a chair, "been a while. How you keeping?"

"Not bad, I guess." She never asked him how he was. It seemed indelicate, somehow.

"What can I do for you?"

She sat with her hands folded. "A girl has died. Do you need me to tell you the details?"

He waved a hand. "Not necessary."

"There's a boy they think did it. He's one of ours, but a pretty bad lot, a *moke*. He *wahahee a he aihue*. If it *was* him I'd almost be relieved. But..."

"But you don't think it is. And you think they're all too happy to pin it on the *kanaka* kid with no big family behind him or business to protect."

"I could be wrong."

"You could. But your heart is in the right place. You're still watching out for our people, Winifred."

"That may not be helpful right now." She bit her lip in frustration. "How can I stay objective when I am so angry? That poor girl. She was the only true *koa la koa* among them. But what if the truth hurts her memory even more?"

Duke nodded. "She deserves that truth, whatever it might be. You are not her judge. Nor do you judge those who harmed her. When you uncover an ancient site, do you shrink from interpreting its meaning even if it seems barbaric to us now? Of course not. What use would a scholar be who made up stories about the past just because they sounded pretty? You are simply the vessel. You uncover the truth and let others judge as they will."

Duke was gazing at her intently, and she felt there was something beyond his words she needed to comprehend. "But what do I do now?"

"Do what you can. Are you a gumshoe detective? Have you caught dozens of criminals?"

"That was you, Duke."

"Nope. That was guys with real training. I was just the old *haku kane* that signed their checks." He smiled gently. "But I learned a few things eventually."

"I don't understand," Winnie confessed.

"'Course you do. You saw those bodies laid out in the sun. What else do you need to know?'"

Light was streaming through the windows and it was becoming difficult to look directly into his face. But Duke Kahanamoku's voice came to her clear and strong:

"Do what you can, Winnie Te Papa."

"A True Account..."

May 9, 1850

I am struck down. The fever crept slowly upon by limbs, weighting them by degree so that I mistook and thought myself merely fatigued. It reached next my bowels and now has my whole person, the work of several days. I have taken to bed. The delirium that I observed in others will, presently, fall upon myself. I write now so that I may leave a plain account of the terrible events and revelations that I have of late witnessed. You shall warrant by the clarity of my words that I am still of my own mind, for it is known to take several hours or even days for the wits to depart. But I must write quickly.

It has been incumbent upon me for some time that there are some, possibly many among my flock who cling unrighteously to their pagan ways. On Sunday last I resolved upon a test. The Scripture lesson was Deuteronomy:

There shall not be found among you any one that maketh his son or his daughter to pass through the fire, or that useth divination, or an observer of times, or an enchanter, or a witch.

Or a charmer, or a consulter with familiar spirits, or a wizard, or a necromancer.

For all that do these things are an abomination unto the Lord.

This was direct enough, I daresay. In my lesson I spoke to them thusly: "You, among all native peoples, are privileged to be received into communion with Christ. You entered into this bond willingly, and in return you shall receive life everlasting in paradise. But to honor any false god or spirit is to dishonor the Lord, and invite His wrath. I allow I have been lax with ye, through my own ignorance of your ways. If any amongst you have fallen from the true path, I alone am to blame. I am your shepherd. I hereby resolve to lead you rightly henceforth." Then I came down from the pulpit and stood amongst them, which I had not yet done afore. "As I have confessed my faults, brothers and sisters, can you not do the same? We are all of us sinful creatures, and there be no shame if it is honestly shared and truly atoned. Come, now. Who will lay bare their transgressions, that they may be forgiven by a most merciful and loving Judge?"

But answer came there none. I repeated my call with increasing fervor, yet was met by naught but sullen looks and downcast brows. So be it, I thought.

That night I waited till long past midnight and, arming myself with a pistol and several rounds of shot, made my way to the village. Prudence did not wish me to go and entreated that I at least take Melchior. But that I would not do, for reasons I have described. It has often been my practice to inspect the dwellings periodically for sanitary reasons, as it is known that vermin carry more disease than a thousand plague ships. Heretofore these inspections were done in the midday when the light was strongest, but that did not suit my purposes now.

I began with Melchior. Rousing him and his wahine from sleep, I ordered them to stand aside while I searched their quarters. This I did most thoroughly, but either he was alerted to my coming or too cunning in his concealment, for I found nothing of note. Occasionally it behooves even a godly man to dissemble in the service of the Lord. I told Melchior I had no doubts about his own fidelity but that it was necessary to be fair. He could now assist me as I searched the other dwellings. Cravenly, he tried to dissuade me and promised he would perform the search himself. I had none of this. So we set off together, moving from one house to the next. I entered first, carrying a lantern before me like Diogenes (the pistol tucked into my waistband was more for show than anything, as it is very much antique). Melchior was given the task of watching over the occupants and keeping them silent—as much, I reckoned, as he could be trusted with.

I will not sully these pages with a catalogue of the monstrosities I uncovered. Suffice to say nearly every hut revealed some grimacing effigy or totem, often with locks of hair or bits of bone worked in. Others kept sachets of foul-smelling herbs on their windowsills or beneath their pillows. There were, additionally, not a few objects I immediately recognized as weapons, usually in the crude form of a spear. Most families relinquished these horrors shamefacedly, but a few, I regret, resisted. One old man became so irate when I discovered his little idol—a wretched grinning thing with engorged genitals, a very sinkhole of carnal lust—that he came at me with clawlike hands and I was obliged to strike him with the butt of my pistol. Melchior pulled him off, speaking to him soothingly in that singsong musical speech they affect.

I ordered Melchior to light a bonfire and made a public

burning of these vanities, exhorting all within hearing to witness. The heat of the blaze affected my eyes and for a moment I thought I saw a figure dancing within the flames, but an instant later it was gone. I waited until each object was thoroughly consumed before allowing Melchior to douse the coals. This gave off a powerful cloud of steam, which again writhed itself into a human shape before dispersing to the winds. I thought myself fanciful, or overcome by the emotion of the moment.

I confess I returned to the house that night an embittered man. My perturbation may be well understood. These selfsame people I had ministered through illness and famine, revealed the glories of the Word, received into communion, and offered my own home for them to share— thus had they repaid me. It was gall and wormwood. Yet, as often during life's trials, I remembered the sufferings of the early martyrs. Those that bring the revealed truth to lands of darkness must expect resistance, ignorance, even violence. So I comforted myself.

In the morning I awoke with the sun, though scarcely more than a couple hours had passed. I tried to rise, but found my head strangely heavy and my limbs uncoordinated. It was a sodden day, black clouds moving across a slate sky. Too wet for the hands to work, so Melchior set them to clean the gears of the refinery. I will say, for all his mendacity, he is a capable overseer. With no one else about, I resolved to clear my head of morbid thoughts with a brisk walk through the valley. This has been my cure-all since youth, and many's the time I plodded through the Commons and found much good from nature, even in the depth of winter.

There are trails throughout the island. I followed a deeply grooved route that meandered along the foothills for some distance until at last it came upon an old ruin. I had visited the spot many times, as it was interesting in a grim sort of way. The old fort was quite destroyed, but not far from the site was a cluster of stones around a well, long since dried. It was here I paused to rest.

The skies had been gathering above my head, and while I do not generally object to rain, I was unprepared for the sudden downpour that followed. Taking shelter under a nearby tree, I observed a strange phenomenon. Where the rain fell above the well it seemed to part and slough off, as if a body were standing there repelling it. I shielded my eyes and looked again. There could be no question; something was standing upon the aperture. I could quite clearly make out its shape—human, but of dimensions no human ever reached. It stood, at a guess, perhaps eight or nine feet tall. It was broad of shoulder and long of limb, judging by the rivulets that traveled down its arms. One hand seemed to extend outwards, beckoning. I took an unwilling step forwards, as though summoned. The rain was quite blinding.

After two paces I stopped. The spirit moved within me, and I shouted out: "I will say of the Lord, He is my refuge and my fortress; my God, in Him I will trust!" Instinctively I raised my hands and formed the sign of the cross. The creature did not seem to heed, yet a moment later the rain ceased as abruptly as it came. The forest sounds, which had gone still as the deluge fell, gradually returned. Yet amongst them, like a low thrum, I recognized a single voice. It spoke through the shirr of the crickets and the call of the songbirds, a single word:

Ku.

Mark you, I was not afraid. As in dreams, I pondered this quite calmly. When Prudence and I arrived in the islands I took the trouble to learn the rudiments of the native cult. This is sound practice for those who spread the word of Christ: we must know what superstitions and nonsense need be dispelled. I knew, for example, that Ku was god of war, Lono was god of agriculture, Pele of the volcanos, and so on. The great god of the Hawaiians is a certain personage called Kane, which looks as though it should be pronounced like Abel's brother but actually is Kah-Nay. In the beginning, it is said, there was darkness. Then Kane sensed he was apart from the darkness, and in creating light he created himself. Lono and Ku sprang from him, either as offspring or brothers depending on the tale.

Kane has been a particular bane of my existence. While the natives might keep a small shrine to Kuula, god of fishermen, Kane was forever in their thoughts. He had the temerity to steal intact the story of divine creation from John 1:1 and present himself to the Hawaiians not merely as a god, but God. I had a time explaining to them, in my early days, that their hairy-hocked deity was not the Almighty. I am not sure they ever quite believed me.

On the other hand, I had no particular quarrel with Ku. My natives were not warlike, merely indolent, so they had little need of his ministrations. It was doubly strange, then, that my fevered mind should produce this vision at that particular moment. For of course that is what it was. I comprehend now that by this time the illness had begun to claim me, and exposure to the elements had merely aggravated the condition. I returned home flushed and faint, falling at once into the tender care of my dear wife. I have not raised from this bed for two days. I am weakened and unable to defend myself from these phantasms, which I know to be the work of Melchior and the rebel contingent among the villagers. They have corrupted my food with *noxious compounds that deprive me of my wits. This is no fever. It is the work of man. For all that I have done to protect and succor the people of New Boston, I am repaid with vile conspiracies. But I shall fool them yet. I will take no food or drink of any kind until I am restored to health. It should only take a few days for the poisons to pass from my body and thus I shall emerge even stronger than before.*

Ku comes to me often now. He stands at the foot of the bed—I am quite sure it is he, for his dark head brushes the ceiling beams—yet says nothing. In form he is not unlike the statues of antiquity, well-muscled and clad only in a strip of some coarse material. A fearful specter. But there is no terror in this vision for me. "No weapon that is formed against thee shall prosper; and every tongue that shall rise against thee in judgment thou shalt condemn. This is the heritage of the servants of the Lord, and their righteousness is of me, saith the Lord." He is here now, but I pay no heed as I write. Let him see me thus engaged, indifferent, and mark the fortitude of a Christian who fears naught but God's judgment. Ay, read these words, you black bastard. I have no fear of you, nor all the councilors and ministers of Hell, should they follow thee. For my love they are my adversaries: but I give myself unto prayer. And they have rewarded me

evil for good, and hatred for my love.
    Set thou a wicked man over him
    and let Satan stand at his right hand when he shall be
    judged
    let him be
    condemned
    and let his prayer become
    sin

Chapter 10

IWI, THE BONES

Mr. Po had troubled dreams. They came in saturated colors, murky green and dark slashes of red cleaving through his sleep. He was running through the forest barefoot, searching for the path home. Roots reached out to snare him and the sharp, spiky leaves of firethorn bushes flayed his skin.

But these were nightmares, not visions. Tonight Mr. Po awoke sweating, heart hammering against his chest, and switched on the bedside lamp. Sadie raised her head and sniffed the air, then settled back into a long snore.

One thing Mr. Po hated about getting old was that wakefulness came far easier than sleep. Resignedly he swung out his legs and checked the clock. Just past one. He trudged into the kitchen and put the kettle on. Tea, he thought. Ginger root and honey. The moon was unusually bright, which was odd since there had been no moon at all the night before. He peered through the curtains and saw, to his amazement, figures gathered on the lawn. Their bodies were almost translucent in the pale light.

He left the kettle and went out onto the lanai. They were there, perhaps a dozen of them, but they were also *not* there. Afterimages, like a double exposure. He saw an old woman with her back bent under the weight of a basket, mouth drawn in a thin line of pain. There was a child with her, a little girl of eight or nine, looking fearfully toward the forest rim. Some distance away stood a young man dressed in a loincloth with tattoos covering his legs and arms. He, too, looked toward the forest, his face apprehensive. None of the figures moved. Then, as Mr. Po watched, the slide changed. Now the old woman had dropped her burden and covered her face with her hands; the little girl was crying; the young warrior raised an arm defensively against an unseen attacker. The others around them looked similarly distressed and fearful.

"What is it?" Mr. Po asked aloud. "What are you trying to show me?"

The image changed again. Now the warrior was facing him only a few feet away, looking directly into his eyes. *'A'ole i hele.*

Not gone. Not gone.

"I know you haven't gone. Why should you?"

The image melted and reformed. The warrior, the child, the old woman all vanished. All the figures were gone except for one, a young woman standing alone.

"*Ailani,*" Mr. Po said with a sob.

She looked more solid than the others, as if the greater part of her was still in his world. But her eyes were empty caverns. Her right hand pointed toward him. He understood that it was she who sent these visions, like photographs from another plane.

"Yes, yes," he whispered, "I see. They are still suffering."

Her figure altered; she now pointed toward the ground. *'A'ole i hele.*

It moves within the ground, Mr. Po said to himself. It latches itself to the roots and earth. Shapeless, formless, but still there. Everywhere. They live under its tyranny. *Ku demands a sacrifice.* A hungry ghost, a bottomless well.

"*Maopopo ia'u.* I understand," he told her. "I will make them see."

Lani disappeared and took the moon with her. Mr. Po was standing alone in his underpants, staring at his yard. At that moment the air was rent with a high, shrill screech—prolonged, agonized, enough to make an old man's heart stumble a beat.

His tea was ready.

———

Winnie Te Papa did not believe in drugs. She had seen too often what they could do. In her mind, "drugs" were anything you took into your body that altered reality. This included sleeping pills. "Genevieve Ho," she would say, if anyone suggested such a thing. "Took them one night, k'den, never woke up." If Mrs. Te Papa could not sleep, she would read or fix herself a cup of tea. Or perhaps some pound cake. If these did not work, she resigned herself to staying awake. There were worse things, she knew, than wakefulness.

But there were some nights, such as tonight, where she longed for the respite that sleep gave from her own thoughts. Lately these had become very dark indeed. She lay on her back, arms at her sides, staring up at the ceiling fan and trying to count the revolutions. Yet instead her mind busily supplied images: Lani Kapiaho standing tall and regal like Princess Kaiulani...then broken, her hair black and matted with dried blood... *Daemonibus Corrumptur,* destroyed by devils...a child's skull grinning horribly in the pitiless morning sun... an old man's quavering voice, *Shame, terrible shame. I cannot bear it. It suffocates me...* A young man's cheerful, guileless face staring up at her from the newspaper, *I KNOW WHAT YOU DID...*

Mrs. Te Papa sat up in bed and switched on the light. The bedside clock read 2:37. But the young, she knew, needed less sleep. She reached for the phone and dialed. Marybeth answered on the sixth ring, her voice muffled. "Mmm, hwah? Wazzit?"

"My dear, I am so very sorry to wake you. But I need your help."

Marybeth became instantly alert. "Oh, my God, have you fallen? Did you break something? Is it a heart attack?"

"No, no, nothing like that." Mrs. Te Papa grimaced. She hated being thought infirm. "I just need you to look something up for me."

There was a pause as Marybeth considered and rejected several impertinent responses. Finally, she said: "Okay."

"A boy named Steven Shimazu was beaten to death. I don't know how long ago. I need you to find out *da kine* about him." Only when Mrs. Te Papa was tired did she allow herself to lapse into slang.

Another pause, punctuated by the faint sound of clicking. "Oh, I remember this," Marybeth said at last. "It was about three years ago. The case got a lot of attention because the victim was a state senator's son. He was a senior at Punahou, that fancy prep school in Makiki."

"What happened exactly?"

"Nobody knows for sure. He left lacrosse practice at around five thirty and was driving home. His parents live near Ala Moana, but he never made it. Police found the car abandoned in a parking lot off the Lunalilo freeway. No signs of struggle, and his backpack and gear still on the seat. Two weeks later a jogger found his body in some bushes off the Na Ala Hele Trail. You know, the one in the state park."

"Yes, yes, go on."

"He still had his wallet and keys and was wearing his gym clothes. Contusions all over his body, three ribs and an arm broken, and his neck snapped clean in half. Police think it was two or maybe three guys that did it, with baseball bats."

Mrs. Te Papa repressed a shudder. "Why do they suspect the Yakuza?"

"It says here," Marybeth was reading from a news article, "that Steven had claimed numerous times that he was either a member of or was being recruited by the Yakuza. He boasted about it. Police think they changed their minds about recruiting him and murdered him instead."

That sounded rather thin. Or was it just that she didn't wish to believe David Tanaka could do such a thing? "What about this boy Steven Shimazu? You say he went to Punahou. Can you look up his classmates?"

"Sure, that's easy. Give me a sec."

More clicking. "Okay, I've got the page from the high school yearbook. It's a pretty small class, I'm checking n—"

Suddenly the phone went silent. Mrs. Te Papa waited a moment, then said gently, "Marybeth?"

A small sound, asthmatic and sharp. The sound of breath caught in the throat. "I'm here."

"Are you all right? What's happened?"

"Nothing. I'm fine. The computer froze, though. I think it's offline for the night. We'll probably have to try again tomorrow."

Mrs. Te Papa knew little about these machines, but she was aware they broke frequently. "That's fine, dear. Thank you for your help."

"K'den, no problem." Marybeth hung up, rather curtly, Mrs. Te Papa thought.

She did not go back to sleep at once. Yes, she said to herself, computers often broke down. But when they did, you pushed buttons, or restarted them, or checked the wires that ran into the house. Why had Marybeth done none of these things?

Mrs. Te Papa had a computer of her own, an ancient IBM that lived an unloved existence in a broom cupboard. She heaved herself out of bed and switched it on. After several minutes and several false starts she found Punahou Academy. After several more, and a revivifying slice of guava cake, she arrived at the yearbook page. There, near the bottom, was Steven. The photograph was the same as in the cutting. Slowly she moved the cursor upward, letting the faces scroll past. Some grinned broadly, others tried to look ironic, a few gazed stone-faced at the lens. Halfway up she paused. *Ah,* she thought.

There, looking slightly younger and even more freckled, was Roger Lathrop.

———

Marybeth had not gone back to sleep, either. She stared blankly at the smiling face on the screen. No, she thought. Not possible.

But how much did she know about Roger, really? Or any of them? The island had seemed enchanted, with its waterfalls and jungles and old manor house. And Roger had been...kind. Yes, that was the word. Kind and sad and surprisingly interested in what she, Marybeth, had to say.

Her life had not been easy. Marybeth's mother died when she was only three, and the girl was sent to live with an uncle and his family. They did their best, but there were five children already in an apartment with only two bedrooms. Marybeth never knew her father. He sent money every month—not much, but enough that she would not be a burden—and that was all. *Kupuna* Gertrude pursed her lips and looked furious whenever the subject came up. After community college, Marybeth stared grimly at her future: wage slavery in one of the hotels or a brokered marriage with another Māori and the promise of one child per year. Then all at once her godmother swooped in, almost like the fairytale, but not quite. With Mrs. Te Papa she had a respectable and occasionally interesting life. Until now that had been enough.

The Lathrops belonged to a different world. Even their problems seemed wonderfully old-fashioned and romantic. And they had been so kind and generous, all of them. Well, except Ogden. But Roger's grandmother was charming, like an eighteenth-century marquise, and his mother had come by Marybeth's room just before bedtime to see if she needed anything. And Roger...

Marybeth laid back on her pillow, a welter of conflicting emotions rattling in her mind. She imagined Roger here with her now, his head cradled in her lap. Then she imagined herself at Lathrop House, putting on a pair of old clogs to go work in the garden. The back garden was quite nice, really; it only needed sprucing up a bit. And the lanai could use a fresh coat of paint. But the Lathrops would not have Kaumaha much longer—in fact, there might not *be* a Kaumaha much longer, at least in any recognizable form. This led her down a new and uncomfortable path. She remembered Lani's face that night, full of pride and anguish. Roger had been appalled by his father's outburst. But then, a few hours later, Lani was dead.

Marybeth tried to imagine any of the Lathrops as a murderer and found she couldn't. Not even Ogden. Certainly not Roger. But then she thought of the other guests, Dr. Ackerman and Judge Chan, and found it equally hard to picture them bashing in someone's skull. It was a primal act, barbaric even. These people were civilized.

But of course they had not been the only guests at Lathrop House. Somehow she had not thought of Tanaka until now, or his alarming bodyguard. *He* was someone who could break a skull without batting an eyelash. Strangely, she had no trouble imagining Tanaka doing the same, despite his expensive clothes and polite manners. But he was Yakuza; she had suspected as much, and now Mrs. Te Papa believed it as well. The Yakuza had no difficulty cracking heads when the need arose.

Or breaking necks, she reminded herself.

Yet the cold truth made her face tingle: *I have been in the same room as a murderer.* It was like that game they played as children, when one would be the killer and the rest had to discover who it was. But that had been just for fun. Someone at Lathrop House, someone she had spoken with and eaten with, and perhaps even come to have affection for... No, it couldn't be possible.

And so Marybeth's thoughts went round and round, until the first light of morning crept up the counterpane and rescued her.

———

Dr. Ackerman liked order and routine. If some of his colleagues called this hidebound or even obsessive, he neither agreed nor cared. He woke every day at six—he didn't need an alarm clock, his body told him the time—put on a pair of jogging shorts and did a brisk three-mile loop around the gated community in Manoa that was his home. Back by seven, he allowed himself one boiled egg and a slice of wheat toast for breakfast. Showered and dressed by eight, he turned the latch on his front door at precisely eight fifteen and (barring traffic or unforeseen calamities) arrived at his office by eight thirty.

Today, as every day, he strode through the corridors with a brisk step and nodded curtly to the department secretary, whose name he never bothered to learn. No one seeing him on this particular morning could tell that he harbored a powerful excitement. But once Dr. Ackerman had deposited his jacket on the coatrack and answered a few trivial emails, he put a call in to the state laboratory's chief of forensics, who was an old friend. After a few minutes' conversation, all was arranged. An unmarked car arrived to collect him from the university campus, and several undergraduate classes (and three chagrined doctoral candidates) were abandoned without a second thought. Passing the nameless secretary, Ackerman called over his shoulder, "Tell 'em I'm sick." Then he was gone.

The forensics laboratory was just another concrete cube in a faceless office park near the highway. Its only distinction was a loading dock where mortuary vans could offload their grisly cargo in privacy. Dr. Michael Parkiss, chief of forensics, waited for Dr. Ackerman in the lobby. "It's a hell of a business, Bob," he said.

"Ghastly," Ackerman agreed. But both men could barely refrain from grinning.

"We've had our best people working on the reconstruction, and I think you'll be impressed with the job they did."

"I'll see about that." Ackerman was noncommittal. "Any preliminary conclusions?"

"Just that the skeletons range from about four to twelve years of age, both genders. All in reasonable health, from what we can make out. No signs of malnutrition or scurvy. Teeth are mostly in good shape—well, of course, they would be, being children."

"And the manner of decease is identical?"

Parkiss nodded. "Yes. All had their throats cut. No broken or fractured bones, which suggests they may have been smothered or drugged first. No traces of rope or anything to bind them, which reinforces that hypothesis."

"Very well. Let's have a look."

They had been striding down a long, hospital-like corridor. Dr. Parkiss pushed his way through a set of double doors into a vast space that look like something between an operating theater and a warehouse. Arc lights illuminated row after row of polished metal tables, on which the mortal remains of Kaumaha's dead were displayed.

At the far end of the room, a large elderly woman in a bright pink muumuu bent closely over one of the bodies, an old-fashioned brass magnifying glass in her hand.

Dr. Parkiss was shocked. "Excuse me, ma'am, can I help you?"

She looked up. "Yes, thank you. This glass of mine really isn't good enough. I use it for reading, you see. Maps and dictionaries. Might I have something stronger?"

"This is a secured area. Do you have clearance to be here?"

The old woman sighed. She drew out her official Office of Hawaiian Affairs badge and began shuffling toward them. As she drew closer Dr. Ackerman let out a startled bark. "Mrs. Te Papa! What—" He was going to say, 'What are you doing here?' but amended it to: "What a delightful surprise."

"Dr. Ackerman! I am very glad to see you, too. How was Cincinnati?" Her tone was light, but the eyes were watchful. Up close, Robert Ackerman seemed grayer, frailer than she remembered. There was a cloudiness in his eyes that had not been there on Kaumaha. She wondered if it might be strain. Or guilt.

"Oh, fine, fine!" he answered, a little too heartily. "Cold as the devil, you know, but needs must."

"Ah, but it was a brief trip, I'm sure. You were there for, what, two days?"

"Yes." He looked to Parkiss, who now seemed both scandalized and confused. "Mrs. Te Papa was with me on Kaumaha when the bodies were discovered," Ackerman explained. "She is an expert on Hawaiian culture."

"But she still needs..."

"If you call the office of the governor, I'm sure they can sort it out for you," Mrs. Te Papa said serenely. "And once you have done that, perhaps you could find me a glass or microscope?"

Parkiss bustled off, his feathers still ruffling. Dr. Ackerman, who had a contrary nature, was amused. "Do you really know the governor?" he asked.

"I taught him in elementary school. I've probably taught half the island at one time or another. It comes in handy."

Ackerman chuckled. "I'll bet."

"I'm glad you're here, Professor." She looked up at him with a small frown of concentration. "I need your help. Would you say, based on what you've seen so far, that these bodies were deposited before or after the construction of the bone feast house?"

Ackerman had not expected this immediate plunge. Nevertheless, he answered readily enough: "Most likely after. All evidence suggests that the Asmat tribe were the first settlers on the island. They built the house for a manhood ritual, not human sacrifice."

"Did the Asmat, in fact, perform such sacrifices?"

"Very rarely. And usually only after warfare with another tribe. It surely would not be children."

"Yes," Mrs. Te Papa agreed. "That struck me, too. The ancient Hawaiians sacrificed often to the god Ku, but usually either young men from their tribe or defeated warriors from another. Ku was the god of war, after all."

"Other cultures sacrificed children for fertility and to ward off disease," mused Ackerman, "The Maya, for example. A child was considered pure, untainted. Their very health was supposed to cure the people of their plague."

"Did any Oceanic tribes believe this?"

"Possibly a few. But none that would have made contact with Hawaii between the fifteenth and seventeenth centuries, when these structures were built."

Mrs. Te Papa considered him for a moment. Finally she asked, quietly, "Were you surprised when they discovered the bodies?"

Ackerman raised an eyebrow. "Yes, of course. I was astonished."

"And yet you do not seem at all shocked or appalled by the act, even standing as we are, surrounded by their corpses."

The professor shrugged indifferently. "Tribes have been bashing their children on the head or slitting their throats or throwing them into volcanoes since time immemorial. Sacrifice to the gods is almost a universal constant in early faiths. What was Christ, after all, but a sacrificial victim offered up to appease a hungry god? 'Take and eat this, my body, in remembrance of me.' It's just the same."

Mrs. Te Papa did not think it was the same at all, but held her tongue. "You are not a Christian yourself, then, Professor?"

Dr. Ackerman snorted. "Not likely. Had enough of that from my parents, and that cold wet hell of a public school in Leeds. I'm an atheist." He thrust out his chin.

"Yes," said Mrs. Te Papa, "I thought you might be." She gestured to one of the most complete skeletons, a child of about four or five. "My glass is not very good," she apologized, "But I would be grateful if you'd look at the marks on the first vertebrae and tell me what you think."

Still dubious, Ackerman took the lens from her hand and bent closely over the skeleton. He saw at once where the tip of a blade had struck bone. "A clean cut," he surmised. "One stroke and very deep, almost enough to decapitate. But, of course, the throat would have been very small."

"Do you see the grooves?"

He studied the knife marks carefully. Yes, there it was. A tiny corrugation where bits and splinters of bone had broken off. He pored over the spot again, playing with the glass to catch it in different light. But there could be no doubt.

Ackerman rose slowly. Their eyes met. "A serrated blade," Mrs. Te Papa said quietly, as if she had read his mind.

The professor had been prepared to regard this woman as a nuisance. Now, with grudging respect and a certain amount of awe, he said, "I think you may be right." But, being himself, he instantly thought of an objection. "It could just be the angle the blade struck. Have you found traces elsewhere?"

"I have examined twelve bodies so far," Mrs. Te Papa told

him placidly. "Not all bear obvious wounds. That would make sense if the blade severed the trachea but did not reach the vertebrae. But of the four where it did, each has corresponding marks. These are younger children with, as you say, smaller necks."

She said this with admirable detachment, Ackerman thought. "We will have to examine them all to be sure," he demurred. But his excitement was palpable.

"Yes, of course. There are also the teeth."

"Teeth?"

"See for yourself. Here, try this one." Mrs. Te Papa indicated a larger skeleton, probably a boy of twelve or so.

This time there was no hesitation. Dr. Ackerman ran the glass over each tooth separately. They were, he noted, in an excellent state of preservation. There was even some dark matter that might once have been cartilage. Yet other than a certain roundness to the molars, and a sharp set of incisors, he saw nothing unusual. He looked up at her questioningly.

"The incisors," Mrs. Te Papa explained. "This is an older child, otherwise you would not notice the effect. On an adult it would be obvious. The teeth would be filed down almost to points."

"Why? Was that ritual?" Ackerman was uncomfortably aware that, while his expertise was global, he was speaking to a woman who knew more about Hawaiian culture than he did.

She shook her head. "Not ritual. Diet. A diet of raw sugarcane, consumed daily to clean the teeth and extract the juices. One finds examples of this in the Caribbean, but it is quite common here also. Over time the cane grinds down the incisors."

Mrs. Te Papa waited as Dr. Ackerman processed this information. Again it occurred to her that the man seemed somewhat diminished. But when realization finally came, his eyes opened wide and a look of pure wonderment flashed in them. "Good Lord," he said, awed. "So that means…"

"Yes, Dr. Ackerman."

Ackerman smiled. It was the first time she had seen it, and it transformed his face. Suddenly he looked almost boyish.

"Call me Bob," he said.

"A True Account…"

May 18, 1850

Praise be to God, I am spared. The fever has passed. For some days I lacked the strength to put pen to paper, and even in recovery my mind was much disordered. Now, thanks to His Most Merciful Grace, I am restored to health.

Alas, sickness still flames throughout the island. With me abed, Prudence has taken on the tasks of both nurse and minister. What a wonder she is! In these efforts she has been ably assisted by Melchior. I am sorry I ever suspected him, for I understand now that he is as good a Christian as any I have known. Blameless, too, are the children of Ham, my beloved villagers, whom I have much abused and maligned. Their errant courses are not of their own doing. Blind, blind have I been! Oh, most merciful Father, forgive me for my ignorance, and pride. I have born enmity to your children and suspected them of great wrong, where in truth I should have looked to my own self first.

Throughout this long confinement my one constant companion has been the Gospel, which sits patiently by my side as I write these words. Strange to tell for a minister in orders, but the plain truth is that it has been many years since I truly read it from cover to cover. A dangerous thing, that—we think we know whereof it says, yet its wonders are boundless. Thus have I read it once again, thus has it sustained me. More, it has given me the answer to the terrible mysteries that have plagued this island. My sufferings have a name and a cause. Old King Saul knew of it, for as the

Book of Samuel relates, "an evil spirit from God came upon Saul, and he prophesied in the midst of the house—and David played with his hand, as at other times—and there was a javelin in Saul's hand." An evil spirit from God. A test, by thunder!

I know now. The gods of these islands are not fantasy. They are real, real as the rocks and earth. They are nothing more or less than demons. How wrong I was to blame the converts for clinging to their false idols! It was not ignorance that claimed them but the wiles of the Evil One. For centuries these unfortunate tribesmen have propitiated their deities, offering them sacrifices and quaking in fear. How could the poor fools know any different, without the Holy Word? See you, it was no accident that placed me amongst them. Nor was the plague mere happenstance. I observe the hand of God in this, moving subtly but surely. He brought me to the Sandwich Isles just as he brought the pestilence—a dreadful tide that deposited this flock upon my welcoming shore.

He brought the demons, too. The Bible tells us that incubi are thrown up from Hell to serve Heaven's purposes; if God is truly omniscient and omnipotent, the war of fallen angels must also be part of His infinite plan. That is cold logic. Indeed we may divine the reason for such horrors: Satan and his minions tempt us so that in resolution we prove our abiding faith and fidelity. There are no accidents. If a demon is loose upon New Boston it is because GOD has placed him there. This is the only logical conclusion possible.

Just as God has placed the demons upon these islands, surely He has placed me to free the natives from their fearful sway. Little wonder my efforts thus far have failed. This is no ordinary conversion, but a righteous battle between Light and Darkness. I must think carefully on how to proceed.

Chapter 11

HŪNŪ, GHOSTS

On Kaumaha, the endless pageant of life and death continued. Gilbert Kapiaho shuffled about the nave of the tiny village church with a broom and dustpan. The space was only about thirty feet long and ten wide, with shuttered windows on each side. The ceilings and stanchions were koa wood that had become almost black from centuries of damp and tobacco. The walls were lined with dusty glass cases holding various relics from the last century: a machete with a rusted handle, several bits of broken pottery, a much-thumbed Bible, a few examples of local palm weaving. Most came from Gilbert's family. The Kapiahos were among the first families to settle Kaumaha with Reverend Lathrop. Melchior Kapiaho was the plantation's first overseer, a tall and broad-shouldered man who had, it was rumored, Austronesian blood. A photograph taken of him late in life, sometime in the 1880s, revealed a face more African than Hawaiian. There were traces of that square jaw and stern expression in Gilbert, his descendant. Lani had them as well.

Gilbert moved about the church like a sleepwalker, emptying the dustpan and straightening the altar cloth. His wife, Agnes, thought giving him tasks would distract from his grief. For days he pottered around the garden, pruning, mowing the lawn, building a bird feeder for the banyan tree. But this work, at least, had meaning. The church was his sanctuary. It was only fitting that Lani should be here at the end.

Black bunting draped the pews and pulpit; two large urns flanked the bier where Lani Kapiaho's coffin would rest. The old man's eyes flickered again to that spot, as if in disbelief. The front doors were ajar, sending shafts of light down the central aisle. Suddenly a figure entered. "Detective Roundtree," Gilbert said, unsurprised.

"I'm so sorry to disturb you again, Mr. Kapiaho."

"S'ok. I'm almost done here." He waved a hand vaguely.

Roundtree looked around him with approval. "It looks lovely," he said, and meant it. There were not many of these village churches left. "Is there anything I can do?"

Gilbert bit back the obvious retort—*You could find my granddaughter's killer*—and said instead, "Thanks, but I got *uku* help. What can I do for you?"

He was conscious of a certain unease in his visitor. Most of the time Detective Roundtree loved his job. At this moment he hated it. "I just heard back from our forensics people," he said reluctantly. "They tested residue from the explosion. There were a few bits and pieces of the blast caps left." He drew a breath, braced himself. "Lani's fingerprints are on them. And on the unused ones back at the construction site. I'm afraid it looks as if she set the explosion herself."

Kapiaho had been absently straightening objects on the windowsill. He paused, looked up. "She did?"

"We think so."

"I don't understand. Does that mean she wasn't murdered after all?"

Roundtree shook his head. "No, it is still very possible she was murdered. But it had to be after the explosion and possibly because of it."

The older man leaned against one of the pews for support. "But why?" he demanded. "Why, when it was just a damn statue?"

"We both know it was more than that." Randall Roundtree did not mention the call he had received from Robert Ackerman. Instead he said, "You are the village historian, aren't you? Could you think of any explanation for how those bodies got there?"

"Everyone keeps saying it was some kind of sacrifice. But if it was, it happened hundreds of years before my people arrived. I wouldn't know anything about it at all."

Roundtree nodded absently. "Sure, sure."

Gilbert Kapiaho was no fool. He knew the detective was concealing something. "What's going on?" he demanded.

Roundtree spread his hands. "I wish I knew. Until today we had a pretty good working theory. Peter Pauahi blew it up, Lani saw him, and he killed her. Or he killed her and then used the blast as cover. Now both of those are out the window."

Gilbert frowned. "Peter is *moke*. He could have forced my granddaughter to steal those caps. That way her prints would still be on them."

"That's true. Or they might have been working together, and he killed her afterward."

Her grandfather liked that idea less. "I can't imagine her still working with him, once she knew what he was."

The detective nodded again. "That's fair. But we still need to explain why the statue was blown up in the first place." He gestured to one of the pews. "May I?"

"Sure."

Both men sat. "We have," Roundtree began, "three separate events to account for. The destruction of the statue, the discovery of the bodies, and Lani's murder. Are they all related? Or could some have been happenstance?"

"I don't understand," admitted Gilbert.

"Think of it like this. Lani might have blown up the statue

and then been killed by someone else, with both murderer and victim unaware of the skeletons underneath. Or someone who knew about the bodies might have convinced her—even forced her—to destroy the statue and reveal the truth."

"And then murdered the only link back to himself."

"Exactly."

Gilbert considered this. "It doesn't make sense, though. Who cares about some old bones?"

"At the moment, a great many people. A twenty-million-dollar sale and a thirty-million-dollar development have both been halted because of them." Roundtree thought of his recent interview with Rodrigo Roxas, a small, pale, smiling man with false teeth and reptilian eyes. Roxas met the detective in his Honolulu office with a lawyer on either side of them, like Dobermans. He answered Roundtree's questions with polite, intractable negatives. No, he had never heard of Peter Pauahi. No, he had not given this individual any money. No, he had never met the Lathrops. Or Dr. Ackerman. Or Judge Chan. Winnie who? No, no, no. Yes, he finally admitted, he did have a property in Kailua. The blueprints for the hotel had been submitted to the town council for approval. His subordinates could furnish the details. No, the sale of Kaumaha did not impact his plans in any way. There were plenty of tourists to go around. Roundtree came away from the interview coldly furious. Practically everyone in his office had tangled with Roxas at one time or another, and more than a few were suspected of taking bribes from him. Every time they came close, the little man retreated into his plush-padded Waikoloa cavern and turned three separate law firms loose on them, like an octopus squirting ink.

Gilbert Kapiaho was still thinking. "Wait a minute. You're saying someone knew about the bodies and set Lani up, right?"

"Potentially, yes."

"But that's impossible! That statue's been sitting there for a hundred and sixty years. How could anybody have known what lay beneath?"

Roundtree smiled. It was, Gilbert thought, a rather sad smile. "That's exactly what I came to ask you, Mr. Kapiaho," the detective said quietly. "How could they?"

———

That same afternoon Mrs. Te Papa received a text inviting her to the funeral, which would be held the following morning. Once again, the Lathrops were opening their house to guests. "I will not need you this time," she told Marybeth, much to the girl's disappointment. But Marybeth received a text a moment later, from Roger. Both women looked at each other, embarrassed. "I didn't know you were so well acquainted," Mrs. Te Papa remarked.

"We weren't," Marybeth averred. "Not when I left, anyway. But we've texted and FaceTimed a lot since then." It never ceased to amaze Winnie Te Papa that relationships, which in her day needed as much care and attention as a tiger orchid, now blossomed even when both partners were dozens of miles away from each other.

When they arrived at the pier they found Dr. Ackerman and Judge Chan waiting. "Well," said the judge, with a trace of her usual bonhomie, "the gang's all here." Ackerman looked sour but said nothing. The waning sun made his skin seem waxy.

The seaplane was as jarring as before, and again it was Roger—more subdued now, wearing a dark navy pullover—who greeted them. Mrs. Te Papa tried not to notice the long, lingering look he shared with Marybeth. A separate car waited behind his jeep; Judge Chan and Dr. Ackerman climbed in. Marybeth looked pleadingly at her boss, but received such a cold glance in return that she jumped into the car after them without protest. Mrs. Te Papa sat next to Roger as they made their procession through the village. "I'm sorry," she said, "but I have to ask you a few questions."

Roger thought he understood. "I really like Marybeth," he asserted, "I know you're her godmother and all. But we haven't *done* anything yet, I promise."

Mrs. Te Papa smiled a little in spite of herself. "I'm very glad to hear it. But that is not what I needed to know. Do you remember a boy in your high school class called Steven Shimazu?"

Roger's eyes remained fixed on the road, but his grip on the steering wheel tightened. "Of course. He was murdered in my senior year. Why do you want to know?"

Mrs. Te Papa wasn't about to show her hand just yet. "There may be a link between his death and Lani's," she said, as gently as she could.

"But that's crazy!" Roger protested. "They said he was killed by a gang!"

"Yes, that is what they said." Mrs. Te Papa paused a moment before asking, "What was he like?"

"Steven? I didn't know him that well. He seemed okay."

"You were on the track team together, I understand. And the hiking club. And volleyball. And..."

"My God," Roger breathed, "did you memorize my high school yearbook?"

"Some of it," Mrs. Te Papa admitted. "Were you shocked when he was killed?"

"Of course I was! Jesus, I just had practice with him before he disappeared!"

"Yes, naturally. But I mean...when you heard he might have been mixed up with a gang, was that news unexpected?"

There was a longer pause this time, as Roger considered. "Not...entirely, no." Mrs. Te Papa waited, and finally he went on: "Steven was kind of an asshole. I hate saying it, because of what happened, but it's true. Always making out that he was a tough guy. He got suspended once for bringing a knife to school; that was back in freshman year."

"Was he a bully?"

"I suppose. He wasn't all that big or strong. But he had a nasty sense of humor. Always finding your weak spots. I think he liked to watch people squirm."

"Did he ever go after you?"

"No, I was too big for him." This was said with simple confidence. "I just told him to go shove it up his ass... Oh, sorry."

Mrs. Te Papa waved this aside. "I've heard worse," she said, which was true. No *haole* curse could begin to compare with native Hawaiian. "So, he was vicious. Did he tell people he was part of the Yakuza?"

"More like hinted it. We all knew his dad was actually a state senator, but Steven talked big about the Yakuza helping him get elected. For all we knew, it might have been true. But I doubted it."

"Why?"

"Because he was a terrible liar. The tough-guy thing was all bullshit. He never went after the big kids, or anyone he thought might actually hurt him. That knife he brought was to scare some middle-schooler."

"A bully *and* a coward," Mrs. Te Papa mused.

"Yeah, and that wasn't the worst of it," he muttered. They were just beyond the town, with the darkness of the forest canopy settling around them. Roger seemed to be concentrating on avoiding ruts in the road.

"What was the worst of it?" Mrs. Te Papa pressed.

He waited a moment before answering. "There were rumors about a girl."

"Oh?"

"We never knew the whole story," Roger said repressively. "And I never knew which girl it was."

"Tell me that part of the story you do know," Mrs. Te Papa encouraged.

"It was after homecoming, or so I heard. He wasn't on the football team or anything, but he liked to come to the games. He offered her a ride home." Roger stopped, unable to say any more.

"When was this?"

He thought for a moment. "Maybe a few months before he disappeared. It went all over the school. Someone said the girl's parents were going to sue, but I guess they never brought charges. After a while people just stopped talking about it. Like it never happened."

"But you think it did," Mrs. Te Papa said, and Roger did not reply. "Are you sure you never knew the girl's name? It seems odd to have a rumor like that circulate without..."

"I'm sure I never knew her name," Roger said firmly. Then he added: "And I'm sure he raped her."

Lathrop House loomed ahead of them like a bad dream. The newspaper clipping was still in her purse, snatched at the last moment from Tanaka's desk. *I KNOW WHAT YOU DID.* Mrs. Te Papa discreetly studied Roger Lathrop's profile. Gentle gray eyes offset by a determined chin. Not the face of a black-mailer, she thought.

But a blackmailer's victim? That was a different story.

———

Eleanor's bedroom faced the sea. She watched the procession of cars as it moved through the village, disappeared into the jungle, then reemerged at the gates of the drive. Marnie joined her on the lanai. "Not coming down?"

"No, dear, I think I'll stay a bit and watch the sunset."

"Are you feeling okay?" Marnie asked solicitously.

Eleanor favored her with a smile. "Just a little tired. Is everything ready for tomorrow?"

Her daughter-in-law absently brushed a lock of hair away from her face. "I think so. We've just got this lot for tonight; Tanaka's not coming till the morning."

"Tanaka!" Eleanor sat up straighter in her chair. "Who invited him?"

"I dunno, must have been the Kapiahos? Agnes has been just wonderful, by the way. I told her not to do a single thing, but she wouldn't listen. She's been up here for hours, getting out the linen and tidying up the bedrooms. Honestly, I don't know how I'd manage without her."

"Probably better that she has something to do." The old woman was silent a moment. "You're a good woman, Marnie," she said unexpectedly. "My son doesn't deserve you."

Marnie made an abrupt motion with her hands. "I don't care about *him*," she answered with frankness. "But I do feel sorry for Roger. He loves this place so."

"You did what you could. We all did. But I suppose in the end it wouldn't have mattered anyway."

"Ogden." His wife made a dismissive face.

"Not only him. Our world is passing away, with or without his help. Maybe we could have kept it going a little longer. But I doubt it." Eleanor looked toward the sea, where the sun was just beginning to emerge from a dark blue cloud. *How I will miss this,* she thought.

Gradually, Eleanor became aware that the other woman was watching her intently. "There's really no hope, then?" Marnie asked. Her eyes looked almost hungry.

"None. The state will demand our back taxes next week, and once we default they'll move in. Those damn skeletons," she added, almost to herself. "That's what brought everything to a boil. If only they'd stayed good and buried just a little longer..."

"I still can't believe," Marnie cut in wrathfully, "that everything we worked for, everything we *are*, will be destroyed because of some barbaric nonsense hundreds of years ago. It isn't right."

Eleanor was about to make an ironic comment, but then she saw the look on Marnie's face. The agony was palpable. "It means so much to you," she said kindly, "doesn't it?"

"Kaumaha?" Marnie seemed almost surprised by the question. "Of course it does! It means *everything*..."

———

Once they were inside and the bags taken upstairs, Mrs. Te Papa was not entirely surprised to see Marybeth and Roger disappear in the direction of the study. They closed the door behind them. Judge Chan declared she had a headache and went upstairs. Ogden was nowhere to be found. Mrs. Te Papa announced that she would rest before dinner. But once she was in her room she did not lie down. Instead she waited until she heard the creak of footsteps descending the staircase, then—with a surprisingly light step for someone her size—eased into the hallway and along the passage until she came to Eleanor Lathrop's room.

The bedroom door was open. The lights were switched off, but a set of French doors admitted the last of what must have been a magnificent sunset. Through them she saw Mrs. Lathrop seated on the lanai. A figure bent over her, tall and stork-like. For one moment Mrs. Te Papa had the mad impulse to cry out in warning, but then Dr. Ackerman planted a chaste kiss on Eleanor's silver head. She reached up and stroked his arm affectionately. They had watched the sunset together.

Mrs. Te Papa waited until a minute or so had passed, then with deliberately heavy footsteps she entered the room. She also contrived to bump quite heavily into a writing desk, which gave out a satisfying groan. The two figures turned around, and Ackerman's hand dropped casually from Eleanor's chair. They moved, ever so slightly, apart.

"Sorry to bother," Mrs. Te Papa said, "I was hoping for a word with Mrs. Lathrop before dinner. But of course it can wait."

"Nonsense," said Eleanor stoutly. "Bob's just checking up on me. Everyone gets so solicitous when you're old."

"Next time I'll bring a mirror to check if you're breathing," Ackerman told her. She made a shooing gesture at him and he departed, with a nod and a wink to Mrs. Te Papa.

"He really is the most horrible man," Eleanor said. "I don't know why I put up with him. He was so rude to Marnie last time, and now he's demanding a staple gun to pin mosquito netting up around his bed. Do sit down."

Mrs. Te Papa took the chaise next to her and spread comfortably. "I did not expect to be back so quickly," she said, "but I'm glad of the chance to speak with you. I have not had the chance to say how sorry I am for your loss. From everything I've heard, Lani was an extraordinary young woman."

Eleanor inclined her head. "Thank you. She was. What did you wish to speak to me about?"

Mrs. Te Papa folded her arms over her chest. "There have been some developments. Did Dr. Ackerman tell you?"

"No, he just came to chat." Eleanor was alert now. "What developments?"

"The professor and I examined the remains found beneath Reverend Lathrop's statue. We found two suggestive things. First, some of the bodies had knife wounds consistent with a serrated metal blade. Those were not introduced into Hawaii until the late eighteenth century, as you may know." She waited, but the other woman made no comment. "Second," she went on, "several of the older children we examined had teeth shaped by chewing raw sugarcane."

Mrs. Te Papa heard a tiny sound, a creak. Eleanor Lathrop had shifted uneasily in her chair. "You see what this means?" she pressed. "The wounds prove that the bodies were deposited in the site long after its construction, after the original tribe had departed. The next to arrive were the missionary natives whose descendants still live in the village. The dental evidence puts the issue beyond doubt. Sugarcane was not introduced on this island until 1843 and did not become a staple food source until 1848. Those children belonged to the village and were sacrificed to the god Ku."

Eleanor jolted upright. "How do you know that? Where did you hear that from?"

"Mr. Po said it when we discovered Lani's corpse. *Ku has taken his sacrifice.*"

"You base your theory on the rantings of a deranged old man?"

"Not at all," Mrs. Te Papa answered calmly. "Ku is the only god that demanded human sacrifices from the ancient Hawaiians. They were still sacrificing to him well into the nineteenth century. You said yourself that Amyas Lathrop discovered—how did you put it?—"a practice among them so revolting that he could not even bring himself to say it aloud." What else could it be but that? It is not hard to imagine the circumstances. Fevers struck the island every year. It is quite possible the veneration of Ku became intermingled with prayers for health, especially after the plague of 1848. Other tribes sacrificed children to ward off disease; Dr. Ackerman told me this just the other day.

"I was thinking about the story you told me of Amyas's death. 'Murdered and martyred,' you called it. But what actually happened? The fever had come again to the island. One of the children was ill, and Amyas removed him from the village to place him in quarantine. The villagers got him back, *and then the boy died.* What if he had been the sacrificial victim? And what if Amyas, coming upon what he supposed was a funeral, found instead a ritual execution?"

Eleanor rose from her chair. "That is outrageous!" she cried. "It's slander! How dare you make such accusations against a people who are dead and cannot defend themselves?"

Mrs. Te Papa rose also. She was not quite as tall as Eleanor, but in her girth there seemed a latent and powerful force. "I will tell you some more rantings of a deranged man. You wondered what Po said to me. His last words spoke of a terrible shame, so great that it choked him. I am quite sure at that moment he was channeling a spirit on this island. You may not believe in such things, Mrs. Lathrop, but that does not mean they don't exist."

"I never said I don't believe in them," Eleanor protested. "I know there are unquiet spirits on Kaumaha. My God, how could there not be? But to claim this dark business is the work of the villagers..."

Mrs. Te Papa was unsparing. "The evidence of the wounds and teeth is incontrovertible. Those children went in the ground after 1848. Do you think I am the only one to see the significance of this? Dr. Ackerman knows as well. If he did not tell you, it is only because he's trying to spare your feelings. But it is out in the world now!" She gestured at the darkening sea. "We told the Honolulu police what we found, as we were obliged by law to do. It's only a matter of time before someone talks to the press. Can you see the headlines?"

"There is no proof," Eleanor blustered, "Just stories. Old, old stories that don't matter anymore, anyway."

"Don't you understand what people are going to say? That Lani Lathrop blew up a hated symbol of Colonial oppression... and revealed horrific evidence of her own family's barbaric—"

"Stop!" Eleanor Lathrop almost screamed. "Enough! I won't hear any more of this."

"I'm afraid you will, Mrs. Lathrop. A great deal more, but

not from me. That story will be across the front pages in less than a week, and the memory of Lani and all her ancestors will be tarnished forever." Mrs. Te Papa's voice was cold, pitiless. "I would not be surprised if the state just shuts down the island and lets it rot."

There was a long pause. Eleanor Lathrop turned and looked down at the village, where a few twinkling lights began to glow. "Until everyone forgets again," she murmured, almost to herself. Her voice lost its vehemence and now sounded almost wistful. "Like a madhouse or a massacre site. Which it is." Below them a solitary figure appeared, moving determinedly down the driveway. From the lanai Mrs. Te Papa could only see the top of her head and a blue skirt. She thought it was Judge Chan, until Eleanor called out, "Night, Agnes!" Agnes looked up, waved. This brief moment of normalcy broke the spell. Eleanor's gaze traveled until it found the short, angry woman in front of her. "How much do you know?" she asked quietly. "The truth, I mean."

Mrs. Te Papa lowered her eyes. It was not a gesture of defeat, but victory. "A great deal. But as you say, I have no proof. I cannot control the story once it's released into the world."

"And once it is, no other story will matter."

"I'm afraid that's true."

Eleanor Lathrop sighed. "Wait here," she said, and disappeared into the bedroom. The lights clicked on. She returned after a few moments holding something close to her chest, and without a word handed it to Mrs. Te Papa.

A green notebook, crackled with age. The leather binding had gone soft and tiny flakes came off in her hands. She opened to the first yellowed page and read, *"A True Account and Journal of the Settlement of New Boston Island, Formerly Kaw-maw-ha, Begun This 23 of January, 1848, by Reverend Amyas Lathrop."*

The Reverend wrote in a neat hand. Even by the light of

the windows she could decipher it easily. "Sit," Eleanor commanded. Mrs. Te Papa sat, balancing the book in her lap. The old woman dropped into a chair across from her. As Mrs. Te Papa read, Eleanor kept her gaze fixed on the horizon, watching the stars appear one by one.

> *"A True Account...by Reverend Amyas Lathrop,*
> *And Postscript by his Wife, Prudence Lathrop"*
> *(Access to these materials is restricted. Please*
> *contact Chief Archivist for further information)*

May 25, 1850

I have arrived upon a happy answer to all present difficulties. The solution, as for all things, is to be found in scripture. How comforting are the counsels of the ancients!

The interconnectedness of nature has been much on my mind. If God sends us these fevers each season, there must be a reason for them. I observe that the fevers bring out the very worst in the villagers. They cling to their familiar idols even as they quiver in fear of the dread gods that visited this scourge. Hence, thinking the matter over, I resolved that the best way to win the people back to the True Faith was to deal, firmly and finally, with the fever. But here I hit a snag. I am no doctor, and Prudence's ministrations rarely do more than provide comfort. I cannot heal the sick through prayer, much as I wish it. Worse yet, it is my conviction that the demons on this island welcome the illness, as it brings the villagers back—through terror—into communion with them. Even if I had a solution, the fiends would doubtless resist me. It was a pretty problem.

Then last night I experienced a revelation. It has long been our practice to quarantine the sick, and a well-ventilated warehouse near the wharf has hitherto served this purpose. But children bear the worst of the fever, and it seemed unkind to let them expire with the rest. There is a cooking shed adjacent to the main house with quarters for the cook and scullery maid. This I gave to little Baptiste Maheha, a boy of six years. He arrived flushed and delirious, calling for his parents and wailing piteously. Prudence calmed him with cool towels and laudanum, but such panaceas were fleeting. He awoke again in the night with renewed cries, such that none of the household could sleep. This went on another day. In the evening I went myself to the cookhouse. The child had eaten nothing and could not even be induced to drink water. Yet somehow his lungs were unimpaired. I tried to calm him so that he might receive the comfort of the Twenty-Third Psalm, but it was no use. This worried me, as at any moment the boy might be lost and not receive the spiritual guidance that was his due. Finally I placed one hand gently over his mouth, dulling the sound, so that he might hear words of solace. He quieted almost at once, I am glad to say. I read several passages, noting that his skin, which had been hot as a coal stove, began to cool.

It occurred to me that my hand, which is quite large, might inadvertently have obstructed the boy's breathing. Yet his passing was so peaceful, the expression on his face so serene, that verily I could not think I had done harm. I looked up and saw a great shadow over the corpse. The room was entirely filled by the spirit I knew as Ku. But I was not afraid. It lingered for a moment, as if gazing at the child, then there was the tiniest rush of air from the boy's lungs, a little sigh. Something had left him, and at that same moment Ku vanished.

Had it mistaken my charity for an offering? The thought was monstrous. But I could not rid myself of the conviction, and later that night I had occasion to read in the Book of Judges the story of Jephthah the Israelite. On the field of battle, Jephthah swore an oath that if God granted him victory over the Ammonites, whatever greeted him first on his return to Gilead should immediately be sacrificed as a burnt offering. Jephthah triumphed and returned home, whereupon his daughter rushed to embrace him. But an oath with God is a solemn thing, and Jephthah did as he was bonded to do. And God was pleased.

I closed the Book with a grateful sigh. Now I knew what was to be done. When Boniface was among the Frisians, he paid homage to their god Wotan, even presumed to make a pact with the high priests of that barbaric tribe. They could worship the devil spirits as they pleased, so long as the One God was understood to reign over all. The early history of our faith is rife with such concessions. And here was I, among a more savage race than ever roamed Thrace or Gaul. The essential thing, I understood, was to break the villagers' bond with Kane. Kane brought the fever, but also succor and health. He presumed to raise himself to the throne of the Almighty, and this was the greatest threat. If I could bargain with Ku, perhaps he would help banish Kane once and for all.

This night I tested my proposition. I chose a boy from the village—the younger brother of Baptiste, in fact—and fed him sweetened cake laced with a powerful emetic from my own stores. He commenced to vomit at once, and I took him from his parents and brought him to the cookhouse, where he remained for some hours under the opiate of laudanum. Just past midnight I removed him from that place and carried him to the well site where Ku had first made itself known to me. There I placed the child on the curved stones. He was still drowsy and fretful, but with one hand I smoothed his brow while the other sliced cleanly through his throat. It was very quick. The boy looked startled, but then I had the satisfaction of hearing that same tiny sigh and seeing the infinitesimal particle leave his body and become absorbed in the ether. Ku had taken his sacrifice. The bond was sealed.

February 2, 1855

It may be of some interest to my successors to know the exact method by which the ritual is performed, in the event some future propitiation be needed. First, note that the sacrifice must otherwise be healthy; a sickly child is no sacrifice at all, as they will likely die in any event. When the first fever arrives on the island—every change of season without fail—I invite the village children to the house for Sunday tea and Bible lessons. One amongst them is given a compound of herbs that, when strained through hot water, produces symptoms not unlike the fever: flushed cheeks, shortness of breath, delirium. The child is then brought to quarantine, where I administer two tablespoons of laudanum dissolved in sugar syrup. This is sufficient to induce a gentle sleep that lasts well into the night; even when roused, the child is drowsy and tractable. It is necessary to remove the clothes, lest they be stained. Once unclothed, the offering is laid upon the altar and quickly dispatched. The remainder is placed in the well and a short prayer is said. The next morning, I present the clothes to the parents and explain that the fever claimed a life, and the body had to be buried quickly to prevent spreading the contagion. That is usually sufficient to remove the plague from the island, although occasionally a second sacrifice is needed. The children have made excellent progress in their Scripture lessons, and I am minded to continue the teas every Sunday.

October 29, 1861
   Catastrophe. No time to write more.

Memorial by Prudence Lathrop, dated November 3, 1863

On this day I have raised upon the island a statue of my late husband, the Reverend Amyas Lathrop, who departed this earth two years previous. Mr. Henry Kirke Browne of New York completed the work and shipped it, for a total cost of $375. I have attached the bill of sale and manifest of the vessel Andromeda, which carried the piece. It is a handsome statue and a very good likeness.

I am compelled to provide a short postscript explaining its presence. I do so not that these facts be generally known, which is the very opposite of my intent, but that my son and his descendants, as custodians of this island, should understand why the statue must remain undisturbed. Accordingly, upon completing this account I shall have it sealed with the journal and entrusted to my Honolulu attorneys, Messrs. Wentwhistle and Thorpe, with instructions that they shall only divulge its contents to my son on occasion of my death or incapacity.

I have long been aware that there existed in my husband, alongside his many admirable qualities, an unnatural severity. I do not mean that he was cruel. In truth, he has never exhibited towards me or my son anything but kindness, compassion and good-will. Yet being in all things an upright man, he could not abide weakness in others. And being a Christian, he believed he could reform them. His fervor for Christ was, I am sure, entirely sincere. Yet it could also be quite overwhelming, especially for the congregants of Lowell, Massachusetts. They resented his attempts to curb their ways, and when he pressed the point, they demanded his removal. *I recommended missionary work, which would—I believed—afford limitless opportunity to tap his crusading spirit. For this much I will say of him: he was never unjust. His punishments were harsh but never unmerited, and arose from a profound belief in the perfectibility of man.*

If Amyas was a stern judge of others, he judged himself most. The success or failure of the Kaw-Ma-Ha community rested entirely on his shoulders. I never ceased to wonder at his passion, even as I felt it sometimes went too far. The people of these islands are playful, docile, mischievous, and childlike. They will obligingly mimic whatever manners or speech or beliefs you press upon them, but strict obedience in all things makes them sullen. If Amyas had made a halfway covenant, I am sure both he and they would have gotten along amiably. But he could not do so. His disappointments were many, and it is my belief they eroded the citadel of his faith until it was a mere shell.

There are those who might say the island corrupted his wits, that the savagery of its people infected him. In Lowell we heard tales of missionaries in Africa who abandoned all decency and comported themselves like beasts. But I do not think he went mad. His was an inflexible nature—it could not bend, only break—and once broken, could not be mended. He tried to reveal the mysteries of the Faith to the Hawaiian people, but—in his view—failed. That failure, like a cancer, grew within him until it consumed all else.

It was good Melchior Kapiaho, the overseer, who warned me of my husband's excesses. He said the villagers had come to fear Amyas, that some believed he had congress with the gods. They blamed him for the fevers that struck the island, claiming that he brought them down with witchcraft. I told Melchior this was nonsense, and he agreed, but something in his tone made me wary. I resolved to watch Amyas more carefully in future. When the fever struck again, my vigilance was rewarded. I observed him put a substance into a child's drink at Sunday lessons; not surprisingly, the child fell ill at once. After Amyas placed him in the cookhouse, I allowed Melchior to free the boy and take him back to his people. I intended to say only that the child had recovered and been sent home, but I was not prepared for my husband's reaction. He became enraged, almost incoherent. Perceiving my distress, he locked me in his study (being the only room to which I do not possess a key) and left for the village. Once there he demanded they return the child, but the unfortunate boy had expired. An ugly scene followed, when my husband accused the villagers of faithlessness and blasphemy. It was not clear, however, to which deity he referred. They flatly refused to relinquish the boy's body and Amyas was forced to retreat, in fear of his life.

Meanwhile, having been imprisoned in his chambers, I passed the time by making a thorough search. I uncovered this journal and read the horrors within. My thoughts may be imagined, but I assure you the shock was far greater. I loved Amyas, and still do, but this vile creature was not he. From my husband I had nothing to fear, and yet I was terrified. By the time he returned I had replaced the book carefully in its position and pretended to be much astonished by his behavior—indeed, it was not all pretense. I asked him why he carried on so, and he replied that the villagers had learned nothing of the Holy Word, that they were mired in anathema, and that he could do nothing more to save them. I soothed him as best I could and pressed upon him a cup of tea to settle his nerves. He accepted it gratefully and fell asleep almost at once—I had followed his own recipe and given him not two but four teaspoons of laudanum.

The rest may be briefly told. While Amyas slept upstairs I had an anxious council with Melchior. We agreed my husband could not be allowed to continue his barbarous practices. I offered to administer poison and let out that Amyas died of the fever. This would explain his sudden madness. But Melchior demurred. He had brought with him a native weapon of curious design which, he promised, would cauterize and banish any unnatural thing it touched. Melchior had become convinced that an evil spirit inhabited my husband's body, and in truth I could not entirely reject the idea. After some debate, I agreed upon the spear.

A curious scene then unfolded. Melchior intended to do the deed himself. I objected, saying he was blameless in this monstrosity and it must be myself that bore the burden. I was Amyas's wife, his counselor and helpmate. I loved him and I had failed him, just as he had failed his people. Melchior became quite agitated. Such a task was not for a woman, he insisted, much less a wife and mother. He declared that he loved my husband also, and the business of dispatching him was nothing more than releasing him from the confinement of his own diseased mind into the mansions of everlasting rest. Finally, we compromised. I struck the initial blow, but Melchior with his powerful arms grasped the spear and drove it home. My husband's eyes opened and he gave a small cry, but that was all.

We laid him to rest behind the chapel, and on the same day I ordered Melchior to fill the sacrificial well with heavy stones. The natives were told only that Reverend Lathrop had died suddenly; they chose to believe their pagan gods struck him down. But I knew this story could not last forever, nor rocks keep the truth from emerging sooner or later. I began inquiries for a sculptor to fashion a suitable monument. Fortunately, my dear friend Evangeline Winthrop knew

Mr. Browne well, and a deal was struck. I took over Sunday services myself, with Melchior retaining his post as deacon. In time I shall see to it that he is ordained, so that he may look after the spiritual needs of the island after my decease.

Today I saw Amyas's statue raised over the grave of thirty-two innocent souls. It rests upon a bed of concrete four feet deep. I requested of Mr. Browne that he make the figure's arms extend into a cross, and I have asked Melchior to carve a few appropriate words in his native language upon the tomb. I wish I could do more. But the story of their death and interment would be the undoing of this place, of that I am certain. Melchior agrees with me. It was Amyas Lathrop that brought Christianity to these people. He proved a flawed vessel, but the work was just. How could I allow the people of Kaw-Maw-Ha to fall back into their pagan idolatry, as they surely would do, if the truth become known? It would be nothing less than condemning their souls.

It grieves me to mark the place of desecration with an effigy of the culprit. But a monument is inviolable; as long as it stands, the colony shall stand. I look at it now and think of the great hopes Amyas had arriving here. The statue represents the best that was within him, even as it conceals the worst. Ecclesiastes 9,5.

Reverently,
Prudence Lathrop

Chapter 12

NĀ LEO PŌ, NIGHT VOICES

Mrs. Te Papa lifted her eyes from the book and found Eleanor's waiting.

"'For the living know that they shall die: but the dead know not anything, neither have they any more a reward; for the memory of them is forgotten,'" Eleanor intoned.

"Ecclesiastes," Mrs. Te Papa sighed. Her expression was grave, but unsurprised.

"You knew."

"I suspected. Not the whole, but part. You told me that the dead boy's family removed his liver before he was cremated. That was only done in cases where witchcraft was suspected. But it was a chance remark of David Tanaka's that really got me thinking."

"Oh?"

"He mentioned how George Pullman's widow had his body encased in concrete so the socialists couldn't dig him up. I thought at once of Ackerman saying that concrete was poured into the aperture to hold Amyas's statue. It seemed unnecessary at the time. But if the concrete was there to *seal a tomb*, it made perfect sense. The statue ensured no one would ever disturb what lay underneath."

"So why that rigmarole about suspecting the villagers?"

Mrs. Te Papa spread her hands. "I knew you were protecting the Lathrops, especially Roger. I had to show you the cost of that choice. I'm sorry."

"Don't be." Eleanor shrugged. "You were right. It couldn't stay buried forever. Neither the bodies, nor the truth. Poor old Prudence."

"Yes. She did what she could. The statue in the form of a cross, the Guinean words on the base—it was as close as she dared to a Christian burial. And who'd have believed that anyone would blast blessed old Reverend Lathrop off his perch?"

Eleanor smiled grimly. "He got what was coming to him. In every sense."

"Not entirely. Mr. Po spoke of a black shadow that moved within the earth, infecting it, he said. I am not sure the Reverend is as gone as we would like. Or Prudence, for that matter. It was her shame and helplessness that Po channeled, I am certain of it."

"Can anything be done?"

Mrs. Te Papa considered. "A few things, possibly. How did you come into possession of this journal, by the way?"

"I was a Fisk before I married Ogden's father."

"Ah." The Fisks, Mrs. Te Papa knew, had an entire museum devoted solely to their collection of artifacts.

"The journal remained in the Lathrop family for three generations. It was Prudence's great-granddaughter, Caroline, who donated it to the Fisk collection, with a strict injunction that its contents remained sealed for fifty years. That seal was lifted in 1968, five years after my marriage. Ogden had already been born. My mother was still alive then. She sent it to me." Eleanor chuckled. "She didn't think much of my choice of husbands."

"Did you share its contents with him?"

The old woman shook her head vehemently. "Never. He had troubles enough, poor man. I intended to keep the secret entirely to myself. Even when Bob Ackerman came as a graduate student and built up his lovely theory of the House of the Bone Feast."

"I was thinking of that, too," Mrs. Te Papa admitted. "The Guinean markings. 'Gathering,' 'flesh' and 'quantity.' Melchior Kapiaho wasn't describing a feast, but a mass grave."

"But then Bob came back a few years later, after his book was published. Sometime around the Watergate hearings. He wanted permission to remove the statue and examine the inside of the base. I told him no, but then he threatened to petition the state government. So, I had to tell him the truth." Her face lit up with a kind of wicked glee. "He wasn't *quite* as uppity back then, but almost. I wish you could have seen the look on his face when he found out. Like he'd been slapped with a haddock."

"So Dr. Ackerman knows?" Mrs. Te Papa was astonished.

"He does. He was all for coming out with the truth, book or no book. I had to work on him for days to change his mind. His was an honest mistake, after all. And the truth would help no one. After a lot of arguing—well, you can imagine, you've met him—Bob finally agreed. He's kept that secret for me ever since."

Mrs. Te Papa was not as certain, but she asked: "Does anyone else know?"

Suddenly Eleanor's face fell. In that moment she seemed ten years older. "One other," she answered, so quietly Mrs. Te Papa almost did not hear.

"Lani?" she guessed.

"Yes. I told her the same night she died. She was so downcast after the hearing. Blamed herself, said it was her fault the village was getting destroyed. Well, I couldn't have that. So I showed her the *ihe* that Melchior used on Amyas and told her the whole story. I wanted to make her understand. This whole colony was founded on a monstrous lie. She wasn't destroying the village, she was liberating it. Just as her ancestors Melchior

Kapiaho and Prudence Lathrop saved it from a psychopath. She was the best part of both of them. That was what I told her."

"How did Lani respond?" Mrs. Te Papa wondered.

Eleanor did not answer at once. She looked out at the moon, and Mrs. Te Papa was amazed to see tears glistening in her eyes. "I should have known," she murmured. "Should have seen it coming. The poor child spent her whole life in our shadow. Ogden was horrid, and Roger…well, Roger was always very kind, but it was him that got to go to the fancy prep school and college. He was the heir. I thought she was better off with Gilbert and Agnes; they adored her. But Lani was still a Lathrop, and she never forgot it.

"I thought that the truth would comfort her, but I was wrong. She was furious. How could I keep this secret from her, from everyone? How could I let the villagers and the family go on believing this horrid lie? How could I let his statue continue to desecrate the victims buried beneath it? She was right, of course. But you see, Winnie, I have a responsibility to both my grandchildren. After Roger's speech that night, I could not let him learn the truth. He was the last of the Lathrops; he deserved to take that with him, for it was all he would ever get from this place."

"You told Lani this?"

She nodded sadly. "I did. I told her that if the truth were known, Roger and the rest of the family would be ruined. The island could never be sold. I said…God help me…I said that the truth was my gift to her, and the lie was my gift to Roger."

"I think I can understand that," offered Mrs. Te Papa.

"But Lani couldn't, and I don't blame her. By telling her the truth, I made her complicit in protecting the lie. She screamed at me then. Said that I had betrayed her, then stormed out of the room. That was the last I saw of my…my only granddaughter." The dam broke suddenly, and Eleanor began to weep, great heaving sobs that convulsed her entire body.

Instinctively, Mrs. Te Papa got up and wrapped her arms around the old woman. They remained so for some time. "It was not your fault," she murmured consolingly, "You did what you thought was best."

Wiping her eyes with her sleeve, Eleanor answered, "But don't you see? I didn't show Lani the journal, I just told her what it said. She thought the only way to expose the truth was to destroy the statue. That's how I knew she'd done it. Can you imagine what it's like to know your grandchild died because of something you told them?"

"You can't blame yourself for that. We still don't know how or why she died."

"Oh, but I do." Eleanor was dry-eyed now and solemn. "I've known for some time."

Mrs. Te Papa released her. "What do you mean?"

"Lani was overwrought that night. With the hearing, and what I told her, and that horrid scene at the bonfire...plus it seemed like there was some argument with that wretched boy Peter..." Mrs. Te Papa nearly interrupted but held her tongue. "And carrying around the weight of this terrible decision on her shoulders. It was all too much. She set the explosives herself and stood too close. Then, at the very last second, she may have changed her mind. That's why the stone hit her from behind."

"And the angle of the blow?"

Eleanor shrugged. "It could have been a stone that shot upward from the blast and then fell down on her."

"A suicide..." Mrs. Te Papa considered this.

"Or an accident. Or some combination of the two. But not murder. There was never any reason for anyone to kill her."

The solution had its merits. David Tanaka, the obvious suspect, had given up trying to buy Kaumaha gracefully and quickly as soon as the bodies were discovered. Roger loved his home, but he loved his cousin also. Ogden, on the other hand...but Ogden was drunk and insensible. It was hard to imagine him staging the elaborate tableau in his sodden state. No one else on the island could have had any reason to kill Lani or destroy the statue.

But there was one person, not on the island, who did. And Eleanor Lathrop had just inadvertently revealed how it might have been done. "It may not be that simple," Mrs. Te Papa said slowly.

———

In another part of the house, Roger and Marybeth were thinking of the future. Roger's bedroom looked out toward the valley. Marybeth sat with him on the lanai, her fingers interlaced with his. She stared at the hills, deep purple with pockets of shadow like a cloak thrown casually over a chair, and sighed deeply. "I'm glad to be back."

"I'm glad you're here."

Marybeth squeezed his hand. "How long will you stay after the burial?"

"Not long. Couple weeks at most. Gran wants Mom and me to take a trip to the mainland after, just to get a break from all this." And from his father, he didn't add.

"What about after you get back?"

He shrugged. "Start looking for a job, I guess. Nothing in Kona, so it'll probably have to be Honolulu. Gran's making some calls."

"What about your mom?"

"I'm not sure. She and Dad may patch things up. They've been together for almost thirty years. And I think he loves her, in his way." But Marnie loved Kaumaha, and soon Kaumaha would be gone. For all its troubles, the island had kept them together. Now they were flying apart.

"You can stay with me, if you'd like," Marybeth offered shyly. For a moment he did not answer, and she wondered whether he had heard. Roger stared off into space, lost in private abstraction. But then he turned slowly in his chair until they were face-to-face. Marybeth resisted the urge to look away. She knew she was not conventionally pretty. Her nose was broad, her mouth wide and generous. Yet Roger was thinking to himself that there was a vitality in this girl he had never encountered before. The Lathrops had an elfin coldness; Roger had it himself. Marybeth radiated warmth. "You mean that?" he asked.

"Yep. It's only a studio, but once you've got your job we can find something better. If you want."

He wanted to say yes, and very nearly did. But it seemed indecent to be making plans while somewhere in a Kailua mortuary his cousin spent her last night aboveground. "Your Mrs. Te Papa," he said instead, "Does she know something about Lani's death? My gran reckons she does."

Marybeth felt the dizzying sensation of having come close to happiness, only to feel it brush past. "I think she figures it was Tanaka," she answered flatly. "She wanted to know all about the Yakuza, and whether they were mixed up in that boy's murder. The one you knew." There was the tiniest hint of acid in those words.

But Roger didn't notice. "Tanaka?" he repeated. "But he withdrew the offer. He doesn't get anything out of this at all."

"Wouldn't you rather him than...someone else?"

"I never really thought about it." He raised his arms and let them fall. "I know the police think it was murder, but I never did. It never made sense to take a human life just for some old rocks and trees."

"But what else could it be?" Marnie asked incredulously.

"Well..." He crinkled his nose in thought. "I always figured they'd decide in the end it was an accident. Or even suicide. Anything other than murder—that just seems so outlandish. I don't believe it."

———

On the opposite lanai, Mrs. Te Papa could have been answering both generations of Lathrops. "It may not be that simple," she said.

Eleanor stiffened. "Why? What do you mean?"

"I mean, it's possible someone else knew what was buried beneath the statue. Someone who was never intended to know." She leaned back against the railing, resting on her elbows. "I cannot be certain, however."

"Go on," Eleanor commanded.

"There is a man named Rodrigo Roxas who owns a large property in Kailua. Have you heard of him?"

Eleanor considered. "I think Ogden might have mentioned him at some point. David Tanaka's competitor, right?"

"Yes. It was Roxas who bribed Peter Pauahi to create Save Kaumaha and try to frustrate the sale. Peter told me this himself." The other woman's nose wrinkled in distaste. "That gives you an idea of Roxas's methods. It was his idea to try to have the bone feast site declared sacred, blocking any development. That didn't work, obviously. But what if Roxas knew what was buried under the statue? The only way to expose the truth was with dynamite."

"Are you suggesting that Lani worked for this man?"

"No. But it is certainly possible he put the idea in her head, directly or indirectly. Or she might have been a witness to the deed."

"But how would Roxas have known?" Eleanor objected. "No one knew except me and Bob."

Mrs. Te Papa nodded slowly. "Exactly." She shifted her bulk against the rail. "Let me tell you something. The day that Dr. Ackerman was supposed to be in Ohio, I saw him enter an office building near the First Hawaii Center. That building has a number of tenants, but only two of interest: David Tanaka and Rodrigo Roxas. There is no particular reason why Ackerman would visit Tanaka, and I later confirmed he did not. That leaves Roxas. If Roxas bribed Peter, it is certainly possible he tried the same trick on others. Dr. Ackerman was in possession of a secret that could make him a rich man, and Roxas richer."

Eleanor studied her through half-closed lids. "You think this Roxas bribed Bob into telling him about the bodies?"

"Dr. Ackerman lied about the conference in Cincinnati. There was no conference. He visited the building where Roxas is located on that same day. And the destruction of the statue has accomplished all Roxas could have wished: development on Kaumaha is halted, probably forever. But it might be worse than that."

"Oh?"

"For some time I wondered if Roxas had ordered Peter to blow up the statue. But Ackerman would be the logical choice for that job. He knew the statue and base better than anyone. If Lani saw him set the explosion, he may have killed her to keep her silent."

"That's pure conjecture," Eleanor scoffed.

"Yes, it is. But I'm afraid it all adds up."

"I suppose it does," the other woman mused. Then she rose, leaned into the bedroom and shouted, "*Bob!* I need a word!"

Mrs. Te Papa stood mute. A moment later Ackerman appeared, looking disheveled. His white hair was flattened on one side. "For God's sake, what is it, Ellie? I was trying to rest."

Mrs. Lathrop sat back down and gripped the arms of her chair. "You lied to us, Bob," she said coldly. "There never was any conference in Cincinnati."

Ackerman looked from one woman to another. "What is all this?" he said, confused.

"I saw you that day," Mrs. Te Papa explained apologetically. "You were going into the Queen Kalama building just as I came out. I believe you were going to see Rodrigo Roxas."

It was interesting to watch the battleground of emotions on Robert Ackerman's face. Confusion gave way to astonishment, irritation, indignation, embarrassment, and something that looked implausibly like whimsy. With that same expression he turned to Eleanor. "So it's like that, is it?"

"You tell me," the old lady answered with spirit.

He cocked an eyebrow. "Will you do the honors, or shall I?"

Mrs. Lathrop grinned. Her face illuminated, and there was the merest flash of the ravishing woman she once had been. "Oh, all right, you old coot." To Mrs. Te Papa, she said, "Bob's appointment wasn't with Tanaka or with Roxas. It was with me."

For one mad instant Mrs. Te Papa imagined a lovers' tryst in some empty office. But Eleanor went on: "We always schedule our visits at the same time. They say it's easier to endure the treatment when someone is doing it with you."

"Which is a lie," Ackerman put in.

"Well, anyway, it gives you someone to talk to. Or scream at, as the case may be."

For once in her life Mrs. Te Papa was completely at sea. The other two seemed to be sharing a private joke at her expense. "Treatment?" she repeated blankly.

"Your researches were incomplete," Dr. Ackerman said, addressing her like a subpar pupil. "There are other offices in the Queen Kalama tower. Including the only decent oncologist in Hawaii." As Mrs. Te Papa watched, Robert Ackerman reached up and tugged his mane of white hair. It came away in his hand. Smiling, he offered it to her for inspection.

"Not that it makes much difference in our cases," Eleanor added. She, too, removed her wig. Together they looked like members of an odd cult.

"My God," Mrs. Te Papa breathed. "I am so sorry."

"It's quite all right," replied Eleanor, replacing the wig and adjusting it. "You didn't know. Nobody does."

"That's how it started, you see," Ackerman explained. "I ran into Eleanor in the waiting room a few months ago. Recognized her at once—she hasn't changed all that much." Mrs. Lathrop rolled her eyes. "At first we were both embarrassed. Mine's pancreatic. Hers is lung. Ellie hasn't told her family yet."

"I didn't think they needed another thing to worry about," Eleanor sniffed.

"And I haven't told the college. No point, really. There's only a few weeks of the semester left, and I'll be a portrait in a hallway by the time summer's over. Eleanor might have a bit longer."

"Two packs a week for fifty years? I don't think I'll win this particular horse race."

"So we made a kind of pact," Ackerman went on. "Didn't want to go through the chemo alone, you see. We coordinated our schedules so we'd get treated on the same day. Then we'd spend a couple nights at the Royal Hawaiian together, recuperating. I've watched the dinner show eight times."

Eleanor cut in, "But the treatment you saw, Winnie, was our last. Bob's already got his affairs in order, and I've made arrangements to stay in Kona for a few weeks. There's a decent hospital there, when the time comes. I just needed to see the family through this latest horror show."

"Didn't they wonder where you were going?"

"Let 'em," replied the lady with vigor. "Ogden couldn't give a damn, and Roger thought I was having some kind of geriatric dirty weekend. Which I suppose it was."

"If only," Dr. Ackerman muttered.

"Thank you, Robert," Eleanor said. "You may leave now."

"Oh, am I being dismissed? What are you two talking about, anyway?"

"Girl stuff. Periods and tampons. Go back to bed."

Ackerman shot her a dirty look, which transformed into an affectionate smile. They touched hands briefly. "See you at dinner," he told Mrs. Te Papa, and the warmth in his blue eyes was such that for a reckless moment she nearly embraced him. The moment passed, and he was gone.

The two women looked at each with new understanding. "So you see," Eleanor said, "Bob Ackerman and I are used to sharing secrets." She settled comfortably in her chair. "I'm pretty sure mine are safe with him."

———

For this task Mr. Po dressed carefully. There was a bureau in the bedroom that held his Sunday suit, a few shirts, and a spare pair of gray striped trousers. These had been pressed and folded by his late wife, Sadie, and had not moved since. Carefully, with a pang of regret, he drew out the trousers and a white shirt. He ran a comb through his sparse hair, squinting at the reflection in the mirror. Then he put on his sandals and set out for the village.

There were no streetlights to guide his walk, but Mr. Po didn't need any. He was used to moving in the dark. In no time at all, he stood before the periwinkle-blue cottage with neatly trimmed flowerbeds. It was not late, but only the kitchen light was lit. He knocked softly.

Gilbert Kapiaho answered almost at once. His face looked drawn and tired. If he was surprised to see a visitor at this hour he did not show it. "Evening, Edgar. Howzit?"

Gilbert was one of the only villagers left who remembered Mr. Po's first name. "Hey, Gil," he answered. "Got a minute?"

"Sure." He drew back to let Mr. Po inside. The kitchen was bright and gleaming—too clean, really. It looked as though every pot had been polished twice. "Agnes is asleep," Gilbert explained, "I was gonna head up soon, but, you know." He pulled out two chairs from the kitchen table and sat down. There was a bottle of Dewar's in front of him. Without asking, he poured them each a double.

The men drank silently. There was no need to rush into speech. Gilbert Kapiaho knew that Po did not come without a reason, and he had a pretty good idea what it was. They had been boys together, after all.

"Everything ready for tomorrow?" Mr. Po asked.

"Think so. They're bringing her over in the morning. Tanaka loaned us his digger, so we can get the job done quick. Got a nice spot picked out right behind the east wall." This was not a question, but a faint interrogative hung at the end of it.

"Yeah. About that." Po frowned, and Gilbert felt his insides go cold. So he'd been right after all. Mr. Po said, "She's not happy, Gil. I couldn't understand all of it, but I got that much." Unconsciously, he lapsed into Hawaiian. *"Said she would not rest if she was near that bad man. The Reverend. Lani was very angry, not peaceful like they usually get. Just as she was alive, lots of opinions."*

Lani's grandfather tried to digest this news as if it were normal. He asked quietly, *"Does she want to be buried somewhere else?"*

"No. She says you must remove the bad man. Take his bones and throw them into the sea."

"Are you crazy?" Gilbert was startled into English. "I can't go digging up graves!"

"You must." Mr. Po was implacable. *"The children told me. They can speak now, since the statue is gone. It was the preacher, he sacrificed them to Ku. Lani knows this also. How could she rest near such a man?"*

"What? I don't understand."

"Amyas Lathrop was deranged. He still is. I hear him, too." The old man shuddered. *"It sounds like water moving underground.*

An endless stream of obscenity and hate. He's trapped in the earth, and the earth speaks with his voice. Not words, but the meaning behind words, more terrible than any word could express. Pray-lust-hands-fuck-God-pain-touch, all mixed up together. It's revolting, like hearing a disease talk to itself."

Gilbert wondered: did the voices of the dead degrade over time, like their bodies? Or had Reverend Lathrop simply been gone from this world so long that his speech became intertwined with the roots and rocks and dirt? "So," he said in English, bringing them back into the living world with a thud, "Lani wants me to dig up the Reverend. Aside from the whole grave-robbing thing, how do we know that chucking him in the sea will work?"

"Lani doesn't know. She just wants him gone."

The other man pondered this for a moment. "Right away?"

"Before she joins him in the ground. She says she can't rest. None of them can." He stood to leave.

"Edgar." Gilbert suddenly reached out and caught the old man's wrist. His impassive face melted into agony. "For God's sake, I need to know. Is she...is she okay?"

Mr. Po freed himself gently and looked down at his old friend. His expression was entirely sane and almost amused. "She's still Lani," he answered with certitude. "She's still on Kaumaha. Just a different Kaumaha from ours." He patted Gilbert's shoulder. "I'll be back later tonight. I have an idea."

"But—"

"Enough, *hoa*. It's okay for you to miss her and wish she was still alive. But the rest...it's not anything to worry about. It never was." The little man finished his drink and went out into the night. He strode sure-footedly into the darkness.

Watching him, Gilbert Kapiaho felt strangely comforted.

Chapter 13

KAKAHIAKA PIHOIHOI, MORNING SURPRISES

Light sleepers on Kaumaha might have awoken to the rumble and growl of Tanaka's mechanical excavator moving the earth behind the old chapel. But if they did, they rolled over and went to sleep again. They knew Lani's funeral was planned for later that day.

Yet upon the morning there was no grave. The grass around Amyas Lathrop's plot had been neatly fitted back into place like a toupee, resting lightly on the loosened soil. The digger stood mute and innocent in Gilbert Kapiaho's driveway. He had a story prepared about testing the motor, but it was never needed. The villagers hadn't heard a thing.

For them, events began not long after dawn, when a familiar figure nosed its way alongside the pier. The *Princess Likelike* began life as a car ferry in San Francisco after the Second World War. Her bulbous bow had a hinge and hydraulic lift, exposing the ship's insides like a doll house. Sometimes Captain Mike flipped the switch to startle the children onshore; it looked for all the world as if the *Likelike* was going to devour them. A varied career in the islands saw her serve as everything from floating grandstand to garbage scow. Now in rusting senescence, she hauled supplies out to Kaumaha every Monday and picked up the trash. But on this particular morning her cargo deck had been scrubbed clean. Waiting on the pier as she came alongside were Gilbert and Agnes, Eleanor Lathrop, and Roger. They stood in a tight knot, dressed soberly in black.

The *Likelike*'s bow lifted majestically into the air. A smart black dray emerged decorated with leis, pulled by two chestnut mares with black feathers on their forelocks. The coffin lay on a brass-railed bier, surrounded by orchids and hydrangeas. Gilbert wondered if his granddaughter was watching this odd procession. Captain Mike approached him, twisting his cap in his hand. "I'm damn sorry about all this, Gil. We did the best we could for her."

"I know. I appreciate it."

"If you're ready, we can get moving on the others."

Gilbert raised an eyebrow. "Others?" He looked over Mike's shoulder and saw to his astonishment that the cargo deck was covered with identical polished pine boxes, not as elaborate as Lani's but fine, nonetheless.

"That was my idea," Eleanor said, stepping forward. In the early morning light she seemed very much herself. But her arm rested lightly on Roger's for support. "I thought Lani would want to be with her people. They need to be reinterred anyhow, poor souls."

"But will there be enough room in the churchyard?" Agnes wondered.

"Oh, don't worry about that. I spoke with the State Parks office last week. They're quite happy to let us use as much of the valley as we need. Tanaka's letting us use the heavy equipment on the island and sending over a crew to dig the graves, all thirty-two of them. Lani's will be the thirty-third."

"And he helped us out with the coffins," Roger added.

Gilbert blinked away tears. "Eleanor...I don't know what to say."

"You don't need to say anything. It's their land, after all, hers and theirs. All I ask is that Lani's grave be closest to the house. For all that's happened, I think she would still like that."

Her grandfather nodded slowly. "I think she would."

There weren't enough carts to move all the coffins at once, so it was a piecemeal procession that saw each one hauled along the path through the village and toward the valley. Eleanor returned to the house and watched from her lanai. Roger sat with her. The dark figures with their melancholy burden reminded him of ants carrying twigs. "I wish," he said, "we had enough money to raise some kind of monument."

Eleanor said wryly, "Another statue?"

"God, no." He shuddered. "But they deserve something, don't they?"

"Yes. They'll get a Christian burial. They *were* Christians, after all."

"Were they?"

"Oh, yes." His grandmother was positive. "The very best kind. Christian martyrs."

Roger's eyebrows went up. "But I thought…I mean, I assumed…"

She took his hand. "I know what you thought. But I can't let you believe that anymore. It isn't right, or fair. Not to them. Not to Lani."

Then, as the bodies passed by them one by one, she told him the truth.

———

Mrs. Te Papa heard the sound of heavy equipment, and in her sluggish state she thought of tanks rumbling across a battlefield. She woke with a sense of dread and a vague determination to spread the alarm: *They are coming.*

But when she lifted herself on her elbows and looked out the window, she saw instead a caravan of excavators and back-hoes, each painted alpine white with the distinctive Diamond Head Holdings logo emblazoned on their flanks. They rumbled benignly past.

Still feeling discombobulated, she wrapped herself in a bathrobe and came downstairs in search of coffee. The house seemed quite deserted. Yet, as if by magic, a coffee tray had been deposited in the library. Mrs. Te Papa poured herself a cup and stared out the window.

"Impressive, aren't they?"

It was Judge Chan, beaming brightly under a nest of pink curlers. "Is that coffee? I'll have some. Need to wash down the aspirin." She shot a whimsical glance at the lumbering machinery.

Mrs. Te Papa handed her the pot. "It's so silly," she said, "but when I woke this morning I really thought I was hearing tanks."

"Goodness, no." The judge was surprisingly definite. "Tanks make a *much* different noise. Like chains rolling around in a cement mixer."

This seemed unusually precise. "You've been around them, have you?"

"Oh, yes. There were quite a few in Beijing when I was growing up."

Mrs. Te Papa took a careful sip. "Tiananmen?" she ventured.

"Not for very long. I was gone before the worst of it."

They drank for a few minutes in silence. "Maybe that's why I went into the law," Judge Chan mused. "That tank was the nega-tion of everything—justice, mercy, civilization itself. I always imagined myself standing before it every time I came into court."

Mrs. Te Papa sympathized. "Sometimes," she admitted, "I imagine that all my ancestors are crowded into the room with me. Even if it is only a little office. I'll be trying to give a deposition to the Planning Bureau and there they come tromping in, dozens of them, dressed as warriors and making the most awful racket."

The two ladies laughed. "I suppose each of us has our own methods of encouragement," Judge Chan said. "But you are lucky. You get to defend your people. I wish I could always be so sure of my cause."

"Isn't justice a cause?"

"Perhaps, but it can be a messy one."

"Yes," Mrs. Te Papa mused, fingering the spines of the books absently. "I'm sure it can."

"You're thinking of something," the judge observed. "What is it?"

"I was thinking of how easy it can be to mistake justice for something else. Or vice versa. Just last night, for example, I accused poor Dr. Ackerman of being a stooge for Rodrigo Roxas. As it turns out, I was completely wrong."

The other woman smiled. "I could have told you that. I've spent almost thirty years staring at defendants in the dock. Bob Ackerman is not anybody's stooge. He's proud as the devil and completely impervious to the rest of humanity."

"As I discovered," Mrs. Te Papa agreed. "I also nearly accused Roger Lathrop of complicity in the death of one of his classmates. And, as long as I am being honest, at one point I suspected Lani of blackmail."

The judge's cup froze on its way to her lips. "Blackmailing Roger?"

"No. At first I assumed she was blackmailing Tanaka. But then I realized that was quite impossible." Slowly she withdrew the newspaper cutting from her bathrobe pocket. "I found this on the night of the hearing, tucked in between two library books. Would you care to look at it?"

The judge took it from her and read it silently. Her expression was wooden. "I remember this case," she said at last.

"I thought you would. When I discovered it, I assumed someone was trying to force Tanaka to abandon the sale. He is, as he later admitted, Yakuza. Both Lani and Peter were in this room during the hearing. But that didn't make any sense. If Tanaka was dangerous enough to kill a teenager in cold blood, why wouldn't he do the same to his blackmailer?"

"That seems logical," Judge Chan concurred.

"Thank you. But there was still another objection. How did the clipping end up being left in this room?"

"Surely there's no mystery in that," the judge objected. "Someone passed it to their victim and he hid it in the books."

"Yes, but *why*? Why risk exposure handing over this document in so public a setting, and why was it left here at all?"

Judge Chan was inclined to be dismissive. "You are assuming that the handover was done publicly. But there is no reason to believe it could not have happened when only the blackmailer and victim were in the library."

"On the contrary, if that were the case, the recipient would have taken it away with them. Since it was left here, it had to be because *there was no other choice*."

Chan sat down on the leather chesterfield and balanced her coffee in her lap. "How could that be?" she wondered.

"I asked myself the same question. Then I went back over the events of that evening in my mind. If the exchange was done publicly, I must have witnessed it. But I could not remember anything of the kind. Then, quite by accident, I learned that Roger Lathrop had been in the same class as the murdered boy. Could Roger have been responsible for his death? Or, alternately, could Roger be blackmailing the killer?

"I thought very carefully about his movements. But there was nothing there to help me. Aside from his one speech, he remained in his seat all evening. It was only some time later that I remembered a chance remark made by the bonfire. After

Ogden's outburst, Dr. Ackerman asked if you had any children. Yes, you said, a daughter. And Roger added that she had been in his class."

The judge did not speak. Her lips parted but no sound came out.

"I know what Steven Shimazu was accused of," Mrs. Te Papa said gently. "Roger told me, though he said he did not know the girl's name. I think he was lying. Out of the noblest of motives, to be sure. But I think her name was Gwendolyn Chan."

The judge was only a fraction of Mrs. Te Papa's size, yet even seated in an overstuffed chesterfield, she seemed to radiate danger. Her eyes were basilisk. "There's no proof of that," she said with deadly calm.

"That was the problem, wasn't it? It was her word against his. His father was a state senator, the family was rich. It's an old, old story. Your daughter could have made the accusation public, but she risked ruining her own reputation in the process. No, don't say anything. Let me tell you what I think happened. You knew the truth, but you also knew there was nothing to be done about it. Your sense of justice was outraged. So you, a pillar of the law, went beyond the law to find that justice. You went to the Yakuza. And you ended up putting your case to David Tanaka.

"Tanaka's sense of justice is, I suspect, as acute as yours. He sympathized. He also saw the opportunity to gain the support of an influential judge. So he acted, decisively."

"No!" The word burst from Judge Chan's lips. "It was not like that!"

"How was it, then?" The other woman did not respond, so Mrs. Te Papa continued: "You came here at Tanaka's request, just as I did. But now that I knew of the connection between you, it seemed certain that you had been chosen because you would allow the development to proceed. That meant whomever was blackmailing you was presumably trying to block the sale. And there I was, back to Lani and Peter. But Peter had no connection to the Shimazu story at all, while Lani might easily have learned it from Roger. So I began to imagine a scenario. Lani presents you with the blackmail note, just in time to prevent you from ruling in Tanaka's favor. Instead, you decide to let the villagers vote on the matter—which seems like a victory for Lani. But to preserve the veneer of impartiality, you rule that the statue may remain.

"Maybe Lani demands to see you in order to force you to change your mind about Amyas. Or maybe you had already thought to eliminate this danger to yourself. Either way, you both meet under the statue late at night. You kill her, and then fake the explosion to cover your traces. Nothing could be simpler."

All the color had drained from the judge's face. She stared blankly over her coffee cup. "It's not true," she whispered. "It's *not.*"

Mrs. Te Papa smiled. "I didn't say it was. I just said it was a plausible scenario. But it still didn't explain how she passed you the newspaper cutting, or why it was left in the library. I went back to that moment in my mind. Who could have known the Shimazu story, and used it? The most obvious answer was Roger, but as I said he was in my sight the entire evening. So Roger was out. Then I remembered something. The look on Ogden Lathrop's face when you promised, out on the lanai, that you would not make any decision until you weighed my testimony and Dr. Ackerman's.

"At that moment I think Ogden panicked. He knew the story of Gwendolyn from his son, and naturally assumed Tanaka had pressured you to rubber-stamp the sale. But you did not sound like you were willing to do that. So he took out his newspaper cutting—which I expect he was saving for just such an emergency—and scrawled "I KNOW WHAT YOU DID" across the top. Then he held on to it, waiting to see if it was needed."

Judge Chan swallowed. "How do you suppose he gave me this horrid thing? Isn't it likely he just tucked it into the library books and left it there?"

"I considered that possibility. But why leave it out in the open? No, he gave it to you. And we all watched him do it." She waited for a moment, but the judge simply stared. "In a way it was my fault. During the hearing I suggested that the Lathrops had a responsibility to the villagers that ran with the land, and you seemed receptive to that idea. At once Ogden jumped up and thrust a sheaf of papers under your nose, which he claimed were proof the tenants hadn't paid their rent. The cutting was on top of that pile. You read it, knew what it was. But you couldn't risk leaving the room with it. After all, anyone might ask to see the file. So you waited until no one was looking and shoved it quickly between two books. I'm sure you intended to come back for it later that evening when everyone had gone. But Marnie told us she was in here reading most of the night, and not long after she left, I came in myself and found the paper. Don't you see? You're the only person who could have received the paper, and the only one who had to leave it in the room."

The judge considered this for a few moments. "If what you're saying is true," she said at last, "both Tanaka and Ogden Lathrop expected—indeed *demanded* that I acquiesce to the sale. Instead, I allowed the villagers to vote on the proposal. How can you account for that?"

"Very simply. The blackmail threat didn't work. And Tanaka didn't choose you just to give him what he wanted. He chose you because he knew you'd be fair."

Chan looked startled. "But, Winnie, if you understand that..."

"I think I do. It's the same reason he chose me. David Tanaka is a very unusual man. He is, I'm sure, ruthless in his way, but he has an almost preternatural sense of fairness. I learned that from talking with him. I don't think he pressured you into taking this case. He just asked you to make an honest appraisal. Which was, of course, what Ogden dreaded most." She paused for a moment. "There's only one thing I don't understand. How you and Tanaka, two upright people, could together cause a teenage boy to be beaten to death and left to rot in the woods."

The judge winced as if in pain, but soon rallied. "You're hanging an awful lot on a piece of paper tucked between two books," she answered tartly. "In court I'd call that circumstantial evidence and probably toss it out. Any good lawyer could argue around it in five seconds."

"I'm not a lawyer, Rosalind. I don't want to judge you, and I don't, God forbid, want to trap you. There's no one here but ourselves. Look, let's say that this is just storytelling, like we do with the *keiki*. Not real, just legend. Tell me a story."

This time the silence was absolute. As Mrs. Te Papa watched, the judge's iron composure began to crack. She slumped in her seat. "It was never supposed to happen," she said, so quietly that the other woman had to lean in to hear. "It wasn't what I wanted at all. But I was so terribly angry. Roger never told you what Steven Shimazu actually did, did he? No, of course, he wouldn't have known. Steven was always pestering Gwen, trying to get her to go out with him. She told me later she felt sorry for him—this odd little kid in his chains and cap with his faux gangster swagger. But when it became clear she had no interest, Steven was angry. Told her how big and important he was, how any girl would be lucky to be chosen by him. She actually laughed at that. So that night he drove my daughter out to Na Ala Hele Trail, deep in the woods. She struggled, and he tied her wrists to a tree. It was past dark and there was no one around for miles. He raped her, not once but several times. Many times. When he was finished, he cut her down and drove her home. Left her in my driveway, shaking and almost unable to walk." She paused, took a sip of coffee. The cup shivered in her hand.

"For weeks she told me nothing at all. I saw she was limping but I assumed it was a field hockey injury. I could tell she was depressed, but what teenage girl isn't? I was very foolish. My husband had died years before, so there was no one else to talk to. Not until several months had passed did she finally tell me. But by then there was no proof, nothing but her word. I contacted the school, and they referred me to the police. I contacted the police, and they said there was nothing they could do without evidence. So there I was.

"Gwen didn't get better. Her body healed, but her mind was broken. She became quiet, withdrawn. Her grades fell. She dreaded going to class each day. I offered to transfer her to a different school, but it was senior year. There was nothing to be done. Gradually, I grew even more afraid. There was something new inside her, something dangerous. A recklessness. Like driving through red lights and not checking to see if there were any cars. I became convinced that if she continued to see this boy Steven Shimazu in school, she would eventually kill either herself or him."

Mrs. Te Papa shook her head in sympathy. "I can't imagine how must it have been to look into that smug, smiling face every day. I might have done the same."

"You do understand. That's good. So, you see, I couldn't lose my daughter over this. Or stand by and see her destroy her life. I went to a man I had once seen in my court, a small-time racketeer whose child custody case I decided. He was a villain, I suppose, but wonderful with his kids. I quite liked him. I asked for an introduction. Two days later I was sitting in David Tanaka's office, pouring out my problems to him.

"It was David who came up with the plan. If this boy Steven was so intent on becoming Yakuza, let him think they were recruiting him. He'd do anything they liked. So Tanaka sent a few of his men to meet with him, and they came back saying the boy was entirely willing. The plan was to meet at a prearranged spot, then drive him out to Na Ala Hele Trail, the same spot where he violated Gwen. I liked the symmetry of that. They would march him at gunpoint into the woods and give him a solid beating. That was all. Nothing permanent or scarring, but enough to keep him in hospital for a few weeks and dead scared for life."

"Justice," Mrs. Te Papa said.

"Exactly. The plan worked perfectly at first. Steven met the men and practically jumped into their car. They drove him into the woods, telling him it was an initiation ritual. Finally, when they reached the trail, he understood. He jumped out of the car as it was still moving and tried to run for it. Tanaka's men chased him down; it wasn't hard. But that small act of defiance angered them and they were rougher than they planned to be. It was sheer accident his neck was broken. Tanaka was furious when he heard."

"And you?"

"Oh, I was devastated." She shook her head, sighed. "The whole point was to punish him in such a way that he'd be too scared to say anything afterward. Let everyone think he'd blundered too close to the Yakuza and got burnt. Which is what they *did* think, though not how we intended."

"You were lucky that the media followed the Yakuza connection, rather than tying his death to your daughter."

"That wasn't luck, that was David. He deliberately leaked the story to protect Gwendolyn and me."

Mrs. Te Papa marveled at this. "Extraordinary," she breathed.

"He felt it was his responsibility, given what occurred. There was no direct evidence of Yakuza involvement, just Steven's own bragging. The police concluded he'd gotten mixed up with some gang and that was that."

"How is Gwendolyn now?" Mrs. Te Papa asked solicitously.

"Better. She'd already gotten her acceptance letter to Cal Tech, and I thought the change of scenery would help. It did. She graduated with honors and is finishing up a master's in industrial engineering at Stanford." There was more than a hint of pride in the judge's voice. "But there've been no serious relationships. Not many casual ones, either, as far as I know. I try not to ask. She's very career-focused, and I'm not going to turn into one of the Asian mamas whining about grandchildren, but...I worry."

"It's a mother's job to worry," Mrs. Te Papa consoled, "and her right. If my opinion matters, I don't blame you for what happened. I'm not sure I can blame Tanaka, either."

"Oh, please don't! It was such a horrible thing to have happen. I know it haunts him still. As it does me." She lowered her gaze.

"What about Ogden?" Mrs. Te Papa asked, then looked around. "Where *is* Ogden? I haven't seen him since we arrived."

"I saw his wife. She said he was wrapping up some business in Kona and wouldn't make the funeral. I get the impression he was warned off."

"By whom, I wonder?"

Judge Chan gave her a tentative smile. "Perhaps you can use those marvelous powers of deduction and find out," she said playfully. "I am quite impressed, you know. But I still wonder why you never showed the newspaper clipping to the police."

"I considered doing so," Mrs. Te Papa admitted. "But blackmail is a dirty business. Innocent people may get hurt. I wanted to know whether it had anything to do with the murder before I got the police involved. Until then, it was, I suppose, a *private* secret. And still is." She handed the clipping back to the judge.

"Thank you, Winnie." The paper disappeared into her purse. "I was serious a moment ago. I've read every murder mystery I can get my hands on, but when it comes to the real thing, I'm stumped. You really are good at this."

Mrs. Te Papa smiled modestly. "Thanks, but the truth is I would not have become involved except that the boy Peter Pauahi was accused. He is one of my people, and I think he is innocent. So, I had to help him. My job is helping other Hawaiians, you see." But she pondered the judge's words for a moment. "Many years ago the chief of Honolulu police thought I had a talent for understanding people. Not quite the same thing as detection. I don't know anything about cigar ash or blood-stains. Maybe, though, if I understand all the people involved in this affair and the relations between them, one bright thread will stand out among the rest. Because what is murder, really, except the end result of all the human interactions that preceded it? Understand them, and you'll understand the crime. That's my hope, anyhow."

"Bravo!" Judge Chan applauded.

———

Ogden Lathrop was not, after all, in Kona. He was in Honolulu at the office of his lawyer, a long-suffering man named Bludge. The office was small and dim, its windows facing the brick wall of a Chinese restaurant across the street. Stacks of paper covered every surface, including Bludge's chair. He perched himself on the edge of his desk. "Ogg," he said plaintively, "I don't see what you expect me to do here. I'm not a title attorney. Even if I was, I don't think there's a law anywhere that says you can force someone to buy a property after you misrepresented it to them."

"I didn't misrepresent it!" Ogden shouted. "I thought it was a clean sale. I had no idea about that trustee thing."

Bludge forbore reminding him that he had advised legal counsel on precisely that point, only for Lathrop to scream in his face. "Anyway," he said, trying to bring the conversation back to some recognizable plane, "now that the land is held up by the state, I doubt he could buy it even if he wanted to. And you couldn't sell, once the tax lien is placed."

Ogden's feral mind worked rapidly. "Couldn't I sue him for tying up the property and making it impossible to raise the tax money?"

"There's no law against negotiating, Ogg. Especially when it's in good faith, as this seems to be. And I don't know if you've heard much about Tanaka's reputation—"

"He's a murderer!" Ogden exploded. "A damned, dirty gangster. And I know that for a fact."

"Then why the hell are you talking about suing him? Leave him alone, dude."

But Ogden Lathrop was congenitally incapable of leaving anything alone, man or object, and proceeded to demonstrate that fact by taking up another half hour of his attorney's time. Bludge repeated the same platitudes, taking comfort in the knowledge that these were billable hours. Except Ogden rarely paid his bills.

When Lathrop finally emerged onto Herbert Street his foul mood had entirely claimed him. He swore lustily at the bicyclist who dodged past and turned to vent the full measure of his fury at a black Escalade that pulled up onto the curb, nearly running him down. His mouth was still open, a denunciatory breath lodged in his throat, when three men jumped from the moving vehicle and, in a single acrobatic movement, tossed him head-first into the back. The Escalade accelerated onto Kapahulu Avenue and disappeared into traffic.

When Ogden recovered his wits, he found he was staring into the expressionless eyes of Kaito. Tanaka's bodyguard was dressed as impeccably as ever. Not a single strand of misplaced hair suggested that he had just kidnapped a two-hundred-pound man right off a busy Honolulu street. "What is this?" Ogden demanded. "Where are you taking me?"

"Mr. Tanaka hopes you will give him the pleasure of accompanying him to the funeral at Kaumaha." It was the first time Ogden heard Kaito speak, and the voice was soft and surprisingly pleasant.

"Why the hell couldn't he have just asked me?"

"Apologies. Mr. Tanaka is very pressed for time. He communicated his wish to speak to you urgently on a matter of business."

Now that was more like it! Ogden leaned back in the leather seat and smiled inwardly. Tanaka was finally coming around. For a brief moment he had worried about handing the judge that cutting—it seemed a trifle, well, reckless. But now he knew he had been right. Thugs like Tanaka only understood force. Ogden had shown him where the whip handle lay, and patiently waited until Tanaka got there himself.

Wrapped in these comforting thoughts, Ogden was unsurprised when the Escalade made a sharp left onto Earhart Field. A crisp white helicopter was waiting, its blades already beginning to turn. Just like the movies, he thought. Kaito helped him out and the two other men formed a cordon around him as they walked. When the helicopter door slid open, Tanaka was there with a smile on his face.

"Mr. Lathrop! Ogden, if I may. Thank you so much for coming."

Ogden might have replied that he didn't have much choice, but his peevishness was overcome by greed. He answered the smile with one of his own. "I'm glad we have this chance to talk," he said.

"As am I. Which reminds me. Here." He handed Ogden a headset. As if on cue, the blades accelerated into a roar.

Ogden donned the headset and the noise stilled at once.

Tanaka's voice spoke calmly into his ear. "Ever been in one of these before?"

"Once. Did a flyover tour in Kauai a few years ago."

"Good. Some people find it jarring, but I didn't think you'd be one of them. Just in case, there's sick bags under the seat."

Ogden tried to look disdainful, but a moment later when the helicopter lurched into the sky he began to have second thoughts. They climbed rapidly. After a few minutes there was nothing to be seen from the windows except open sea. In his ear, Tanaka kept up a steady stream of chatter. Ogden responded appropriately but began to wonder when the other man would get to the point. The journey to Kaumaha couldn't take more than half an hour, and Tanaka was resolutely discussing golf.

Finally, when he could stand it no longer, Ogden broke in: "Your bodyguard told me you wanted to talk business. I'm ready to listen."

"That's very good. Listening is exactly what I need from you right now." It was disconcerting to see Tanaka's lips move and have his voice resonate inside one's head. Almost like mind control. "I want you to know," Tanaka went on, "that yesterday morning I paid all your outstanding taxes to the State of Hawaii. You now own Kaumaha free and clear. I also persuaded them to hold off on declaring it a state park, for the time being."

Ogden's mouth fell open. "That is...wonderful," he managed.

"Let me be clear. Just because I paid the taxes, that gives me no claim on the property. You can choose to dispose of it how you wish."

"I'd still like to make a deal," Ogden said quickly. "If you're interested."

"Yes, indeed I am. But not with you."

There was a pause, as both men's headsets crackled with static. "I don't understand," said Ogden at last.

"Do you know the penalty among the Yakuza for betraying another's secrets?" Tanaka asked him pleasantly. "I thought you might, since you researched us so carefully. The bottom three fingers of the right hand are considered essential to hold a sword. So we start by chopping them off. It is called *yubitsume*. But that is for minor transgressions. The greater the dishonor, the more we take. First the hand, then the wrist, then the whole arm. Betraying a secret is the second-worst crime. The worst is profiting from that betrayal." He turned in his seat to look at Ogden, whose face was pale and glistening with sweat. "For that, we go all out. Tie you down and start hacking away with a fire axe. There's a butcher shop in Kalihi that we use for this sort of thing. It takes a while, depending on your size. I've gotten pretty good at gauging. With all that blubber I'd give you about three hours. But we'll see."

Ogden's body seemed to have collapsed upon itself, and now looked like a gelatin mold in vaguely human form. "I don't understand... What did I do?"

"You tried to blackmail a high court judge. And you caused me great embarrassment with a person I admire." Tanaka did not say anything more of his meeting with Winnie Te Papa. The headset whistled with a sigh. "How could you hold me in such small account? Did you really think I would let this insult stand?" He did not sound angry, only puzzled.

Ogden nervously ran a hand over his glistening face. "I'm sorry. I misunderstood. We can still make a deal, a good deal, anything you want," he burbled.

"I have no interest in doing deals with you. I intend to resume negotiations with your son. And heir."

The last word scythed through Ogden. "You can't do this!" he bleated. "I haven't done anything wrong! It's not fair!"

Tanaka appeared to consider. "You may be right," he answered. "It doesn't seem entirely fair. After all, you're *not*

Yakuza. But on the other hand, you are a blackmailer and a scumbag, and the world will be a better place without you—my world, especially. Let's make this easy." He flicked a hand at Kaito, who leapt from his seat at once and disarmed the crossbar on Ogden's door. The frigid wind hit Ogden like a blow to the face. Casually, Kaito released his shoulder restraints and began tipping Ogden toward the void. "Oh, my God! Oh, my God!" Ogden screamed, his voice high and shrill. "You can't! No! *Please!*"

Tanaka's voice was still in his ear. "Sure I can," he said calmly. "No one saw you on Herbert Street. No one saw you board this chopper. You just walked out of your lawyer's office and disappeared. Look down."

That was easy, as Ogden's head and shoulders were now completely outside the aircraft. "At this altitude," Tanaka told him, "your body will flatten on impact. The ocean under you is part of the equatorial current. That means whatever is dropped into it gets pulled out into the Pacific and winds up in the Great Pacific Garbage Patch. Personally, I can't think of a more fitting place for you."

Ogden Lathrop had now lost all coherent speech. He was blubbering, screaming, struggling feebly against the iron grip of the hands that held him. The wind swallowed his cries. *"I'll do anything! Anything!"* But he could feel his body slipping through their grasp. He was pouring out of the helicopter like milk from a jug.

The aircraft lurched again, and Ogden experienced a moment of weightlessness. His eyes were closed in terror. He was falling, moving through an infinite vacuum. His mouth was opened to scream, but the air rushed in and stole it. Then, suddenly, he landed. He lay facedown on the floor of the helicopter. The fall had only lasted a second.

"Get up," the voice in his ear commanded.

Ogden rushed to comply, but his bladder had let him down. He feebly tried to cover the spreading stain with both hands.

"Never mind that," Tanaka said. "Keep your hands dry." The door was still open and wind shrieked around them. Kaito, back in his seat and perfectly composed, handed Ogden a clipboard with a sheaf of papers on it. "This is a transfer of title," his headset told him. "You are hereby relinquishing all claim on Kaumaha Island, its buildings, outbuildings, air rights, navigable rights, and resources, and transferring it to—"

"You?"

"No. Your son, Roger. I will not speak with you ever again. You may remain on the island if your family consents. But you will absent yourself whenever I visit. From this moment you have no interest in the property at all. All matters relating to Kaumaha will be handled between Roger and myself. Is that clear? Very good. You may sign."

Ogden signed willingly, gratefully, joyously. His hand was slick, whether from sweat or piss, he didn't know.

"There is a towel and a change of clothes in the plastic bag in front of you," Tanaka told him. "Wipe yourself off and put them on. Place the soiled ones in the bag and tie it." Ogden started to thank him—for the clothes, for his life—but Tanaka had already taken off his headset. He shouted something in Japanese to Kaito, who laughed rather cruelly and shouted back. The two men ignored him for the rest of the flight.

———

Tanaka was lighthearted, joyful. What he had shouted was: *"That was a good idea of yours about the spare clothes and the trash bag."*

To which Kaito answered: *"It wasn't my idea. The pilot said he wasn't going wash the seats again, not after last time. The smell was terrible."*

Chapter 14

HALE KANU, RESTING PLACE

Just past noon a storm cloud rumbled over the hills of Kaumaha, blotting the sun and covering the valley with a fine canopy of spray. The diggers paused in their work as men wiped their faces, sipped coffee from thermoses, and listened to the machine-gun rattle of rain against metal roofs. Then, just as abruptly, it passed, and the ground glistened as if Lono had strewn it with jewels.

Mrs. Te Papa took shelter under a large banyan and watched them as they worked. The process had a vaguely agricultural air, like grim seedlings planted in the ground. Three or four graves were dug at once. Then the excavators retreated and the golf carts trundled up, each carrying a polished pine box. An elderly man in a black cassock—a Methodist minister from Hilo, she heard—said a prayer over each grave, solemnly raising his cross before moving onto the next. The backhoes waited a respectful few moments before moving up and shifting the soil back into place. The burial mounds made long symmetrical rows in the earth.

Could the children sense what was happening? Was there any sigh of relief as the ground closed over them once again? It sounded fanciful, until she thought of old Mr. Po. She would like to ask him.

By four p.m. the melancholy business was done, and the excavators rumbled back toward the village. Mrs. Te Papa saw the Lathrops emerge from the house, Eleanor taking her grandson's hand while Marnie followed. Judge Chan and Dr. Ackerman walked side by side, deep in conversation. Then she saw Tanaka and Kaito, dressed in identical dark pinstripes, with the unmistakable figure of Ogden Lathrop between them. He seemed to cringe. Mrs. Te Papa fell in step behind. The odd little procession made its way down the hill, through the forest glade and into the village, where the doors of the chapel were open to receive them. Gilbert Kapiaho stood at the entrance, Agnes at his side. Her round face looked pinched. She embraced Eleanor fiercely, then drew in Roger, and even Marnie. Gilbert and Tanaka exchanged curt nods. Everyone ignored Ogden.

The tiny chapel was completely full, with congregants lining every wall. Fortunately, Marybeth had saved her a seat at the rear. Mrs. Te Papa noted with approval that she was dressed in charcoal gray with a discreet black hat that might have been her grandmother's. "The governor is here!" Marybeth whispered as her employer sat down.

Mrs. Te Papa did not crane her neck, but she managed to look around. Yes, indeed the governor was present, along with several state senators, a cordon of police, and the mayor of Honolulu. Kaumaha had become famous. The sleepy island with its ramshackle village and faded manor house had now become the latest battleground of an age-old struggle between native and settler, past and present, meaning and memory. But today was about honoring the dead.

A children's choir, borrowed from Kailua Congregational, rose and began to sing. The song was ancient, older than this chapel or even the English settlement on the islands. It touched a distant chord from Mrs. Te Papa's own childhood:

"How firm a foundation, ye saints of the Lord,

Is laid for your faith in His excellent word!"

She tilted her head back and let the words wash over her. Suddenly she was eight years old again, and her grandmother was smoothing the pleats on her gingham dress.

"The flame shall not hurt thee; I only design
Thy dross to consume, and thy gold to refine."

No, it was not the flame that had hurt Lani Kapiaho. Someone—very likely one of the people in this room right now—had ended her life. Mrs. Te Papa looked from one to the other, asking the same question each time. But the answer seemed ludicrous, impossible. Now that Mrs. Te Papa knew them better, they no longer seemed like pieces on a game board. She saw them lit with the warm glow of humanity inside them: a brokenhearted mother protecting her child, a courageous young man, two old friends trying to find a quiet place to die together, and a gangster with feudal ideas of honor and justice. Ogden was, of course, unspeakable, and his wife remained an enigma. Yet what could any of them hope to gain, when so much had already been lost?

Of course, there was one more suspect. Peter Pauahi was still in a Honolulu jail, but Mrs. Te Papa noticed his parents seated not far from the Kapiahos. They wept openly. A nice couple, she thought. Odd that they had produced such an unsatisfactory son. Perhaps he killed Lani, after all. But even as she considered that possibility, she rejected it once again. There was a defeated look in his eyes that day; if he had been concealing anything, she would have known. Or so she hoped.

The Methodist minister came forward and offered a short prayer. Mrs. Te Papa bowed her head, but her thoughts were still moving among the characters in this strange little tragedy. Was there anyone left? It was always like that in books—that one person whom you never suspected who was right in front of you all along. But aside from herself, the only other people in the house not yet considered were Tanaka's man Kaito and, of course, Marybeth. Kaito looked capable of almost anything, but there was a rigid discipline to him. He would not act unless his master ordered it, and she could not picture Tanaka doing so. In fact, she could not really imagine it of any of them.

This was not wishful thinking. Mrs. Te Papa had spent the better part of fifty years counseling her people. She sat in jail cells with men who had murdered their wives, friends, even—in one horrifying case—children. She arrived in barrooms when blood was still fresh on the floor and comforted both the survivors and perpetrator. Once she was summoned to a house in a posh neighborhood and found a man staggering in the driveway with a lit blowtorch while his family cowered in the garage. There were, she knew, certain kinds of people who were predisposed to take life. Some were violent, others irrationally fearful, and a few who genuinely enjoyed causing pain. But the ordinary person did not murder for any of those reasons—because, of course, the ordinary person did not murder. If they did, it was not themselves but the circumstances that were extraordinary.

"Melveen Sai," she muttered to herself. A lady in her bridge club at the First Episcopal. Midforties, rather plump, unremarkable. Two children, a girl and a boy, both in their teens. Husband was an accountant for Edward Jones. Melveen poisoned him by mixing her diet pills with his blood pressure meds. *"I sat next to him on the couch watching* Wheel of Fortune, *waiting for him to die."* She told Mrs. Te Papa this one night after swearing her to secrecy. Her husband, she discovered, had been molesting both children for years.

For a normal person to commit murder, Mrs. Te Papa reasoned, they had to believe that there was *no other choice.* Then murder became a rational decision, perhaps even a necessary one. But what could have prompted anyone to kill Lani Kapiaho? She had no great wealth or secrets to protect. She held no one's destiny in her hands. There could be no sane motive for this crime. And the old lady had no doubt: of the persons she encountered at Kaumaha, some might qualify as eccentric, boorish, or mysterious, but all were eminently sane.

Yet the coffin on its bier was an objective reality. So, too, were the thirty-odd graves freshly dug in the valley. *"For My thoughts are not your thoughts, nor are your ways My ways..."* the minister reminded her. He was quoting Isaiah, a common verse for reckoning with unthinkable tragedy. Mrs. Te Papa supplied another: *"The secret things belong unto the Lord our God, but those things which are revealed belong unto us and to our children forever..."* A powerful thought, that. The truth, once known, cannot be unknown. That is the will of God. So when the sacrificial site was revealed, a new and dangerous truth emerged.

Benedictory music began playing, and Mrs. Te Papa realized with some embarrassment the service had ended. It took a few moments for her to gather her belongings and adjust her muumuu—she was not slow, merely deliberate—as the church emptied around her. Marybeth departed in search of Roger. But when Mrs. Te Papa finally looked up, a small figure waited.

"Could I have a word?"

Agnes Kapiaho stood awkwardly, turning a black pocketbook over in her hands. Her round, moon-shaped face seemed designed by nature to beam, but today it was bunched up and fretful. One could hardly blame her. "Of course," Mrs. Te Papa said. "I am very sorry for your loss. What can I do for you?"

Agnes threw an anxious glance toward the door, but they were quite alone. Her husband had gone with the body. "They'll need me for the procession," she said quickly, "but I wanted to talk to you before I go. Have you heard what Detective Roundtree has been saying?"

"I haven't spoken with the detective since I left Kaumaha."

"Oh! I thought perhaps...well, I heard a rumor...that is,

Grace Pauahi said you've been trying to help her son. Find who really killed our Lani."

Mrs. Te Papa nodded gravely. "So you don't believe it was Peter?" she asked.

"Of course not! He's a *moke* and a prize idiot, and I wish Lani had never met him, but he's no killer."

"I agree."

"But that's just it. Yesterday the detective came by and spoke with Gilbert. He said… Oh, it's horrible! He said there was no question Lani set the explosion herself. Her prints were on the blast boxes, or whatever they call them."

Mrs. Te Papa made a startled exclamation. "Roundtree said that? You are sure?"

"Yes, absolutely. Now the detective thinks maybe Lani and Peter did it together, or he convinced her somehow. But I know that isn't true. I saw her face that night, after she got home. She was furious with him. Said never to speak his name to her again. I never knew why, though."

"Because she had discovered Peter was being bribed by one of Tanaka's competitors," Mrs. Te Papa explained. "'Save Kaumaha' was a front."

Agnes Kapiaho did not look surprised. She nodded thoughtfully. "That fits, then."

"With what?"

Agnes did not answer immediately. She cast another nervous glance toward the door, then began digging though the contents of her purse. "Do you need a tissue?" Mrs. Te Papa offered.

"No, no." Her tiny hands rooted about in the crevices and finally emerged with a sheet of notebook paper, folded. "I haven't shown this to anyone. Not Detective Roundtree. Not even my own husband. I didn't want them to think less of her. But if Peter really is in trouble…well, you just read it and tell me what you think."

Mrs. Te Papa unfolded the paper. The breath caught in her throat. "Where did you find this?" she asked quietly.

"It was on the floor next to Lani's desk. I didn't see it until after the police left."

Mrs. Te Papa recognized the same strong, clear hand that had made annotations to Dr. Ackerman's book. Her lips moved with the words in green ink:

Dearest Gram and Gramps,
    I think this is probably the best way. Please don't feel too bad, and don't blame Peter. It's not his fault. There's nothing left for me in this world of lies. I'm sorry

So Eleanor had been right. Lani was determined to end her life and set the truth free. Maybe she changed her mind, tried to run. But it was too late. The stone, making a high arc through the sky, came down and claimed her.

Agnes thought the same. "When I found this, I figured— well, I don't know what I figured. But everyone kept saying Lani was killed by someone else. Something about the angle of the blow. And if that were true, then maybe this letter didn't mean anything—she might have just been venting steam."

"But now that there is proof she set the explosion herself," Mrs. Te Papa finished, "you feel you must tell the police."

The other woman made an expressive gesture with her hands. "I don't know *what* to do. It looks, doesn't it, like there was no murder at all? And if not, then that boy Peter must be released at once. And the shadow over the Lathrops can finally lift. Oh, it's been monstrous, going up to that house very day, wondering if one of them might have—but this saves them, don't you see? It must."

There was an earnestness in her voice that reminded Mrs. Te Papa of Lani herself. Like her granddaughter, Agnes Kapiaho was caught between two worlds. "Ye-es," Mrs. Te Papa said slowly, "it does seem as if we were all wrong."

"Do you think that if I show it to them, the police might keep the contents secret? I don't want it getting out. Not more than it has to."

Mrs. Te Papa made a noncommittal sound. Exculpatory evidence like this—if indeed that was what it was—might lead the police to close their case. The girl was overwrought. The knowledge of what lay buried beneath the statue, coupled with the perfidy of those around her, became too much to bear. Mrs. Te Papa took a step back from this solution and paused to admire it. Neat, logical, almost beautiful in its pathos. No need for blackmailers or moles or murderers blundering around in the dark. Just a terrible tragedy and everyone telling the truth. "Do you think I could take this with me?" she wondered. "Just for a few hours. Then we can talk to Detective Roundtree together."

"Oh, *yes*," said Agnes, relieved. "That would be such a comfort, thank you."

Mrs. Te Papa pocketed the note. "I will join you at the grave in a moment," she said.

But after the other woman left, she did not move. Slowly, she pulled the letter out again and examined it. Simple and straightforward. But one detail seemed incongruous. The abrupt end after *sorry*. Who would write a suicide note and forget to sign it, or even put in a period? An anguished voice echoed in Mrs. Te Papa's mind: *"Good God, if I could open my veins right now and drain out every precious polluted drop of Lathrop blood..."* Lani had known the truth by then. Was that presentiment, or warning? Other voices crowded Mrs. Te Papa's thoughts: Eleanor's, Judge Chan's, even Peter Pauahi's. *She said everyone on this island was a liar, that none of us were who she thought we were....* Yet one voice was clearer than the rest, and it might not even have been real. Duke Kahanamoku, sitting in his dusty office somewhere between Honolulu and Hades, studying her intently with his dark, intelligent eyes. She could feel him watching her now.

Mrs. Te Papa stood irresolute, gazing with sightless eyes at the colored patterns crisscrossing the polished pine floor of the nave. Suicide…or murder? From somewhere came the distant echo of a hymn. She returned to herself with a start. They were laying Lani to rest, and it would not do to be absent. If she hurried she could reach them before it was over, melt into the crowd at graveside; it could not be more than a mile…

Her body froze in the act of turning, with one hand still balanced on the pew rail. Not more than a mile to the valley. And half again to Amyas's statue. How long would it take? But she was an old, fat lady—honesty was one pleasure she allowed herself—and for a younger, fitter set of legs, it could not take more than…fifteen minutes? Yes, possibly. But one must be sure. Did she have her watch? No. Marybeth had been insistent. The dreaded "smart" phone had a clock. Did it also have a second hand? Of course not. Mrs. Te Papa fumbled with the thing for several minutes, until miraculously she discovered something called "stopwatch." It would measure to the half-second. For the first time in her life, Mrs. Te Papa regarded the device with something like approval. They were allies now. It was necessary to be precise in such matters, she knew.

Especially for a charge of murder.

—

Roger Lathrop stood by the grave of his cousin, a whirlwind of thoughts in his head. He was remembering when he and Lani played in the tide pools as children, skipping from one to the other and peering into the depths. *Can you see all the way to the bottom?* Roger could not. Everything seemed murky now, stirred up. Lani's death—*murder*, he reminded himself—and selling Kaumaha and thirty-two bodies that had risen from the earth and now, improbably, rested there again. Amyas Lathrop, a serial killer! It was incredible. Yet Roger had taken it better than his grandmother expected. Yes, it was a formidable shock, but there had been so many shocks in the last week. The reverend's perfidies, at least, happened a long time ago. But why had Eleanor looked at him like that? Did she have some crazy idea of tainted blood running in families?

He could feel her eyes on him now. Roger looked past her and saw his father, still sandwiched between Tanaka and Kaito. He would give a lot to know what the three of them discussed on the trip over. There was something about his father that reminded Roger of a very small boy who has just been chastened. He avoided looking at the grave and stared at his shoes instead.

"I am the resurrection and the life, he that believes in me..." Marybeth's hand slipped into his and pressed gently. She could feel his distress, even if she misunderstood its cause. He looked sideways at her, nodded. Here, at least, was something real, something he could cling to. Marybeth had known about his connection to the Shimazu boy, yet still never suspected him. Nor of this death, either. Roger was truly touched. Then, over her shoulder, he saw something alarming. That big Hawaiian woman, Mrs. Te Papa, was moving up the path in long strides. She did not even turn to look at them as she passed. Her head craned forward and she swung her arms with abandon. She was not actually running, but there was an urgency in her gait that suggested she would if she could. In other circumstances she might have looked ridiculous, but the word that flashed in Roger's mind was not ridiculous at all.

Nemesis.

Now why had he thought of that old Agatha Christie novel? He had a collection tucked away in the attic. He remembered the scene: Mrs. Marple appearing in the window of old Mr. Rafiel's bungalow wrapped in a fluffy pink scarf but with eyes like cold steel.

Roger felt a pang of unease, though he could not have said why.

Chapter 15

MANAWA MĀLIE, AN INTERLUDE

It was evening now. Two old women sat on the western lanai, fanning themselves with memorial programs, watching the sunset.

"It was a beautiful service," Mrs. Te Papa said.

"It was," Mrs. Lathrop agreed. "You missed the burial, though."

"I'm sorry. I had to take care of something first."

Mrs. Lathrop didn't ask the obvious question. She looked out at the sky instead. Only a sliver of golden light remained. They watched the Pacific claim it, leaving behind a mourning sky of deepest purple. "Always loved this time of day," she mused. "Never wanted to miss it, even when I was a girl. Now I watch them every night."

"It's a fine idea," Mrs. Te Papa agreed.

"Always different, that's the wonder. I thought to myself: here is a painting on God's canvas, made just for me. Isn't that silly?"

Slowly the other woman shook her head. "No, it is not silly."

"I tried to teach my boy Ogden. Took him out here, told him all the old stories of Lono and Hina. I failed there. Too late now, I guess." Eleanor sighed. "Ah, well, just listen to the old bat wishing for more time. But there's never enough, is there?"

"There is still your grandson," Mrs. Te Papa said comfortingly. "He understands."

"He does. Lani did, too." She was quiet for a moment. "Did you ever think of having a family yourself, Winnie? Sorry, didn't mean to pry."

But Mrs. Te Papa was not offended. "I had a husband," she answered. "We were married for almost forty years. I wanted children, as one does. We tried many times. Perhaps now it would be different. But back then there were—complications. I spoke with doctors. I spoke with healers. I tried herbs and roots and teas and sitting in strange positions. Nothing worked." She shrugged. "Later, as I came to know my husband better, I decided this was a blessing. Winston was a very disappointing man. As a husband. And as a father."

"But I thought you said... *Ah.*" The old woman nodded shrewdly.

"He was a big man with a big laugh. The kind you always want at a party. He flirted outrageously with old *kupunas* and little girls and everyone in between. I figured it was just his charm—those big arms that embraced everyone. I should have known. His appetites were not a normal man's. The luncheonettes banned us eventually—he could demolish a buffet singlehandedly." She sighed, shook her head. "I heard rumors. But the truth was worse than I could have imagined. He screwed like he ate, great bunches of women, friends' wives, high school girls, and haole tourists just off the boat. But the worst was..."

"Your best friend?" Eleanor guessed.

"Her daughter."

"Jesus Christ."

"She was only fourteen. Came crying to her mother afterward. But they were good Catholics, so there was nothing to be done except wait. Then the child was born and the poor girl died herself a few years later. Drowned in Kaneohe Bay. They said it was an accident." Mrs. Te Papa's face darkened. "I hated my husband then. He wanted to bring the child into our house, but I refused. How could I live with such shame? The little girl was three already. Everyone would know the truth. I told him to give me money, which I gave the child's grandmother, my friend. And so it went for many years, until my husband died."

"And the girl?"

"She went to HCC on a scholarship, but it was difficult when she graduated. Not a lot of jobs except the hotels, and she was too smart for that. So I asked her to come work for me about five years ago. I was her godmother, after all. Her grandmother's best friend. Marybeth has been with me ever since." Mrs. Te Papa sighed. "Some days I think I will tell her. Perhaps I will."

The light faded from purple to blue. The ladies sat in companionable silence, content to let the night come. "Thank you for that," Eleanor said finally.

"I would prefer…"

"Don't worry. I'll take it to my grave." She chuckled. "Isn't this fun? They say you hit a certain age and become a child again. Right now we could be a couple of teenagers out on the porch exchanging secrets."

"Our secrets are more interesting than theirs," Mrs. Te Papa said.

"True." Eleanor thought for a moment. "Tell me another," she demanded.

"Isn't it your turn?"

"I showed you Amyas's diary. That's worth at least ten secrets. Plus, I'm dying. Humor me."

Mrs. Te Papa chuckled. "Very well, one more secret. But this one you know already—or would, if you ever stopped to think about it. You were right. Lani did blow up the statue. Her fingerprints were on the blast caps."

Eleanor's hands gripped her chair. But she said merely, "That's not a secret. I've said so all along."

"Yes, but now we have proof. It happened just as you

thought. Lani was probably horrified by what you told her about Amyas, and resentful that you insisted she keep it from Roger. Not long after, she learned that Peter was taking bribes from a rival developer. 'Save Kaumaha' was a fake. These were two formidable shocks. As she herself said, the two people she trusted most had lied to her."

"I'll never forgive myself," Eleanor agreed sadly.

"Then came the bonfire, where Ogden confirmed her worst fears. I can't imagine what was going through the poor girl's head. Feeling unwanted and betrayed by both the Lathrops and the villagers—and, worse yet, hearing she was the author of their misfortunes simply by being born. You wondered if she might have committed suicide. She did, in fact, consider doing so, and left a note which her grandparents later found. But the note was *unfinished*. You see what that means? A different idea must have come to her. She promised you she would never tell Roger about Amyas. But if she destroyed the statue, she wouldn't have to. At the end I think Lani was overcome with a passion for truth. She could not leave it buried any longer. So she came up from the village…"

"You remember, I saw her."

"No. The person you saw was Peter Pauahi."

For the first time, Eleanor was surprised. "What?"

"It was nighttime, and you were looking down from the lanai. I noticed the same effect myself yesterday. You can only see the top of someone's head and a bit of their clothes. Lani and Peter wore nearly identical outfits: a gray shirt and shorts. Their hair is similar. By the time you came out onto the lanai, Lani had already blown up the statue. You couldn't hear because of deafness, and your bedroom faces the wrong direction. But Peter heard the explosion and followed immediately. You told Detective Roundtree that you saw only one person, whom you thought was Lani, go up the path. No one came down afterward.

Which means that by the time you saw Peter pass by, Lani's murderer must have already returned to the house. Otherwise, you would have seen them pass under the lanai."

Eleanor was thinking. "So if she was murdered, it had to have been sometime between when Peter heard the explosion and when I came out. By which time her killer was already back in the house, safe and sound. But Peter passed by about ten minutes after I sat down. That's a pretty narrow window of time."

"Exactly. Say about fifteen minutes. Which means that the killer was either with her when the explosion took place or arrived immediately after, and her murder must have occurred no more than five minutes after that. And that fact is tremendously important."

"Why?"

Mrs. Te Papa leaned back in her chair. "Detective Roundtree once said there were three possibilities. First, Lani set the explosion herself and was murdered afterward. Second, she witnessed the explosion and was killed by the arsonist. Third, someone murdered her first and staged the explosion to cover their traces. We now know which is correct: Lani *did* set the blast, and was killed almost immediately afterward by someone who witnessed it. So the statue *had* to be the motive. Or at least the proximate cause."

"You're saying she was murdered by someone who saw what she did and was so incensed that they brained her?"

"Exactly, the five-minute gap proves that. This was not a premeditated crime. It was someone who acted rashly out of pure rage. Someone who knew exactly what destroying that statue would mean to them."

Eleanor felt a sudden chill. "I don't think," she said, "that I want to hear any more."

Mrs. Te Papa nodded. "I understand. Actually, I don't think I want to say any more. I made a promise to protect someone I knew to be innocent, and prove the guilt of another. I failed. If I go to Roundtree now, all I can give him is a plausible theory. And two pieces of circumstantial evidence." From her pocket she drew out Lani's unfinished suicide letter and the Post-it notes from the library book.

Mrs. Lathrop took both and studied them intently. She lingered over the letter, and sighed. But when she read the notes, she merely looked puzzled. "Where did you get these?" she asked.

"From one of your books. I think Lani was trying to find a way to save Kaumaha. Taken with that letter, I believe the whole thing speaks for itself."

Eleanor was silent for several minutes, but Mrs. Te Papa heard her thoughts as if spoken aloud. "If I'm right," she pressed, "this may not be the end."

"You have no proof." The voice was harsh.

"Only the papers in your hand."

Eleanor considered them for a moment. Then she reached into her pocket and drew out a cigarette lighter. Before Mrs. Te Papa could rise or cry out, the letters were aflame. Eleanor stood, tossed them over the rail and watched as the trade wind carried them away. Her face was expressionless. "Thank God I decided to start smoking again."

"That was very foolish," Mrs. Te Papa admonished.

"The cigarettes won't kill me, Winnie. For all intents and purposes, they've killed me already."

"You know what I mean. If I understand your actions just now, you may be placing us all in terrible danger. Yourself most."

Eleanor laughed. It was not mocking or derisive, but a genuine guffaw that ended in a coughing fit. She poured herself a glass of water and drank it in one gulp. "I'm sorry," she said, still chortling, "but you've got to admit that's funny. A knife through the heart would be a fucking goodnight kiss compared to what's coming my way."

Mrs. Te Papa disapproved. She had her own opinions on life and death. But she was also merciful. "Do you have anything to make it...easier?"

"Only a whole cabinet. Muscle relaxants, oxycodone, hydrocodone, and something I think might be horse tranquilizers. If I had more time, I'd sell them on the black market and make a fortune."

"You must be very careful, Eleanor."

"Good God, why? At my age, just getting in the bathtub is an act of sheer recklessness."

"You must be careful," Mrs. Te Papa repeated, "because you have a grandson who loves you very much."

The wicked gleam died from Eleanor's eyes, and she became solemn. "It's him I'm thinking of," she answered coldly. "Why'd you show me these, Winnie? You must have had some kind of plan in mind."

"No, no plan. I just wanted you to know. But there is something else I must tell you. The boy Peter is still in jail. He's a disgrace to our people, and I'm ashamed to call him Hawaiian, but he is innocent of this crime. More to the point, I promised to protect him."

"Does that make us enemies?"

"Only if you remain silent. It isn't like the statue. This is not a secret you can take to the grave."

Eleanor leaned back and studied her. "You know," she said, "it's a goddamn shame we had to meet now. I think if we had met twenty years ago, we might have become great friends."

"I'm sure of it."

Eleanor was about to respond, but a movement from below startled them both. A figure appeared on the path leading up from the village. They watched as it moved out of the shadows into the warm yellow light.

"Evening, all."

Mrs. Te Papa raised a hand, while Eleanor merely nodded. A casual observer might have wondered at the coolness of their response. But really, what was there to see?

Just two old women out on the lanai, fanning themselves from the heat.

Chapter 16

NĀ 'UHANE 'INO, RESTLESS SPIRITS

Roger had strange dreams. Lani was with him. They moved through the forest on silent feet along an old trail he had never seen before. She glided sure-footedly, and the roots themselves jumped out of her path. *I want to show you something.* But I can't keep up, he said. I don't know this trail like you do. Lani looked over her shoulder and laughed.

Sure you do.

Shapes appeared, mounds rising from the dense underbrush covered in vines. They had always been there, Roger knew, but he had never seen them. Great *heiaus* with palm-thatched roofs and stark lava walls, cookhouses, and even little huts with totems dangling from open doors. He knew this was the village as it had been many centuries ago. He assumed it was abandoned, yet his nose caught the definite scent of woodsmoke. There were people here. But how?

Lani brought him to a neat little cottage painted coral with a pocket garden in front. It seemed newer than the rest. He understood this was her home. *It's small, but there's lots of land out back. I'll be putting in an addition soon.*

I'm sorry, Lani, he told her. You wanted to tell me that

night, didn't you? About the children. About Amyas. I should have pressed harder. Maybe I could have saved you.

Saved me from what, Cuz? From this? Does this look so bad to you?

It looked beautiful, he admitted. But it was not life.

His cousin studied him for a moment, quizzically. He recognized the expression: head tilted to one side, mocking smile. It was how she always looked when she explained the world to him, even when they were children. Lani reached up and snatched from the air a long stalk from a bingabing tree. Its leaves were shaped like spades and big as dinner plates. *You see this leaf? Is it alive?* He agreed it was. *How can you tell?*

As this was only a dream, Roger humored her. Lani had always been bossy. I can see it for myself, he replied.

Ae, you can see it. Now, is the other side of the leaf alive, too? Really? How can you tell, if you can't see it?

Because it's the same leaf.

Pololei, *Little Bra. One side reveals itself to you, the other remains hidden. You see only what the light touches, but you know there is another part beyond what your eyes can see—just as real, as alive. Would you feel sorry for the other side of the leaf? Of course not. So why feel sorry for me?*

They were moving through the woods again. Roger wasn't conscious of walking, yet somehow he kept pace with her.

I need to show you something.

Now they were gliding, not past the trees but through them. It was a strange sensation, not unpleasant. The forest parted, and they were in the valley. Before them was something that was, and also most definitely was not, Lathrop House. It was as if the house had been rendered by a different hand, recognizable but distinct. A few windows were missing their panes, and a pile of lumber lay in the yard. The building was nearly complete.

Do you know whose house this is?

Roger did. But he could not bring himself to say it aloud.

Lani grinned. It lit up her face, and like the house, she was transformed. Roger realized with a pang that he had never seen her so perfectly, transcendently happy. *Don't be afraid,* she said. *That's why I brought you here. So you could see for yourself.*

Even as he watched, the structure seemed to become a little more solid, its profile sharply defined against the cliffs. How long? he wondered.

Almost ready. But with plenty of room to expand. You know, when the time comes. She winked at him roguishly. *And there'll always be a spare bedroom at my place, too.*

Roger felt the sun on his face. Late afternoon, time to go home. But he could not bring himself to look away. The cliffs of Kaumaha glowed with a light he had never seen, and the waterfall was a silver band studded with pearls.

Is it really like this? he wondered.

It can be. It will be.

There was something else he needed to ask her, something desperately important. But the sun was blinding, he couldn't think clearly. Lani was singing a lullaby. He recognized it; his grandmother sang it to soothe him when he was a boy. Something about a princess trapped in a cave and her brother who summoned all the sea creatures to save her.

Ōpae ē, 'Ōpae ho'i
Ua hele mai au, ua hele mai au
Na kuahine.

Roger awoke with the sun on his face and the song still whispering in his ear. He rolled onto his side, disturbing the slumbering figure next to him. Marybeth opened one eye and muttered, "Mhwhah?"

"It's okay. Go back to sleep."

He waited until her breathing became deep and heavy, then rolled gently out of bed. The floor was already warm; the sun had been up for a while. Without pause, without thinking why, Roger pulled on a tank top and a pair of boxer shorts and went to Eleanor's room. The door was ajar. He saw the bed neatly made, one corner thoughtfully folded down. Agnes always did that before she left for the night. The bed had not been slept in.

Roger took a deep breath, tried to control the rising panic inside him. She had probably slept on the lanai. She did that quite often these days. He looked through the French doors to see if her afghan was thrown across the chair, but it lay folded on the side table.

"Gran?" His voice sounded hollow in his ears. "Gran?"

He came downstairs and put his head in the dining room, where Mrs. Te Papa and Judge Chan chatted over coffee. "I'm so sorry," Roger said, calmly as he could, "but have either of you seen my grandmother this morning?" Both ladies shook their heads. "Is my father or mother up, do you know?"

"Your father left early this morning," said a deep voice behind him. He turned and saw David Tanaka clad in a garish silk bathrobe. "He had an urgent appointment, it seems. I loaned him my helicopter."

"I think your mother is down at the village with the Kapiahos," Mrs. Te Papa added helpfully. "She said she was going to bring them some tea cakes."

"And Ackerman?" He and Eleanor were friends, Roger remembered.

"Upstairs, still dead to the world," Tanaka said with a grin. "The good doctor likes his beauty sleep."

"Why the urgency, Roger?" Mrs. Te Papa asked. "Is something wrong?"

He swallowed. "Her bed hasn't been slept in. And I dreamt..." He stopped.

But Mrs. Te Papa's eyes were suddenly very gray and deep. "Yes? What did you dream?"

Roger suddenly had a very clear image of himself standing wild-eyed in his boxer shorts with his hair tousled from sleep, like a six-year-old boy roused from a nightmare. "It doesn't matter," he said repressively. "I just want to make sure she's all right, that's all. She's not a young woman."

"I should say not," said a voice from the lanai. Eleanor stood in the doorway, her gardening hat perched at a jaunty angle. She surveyed the company with an arched eyebrow. "Did I miss something?"

"Gran!" Appearances be damned, Roger thought. He rushed to his grandmother and enveloped her in a hug. Eleanor looked rather bemused but patted his back reassuringly. "I thought...I thought... Where were you anyway?"

"I just took a walk, that's all. Is something wrong?"

"Not now, but I thought...well, I saw your bed hadn't been slept in, and..." He found he couldn't go on.

Mrs. Te Papa said calmly, "Roger had a disquieting dream. I gather it was about you." Her eyes met Eleanor's, and they exchanged a meaningful look.

"Well, as you can see, I'm totally fine," Eleanor said bracingly. "And the bed wasn't slept in because I never went to sleep. I was out on the lanai most of the night and went for a walk around the island this morning."

"Then that's settled," Judge Chan said brightly. She beamed at them all. "It's such a lovely morning, isn't it? I don't blame you, Eleanor. I'd love to see the sunrise over those cliffs. Maybe next time." This was a lie. Rosalind Chan hoped she never saw this cursed island again as long as she lived.

"When is the seaplane coming?" Mrs. Te Papa asked Roger.

He glanced at the hall clock and was astonished to find it was nearly ten. "About an hour. I'll drive you all down myself." Relief was rapidly giving way to embarrassment in him.

"I'd better tell Ackerman," said Tanaka. He disappeared upstairs.

Eleanor was still confused. "What's all this about a dream?" She looked to Roger, who found he couldn't speak.

Mrs. Te Papa had joined them. "You should tell her," she said quietly.

"Why? It doesn't matter. It was just a dream."

"Yes, but sometimes dreams are important. I had one myself, last night. I saw a house standing alone in a green valley, much like this one, but with fresh paint on the walls and a koa wood lanai still green from the cutting. Empty now, but almost ready to be lived in..."

Roger's eyes widened. He opened his mouth to speak, but from behind them came Tanaka's voice, quietly urgent: "Please excuse me. Roger, is the telephone still working?"

Still in a daze, Roger nodded distractedly. "I think so. Why?"

The corners of Tanaka's mouth turned down in disgust. It was a fastidious gesture, as if he had taken a spoonful of something rotten. "I need to make a few calls. And you'd better cancel that seaplane."

"Ackerman won't like that," Roger demurred. "He told me at least a dozen times he's got a faculty meeting later today."

"What now?" wailed the judge.

Considering the circumstances, Tanaka's reply was a model of restraint. "Professor Ackerman won't mind," he said coolly. Then, because he was only human, he added:

"He's up there right now, pinned to his bed like a butterfly with a spear through his throat."

———

It was not a spear. It was an *ihe*. Mrs. Te Papa recognized it at once. She stood over the body with Marybeth, pale and liverish, at her side. "I'm not sure we should be doing this," her assistant said nervously.

"Probably not. But Detective Roundtree will not be here for some time. And I had to see for myself."

Robert Ackerman lay atop the sheets, dressed in a navy polo and khakis. His hands were at his sides and his head rested on the pillow in an attitude of repose. The weapon stood like a flagstaff atop his corpse, entering the soft triangle of flesh just below his whiskery chin. A well of blood, now dried, erupted from the open mouth and trailed down the pillowcase and duvet. His eyes stared unseeingly in frozen horror.

"It doesn't make any sense," whispered Marybeth. "It can't have anything to do with the statue or the sale, it can't. That's all over and done with. So why now?" She looked to Mrs. Te Papa. "Do you think it might be a serial killer?"

Slowly, Mrs. Te Papa shook her head. She seemed strangely wooden, inert.

Marybeth had overcome her fears enough to take a closer look. "He didn't struggle much, did he?" she remarked.

"No."

"Maybe the stabbing was so fast he never had time to react."

"Perhaps." But surely even in that moment the victim's hands would fly up to his throat to protect himself. Roundtree would see that at once. Her gaze traveled around the room and fell upon an empty water glass on the washstand. "My dear, will you go and see if Roger has the key? The crime scene should not be disturbed until the police arrive."

Marybeth thought that a little cheeky, considering they were already standing in it, but did as instructed. She returned a few moments later with a large brass key. "Roger says the detective will be here in an hour or so. His grandma is lying down now. Funny how worried he was about her, wasn't it?"

"She's not well," Mrs. Te Papa answered. But her mind was on other things. "This room faces the valley," she mused. "Do you know who else has this view?"

"Roger does," Marybeth answered promptly, and reddened. But Mrs. Te Papa merely shook her head. "No, that won't help. Anyone else?"

"Ogden and Marnie each have a room, then this one, then Judge Chan on the end. The rest face the sea, like yours. Five on each side."

Mrs. Te Papa considered this for a moment. "Very well," she said at last. "That should be all right then. Come, child." She ushered Marybeth through the door and locked it behind them. Dr. Ackerman would remain undisturbed until his tryst with the Hawaiian State Police, and the ladies made sure to leave everything exactly as it was—with one small omission.

The glass was no longer on the washstand.

———

The dreams that so unnerved Roger and Mrs. Te Papa never reached Gilbert Kapiaho. He had not slept at all. The reserve of his will was enough to see Agnes home from the funeral and stay by her side as she alternated between manic bursts of cleaning and paroxysms of grief. He remained calm, patient, stoic. At eleven he put her to bed with a sleeping pill and came down to the kitchen to wait. He did not know for what.

Now he knew. It was a brilliant morning on the Pacific: cerulean skies and waves that slapped playfully against the boat, an acrid tang in his nostrils without the cloying scent of land. These were things he had loved all his life. He wondered if he would ever love anything again.

"Okay," said Mr. Po, "That's far enough."

Gilbert throttled down the engine of his Boston Whaler. They were creeping along, just fast enough to keep steerage. Mounted on the stern, where he usually kept lobster pots, was a dirty and very old casket wrapped in several lengths of iron chain. The chain was to weigh it down, or so Gilbert told himself. But looking at the thing it was not hard to imagine an ancient evil trapped inside. "You sure this will work?"

Mr. Po shrugged. "I'm not sure of anything anymore," he answered indifferently. "But what else can we do?"

This was old ground. Gilbert had suggested cremation, but Po thought it too risky. If any particle of Amyas remained on the land, it could still be contaminated. Or so he supposed.

Mutely, Gilbert went to the stern and began working the hydraulic hoist. The coffin rose jerkily, tipping this way and that. He tried not to notice the clattering within. The crane swung out over the sparkling water. It seemed to Gilbert an abomination to drop so unlovely an object into the innocent sea. "What now?" he asked. "Should we say a prayer or something?"

Mr. Po had taken the wheel. "Couldn't hurt, I guess. You know any?"

Gilbert went to Sunday service on the island as a boy, when the hymnals were the same ones Reverend Lathrop brought from Boston. His father was a lay preacher, just as every Kapiaho had been since old Melchior. But by the time Gilbert was old enough to take his father's place the congregation had dwindled. The chapel became a museum, a dead thing rather than a live one. He still remembered some of the liturgy.

But that seemed wrong somehow. It was in the name of the Christian God that Amyas committed his crimes; if the words could not save him then, what good would they be now? Somehow Gilbert had to reach this terrible man, to set him free so that the island would be free of him. But what could he say? What would Amyas want to hear?

"*Ho'oponopono.*"

It was Mr. Po who spoke, but the voice did not sound like

his. It was deeper, more commanding. And ancient. Po turned from the wheel to face him, and in that moment his features flickered like a mirage, and Gilbert saw the stern, unmistakable visage of his great-great-grandfather. Then it was gone. Mr. Po was looking at him quizzically. "You okay there?"

"Yeah." *Ho'onopono.* The prayer of forgiveness. It wasn't particularly original; New Agers chanted it in ashrams and wore it on lanyards around their necks. But it was old, and it had power. The last of the Kapiahos cleared his throat. "Amyas Lathrop!" he called. "Listen to me! *E ho'olohe mai ia'u!*" The words came to him, and he spoke in a voice that was neither his nor Melchior's, but all voices:

"Kala aku wau iā 'oe!
Kala mai lākou iā 'oe!
E 'olu'olu!"

Again and again he repeated the chant, until consonants became percussive and vowels became song. His voice was a drum to wake the dead. *I forgive you. They forgive you. Be at peace.*

There was no answering groan, no rattle of chains. Nothing but the desiccated carcass of an old Boston preacher. Still Gilbert called to it, on and on, until finally Mr. Po put a hand on his shoulder. "That'll do," he said.

Gilbert felt breathless and drained. "Okay, let's get it over with," he said gruffly.

The two men stood side by side, gazing up at the casket. It still looked ordinary, untransformed, a bit ludicrous dangling in its chains. Gilbert Kapiaho pressed a switch and the restraining cord gave way. The mortal remains of Amyas Lathrop hit the surface with a flat splash, turned upright and bobbed for a moment. There was a gurgling, shushing sound. Mr. Po made a sign of the cross as the coffin sank from view. It gave up a last glutinous bubble and was gone.

Without a word, Gilbert went back to the helm and powered

up the engines. The twin Evinrudes bit into the water and the bow lifted clear. For several minutes he let the motor race, putting two solid miles of sea between himself and the grave site. Only when he saw the familiar crescent harbor with its ramshackle pier did he reluctantly drop a gear. Po handed him a bottle. "I promised Agnes I wouldn't," Gilbert said, and took a long pull. "But I guess we're outside the three-mile limit." He took another.

"You sounded good back there, braddah. Like a real holy roller kahuna."

"Did it work?"

Mr. Po shrugged. "Not sure. Thought I felt something for a moment, but it was gone before I could tell. You conjured up quite a crowd, though." He grinned toothlessly.

Gilbert shook his head in wonderment. There were times he would give his right arm for even a glimpse of the world his friend saw. He and Agnes had reached the age where, as she put it, they had more friends on the other side of town. And family, too: his parents, the brother he lost in Vietnam, his only son. Now Lani. How comforting it must be to know they were so close by.

But Eddie Po never seemed comforted by his visions. They haunted him, perhaps even made him a bit mad. It did not escape Gilbert's notice that Po never mentioned seeing his own family there. If he had—and he must—he probably didn't like what he saw. This terrified Gilbert, on the rare occasions when he allowed himself to think of it.

"Who was the old guy?" Po asked. "He didn't look Hawaiian, but he seemed to know you."

"He was Guinean. He was my great-great-grandfather."

"Huh. That figures." Po digested this for a moment. "He's proud of you. Like, *loa* proud."

Gilbert's heart skipped a beat. He desperately wanted to

hear more, and was about to ask, but stopped himself. Years ago he learned to take what Eddie offered him and nothing else. Partly because he didn't want to turn his friend into a human weather vane. Partly because he didn't want to know.

But he could help smiling to himself a little, now. He was still smiling when they pulled up to the dock.

Chapter 17

TALKING STORY

Detective Roundtree's mustache drooped more than ever. He inspected the body of Robert Ackerman without comment, sighed, and gathered the household in the library to take statements. His resigned melancholy reminded Mrs. Te Papa of a basset hound left out in the rain. "Anybody want to tell me about the weapon?" he asked, without enthusiasm.

"I will," said Mrs. Te Papa. "It is an ancient *ihe*, dating back several hundred years. It belongs to the house."

It was too much to hope otherwise. "Who saw it last?"

"Professor Ackerman had it," Tanaka supplied. "I was in the library when he asked to see it, and Mrs. Lathrop let him bring it to his room. I think he wanted to draw some of the markings."

Roundtree nodded, surprised. So the murder weapon was already in the bedroom. They were making progress. He'd have to confirm Tanaka's story with Mrs. Lathrop, who was still in her room suffering from shock. But that was a minor detail. "Okay. So, anyone hear anything unusual last night?"

"What do you mean by unusual?" Mrs. Te Papa wanted to know.

How about the sound of a man being impaled to his own

bed? "Loud voices, sounds of a struggle, a cry, something like that."

They all looked blankly back at him. "Whose room is next to his? Isn't it you, Judge Chan?"

The judge looked startled, but answered readily enough: "Yes, but I don't think I can help you. All I heard was talking. I thought it was the television. But a struggle or a cry, no."

Roundtree's pen paused in midair. "Talking? You mean you heard voices?"

"Yes, not very clearly. I'm afraid I wasn't paying much attention. I only heard a few words."

The detective had gone completely still, like a tiger surveying its prey in the veldt. He hardly dared move his lips. "And what exactly were those words?"

Judge Chan frowned in thought. "Something like 'sends regards,' I think. It was the only time the voice was distinct. I didn't hear anything after that."

"Could you recognize the voice? Did you know who it was?"

"I just told you, Detective, I thought it was the television," the judge replied with a touch of asperity. "It was a man's voice, rather low. I really couldn't tell any more."

"Anyone else hear this conversation?" Roundtree asked.

To the astonishment of all, the ever-silent Kaito stepped forward. "Excuse me," he said, in excellent English, "but I think I might be able to assist here."

"You heard the voices, too?"

"No, sir. My experience was different. It is my job to guard Mr. Tanaka while he sleeps. His room is next to mine. There is no connecting door, but I always leave my door open to the hallway. My bedroom is the first on the landing; no one can go by without my seeing. It is also directly across from Professor Ackerman's. I could see it quite clearly. No one entered it that night."

"But then how…"

"I think I know," Mrs. Te Papa said. "I was awake myself until quite late, sitting on the lanai outside my room. Sometime past one I thought I saw someone on the path leading up from the village. The moon wasn't out, but I got the definite sense of a shape. I stood up to get a better look, but whoever it was—if indeed it was anyone—moved into the shadows and disappeared. I remained there for a few minutes, but he did not appear. I assumed it was some kind of animal."

"So I'm guessing you didn't get much of a look at him."

"Not at all. He could not have been particularly tall or broad, but other than that I couldn't say."

Still it was a rich haul, and in less than ten minutes. It was beginning to look like an outside job. But if the killer hadn't entered through the bedroom door, he must have climbed up onto the lanai and broken in. Roundtree made a note to examine the latch on the French doors. "How difficult," he wondered aloud, "would it be for someone to reach this island without being seen?"

Roger, who had seemed oddly dazed when Roundtree arrived, roused himself to answer, "Not difficult at all. The village is barely lit after ten. A fast Zodiac boat could make the trip from Kona in less than an hour."

Detective Roundtree realized he might have been too hasty in dismissing that possibility for Lani's murder. All the people bound up in the fate of Kaumaha had been on the island at that time; why look anywhere else? But since then another figure emerged: the shadowy and thoroughly despicable Rodrigo Roxas. It was Roxas who had bribed Peter Pauahi. If the boy's story was true—and it was beginning to look like it was—then Roxas might well have had other operatives come to the island. Or, to be blunt, assassins. But why go after old Ackerman?

David Tanaka was looking at him keenly. "I told you before,

Detective, that there were other parties interested in this sale. You probably thought I was just trying to discredit a competitor, and I don't blame you. But surely the Honolulu police must have a file on his activities by now."

There was an uncomfortable silence, broken suddenly by Marnie. Until that moment they had all forgotten she was there. "Professor Ackerman was hiding something," she declared. Seven pairs of eyes swiveled in her direction. She reddened uncomfortably.

"Yes, Mrs. Lathrop?" Roundtree encouraged.

"I heard him, too," she explained. "But earlier, when I was going to bed. Around ten or so. I think he was on the telephone."

"Yes? Go on."

"I wasn't trying to overhear," she protested miserably. "I just walked by his door and heard a few words. He was...rather agitated."

Every single person knew exactly what she meant. "And those words were?" Roundtree pressed.

"First he said something like, 'I don't have to do a goddamn thing and I won't be threatened by the likes of you.' He said this quite loudly, you understand. Then there was a long pause..." The image of Marnie hovering breathlessly outside Ackerman's door leapt to everyone's mind. "After a bit he muttered something under his breath, I didn't catch it. Then another pause, and finally he yelled, 'I'll see you in Hell first!' I heard that right enough. After that there was a bang when he slammed the phone down. And that was all."

There was a shocked silence as each of them heard the ghostly echo of the slammed phone.

"Golly," said Roger.

———

Detective Roundtree remained several more hours, interviewing each of them separately and taking their statements. Then he went to Ackerman's room and found that the latch on the French doors was indeed broken. Moreover, there were small scratches and punctures on the railing where the grappling hook had been. Satisfied, he announced that the guests were free to leave the next day, as long as they kept themselves available for questioning. He was looking forward very much to another interview with Rodrigo Roxas.

After his departure a quiet settled over the island. Mrs. Te Papa went to apprise Eleanor of the latest developments while Judge Chan set off toward the village. Marnie, the star witness, fled to her bedroom. Roger was headed to Marybeth's when Tanaka caught him on the landing. "Got a minute? There's a few things we should talk about."

Roger followed him out into the valley. Almost without realizing it, they moved along the old path to Amyas's statue. The late-afternoon sun showed the island to best advantage. Just another thing he would miss.

"I'm afraid I was not completely honest with you earlier," Tanaka said, after they had walked some distance in silence. "Your father did not have a business appointment. The truth is, I asked him to leave."

Roger was puzzled. "Why?"

"He doesn't belong here. He never did. Look, I'm an outsider, but from where I'm standing it looks like your dad did nothing with his inheritance except drive it into the ground and then try to offload it at the first opportunity. Tell me if I'm wrong."

"That's pretty rich, coming from you," Roger said bitterly.

To Roger's surprise, Tanaka chuckled. "I'll admit I was the first jackal at the feast. But it wasn't my kill. Your father hates this island almost as much as you love it."

Roger turned to him, startled. "Why do you say that?"

"Because it's the truth. I've done deals like this before. Usually the family can't wait to get rid of Grandpa's horse farm, or trade the old plantation house for a new condo at Ala Moana. But soon as I arrived here I saw how committed you were to saving Kaumaha. How could I deny you that chance, simply to gratify your father's greed?"

And your own, Roger almost added. Instead he said, "It doesn't matter now. The state will take Kaumaha even if you don't. And everything I believed about this place was a lie."

Ahead they could see the walls of the ancient temple, beyond which the statue once stood. "A lie?" Tanaka repeated. "Really? Weren't you the one that said the villagers came to this island willingly, that they believed in its mission?"

"They may have done, but they were wrong. Amyas was a monster. You have no idea."

"Actually, I do." Roger stumbled over a root and Tanaka caught his arm. "Winnie told me the whole story. Your grandmother doesn't have to keep that secret anymore. Neither do you."

"Then how can you say it wasn't a lie? My God, all those children!"

"What Amyas did was unconscionable. But, as I understand it, it was his own wife—your great-great-great-grandmother—who put a stop to it. Since that time there have been many generations of Lathrops and villagers living here together. Almost one hundred and eighty years of cohabitation. That isn't a lie. Your aunt married a man from the village, an overseer like Melchior Kapiaho once was. If they had lived, you and Lani would already be making plans to inherit jointly. That was the real tragedy, don't you think?"

"True," Roger admitted quietly.

"And, not to keep contradicting you, but you're also mistaken about the tax debt. Your debts are paid."

Roger was thunderstruck. "How?"

Tanaka explained and then told Roger that his father had agreed to transfer all title to him. He did not, however, relate the circumstances. "Your father behaved foolishly, and realized it," was all he would say.

They arrived at the site. The broken column jutted out of the ground like a rotten tooth. "What now?" Roger asked.

"That's up to you. The island is yours, free and clear. Consider it my gift for all the pain and heartache your family has been through. You can shake my hand and I'll fly away in my helicopter and that will be the end of it."

"I have a feeling there's a 'but' in there somewhere," said Roger with the ghost of a smile.

Tanaka grinned boyishly. "Yes, there is. *But* if you take the island back just as it was, the same problems will recur. You don't have enough capital to turn this place into a proper resort, and it can't survive as anything else. Even without the tax lien you'll still be losing money, and the villagers will feel that even more than you do."

"Are you saying you want to buy it back again?"

"Not exactly. Everything I was envisioning here—it won't work. Even if the state gave me permission, which they certainly won't now. In a way I'm grateful. My brand is big, splashy resorts—lots of rooms, lots of revenue, lots of clients. The selling point of Kaumaha is just the opposite: exclusivity. Who wants to go to Shangri-La and find a Hilton?"

"I don't think I follow you, Mr. Tanaka."

"Please call me David." They both sat on the ledge of the *heiau*, and Tanaka adopted a professorial attitude. "Do you know what the first lesson of hostelry is? Don't bother answering; it's a rhetorical question. The first lesson is that there are only two ways for a hotel to make money. Either you get a lot of people to spend a little, or a few people to spend a lot. Nothing else works."

"As Dad seems to have proved," Roger added wryly.

"Well, yes. But I was just as mistaken. For Kaumaha to survive, it needs to become Shangri-La: remote, exclusive, pristine. The good news is that the valley and the waterfall do most of the work for you."

"And the bad news?"

"You'll still need capital. Moreover, not one of you has the faintest idea how to run a hotel, much less a five-star one—no offense." Roger said there was none taken. "You need to develop the property so that the whole island becomes a seamless experience. That means the village needs a redo. Not condos, but something more like Gilbert Kapiaho's place. We can take that as a model and make thirty of them."

"*We?*"

"Yes, Roger. My company is prepared to loan you enough money to transform the village, fix up the main house, put in a decent pier, and build ten or fifteen ultra-luxury guest bungalows along the perimeter of the valley. Once you're up and running we'll stay on as property managers. The profits from the hotel will pay off the loan and our fees—which, in all candor, are going to be steep as hell." Tanaka's grin was infectious.

The young man's mind boggled. "But that would be...that would be..."

"Incredible? Fantastic? Stupendous? Any of those work?"

"All of them," Roger murmured breathlessly. "But why are you doing this, David? Couldn't you make more money by letting us go under and buying the island yourself?"

"You're still looking for the angle, aren't you?" said Tanaka shrewdly. "No, don't apologize, it shows good business sense. Well, for one thing, this project will certainly get approved by the State of Hawaii and probably win me some Good Samaritan laurels, which I badly need right now. No, I'm not going to tell you why. Wait and see. Also there's a certain expert on Hawaiian culture whose opinion I value, and I don't want to piss her off. As a matter of fact, she's agreed to serve as a project adviser if you agree—pro bono, of course."

"I'll have to ask Gran. The island is half hers."

"I am aware," said Tanaka dryly.

"So…how should we do this?" Suddenly Roger seemed very young, and Tanaka was embarrassed to discover certain paternal feelings stirring.

"Once you both agree, the lawyers take over and make a mess of everything. Your Gran probably has an attorney for her personal affairs; otherwise I can recommend a few. There will be lots of contracts and transfers and statements of intent. You'll have to learn how to read that kind of thing, because you'll be seeing them the rest of your life. If you like, I can help. But for now—a handshake will do."

He offered his hand, and Roger took it without hesitation.

———

The ferry *Princess Likelike* was due in Kaumaha at six that evening. Mrs. Te Papa chose to depart on her, as the *Likelike* was slow and comfortable like herself. She had had her fill of seaplanes.

Roger and Eleanor brought them to the pier. Eleanor still looked pale, but rallied enough to give Marybeth a warm smile and a hug. "You're a good girl," she said, patting her cheek, "I think you'll make Roger very happy. If I don't get the chance again, let me pass along the blessing my old Nan gave me. 'May all your babies be as lovely as him and as smart as you. And contrariwise.'"

"*Gran!*" Roger expostulated, rolling his eyes. He took Marybeth's hand to escort her onto the boat. They climbed to the shelter deck and looked out over the stern. From there the setting sun threw its auric cloak over the whole island, touching the jagged cliffs in the distance and two tiny figures on the pier.

"It's so beautiful," Marybeth sighed.

"You will come back, won't you?"

"Of course, but… You mean, you'll still be here?"

Roger grinned. "Looks like it. David Tanaka wants to go into the hotel business with me. With one thing and another, all the repairs and staff hires, I figure I'll probably be here—the rest of my life."

Marybeth squealed with joy and embraced him. Then she made a face. "Damn. I was actually looking forward to sharing my studio."

"Would you be okay with half a bed in a dilapidated old house surrounded by construction for the next two years?"

"Yup."

Roger held her in his arms, perfectly happy. Over her shoulder he saw the two older women embrace briefly. Eleanor Lathrop handed something to Mrs. Te Papa that looked like an envelope. They shook hands one last time, and Mrs. Te Papa crossed the gangplank. "That's my cue," he said. He kissed Marybeth affectionately.

"FaceTime tonight?" she asked.

"As soon as you land," he told her, and was gone.

———

Most of the ferry had been given over to cargo, leaving only a cramped cabin behind the funnel for passengers. Mrs. Te Papa chose to sit on deck instead, spreading herself luxuriously over the bench and letting the sea breeze have its way with her long hair. She tilted her face up to the setting sun and closed her eyes. Her expression was beatific.

"You look very pleased with yourself, missus," Marybeth observed.

Without opening her eyes, Mrs. Te Papa answered, "I am pleased with life. I am pleased to be returning home, and for this day, and for a job well done. I am pleased to have helped my people."

Marybeth thought she understood. "This should be enough to set Peter Pauahi free. Imagine it being Roxas all along! I guess he must have arranged poor Lani's murder, too."

"The Honolulu police will investigate that possibility, certainly. And I'm sure they will uncover any number of unsavory activities in the process. Detective Roundtree was practically rubbing his hands at the thought. No, I see no reason to pity Mr. Roxas."

Marybeth looked at her more closely. The old woman was still smiling, but there was something devilish behind that smile. "You mean... Wasn't it him?"

"No, dear. But it will take them several weeks to prove it. That should be more than enough time."

"Time for what?"

Mrs. Te Papa lifted her large shoulders. "For nature to take its course."

The implications of this gradually settled on her assistant. "But that means...that means we still don't know who killed Lani! Her murderer is still out there." At once she felt the cold touch of dread. Roger...Roger, who now had half of Kaumaha all to himself, who was already imagining a life for them both...

Mrs. Te Papa opened her eyes. They were gray and deep as tide pools. *"Mai hopohopo,"* she said gently, "Don't worry about these things. Justice has already been done. Robert Ackerman is dead."

"Professor Ackerman?"

"Oh, yes. It was he who killed Lani Kapaiho. I've known for some time."

"But how is that possible?"

"Don't forget, child. There were two people who knew what lay beneath Amyas's statue: Eleanor Lathrop and Bob Ackerman. As it turns out, both of them had very good reasons for wanting to keep it secret. In Ackerman's case, it was a matter of reputation. He staked his entire career on the House of the Bone Feast. Which, as we now know, did not exist."

"But didn't you say Dr. Ackerman only found out the truth after he published his book? What difference could it make to him then?"

Mrs. Te Papa smiled. "I didn't say that. Bob Ackerman did. And it was a lie." She shifted more comfortably in her seat. "It is probably best to consider the whole matter chronologically. A young Robert Ackerman arrived on the island in 1972 as a graduate student and developed his theory of the House of the Bone Feast. He genuinely believed that was what the site was, and he must have been elated to be the first to identify it. Then, as scholars do, he went off and published his findings. He returned in 1973 to do more research and asked permission to excavate under the statue. It was then that Eleanor told him the truth, the terrible secret of the Lathrops. Ackerman was forced to stick by a thesis he now knew to be false. Which," she added pointedly, "he's been doing for almost fifty years."

"You think he killed Lani because of a mistake he made in a book published fifty years ago?" Marybeth could not conceal her incredulity.

"Not a mistake, child. Fraud."

Marybeth sat straighter on her bench. "What fraud?"

Mrs. Te Papa settled back and folded her hands on her stomach. "When Ackerman returned the second time, he told Eleanor he had already published. She assumed he meant his book, the same one that now sits on the library shelf at Lathrop House."

"Of course. What else could that mean?"

"That's what I asked myself. Then I remembered my own time as a graduate student. Not many doctoral candidates publish a book right away. Usually it's a paper for a journal. Afterward, if they're lucky and it gets noticed, it becomes a book sometime later—quite often years later."

"But Dr. Ackerman *did* publish a book!" Marybeth objected.

"He did. But Eleanor told me she remembered watching the Watergate hearings with him during his second visit. That meant it had to be either 1973 or 1974. Sure enough, Robert Ackerman published a paper for the *Journal of Anthropological Archaeology* in January 1973. "Evidence of New Guinean Settlement in the Hawaiian Islands." It caused quite a stir at the time. Got him his postdoc at Princeton. Then, once he had a tenure-track job at Manoa, the paper became a book and was published in 1975. I read that in the *Honolulu Star-Advertiser* just a few days before the hearing. 1975."

It took a moment for this to sink in. "You mean by the time the book came out he already knew he was wrong?"

"Worse. He knew before it came out—in fact, *before* he'd even *written* it." Mrs. Te Papa sighed, shook her head. "It is dangerous for scholars to become too attached to a theory. Yet I suppose one can understand the temptation. You think you've found something new, something extraordinary, something no one else has found. It must be like discovering a new continent. You cannot wait to share this knowledge with the world and bask in the glory of your own brilliance. And then—*poof*! It's gone. Your precious theory is blown to bits, and you're right back where you started. All that work for nothing."

Marybeth thought this sounded irksome but hardly a motive for murder. She said as much.

"Ah, but it's more than just the idea," Mrs. Te Papa replied. "It is the idea upon which a scholar builds their career. An idea that distinguishes them from their peers, brings them fame and sometimes even fortune. Think about poor Dr. Ackerman. He published the journal article in good faith back in 1972. But then it got press attention. Suddenly it was not just a dissertation anymore. He came back to do additional research for the forthcoming book, like any good scholar, and that's when Eleanor told him her little secret. Can you imagine how devastated he must have been? Based on the House of the Bone Feast, he had already received a job offer—which would be lost, of course, if the truth became known.

"Maybe there was a moment of doubt. I'd like to think so, anyway. But he was young and ambitious. He was a damn good scholar, in spite of everything. There would be other books, other chances to prove himself. So in the end he decided he'd keep the Lathrops' secret, and his own. After all, there wasn't much risk. He figured that the statue would remain there forever."

"So why kill for it? Eleanor was the only one that knew for certain he was lying."

"One other person knew. *Lani.*"

"What? How?"

"The night she died, she told Peter, '*Everyone here is a liar.*' I wondered about that. Of course, she was referring to him and Eleanor, but was that all? Could she have known something about Tanaka, or Judge Chan, or even me? It was possible, but not likely. The one piece of evidence she had right at hand was Ackerman's book. Her notations prove she had been reading it to bolster her case that the island should be protected. The night Lani was murdered, Eleanor told her the same story she later told me, including Ackerman's involvement. This must have stirred something in Lani's mind, for she came down to the library and pulled his book out again. All the other notes in Lani's hand were written in blue ink. But there is a note attached to the copyright page in green—the same pen she used later that night to write her own suicide note. One word: *"Nixon?"* Quite accidentally, Eleanor gave her granddaughter the power to destroy Robert Ackerman."

"Oh, my God."

"I figure it was something like this. Ackerman told us himself he was up most of the night, killing mosquitoes. His windows, remember, face the valley. He looked out and saw Lani headed up the path. Something in her manner worried him. He remembered the scene at the bonfire, wondered if she was going to do something rash. He followed her. But Ackerman is an old man. It took him a while to navigate the trail, especially at night. He arrived just in time to watch Lani blow Uncle Amyas to smithereens.

"Ackerman, as we all know, had a very prickly personality. I don't doubt he gave her a piece of his mind. That might have been the end of it. But think of what must've been in Lani's mind at that moment. Betrayed, lied to, castigated—all for a secret which Ackerman knew all along. Imagine in that moment, instead of meekly accepting his recriminations, she suddenly turned round and fired back. Told him she knew he was a fraud and, worse yet, had proof of it. At that moment Dr. Ackerman was the living embodiment of all the lies and deceit she was determined to end. She was going to reveal the truth, all of it. Including his."

Marybeth thought of an objection. "Roger told me last night that when they went to move Ackerman's body, the wig fell off his head and he was completely bald. He was dying, wasn't he?"

"Yes. He was dying."

"Then why would he do something so terrible, if it wouldn't matter much longer anyway?"

Slowly Mrs. Te Papa shook her head. "You don't understand this man. Eleanor Lathrop is dying also. Did you know this?"

Marybeth nodded sadly. "Roger told me. He suspected for some time."

"Yes, it is a tragedy. But Eleanor has children and grandchildren who love her and will remember her. She has faith in God to sustain her sufferings. She can approach the end with peace.

"Dr. Ackerman had none of these. No family to comfort him. No faith or hope for the afterlife, for he was a militant atheist. Judge Chan said to me just yesterday that Ackerman was 'as proud as the devil and completely impervious to the rest of humanity.' At the end, what does such a man have left? Only his career, his reputation, his writings. These will survive him after death. Indeed, they will be all that remains of the thing that was Robert Ackerman. It might not sound like much to you, but it was everything to him. A lonely old man whose life was defined by a book written, as you say, nearly fifty years ago. A book that made him famous, respected, admired. That night he watched it all go up in flames. Then, even as the dust fell, Lani Kapiaho confronted him with his deceit and promised to make it known the very next day. Dr. Ackerman would be destroyed. He would live just long enough to see himself be condemned, ridiculed, perhaps even pitied, and then dismissed. Forgotten forever. She turned away from him in disgust. In that moment, he struck."

Marybeth gave an involuntary shudder.

"He remained just long enough to arrange the corpse, making it appear as though she had been killed by the blast. Then he hurried back to the house, entering just before Eleanor emerged on the lanai and narrowly missing Peter, who was already on his way up the hill. The next morning he awoke and began playing the same role he had played throughout his life: the great Dr. Robert Ackerman, eminent anthropologist."

They were silent for a moment. But their silences had a

different character. Mrs. Te Papa's was one of contentment; Marybeth's was apprehensive. "Why didn't you tell the police all this?" she asked.

"I knew there was no point. I could prove Dr. Ackerman was a fraud, and that Lani discovered the fact. There was also circumstantial evidence suggesting the murder had to be committed as a direct result of Lani destroying the statue, which again pointed to him. But that was all. Robert Ackerman was an intelligent and desperate man. Once the truth of Amyas's statue was revealed, he did not dispute it outright but rather tried to fold it within his own narrative of the bone feast. Even when Eleanor informed him that she had told me of his complicity—and I came very close to accusing him of murder—he remained calm. He had no fear of me, nor should he have. I am not a police detective. I know nothing of crime or investigation. I am *kanaka maoli*, a meddling old Hawaiian woman. If I had brought my suspicions to Detective Roundtree, what then? It would just look like I was stirring up trouble."

Marybeth considered this. Finally, in a voice so small it could barely be heard, she asked, "Did you kill him?"

Mrs. Te Papa smiled. It was a strange smile—knowing and somehow ancient. Her brown face looked more wooden than ever. "No, child. I didn't need to. I told Eleanor all that I knew. She understood perfectly."

"You mean..."

"I had no proof, you see. That was a quandary. Of course, I could simply allow nature to settle the issue: Ackerman would be delivered to a greater judgment soon enough. After his death I might have been able to convince Roundtree of the truth and set Peter free—at any rate, I would have tried. But that was not justice. Lani deserved better. And Eleanor, who had befriended this man and possibly even loved him, deserved to know the truth. In the end, the truth was all I could give her.

"So I did. Then, once I handed her the papers with the telltale green ink, Eleanor did something astonishing. She burned them right before my eyes. The meaning was clear: she was taking responsibility for justice upon herself. This frail, dying woman. It was magnificent. Naturally, I did all I could to help her."

"You claimed you saw a man outside..."

"That was a lie, of course. In the morning, after Tanaka found Ackerman's body, I took him and Rosalind Chan aside and told them everything. We agreed it would be for the best if Detective Roundtree could be sidetracked for a little while. So I invented the assassin, Rosalind claimed she heard him speak to Ackerman, and Tanaka convinced Kaito to claim that he had observed Ackerman's door all night and seen nothing. To make the story more plausible, I broke the latch on the French doors and left marks on the lanai suggesting a grappling hook."

Marybeth stared as if her employer had suddenly sprouted dragon wings. "And Marnie, too," she added. "She must have invented that telephone conversation."

"No, Marnie told the truth. What she heard was Robert Ackerman speaking with Eleanor, moments before she killed him." Observing the girl's look of astonishment, she patted her knee reassuringly. "Don't worry, dear, he really was guilty. Eleanor made certain of that before she delivered justice. They were friends, after all."

"But...how? She was so tiny and frail!"

"That was my worry, too. Once I knew what Eleanor planned, my greatest concern was that he might overpower her—after all, she was not a strong woman. But then she disclosed to me that she had various drugs that could render a body compliant. I think she entered Ackerman's room sometime after ten and suggested a companionable drink. Crushed into the glass were a large quantity of muscle relaxants and tranquilizers.

Once he was immobile, but still conscious, she told him what she knew. I think she demanded that he admit his guilt; his confession was what Marnie overheard through the door. By which time, I expect, Dr. Ackerman was too weak to rise from his bed, much less resist what came next. What Marnie thought was the telephone being slammed might well have been the *ihe* entering Bob Ackerman's throat."

"How horrible," Marybeth muttered, thinking of the reddened mouth and staring eyes.

"Justice is rarely an attractive thing to witness," Mrs. Te Papa said sternly. "But it has beauty all the same. Professor Ackerman paid for his crime, just as Amyas did, and by the same means. There are those who would argue that Eleanor, more than anyone, had the right to deliver that justice."

"But it's still murder!"

"Yes, and Eleanor Lathrop was quite willing to confess what she had done. But as we both know, she would never live to stand trial. I decided it would be best to let her spend her last few weeks on the island with her grandson, and after some consultation, I convinced Tanaka and the judge of the same."

Marybeth shook her head wonderingly. "After Roundtree investigates Roxas and comes up with nothing, what then? He could go right back to suspecting Peter Pauahi. Or even Roger."

Mrs. Te Papa removed from her purse the envelope Eleanor gave her. "Well reasoned, child. I thought of that also. That is why I asked Eleanor to write out her confession, which I will give—still sealed—to her attorneys in Honolulu. They have instructions to send it to Detective Roundtree immediately upon her death." Marybeth still looked frightened. "Oh, I know what you're thinking," Mrs. Te Papa said. "But you mustn't worry. I can claim to have barely seen the alleged assassin; Judge Chan might decide it was the television she heard after all; and

Kaito may conveniently remember that he fell asleep on the job. We are not fools."

Her assistant still looked unconvinced. Marybeth grew up in a world where protection meant police and justice meant courts of law. She could not imagine any other. "There is a place," Mrs. Te Papa told her softly, "not too far from here, called Puʻuhonua o Hōnaunau. It is a city of refuge. When our people broke the ancient *kapu,* they could seek this place and, if they found it, were absolved of their crimes. But they could only reach the city by sea, swimming across a hazardous reef with currents that wanted nothing but to throw their body against the rocks, and sharks and eels waiting to feast on the remains. How could this be justice? The wicked might be stronger than the good, and receive their reward unjustly.

"But that is the secret of Puʻuhonua o Hōnaunau. It is not just treacherous to reach; it is impossible. No one can survive the journey. If they did—and some did—it could only be because the gods offered divine assistance. Thus the priests would know that this person was *hoopomaikai,* blessed. You see, my dear, it wasn't the priests that absolved this man, but the gods.

"Now we are much more civilized. We have courts and judges and people like Detective Roundtree. We don't need the gods anymore. Except in rare instances when our systems fail us and evil may otherwise go unpunished. Then we find the gods still waiting, eager to offer their help. Can't you see them, child? They are everywhere around you, in the sea under this boat and the soil beneath that, and in the very flesh of your hand." Marybeth glanced at her hand disbelievingly. "Oh, you think the old *kupuna* is talking story?" Mrs. Te Papa mocked. "You'd rather stay wrapped in that nice cool blanket of fact and science? Very well. Let us agree on this: nature has its own ways to flush out pollutants, often mysterious and unknowable to us.

Twice Kaumaha has suffered an outrage when a *haole* perverted our culture for his own ends. Such acts poison the very soil on which they are committed. They must be expunged. So, in the end, Kaumaha delivered Robert Ackerman to justice when no one else could."

Marybeth's eyes widened. "You think the island arranged all this?"

"I do," said Mrs. Te Papa.

Chapter 18

LOA'A 'AO 'AO O KA LAU,
THE OTHER SIDE OF THE LEAF

Winnie Te Papa was, among other things, a woman of habit. Fortunately most of her habits were good, and those that weren't—the second breakfast that she referred to as "tea time," for example—were balanced by others. She was also a woman of her word, which when given had the ringing finality of chisel against stone. So it was all the more remarkable that when an invitation to attend a certain groundbreaking reached her desk, she accepted with pleasure. The circumstances, she would have said, were unusual.

Five months had passed. It was winter now, but in Hawaii the seasons are observed rather than felt. Winter meant great breakers rolling ashore in Kealakekua Bay, cresting over dolphins as they slept. It meant that La'aloa would appear at sunrise to be nothing more than jagged rock, until the sea performed its daily miracle and deposited a perfect white sand beach by afternoon—hence the name "Magic Sands." Red ginger bloomed and poinciana budded alongside roads on the North Shore. Mrs. Te Papa observed this from the window of the #23 bus, and it cheered her.

On Kaumaha changes were subtler. The forest canopy thinned slightly, letting more sunlight touch the reeds and ferns on the ground. Pueo, the short-eared owl, hunted earlier in the evening, and mongooses dug their burrows deeper into the red soil. The graves in the valley were carpeted with a fine dusting of white naupaka blooms, like snow, except for one newly turned mound.

The celebrants met nearby, at a spot where the land sloped gently upward to reach the first foothills. From here they could see Lathrop House, resplendent in a fresh coat of ochre paint, and the old *heiau* stark against the waning sun. The remains of the well were gone. Instead, a small stone cut from polished onyx was placed in the ground, on which was written: *Here in this place were thirty-two innocents massacred in the years 1850–1861. Ho'omana'o mākou iā lākou.* Mrs. Te Papa chose the inscription.

The villagers came, even old Mr. Po, wearing a nearly clean white shirt for the occasion. Roger and his mother stood among them. David Tanaka and Judge Chan chatted with representatives from the Hawaiian Office of State Parks. For once, Mrs. Te Papa had no official capacity, and celebrated the fact with three glasses of champagne.

Roger Lathrop addressed them from a small platform, behind which stood a shrouded figure some eight feet high. "This is a day of celebration," he said, "but it is also a day of remembrance. We remember those who should be here now to share our joy, and those whose sacrifice transformed this island many years ago. Today we affirm that they shall be forever honored, *e ho'omana'o mau*, by us and by all those who visit this place. Today we consecrate this valley as a sacred burial ground, and I will ask Bishop Grace Cordell and *kapuna* Mike Kahele to perform the blessing. But first I would like to ask Mr. Gilbert Kapiaho to come forward."

Gilbert emerged, dressed nattily in a seersucker three-piece suit and bow tie. "Mr. Kapiaho is the cultural historian of the island," Roger told the crowd, "descendant of the island's first overseer, Melchior Kapiaho. It is with great humility that I have asked him to do the honor of rededicating this island today." He bowed and stepped aside, joining a beaming David Tanaka.

Gilbert Kapiaho ascended the dais slowly and gripped the podium with both hands. "The ancient Hawaiians who settled this island called it Kaumaha, or misery," he said into the microphone. "To be sure, this has been a place of much tragedy. But it also home to an extraordinary community, *kanaka* and *haole*, who have lived alongside one another for almost two centuries. As some of you know, my granddaughter, Lani, was the child of William Kapiaho and Rosemary Lathrop. It was her fondest hope to become a bridge between these families, and peoples. We carry that hope with us now. From today, this island will no longer be known as a place of sorrow. We give it the name of princesses and chieftainesses, the name of hope. In my granddaughter's memory, I hereby rechristen this land…Ailani."

He pulled the cord. The shroud fell, revealing a bronze figure in a heroic stance. Ailani Kapiaho stood tall and straight, her right foot slightly forward. She wore a flowing muumuu that left her arms and shoulders bare, revealing strength in every sinew. One palm turned upward toward the sea in welcome, the other protectively toward the island. Her steady gaze took in the valley and cliffs beyond. The expression was serene.

"Would she have liked it, do you think?" David Tanaka asked Roger afterward.

"She'd have hated the fuss," he answered honestly. "But I think we did her justice."

Mrs. Te Papa approached them with a heaping slice of pineapple cake in her hand and Marybeth following in her wake. "In every sense," she said, "what you have both done here is extraordinary."

Tanaka smiled in gratitude. "Thank you, Winnie. But we are just getting started. Had to get the big house up to code first. Now we can start on the village. I've got crews coming in on Monday."

"I hope," said Judge Chan, "that it won't incommode the villagers too much."

"I was worried about that, too," Roger answered. "But we are only doing two or three homes at a time, and I've asked the residents to come stay at my place until the crew are finished. We've got plenty of room. Mom can't wait to have a full house again." He looked to Marnie, who with Agnes was enthusiastically shaking hands and handing out cake.

"Your grandmother would be very proud," Mrs. Te Papa observed.

"I think about her all the time. The very last days, when she couldn't leave her room, Gran asked me to carry her out to the lanai. One afternoon she pointed to a spot where the sun touched the ground and said, 'That's where you should put Lani's statue.' I hadn't even mentioned it, but somehow she already knew. It was her idea to rename the island. She said we'd had misery here long enough." Roger's face clouded for a moment. "Gran also told me what she had done, and what you three did for her. I couldn't believe it. I still can't."

Judge Chan patted his arm. "You mustn't think about that. She was doing justice."

Roger shook his head. "No, you don't understand. I don't have the words to thank you. You gave me my grandmother when I needed her most. I...I wouldn't have traded that time for anything."

The others looked away tactfully as he wiped his eyes. Marybeth put a comforting arm around his waist. "But whatever happened to Rodrigo Roxas?" she asked, bringing the subject onto less sensitive ground.

"Well, naturally the police had no case against him," answered the judge, "though Detective Roundtree was able to get a warrant to search his offices and turned up all sorts of interesting information. Last I heard, Mr. Roxas decamped back to the Philippines. I gather he's friends with that dictator there."

"But what about his hotel?" Marybeth pressed, looking to Tanaka. "Aren't you worried about the competition?"

"Not particularly," he answered airily. His studied nonchalance dissolved into a grin. "You remember how anxious he was to shut development down here, claiming the bone feast site was sacred ground? Turns out there's quite a significant *heiau* under the dirt where he wants to put his big resort. I had my surveyors do thermal imaging scans. A whole temple complex turned up. Thanks to my new friends in the state house, the property has just been made *kapu*, sacred space. The University of Hawaii is sending a team over to start digging next month."

Judge Chan nodded approvingly. "Well done, David."

Behind them, a group of dancers began to raise their arms and sway to the sound of drums. The blessing was complete. At that same moment the sun caught the bronze threads of Lani's hair and turned them gold. The guests paused, looked up in wonderment at the sight.

Mrs. Te Papa raised her glass solemnly. "To Ailani!" she said.

———

This morning the *i'iwis* roused old Mr. Po even earlier than usual. He muttered a curse into his pillow and rolled over, but the birds kept up their spirited argument until at last he rose, blearily, and slammed the shutters closed.

A fresh papaya awaited him under the mesh dome. He ate it slowly, carving off slices with his knife. He found his cigarettes, but the packet was empty. Not a good start to the day. Worse, Sadie had gone off somewhere, probably hunting voles. Her eyes had cataracts, and half the time she walked into trees.

Mr. Po poured some kibble into Sadie's bowl and gave her fresh water. The light through the kitchen window was blue and soft, halfway between one day and the next. His wife's favorite time. She'd be up before him, putting the coffee on and bustling around the kitchen while he fumbled for his pants and razor. By the time he was dressed she had breakfast ready: not fruit or granola but flapjacks with guava jelly or fresh cinnamon rolls, steam still rising from their folds. He could almost smell them, and pushed the thought from his mind.

Another day. Best to get it over with. Walk up to the ruin and watch the sunrise, then wander round the cliffs until it was time for lunch. Play with Sadie in the afternoon, nap, read a detective thriller until it was time to make dinner. Eat dinner, watch a little television, go to bed. And repeat. And repeat.

He tried to make coffee, but it burned his throat and the grounds hadn't strained properly. It was Kona coffee, the best in the world, but that didn't matter if you couldn't make it right. It tasted like sludge. He poured the rest down the sink. It would be nice to lose his temper, smash the coffeepot against the wall and heave a few pieces of crockery around. But with everything coming from the Big Island, even a cup and saucer could take a week to arrive. Instead he carefully placed the pot on the draining board and rinsed out the basin.

The light was warmer now. He felt it on his skin. Time to get going. He pulled on his trousers and retrieved his sandals from under the bed. Mr. Po was sorry the visitors had left. He liked Mrs. Te Papa; she was the only one who didn't look at him like he was crazy. She reminded him of his wife Sadie. He'd enjoyed the party, too, and what they were planning for the village didn't sound too bad. It wasn't real, of course, just a Disneyfied version, but at least he'd get a roof that didn't leak. And maybe air-conditioning.

Mr. Po stepped out and found the sun had already risen. This was very strange. Stranger still, the village Tanaka proposed had apparently been built overnight. Victorian cottages with ginger-bread tracery stood comfortably alongside seemingly ancient huts with grass roofs. There was a traditional cookhouse in the center of the square guarded by grimacing tikis. Even more remarkably, the village had not only been built but peopled. There were dozens of villagers milling about, exchanging greet-ings, choosing produce, scrubbing their linens in the communal washhouse with a *slap-slap* of fabric against rock, exactly as if they had done so every day of their lives. He staggered into the street and looked around him, blinking.

The villagers were dressed as though for an elaborate pag-eant—or, more precisely, several pageants at once. Some wore skirts made from palm fronds and necklaces of puka shells and polished stones. They tied their long hair into braids. Others wore white cotton shirts with puffy sleeves and breeches held by leather belts. The women had long dresses gathered at the waist that rustled as they walked. But they, too, had elaborate necklaces and laurel wreaths atop their black hair. The two groups blended seamlessly, chatting with one another, petting children, and offering compliments to the wives.

There was a *haole* woman among them. She had a strong face and determined chin, and looked rather like a schoolmistress. Her dress was as long as the others, but made of dark blue serge. Another was with her. Tall, willowy, aristocratic, with beauti-ful flashing eyes. Something familiar about the line of her jaw, the upward ironic tilt of each eyebrow that all the Fisks shared. She gave him a welcoming smile as if they were old friends. He returned it, embarrassed.

Mr. Po turned back to his own house. It was just as he remembered, but also quite different, as if he'd been remember-ing it wrong all these years. The walls were pale green and the shutters bright yellow with cabbage roses that his wife found in a stencil kit. Of course they had always been there; he just hadn't noticed them in a long time. There was a milk jug full of fresh nasturtiums on the porch. Next to the door, two pairs of sandals. The kitchen window was open and a gingham curtain fluttered in the breeze. Music floated out, an old Gabby Pahinui song on the Philco. *"Kumaka ka 'ikena ia Hi'ilawe. Ka papa lohi mai a'o Maukele..."* A woman's voice sang lightly in counterpoint. Sunlight filled Mr. Po's eyes; he could not see inside.

But somehow he knew who he would find there.

Chapter One

Little Compton sits on a tiny spit of land on the wrong side of Narragansett Bay. Everything else—Providence, Newport, URI, and civilization—is west. Little Compton is east. It used to be part of Massachusetts, but they didn't want it, and it got handed over to Rhode Island in some obscure colonial boondoggle back in 1747. The town patriarch was one Colonel Benjamin Church, who led the colonists' war against the Wampanoag and slaughtered two hundred of them at the Great Swamp Fight in 1675. A plaque in the square celebrates this historic achievement.

You don't come here by accident or pass through on the way to someplace else. There is nowhere else. The town is a peninsula. The main road narrows, runs along the coast, passes a few scrubby beaches and the tatterdemalion fleet at Dowsy's Pier, hunkers down into the swamplands of Briggs Marsh, and finally reaches a desolate spot where the only thing around you is gray, sullen ocean. Fog envelops the car. You're not in Rhode Island anymore, not anywhere, really. Little Compton is a void where the North Atlantic should be.

Our town square is a graveyard. I know how that sounds, but it's literally true. Look it up on Google Earth and see for yourself. The United Congregational keeps watch on the graves from the top of Commons Street, a view it shares with the post office, elementary school, and community center. You can't get anywhere in town without passing the cemetery first. It forms the backbone of all local directions.

Here, marked by a Celtic cross with a fouled anchor at its heart, lies my great-great-grandpa Ezekiel Hazard, a captain on the Fall River Line ferry to New York. He spent fifty years at sea and drowned in his bathtub after slipping on a bar of Yardley soap. Just to his left is a little granite wedge for Millicent Hazard, 1909–1918, dead of influenza but *"Resting in the Arms of the Lord."* An imposing obelisk marks the remains of Howland Prosper Hazard, who served one term in the Continental Congress and spent the rest of his life telling the story of how he loaned a half-crown to George Washington for passage on a stagecoach back to Yorktown, where Washington triumphed over the redcoats. Howland's epitaph declares him the *"Financier of the Revolution."*

And, a few paces away, under a blighted beech tree, rests my mother.

The only Hazards left now are me and Grandma. My father, not technically dead, read himself out of the family at Thanksgiving a few years ago, which is also where I received the sickle-shaped purple scar on my left shoulder. I didn't like how it looked, so I covered it with a tattooed rose. Then I didn't like how it made the other shoulder seem bare, so I covered that with a bloody skull. Don't ask what they mean. I got them out of a book. Dad's somewhere in Massachusetts; I don't care to know where.

Grandma's house is one right and two lefts from the cemetery, on Fillmore Road. In her kitchen is the last pink rotary phone in the world. It even works, though we had to pay the electrician to install an adapter. Now when she turns the wheel it connects to a motherboard inside that translates her analog commands into digital language. It's like she's calling from 1974.

Next to the phone is a list of numbers with "Emergency" written on top. I never thought about it until now, but that list is basically her whole life. The first are the pediatrician and vet, both dead, fire department, and police. After that comes a different hand, my grandfather's. It gives the name and number of the electrician, plumber, and a direct line to St. Miriam's. This was when he found out he had lung cancer.

The other names are in her handwriting, shaky but recognizable. There are the Laughing Sarahs—more about them later. My number is there and my father's. These were numbers she used to remember, but not anymore. The last entry is the saddest. It is her name and phone number. Now the emergency is her.

The avenues of my grandmother's mind are closing down, one at a time. Dr. Renzi described it like that: a great city becomes just a town, then a village, then a hamlet, then a single street with a vacant house and broken windows staring blankly. Right now we're somewhere between the town and the village. But the village still has a telephone, and Grandma's phone has become the only link to an increasingly shrinking world. Her calls are incessant and strange. Once she interrupted a meeting between me and the department chair to ask why Ronald Reagan stopped making movies.

"Because he's dead," I answered abruptly.

There was a long, shocked pause. "My God, has anyone told Nancy?"

Another time she dialed AT&T because a zeppelin was trying to dock to her satellite antenna. Then came an endless stream of phantom burglars, mashers, and would-be rapists. The last afternoon Pastor Paige came for coffee, she snuck into the front parlor and called Billy Dyer down at the police station. "He wants to do those sex things again," she whispered, horrified.

At the end of the month the bill would come in, full of bizarre notations. Grandma apparently spent three hours on a Thursday afternoon talking with the office of the governor general of Canada. Cost: forty-five dollars and eight cents. Calls to a florist in Poughkeepsie, to a charter boat company in Nantucket, to dozens of private numbers whose identities I can only imagine; calls going out in all directions, all day long— distress signals from a foundering liner demanding rescue from anyone near enough to help.

Mine comes on an afternoon in early October. I let it go straight to voicemail. Lately Grandma has taken to calling me every time she mislays something—reading glasses, television remote, keys. I've become her Lar, god of the household, even though I haven't set foot in the place for months. Our dialogue follows a familiar track:

"Did you look on top the television?"

"Of course I did. What d'you take me for...? Oh."

But today I'm not in the mood. Back in my little cubbyhole at Faculty Housing, staring at a room that has just ceased to be mine. There is still a tub of peppermint ice cream in the fridge and half a bottle of vodka left over from a welcome-back party weeks ago. It turns out they go well together. So it's not until evening that I finally pick up the phone and listen to her message.

"*...gotta come over here and help me, there's blood everywhere, on the sink and countertop and all over the floor, I don't know what to do. I just found him and I'm sure he's dead and the lobsters and it looks like his head is—*"

She cuts off abruptly. There is a rustle and a thump, like she's dropped the receiver. The next three minutes are static.

Dr. Renzi warned me that her delusions would become more fantastic as the dementia eats away at her sanity. She could become violent or terrified or amorous all in the space of ten minutes, shifting like a one-act tragedian from one scene to the next. "Sooner or later," he said, "you're going to have to bring in professional care. The question is not if but when." It looks like that moment has come. I call Renzi's office and leave a message with the triage nurse, requesting an appointment for Maggie Hazard as soon as possible.

Then I call Grandma.

The phone rings and rings. I imagine it jangling through the house, buzzing the extension in the back parlor, irritating the solemn black Bakelite with its long cloth cord in Grandpa's old office. But there is no answer. Panicking a little, I ring up Irene, Constance, and Emma—Grandma's closest friends. No one picks up. I leave a string of increasingly hysterical messages on their answering machines and end up staring at the quad outside my windows, a bare patch of scrubby grass.

I could call Dad. But I don't. Not yet. Don't open that box. Instead, I take out the overnight kit from my desk drawer—kept ready for just such an occasion—and toss it into a rucksack with a spare shirt and a dog-eared copy of Borodin. Five minutes later I'm on Route 95, heading south past the outlets at Wrentham, the monitory spire of the Fleet Bank building, the floodlit capitol with its naked *Independent Man* glowering down on the shoppers at Providence Place Mall. Over the Mount Hope Bridge, and into the clinging country dark of Tiverton. I didn't bother leaving a note. After all, it's not like anyone will miss me. I've just been fired, but that's a story for another time.

———

It is past ten, and the house is dark as I approach. Even the porch light is off. Grandma's place is the biggest on the block, shaped like a foreshortened T. From the road it looks oddly backward, showing its shingled tail to passersby while its white clapboard face stares out to sea. But there is a reason.

The house was built on a sloping hill by Captain Ezekiel Barrow in 1704. Its tall windows look out to Narragansett Bay, where Captain Barrow could watch the ships sail in and out of Newport. He even added an extra story and a widow's walk with lead-glass windows that opened on a hinge. Old Barrow was a wrecker, and from his lofty perch he watched for ships in distress like a vulture circling carrion. Inside is a patchwork of flotsam from his prizes: a carved Spanish staircase in mission oak with pineapple finials, tall French doors with silver handles, Delft tiles that frame the front room fireplace. Captain Barrow came to a bad end in 1713 when his sloop overturned in a squall as he attempted to claim a prize; his corpse washed up on Breakwater Point.

Gravel and crushed seashells crunch under the tires. The sound usually wakes up anyone within, but not this time. Part of me already imagines the scene I'll find behind the polished oak door: Grandma sprawled out at the foot of her stairs, neck broken; or slumped over the kitchen table; or tucked into bed like a child with one cold hand resting on the pillow. I've seen these visions often enough. When I was young, I used to watch her labored breathing as she napped, counting each breath and waiting, terrified, for the rattle and cease. Now it would be a comfort, and I'm angry and ashamed at myself for thinking such thoughts. Nevertheless, even as I move round the house, trying the doors and peering through curtained windows, a cold, clinical part of me is already making lists: call the hospital, the undertaker, her lawyer Mr. Perkins; get out her best black dress with the piecrust collar and seed-pearl piping. Empty the refrigerator. Call the Sarahs.

"David? Is that you?"

The sound of her voice makes me jump. Grandma is standing on the back porch, cigarette in hand, wrapped in a green tartan bathrobe that used to be Grandpa's. The smoke forms a wreath around her head. She looks at me quizzically, but without surprise. "You all right there, kiddo?"

"Grandma! Are you okay?"

"Why shouldn't I be?"

"You called me. You sounded really upset. You said…" Here comes the awkward bit. "You said there was a body."

She raises an eyebrow. "A body? Whose body? What are you talking about, boy?"

Honestly, I wish I knew. But the bloody corpse has already flitted back into the Lethe of my grandmother's imagination. And I've just driven all the way from Boston for nothing. "What are you doing outside this time of night?" I ask instead. "It's freezing."

She shrugs. "I like to watch the waves." Her cigarette semaphores towards the sea, making a fiery arc. "Want to join me? The *Dixieland* oughta be passing by pretty soon." This is a private joke. The *Dixieland* ferry—ludicrously named, filled with day-trippers from New York—passed by our house every day at noon. Sometimes Grandma and I would stand on the bluff, wait until it approached, and then drop skirts and trousers and let our asses hang in the breeze. She chuckles at the memory.

"Grandma," I say again, bringing her back to the present, "you called me. You said something was wrong. Do you remember?" Even as the words leave, I regret them. Her face darkens. She hates to be reminded of "Fuzzy Acres," as she calls it.

"Of course I remember," she snaps, and we both know she doesn't. "But I'm fine now. You can go along back up to that college. I don't want you failing 'cuz of me." Sometimes she knows I'm an assistant professor now, sometimes not.

"It's okay. Let's go inside."

She shrugs again but doesn't resist as I take her arm. The house is utterly dark. I wonder how long she's been standing on the porch. "Did Emma bring dinner yet?"

"I think so."

But the kitchen is cold and untouched. Aunt Emma always rinses the dishes and puts them on the counter—the counter is bare. "Let me fix you something," I say.

"Whose house is this? You sit down. I'll fix you something."

Before I can protest Grandma puts on the coffee, plugs in the toaster, and pulls out a loaf of bread from the cupboard. While the toast heats, she makes scrambled eggs, a perfect yellow disc at the bottom of the pan. This she cuts in two and sprinkles with a dust of salt and castor sugar. At that exact moment, the toast pops up. I've watched her do this all my life, and it still amazes me that she can time it so well. Even the coffee is brewed. Grandma sits across from me and helps herself to eggs. In a moment they're gone and most of the toast too. She eats ravenously, licking her fingers, all delicacy forgotten. I'm beginning to wonder when she ate last.

"Did Emma give you your pills tonight?" I can see the little orange bottles still atop the fridge. "Here, I'll do it."

"Emma does it," Grandma corrects, mulishly. "You let her do her job."

Emma is Grandma's next-door neighbor and best friend, but lately Grandma has taken it into her head that she's some kind of paid housekeeper. I can't blame her, really. For months now Emma's come by every night to give Grandma her dinner, pick up the clothes she left strewn on the floor, straighten the furniture, and sort the mail. I've learned not to offer her money. Truth is, Emma was always Grandma's guardian, even before Fuzzy Acres. When Grandpa died, it was Emma who chose Grandma's funeral outfit, dressed her, and fixed her hair while Grandma stared blankly at the mirror, numb with grief. When Grandma started forgetting things—little things, appointments and birthdays and children's names—it was Emma that kept track. On my birthday, I received a Hallmark card with a twenty-dollar bill inside. The card was signed in Grandma's handwriting, but it was addressed in Emma's. In her own quiet way she gives Grandma the greatest gift any friend ever could by allowing her to remain herself. But when I tried to express my gratitude, Emma was curt. "Never you mind. You don't know what she did for me." Then she changed the subject.

Now I peer out the kitchen windows, over to Emma's house. Her ancient Buick is parked out front, and there is a light on in the kitchen. It's Thursday night, which means Emma will be watching her shows. Cop dramas mostly, the gorier the better. It's always been a strange side of her otherwise buttoned-up personality. "Give Em a semidecomposed corpse in a lonely field," Aunt Constance likes to say, "and she's a happy woman." A flickering blue light reflects on the grass outside her parlor windows. But why hasn't she come by?

"I'm gonna go check on Emma," I say.

Grandma doesn't look up from her toast. "Tell her those eggs she brought last week were bad. Feathers and blood. Had to throw half away."

Outside the air has a definite chill, and there's a hint of frost on the lawn. I shiver in my shirtsleeves. Emma's house is smaller than Grandma's, a gray saltbox colonial whose austerity and uncompromising squareness always reminded me of Emma herself. A pot of nasturtiums greets callers at the door. I knock, ring the bell.

"My God, what is that? Is that a body?"

The television blasts away in the front room. Emma has grown rather deaf lately. I try the door and, sure enough, it's unlocked. It opens right into the parlor, where a rocking chair is pulled up close to the television set. Dr. Ross and Detective Stone peer down at a mangled corpse on the screen. But the chair is empty.

"Emma?"

"Dead some days I expect. There is hypostasis on the lower back and forearms, suggesting..."

The inside of the house is small and plain, with only a few stick-back chairs in the living room, and a kitchen with a built-in table just behind. A kitchen light with a wicker shade dangles overhead. The light is on, gleaming off a pile of copper pans strewn on the floor. The shelf above the stove is skewed at a cock-eyed angle, one plank dangling loosely from a single bent nail.

"Emma, you there?"

The kitchen island is one of those old-fashioned stainless steel models with ceramic sides and a grooved draining board to catch the juices. On the floor behind the island a pair of bare, bluish legs stick out at an odd angle. Fuzzy pink carpet slippers point upward toward the ceiling. Emma's fingers curl loosely around the handle of a stockpot. The saucepan and braiser lie at her feet. The skillet, polished steel with a weighted iron base, rests gently against her gray curls. A dark smudge on its rim corresponds exactly to the deep wound across her forehead.

"Yes," says a voice behind me, "that's just how she was when I found her."

Grandma is standing in the doorway holding an unlit cigarette and studying the corpse of her best friend with a dispassionate eye.

"How *you* found her?"

"Sure. Came by a couple hours ago to ask if she had any strawberries, and there she was. Head bashed in something awful."

"But..." My brain is working sluggishly. "But you said it was a man!"

"A man? What man?"

"I don't know! You said it was a man, that there was blood everywhere, something about lobsters..."

We both stare as if the other had gone completely insane.

"My God." I take hold of the kitchen island to steady myself. "Why you didn't call the police?"

"I *did*. I called them, and Connie and Irene. I called everybody. I called you, David."

Of course. And Irene, Constance, and Billy down at the police station had all reacted just as I had. Which is to say, not at all. "I kept calling and calling," Grandma goes on, sounding a little peeved, "but nobody answered, so finally I just gave up. What else was I supposed to do?"

"But why didn't you tell me when I got here...? Oh..."

That look comes back into her eyes, half combative and half terrified. The Revenge of Fuzzy Acres. "I'm sorry, Grandma."

She shrugs. "Had to happen someday. And this was quick, at least. She prob'ly never felt a thing." Still, Grandma shudders.

"It's okay," I tell her. "I'll call the police."

"Maybe you'll have better luck."

Grandma decides this is a good exit line and makes her way back to the house. I'm about to follow when something brushes against my shoe. Something large, dark, and prehistoric is scuttling along the floor, making its laborious bid for freedom.

A lobster.

Hawaiian Glossary

ae
An expression of surprise

anela
Angel

aole loa
Not at all

buk buk
(slang) of Filipino descent

da kine
(slang) that, that kind

haole
foreigner, non-native

hapa
mixed race

heiau
temple

hilahila
shame

ho'omaha
to rest

ho'oponopono
forgiveness

hoopomaikai
blessings

ho'opailua
disgust

ihe
spear

I'iwi
species of bird native to
Hawaii, also known as the
scarlet honeycreeper

kahuna
chief, leader

kamaiana
local, native

kanaka
Hawaiian

kanaka maoli
the true people

kapa
a native fabric

kapu
forbidden, cursed

katonk
(slang) of Japanese descent

keiki
children

ko'u akua
my God

koa la koa
brave warrior

kupuna
grandmother

kupunakane
grandfather

lanai
porch

loa
very, much

lolo
crazy

mahalo
thank you

mai hopohopo
don't worry

manong
older person

moke
  (slang) a lowlife

pake
  (slang) of Chinese descent

pau
  finished

pololei
  correct

pookela
  nonsense

puaiohi
  strength

wahi hewa
  the wrong place

PHRASES

A'ole i hele
  Did not go

E ho omana o i kou po e kānaka
  Remember your people

e ho omana o mau
  Remember always

He wahahee a he aihue
  He is a liar and a thief

Ho'omana'o mākou iā lākou
  We remember them

Ho onani i ke akua
  Praise be to God

Maopopo ia'u
  I know

Reading Group Guide

1. When the Lathrop family is divided over the future of the hotel and village, whose argument did you feel was most reasonable, and why? What would you do?

2. Peter Pauahi, a resident of the village and chairman of the Save Kaumaha action committee, wants to block the construction of a hotel and at the same time wants the statue of Reverend Amyas Lathrop removed. What rights and authority do you feel he and the villagers should have?

3. Do you think the Lathrop family has a responsibility to protect the villagers? If so, do you think the sale and distribution of a portion of the proceeds to village families is a reasonable compromise?

4. Why would Eleanor want Lani to make the final decision about selling the island to a resort developer?

5. How would you describe Lani's relationship with the villagers? And the Lathrops?

6. What are your reactions to the coming-of-age rituals thought to have occurred at the House of the Bone Feast?

7. Judge Chan stated that because the Lathrop family had been on the island just as long as the villagers, neither group could be described as indigenous. Do you agree with her assessment?

8. After the explosion, Eleanor spoke to the detective about Lani: "Can you blame her, then? After hearing that she was the reason this whole crisis came about, simply by being born? Can you blame her for lashing out?" Can you?

9. Some readers have compared the plotting of *A Legacy of Bones* to the twists and turns of an Agatha Christie mystery. What similarities do you see, if any?

10. Several of the characters experience dreams, colorful visions, and audio hallucinations. Do you think these devices are effective in informing readers about the characters? Do they enhance or detract from the verisimilitude of the story?

A Conversation with the Author

How has being an academic yourself informed your shaping of Dr. Ackerman's character and the pressure he felt to publish and to "get it right"?

Ironically perhaps, Robert Ackerman is the character I most identify with. His story is not only plausible but common. The great task for all aspiring academics is to uncover something completely new. Depending on your field, this could mean anything from a genome sequence to a lost aboriginal tribe to an undiscovered manuscript. Finding something new and significant establishes your credibility among your peers, and the strange truth is that most academic careers—which can last fifty years or more—are shaped by the very first piece of work we produce, usually in our midtwenties. Mine, for example, was the discovery that nearly every colonial American governor was actively sponsoring and sheltering pirates in the early 1700s. I became "the pirate guy," even going on television to tell Hilary Duff how her great-great-great-great-grandfather hunted down Blackbeard.

The problem, of course, is that one piece of evidence may completely contradict another, and you might be three years into your dissertation before discovering it. What then? Give up, start over, or just keep going regardless? Another mystery author/academic tackled this question long before me. The solution to Dorothy Sayers's *Gaudy Night* hinges on the legacy of a disgraced academic who knowingly concealed evidence of his own error and was uncovered and destroyed. "It was just a piece of paper," his wife tells his accusers. "It wouldn't keep a cat alive. But you killed him for it."

While Misery Island is fictitious, how closely does the racial divide between the villagers—the former plantation workers—versus the Lathrops—the former plantation owners—parallel issues at actual historical Hawaiian sugarcane-growing operations? Or did you base the landownership debate and economic disparity on pre-Emancipation mainland American South?

Oooh, I'm glad you caught that. The inspiration for this book actually began with debates surrounding the removal of Confederate statues in the American South and elsewhere. Statues create a particular narrative of the individual they portray; in many cases, they conceal more than they reveal. I took that concept one step further and made it literal. But I never intended to set it in the South. The premise could apply almost everywhere; in Kinshasa, formerly Leopoldville, Congolese natives were made to walk under a giant equestrian statue of their conqueror and murderer, King Leopold II. But only Whites were allowed to walk in front of the figure; Africans had to quite literally walk under the horse's ass.

The racial and cultural divide in Hawaii is one of America's grimmest stories, and yet it has almost entirely disappeared from our collective memory. It began with Mormon missionaries arriving to Christianize the native Hawaiians in the nineteenth century. These were followed by succeeding waves of American capitalists intent on appropriating Hawaii's rich soil to grow sugarcane, coffee, and pineapples. These men became so wealthy and powerful that they were ultimately able to topple the Hawaiian monarchy altogether, transforming the Hawaiian people into second-class citizens on their own land. I wanted to reacquaint readers with that story and do so in a way that tied it to similar appropriations and atrocities in America itself.

Misery Island is lushly landscaped with many tropical flowering plants. How did you research the flora? Did you visit a Hawaiian island botanical garden?

There is a spectacular botanical garden on the island of Kauai, which I dearly love, but the truth is, it is completely redundant. Hawaii is one big botanical garden itself, and the only task for me was to put the correct name to plants, flowers, and species I had seen my entire life.

Mr. Po has haunting visions and audio hallucinations. Roger, Lani, and Mrs. Te Papa all had dreams that provided impetus for their daytime thoughts and actions. As an author, how difficult is it to construct otherworldly unconscious messages?

Hawaii is a mystical place and operates by its own rules. I don't think I've ever met a Hawaiian—native or transplant—who hasn't come to accept island lore about spirits, demons, even gods. In the book, I make reference to a hotel on the Big Island that had to close because it was simply too haunted. That story is true. There are supposedly "walkers" that patrol the Waipi'o Valley at night, and scores of campers relate stories about encountering them. Whether you believe or not, these stories are all around you in Hawaii and became an accepted part of island culture. So it was not that big a stretch to create someone like Mr. Po, who is just a little more wired-in than everyone else. Also, since you asked about Easter egg references to other mysteries, Mr. Po is one himself—but it would take a pretty careful reader to catch it!

Mustachioed Detective Roundtree seems a classic character—a frustrated, melancholic investigator. Is he based on anyone in literature?

The stolid, earnest police inspector is absolutely everywhere in mystery fiction, often as a contrast/counterpart to the brilliant detective. Holmes and Lestrade, Wimsey and Sugg, Poirot and Japp, the list goes on and on. My personal favorite was a relatively minor character in Christie's *The Hollow*, whose mustache drooped whenever he was particularly depressed. I wrote that detail into the novel because I loved it so much.

The villagers willingly moved to the island back in Reverend Amyas Lathrop's day but continued to pray to Kane and to fear Ku, despite his efforts to convert them to Baptist Christian ways. Did you find examples of this kind of resistance in your research?

Certainly. But it is also a universal phenomenon among missionaries and missions. Every religion that takes itself on the road has to be flexible enough to adapt to local circumstances. Early Christianity was no exception: the saints were a useful stand-in for the pagan pantheon, and festival days were scheduled to fall precisely on the same dates as the old pagan calendar. When the Spanish brought Christianity to the New World, they leveled Aztec temples but used the stones to construct cathedrals on the same spot. As the Thais say, same-same but different. I once did a tour of old Norman churches in England, and the guide delighted in pointing out all the pagan details in the architecture and decoration. The idea was to make a new religion seem more familiar and therefore more palatable. And however you feel about it, it worked—especially in Hawaii. The Hawaiian kings themselves adopted Christianity in the early nineteenth century, and to this day, there is an impressive stone church right across from Iolani Palace in Honolulu. But the old gods never went away, and now they coexist relatively peacefully alongside Christianity in Hawaiian culture and faith.

Do you speak the Hawaiian language fluently? If so, where did you learn?

Very few people speak Hawaiian fluently, and I am definitely not one of them. Nearly everyone who lives on the islands picks up a pretty large vocabulary of pidgin phrases— it comes as naturally as taking off your shoes when you enter someone's house. For the book, however, I had to consult a Hawaiian dictionary and phrase book pretty frequently and then cross-check it with friends who speak the language better than I.

You must have done extensive research on the traditional religion of the islanders—including the custom of removing a corpse's liver and feeding it to a bird, then salting the body and wrapping it in a kapa before it's burned on a pyre. All historically accurate?

Yup. Remember what I said about academics? Even if we sometimes get it wrong, we *really* don't want to. I'm a historian and not an anthropologist, but the research methodology is similar. Before I wrote a word, I researched extensively—at the Bishop Museum, at libraries, everywhere. And after the draft was complete I had one of my university colleagues, who *is* an anthropologist and an expert on Hawaiian culture, proof check for errors. One of the central features of the book, the Bone Feast House, is very real indeed—there is an exhibit on it in the Metropolitan Museum of Art in New York City. I saw that one day and thought "Wow, if that doesn't sound like a murder mystery, I don't know what does." And it became one.

Word is that you've intentionally hidden Agatha Christie-style "Easter eggs" in the book. Is that true? And, if so, how many? Are you willing to identify one or two of them?

The funny thing is I never set out to put Easter eggs in my books, but I've read so many mystery novels, especially from the "golden age," the 1920s through 1950s, that the references just pop up without my realizing it. Mr. Po is one of the few deliberate ones (though not from Christie). There's definitely a bit of Miss Marple in Winnie Te Papa—consider the scene where Ackerman and the forensic pathologist walk in on her as she examines the bones with an old magnifying glass. She knows she's playing a role, "a sweet *kamaaina* aunty," and uses it to bluster her way into places she doesn't necessarily belong. One very deliberate reference, not really an Easter egg but a shout-out, is to a scene in *A Caribbean Mystery* where Miss Marple pops up in Mr. Rafael's window dressed in a pink woolen shawl and describing herself as "Nemesis." I felt like Mrs. Te Papa would see herself the same way: defending the dead and protecting the living from an indescribable evil that transformed her into a kind of mythic warrior.

The characters on the island are well-defined, differentiated. Who was your favorite? Who was the most difficult to write?

Winnie for both, hands down. My favorite scene in the novel was also the most difficult to write: when she revisits

Duke Kahanamoku and asks for guidance. I deliberately left it ambiguous whether he is real or a kind of manifestation of her own subconscious—I'm not even sure myself. But, perhaps more than anyone else in history, Duke *is* Hawaii, and talking with him would be like tapping into her own roots. This was a delicate scene because I'm not a native Hawaiian, and yet I wanted to convey her perspective accurately. Duke became a way to do that and to give the reader an insight into how Winnie became the woman she is. Also, as a historical figure, Duke may actually be the most interesting man who ever lived. Look him up!

Acknowledgments

The author wishes to thank his amazing editors, Diane DiBiase and Beth Deveny, whose contributions to this work have been immeasurable. Thanks also to Kimberley Cameron, who championed this project as she has so many others for nearly twenty years. A debt of gratitude is owed to Professor Jill Katz and the staff of the Bishop Museum for fact-checking the Hawaiian cultural dimension, and to Tonmoy Hassan, my first and best reader always. *Mahalo*.

About the Author

Doug Burgess is an award-winning author of fiction and nonfiction. His critically acclaimed debut novel, *Fogland Point*, was republished as *Dark Currents* (Poisoned Pen Press, an imprint of Sourcebooks) and released in 2021. His short fiction has appeared in *Ellery Queen Mystery Magazine* and other periodicals. Doug lives in the Hudson Valley, New York, where he is a professor of history.